RICHARD P. HENRICK

NIGHTWATCH

HarperTorch
An Imprint of HarperCollins*Publishers*

HarperTorch
An Imprint of HarperCollins*Publishers*
10 East 53rd Street
New York, New York 10022-5299

Copyright © 1999 by Richard P. Henrick
ISBN: 0-380-79028-9

First HarperTorch paperback printing: February 2001
First Avon Books hardcover printing: June 1999

HarperCollins ®, HarperTorch™, and (HarperTorch colophon)™ are trademarks of HarperCollins Publishers Inc.

Printed in the United States of America

Visit HarperTorch on the World Wide Web at www.harpercollins.com

10 9 8 7 6 5 4 3 2 1

The nightmare that could "never happen here" is happening. The next American Revolution has begun . . .

NIGHTWATCH

"HOLD ON TO YOUR SEAT."

St. Louis Post-Dispatch

"AN EXCELLENT READ . . .
with all the right twists and turns . . .
A tautly written thriller that keeps readers on edge to the final pages."

Copley News Service

"RICHARD HENRICK IS A MASTERFUL PLOTTER . . .
The action seems too real as Henrick uses the disenchantment of the military and the suspicions of home-grown militia to create what would heretofore be unthinkable."

Virginian Pilot and Ledger-Star

"A GOOD STORY . . . A WILD ADVENTURE."

Publishers Weekly

"Henrick keeps things moving so quickly you don't stop to ask what's going on. YOU JUST ENJOY."

Houston Chronicle

"WRITING EXCELLENCE . . .
Henrick's becoming a major force in the geopolitical thriller genre and *Nightwatch* proves it."

The Midwest Book Review

Also by Richard P. Henrick

Author's Note

Time references in *Nightwatch* are recorded either in Zulu Time (Greenwich Mean Time), the time unit favored by the military, or in Central Daylight Time (CDT). CDT is six hours behind Zulu Time.

Nightwatch (E-4B) Compartments

1   **Flight Deck and Upper Deck Rest Area**
The flight deck contains the pilot's, copilot's, navigator's and flight engineer's stations. A lounge area and sleeping quarters for flight crews and other personnel are located aft of the deck.

2   **Forward Entry Area** The forward entry area contains the main galley unit and stairways to the flight deck and to the forward lower equipment area. Refrigerators, freezers, a convection oven and a microwave oven give stewards the capability to provide more than 100 hot meals during prolonged missions. Additionally, four seats are located on the left side of the forward entry area for the security guards and the stewards.

3   **Conference Room and Projection Room** The conference room provides a secure area for conferences and briefings. It contains a nine-position executive table with executive chairs. A projection room serving the conference room and the briefing room is located aft of the conference room. It has the capability of projecting computer graphics, overhead transparencies or 35mm slides to either the conference room or the briefing room either singularly or simultaneously.

4   **Operations Team Area** The operations team area contains the automatic data processing equipment and seats and console work areas for 29 staff members. The consoles are configured to provide access to/from the following types of circuits or systems: automated data processing, automatic switchboard, direct access telephone and radio circuits, direct ("hot") lines, monitor panel for switchboard lines, staff and operator interphone and audio recorder.

5   **NCA Area** The NCA area is designed and furnished as an executive compartment. It contains an office, a lounge/sleeping area and a dressing area. Telephone instruments in this area provide the NCA with secure and clear, worldwide communications.

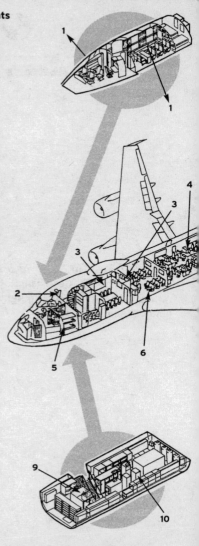

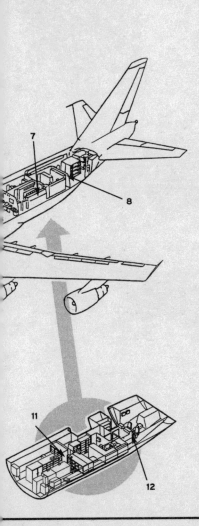

6. **Briefing Room** The briefing room contains a briefing table with three executive seats, eighteen seats, a lectern and two rear projection screens.

7. **Communications Control Area** The communications control area is divided into a voice area and a data area. The voice area, located on the right side of the compartment, contains the radio operator's console, the semi-automatic switchboard console and the communication officer's console. The data area, located on the left side of the area, contains the record communications console, record data supervisor's console, high speed DATA/AUTODIN/AFSAT console and LV/VLF control heads.

8. **Technical Control and Rest Area** The aft end of the main desk is divided into a technical control area and a rest area. The enclosed technical control area, which occupies the left forward part of the compartment, contains a technical control console, multiplexer, SHF SATCOM, console, and patch and test assembly. The rest area, which occupies the remaining portion of the aft main deck, provides a rest and sleeping area for the crewmembers.

9. **Flight Avionics Area** The flight avionics area contains aircraft systems power panels, flight avionics equipment, liquid oxygen converters and stowage for baggage and spare parts.

10. **Forward Lower Equipment Area** The forward lower equipment area contains the potable water supply tanks, 1200 KVA electrical power panels, stepdown transformers, VLF transmitter and SHF SATCOM equipment. Electrically operated retractable stairs, located in the forward right side of the forward lower equipment area, are installed for airplane entry and exit.

11. **Aft Lower Equipment Area** The aft lower equipment area contains the maintenance console and various mission equipment.

12. **Lower Trailing Wire Antenna Area** The lower trailing wire antenna area contains the long trailing wire antenna reel, the antenna operator's station and the antenna reel controls and indicators.

Glossary

(in order of appearance)

C.D.T.	Central Daylight Time
PL	Patrol Leader
BDU	Battle Dress Utility
NVG	Night Vision Goggles
ORP	Objective Rally Point
MRE	Meal Ready to Eat
OPORD	Operations Order
RTO	Radio Telephone Operator
R&S	Reconnaissance and Surveillance
APL	Assistant Patrol Leader
TOC	Tactical Operations Center
EPW	Enemy Prisoner of War
SAW	Squad Automatic Weapon
ACE REP	Ammunition/Casualty/Equipment Report

LBE	Load Bearing Equipment
Demo	Demolitions
OPFOR	Opposition Forces
Zulu	Greenwich Mean Time
MP	Military Police
SAIC	Special Agent in Charge
CAT	Counter Assault Team
SWAT	Special Weapons and Tactics
ATF	Alcohol, Tobacco and Firearms
IED	Improvised Explosive Device
SRT	Special Response Team
MILAIDE	Military Aide
CID	Criminal Investigative Division
NAOC	National Airborne Operations Center
NCA	National Command Authority
NMCC	National Military Command Center
STRATCOM	Strategic Command
CO	Commanding Officer
POTUS	President of the United States
FEMA	Federal Emergency Management Agency
SIOP	Single Integrated Operational Plan
CONUS	Continental United States
NPR	National Public Radio
SITREP	Situation Report
IR	Infrared
FCO	Fire Control Officer
SSGT	Staff Sergeant

RPG	Rocket Propelled Grenade
SATCOM	Satellite Communications
TACAMO	Take Charge and Move Out
DEFCON	Defense Condition
NAS	Naval Air Station
EAO	Emergency Action Officer
MO	Modus Operandi
CG	Commanding General
EOC	Emergency Operations Center
CPR	Cardiopulmonary Resuscitation
DOD	Department of Defense
VLF	Very Low Frequency
ICBM	Intercontinental Ballistic Missile
EAM	Emergency Action Message
COMSUBLANT	Commander Submarines Atlantic
XO	Executive Officer
COB	Chief of the Boat
NSA	National Security Agency
SOSUS	Sound Surveillance System
SINS	Ships Inertial Navigation System
SAR	Search and Rescue
ADI	Altitude Direction Indicator
SOG	Studies and Observation Group
ALCS	Air Launch Control System
ACO	Airborne Communications Officer
NORAD	North American Aerospace Defense Command

PA	Power Amplifier
SOCOM	Special Operations Command
COMSUBPAC	Commander Submarines Pacific
INMARSAT	International Maritime Satellite
SHF	Super High Frequency
CNO	Chief of Naval Operations
IMF	International Monetary Fund
ETA	Estimated Time of Arrival
CRT	Cathode-Ray Tube
PFD	Primary Flight Display
MOUT	Military Operations in Urban Terrain
MIRV	Multiple Independently Targetable Reentry Vehicle

At what point shall we expect the approach of danger? By what means shall we fortify against it? Shall we expect some trans-Atlantic military giant, to step the ocean, and crush us at a blow?

"Never!

"All the armies of Europe, Asia and Africa combined . . . could not by force, take a drink from the Ohio, or make a track on the Blue Ridge, in a trial of a thousand years.

"At what point then is the approach of danger to be expected?

"I answer, if it ever reach us, it must spring up amongst us. It cannot come from abroad. If destruction be our lot, we ourselves must be its author and finisher. As a nation of free men, we must live through all times, or die by suicide."

—ABRAHAM LINCOLN
January 27, 1838

NIGHTWATCH

Sergeant Sam Reed stepped over the fallen oak trunk without breaking his stride. The nine-man Sapper squad that he was following was making the most of the remaining light. They were moving quickly through the forest, in a modified wedge formation, a ten-meter interval between soldiers.

The summer shower that had soaked them earlier in the day had long since passed. A cloudless, powdery-blue sky prevailed in its place, with the remnants of a glorious sunset visible through the tree limbs ahead. The plan was to remain on this westerly azimuth until they reached Penns Pond, where they'd turn north toward the ridge separating Hurd Hollow and Roubidoux Creek. This was where their objective was located—an illegal-weapons cache, controlled by the outlaw Ozark People's Militia, that they intended to neutralize by force, if necessary.

The men of Sapper One were already running well behind schedule, and Reed was somewhat annoyed when, from the center of the wedge, the Patrol Leader raised his open palm overhead signaling the squad to a halt. A slap on the cargo pocket of his Battle Dress Utilities indicated that he was calling for a map check. As the PL quietly conferred with the squad's compass and pace men, Reed reached for the plastic tube that extended from his ruck and took a sip of the cool water stored in a Camelbak bladder. The humidity was fierce, and with his own BDUs long since soaked, Reed knew it was essential for the soldiers in his charge to drink plenty of fluids. With rucksacks weighing over seventy pounds, and the additional burden of their weapons and a full load of ammunition, the danger of heat stroke had to be taken seriously.

Reed watched the rifleman standing directly in front of him take a drink from his canteen, and looked on as the PL stood erect, swung his arm overhead from rear to front, and pointed toward the sunset. A bare second later, the men of Sapper One were on the move once again.

The fiery hues that had previously painted the horizon had faded by the time they reached Penns Pond. They changed azimuth here, and with the ever-gathering dusk, their pace further quickened. The forest was thick, and because of their desire to travel well away from any established trail, the going was difficult. Razor-sharp brambles tore at Reed's jungle boots and the rip-stop cloth of his camouflaged BDU pants. As they began their way up a steep incline, the rocky soil offered little in the way of secure footing, and Reed found himself ducking and bobbing to escape the arched oak saplings. Ever thankful for his protective eyewear, he accepted a hand signal from the soldier in front to tighten their formation.

Upon attaining the slope's summit, the men could see a crescent moon dominating the western sky. They hurriedly climbed off the ridgeline, preferring instead to travel by way of the sloping gradient that graced its far side. It was getting increasingly hard to see, and when they continued down into the hollow, Reed toyed with the idea of deploying his Night Vision Goggles.

It was shortly after an oak limb slapped Reed hard against his cheek, driving home how frustrated he was getting with this march, that the PL signaled for a listening halt. He did so by removing his BDU cap and waving it overhead. The squad removed their own caps, took up security positions, and knelt, their knees protected by pads designed to cushion the weight of their rucksacks.

Reed joined them. The purpose of this halt was to remain absolutely silent and absorb the sights and sounds of their new surroundings. They were finally closing in on their objective, and now was the time to find out if they were being followed, or if they had any unwanted onlookers nearby.

Sam Reed was no stranger to the sounds of the forest at night. He'd grown up in the hills of Tennessee, in a hollow much like the one they currently traveled. The cicadas called to him like old friends, their throbbing chorus welcome and most familiar. When a barn owl began hooting mournfully in the distance, Reed found himself thinking about those first hunting trips with his father and his decision to enlist in the Army on the eve of his eighteenth birthday. The military had been his entire life ever since, with the Combat Engineers his adopted family of choice.

The first visible stars penetrated the forest. A warm gust of wind caused the limbs to sway in unison, the creaking boughs seemingly moaning in protest. His night vision sharpening, Reed scanned the wood line in the direction they would be headed. The Objective Rally Point that the squad had picked lay at the bottom of the next ridge. From there, the militia cache was less than a kilometer distant.

It had taken the better part of the day for Sapper One to plan this operation. The initial warning order arrived at daybreak, along with the morning rains. Over soggy Meals Ready to Eat, the squad created the detailed Operations Order that would ensure their mission's success. This long, complex briefing included the creation of a terrain model, molded from the wet Missouri soil and given additional detail with colored chalk, strands of yarn, and toy soldiers.

By the time the OPORD was completed, every soldier knew exactly how the unit would accomplish its mission from start to finish. The details included the actual order of movement, actions at halts, the precise route, location of rally points, actions at danger areas, response to enemy contact, fire control measures, priority intelligence requirements, and rules of engagement. Each soldier was given a thorough list of the specialized equipment he would be responsible for carrying. In case of a casualty, it was imperative that items such as demolitions, claymores, spare barrels, or star-cluster flares be accounted for. Code words were also distributed, along with radio frequencies for the Radio Telephone Operators, and the proper arm and hand signals. Though time-consuming by its very nature, a proper OPORD could mean the difference between life and death on the battlefield, and Reed emphasized this fact each time a point was skipped over or improperly covered.

The mission had gone off without a hitch so far. The proper azimuths were being followed, the pace count was accurate, and their objective nearby. The only problem was the late start of their movement. Because of Sapper One's tardiness in the delivery of their OPORD, the raid would have to be set up without the benefit of the last light of dusk.

A buzzing mosquito announced the arrival of the night. Reed swatted at the insect as it passed by his ear. He reached for his water tube, and could just see the PL stand, extend his arm overhead, point forward, and rotate it in a counterclockwise direction. This caused the squad to rise in unison, line up in a single-file formation, and continue down into Hurd Hollow, where their Objective Rally Point would be located.

Reed was last in line. From this position, he could clearly see the two rectangular, luminescent "cat-eye" strips sewn into the BDU cap of the Sapper in front of him. The file formation was used when terrain or limited visibility precluded the use of the more tactically flexible wedge. Like a single entity, they snaked their way down the sloping gradient.

Even with the file, it took Reed's full concentration to keep from colliding with a projecting limb or tripping over an exposed root. Night vision was an applied skill. Instead of looking directly at a faintly visible object, one learned to slowly scan it. Yet another technique was off-center viewing, looking ten degrees above, below, or to either side of an object.

By the time they reached the hollow's bottom, Reed's eyes were fully adapted to the dark. This coincided with their arrival at the Objective Rally Point. The ORP was intentionally located out of sight, sound, and small-arms range of the objective. It would provide a temporary base of operations, and the men gratefully slipped off their rucksacks and initiated final preparations for the raid.

Reed removed his own ruck, and watched as the PL positioned his security team. Once this was achieved, the PL assembled the squad's Recon and Surveillance unit. A flashlight with a red lens was used to double-check their position on a folded map, and before leaving to reconnoiter the objective with his R&S team, the PL delegated responsibility for the ORP to the Assistant Patrol Leader.

"Red Dog One, this is Red Dog Two, over," whispered the RTO into the handset of his radio.

"Red Dog Two, this is Red Dog One, over," replied the gruff voice of the soldier occupying the Tactical Operations Center back at Sapper base camp.

"Red Dog One, be informed that Red Dog Two has reached its Objective Rally Point at coordinates Whiskey Mike six-seven-six-five, six-seven-eight-zero, and is preparing to move on objective, over."

"Red Dog Two, this is Red Dog One. Roger, out."

With the conclusion of this brief exchange, silence returned to the ORP. Reed watched a pair of Sappers cache the rucksacks with straps up for quick recovery. Yet another pair of soldiers began preparing demolitions, while the APL went to work crafting Enemy Prisoner of War bindings.

A sudden rustling sound prompted Reed to turn around in time to see a tall, BDU-clad figure break free from the surrounding underbrush.

"Hey, Reed," greeted First Sergeant Louis Stewart in a hoarse whisper. "Are you carryin' long cut or mint?"

"Don't tell me you're getting particular in your old age," Reed answered, pulling out a tin of Kodiak chewing tobacco from his top pocket and handing it to the fifteen-year veteran. Stewart was a fellow observer, who began his career as a tank driver. An incessant moocher, Stewart rarely reciprocated, though Reed could forgive him because of his rotten luck in cards.

"This humidity's a bitch," said Stewart as he tucked a pinch of tobacco behind his lower lip. "The twins are up in Rolla playin' ball tonight, and I sure hope they're pouring down plenty of Gatorade."

"How about getting TOC on the horn and setting up an extra water rendezvous right after the raid?" Reed offered while pulling out his NVGs. "Our Sappers are going to be awfully thirsty after expending all that ordnance."

Stewart took a sip from his canteen and checked the luminescent dial of his wristwatch. "Looks like it's going to be another late one. This group's slower than a pig in molasses."

"At least they're thorough and following the handbook," returned Reed. "Besides, what else do you expect from mechanized?"

Stewart grinned. "Sappers might lead the way, but tankers do it in style."

"Let's just make certain that Sapper One doesn't get too comfortable in this ORP," Reed advised.

Stewart spat out a torrent of tobacco juice. "Why don't I

check the perimeter and see if we've got us any sleepers? See ya up at the raid site, good buddy."

With Stewart's exit, Reed wiped the sweat off his forehead and slipped on his NVGs. The AN/PVS-7D binocular goggles utilized a single passive third-generation image intensifier tube, and when he switched them on, the entire forest was illuminated in a greenish-yellow hue, compliments of amplified starlight. Individual trees and clumps of shrubbery were clearly visible, and as Reed scanned the ORP, he noted the positions of each of the Sappers.

The APL could be seen huddled beside his RTO. Behind them, their automatic rifleman was attending to his M60 machine gun. The squad had only just received a pair of M249 Squad Automatic Weapons. The SAW was designed to replace the venerable M60 in certain units. Both weapons delivered devastating firepower and could engage targets up to eight hundred meters.

Reed watched Sergeant Stewart make his rounds of the security perimeter. The Sappers there were armed with a variety of M16A2 rifles and M4 carbines with M203 grenade launchers, hopefully providing more than enough firepower for the job at hand.

The snap of a tree limb caused Reed to turn in the direction of their objective. He readily spotted the R&S team headed back to the ORP. It took his eyes less than two minutes to regain full-dark adaptation upon removing his NVGs, and Reed joined the newly returned PL beside his ruck.

The results of the recon were most promising. As expected, the militia outpost was located on the adjoining ridge. A trio of armed individuals was spotted there, dressed in tiger-striped fatigues and huddled around a small campfire. A pickup truck was parked nearby, with an assortment of wooden crates stacked in its bed. Ever fearful that the weapons cache was about to be moved, the PL ordered his squad to strike with all due haste.

Sapper One moved out in a file formation, wearing Kevlar helmets and weapons locked and loaded. Their climb was a short one. The flickering campfire highlighted the objective like a klieg light, and Reed accompanied the three-man support element, whose automatic weapons were responsible for securing the right flank.

They had decided on a linear ambush. It would be a relatively basic assault, with the support element initially attacking the campsite with a volley of machine-gun fire. The assault team would then open fire from the left flank. After the PL signaled the support element to lift or shift fire, the assault team would charge across the kill zone to destroy the remainder of the enemy.

Reed watched his Sappers take cover behind a rocky berm. Once they were in position, a red chem-lite was activated to inform the assault team that they were ready to rumble. The assault element answered in kind, and Reed inserted a pair of foam earplugs. No sooner were they in place than a green star-cluster flare arced upward into the star-filled heavens, silhouetting their objective in a pulsating emerald glow. And it was then that all hell broke out.

The support team's machine guns raked the objective with a deafening barrage that delivered a continuous outburst of fire for a full forty-five seconds. The ambush must have caught the enemy by complete surprise; Reed spotted just a single muzzle flash from the direction of the campfire. This feeble response was all too brief, and by the time a red star cluster signaled the support team to lift fire, no enemy activity was noticeable.

An exploding smoke grenade veiled the assault team's charge across the kill zone. Reed left the support team behind at this point and headed for the objective himself.

He arrived beside the campfire just as the PL was calling for an Ammunition/Casualty/Equipment Report. Through the thick white smoke, Reed spotted the bodies of two militiamen lying on their stomachs on the far side of the fire.

Neither one of them was moving. Apparently they never had the chance to put their rifles into play.

He supposed that the sole muzzle flash had originated from the corpse in front of the truck. It too was sprawled out on its stomach, an M4 carbine close by.

Once the team had determined that there were no friendly casualties, the PL called out the EPW search team. All three of the enemy were labeled definite kills, and Reed watched a pair of Sappers prepare to search the body of the militiaman lying beside the truck.

While one of the Sappers stood guard at the enemy's head, his buddy kicked aside the M4 and knelt to roll the body over. Reed noted the way in which he lay prone on the enemy's back before proceeding. This technique was used to shield the Sapper should a grenade booby trap be encountered.

He reached around and grasped the militiaman's lapels, but without waiting for his co-worker to give him the go-ahead, as he should have, the prone Sapper rolled the body over. And there, to the standing Sapper's horror, was a single grenade.

Before the Sapper could brace himself or even curse, the fallen militiaman's eyes suddenly snapped open and he deadpanned, "Boom!"

"Damn it, Sapper, you just went and killed your buddy!" exclaimed Reed. For in reality, the militiaman was only playacting, and he couldn't help but smile as Reed then read his trainees the riot act. "There's no use going to all that trouble if you fail to get your Sapper buddy to step aside. 'Cause where he was standing, that grenade would have cut him in half!"

Reed pulled a flare gun from his Load Bearing Equipment harness, pointed the blunt muzzle skyward, and launched a white star cluster. It activated with a loud pop, its dazzling light now illuminating the objective like a newly risen sun.

"Listen up, Sappers!" Reed proclaimed. "We just had our first friendly casualty over here, and all because of a soldier's carelessness. I realize that all of you are tired and hungry. But this isn't the time to go and get sloppy. You did a great job to this point. EPW search teams, mind your technique! And, PL, how about getting your Demo team in place? We're already running late, and I want that cache blown and us off this ridge and on our way to the Roubidoux within the next thirty minutes!"

The flare faded, along with Reed's anger. He removed a flashlight from his LBE and illuminated the body of the fallen militiaman.

"Nice job, OPFOR," said Reed. "Sorry we had to keep you out here so late."

The fallen militiaman, who was a corporal assigned to Leonard Wood's Military Police detachment, stiffly got to his knees and stood. "Not to worry, First Sergeant. Next time you've got to let me and my boys try a little flanking action."

Sergeant Stewart emerged from the trees, his own flashlight in hand, and addressed the MP. "Hey, Corporal, you carryin' any long cut?"

"My old lady made me give up the habit, Sarge. Care for any M&M's?"

Stewart grimaced and looked to his fellow Sapper instructor for salvation. Without a word spoken, Reed tossed Stewart his can of Kodiak, while the voice of the PL boomed out behind them.

"Demo team's up!"

The plan was to detonate a five-pound block of C-4 to simulate the destruction of the weapons cache. Since blowing things up was one of the things that every combat engineer did best, Reed was content to let Louis Stewart grade their efforts. He watched while the three members of the OPFOR began extinguishing the campfire, and pulled out his two-way to contact operations. Yet before he could activate it, his attention was drawn to the woods, where five heavily camouflaged men were in the process of emerging from the tree line. Each of these armed individuals wore ghillie suits, specially designed fatigues covered with strips of brown and green cloth and favored by snipers.

Reed's first confused thought was, Who ordered the additional OPFOR? But if that were the case, why would two of them be sporting long ponytails, with an associate bedecked in a full beard?

For the first time since being assigned as a Sapper Leader course instructor, Sam Reed wished he had a weapon with real bullets in it.

Friday, July 2, 1311 Zulu

Simferopol International Airport
Crimean Peninsula

The first of a flight of two U.S. Air Force C-17 cargo aircraft landed on the main runway with the barest of jolts. There was a deep, growling roar as its thrust reversers were activated, and the stubby, high-winged, T-tailed jet ground to a halt using less than a third of the runway's ten-thousand-foot-long expanse.

Instead of continuing on to the main terminal, the C-17 followed a pair of black Zil police sedans to an isolated apron. Here, beside an immense hangar guarded by dozens of armed soldiers, the Air Mobility Command airplane braked to a final halt and shut down its four Pratt & Whitney engines.

A side hatch, positioned immediately behind the cockpit, cracked open and a pair of airmen in green flight suits deployed a self-contained stairway. While one of the Zil sedans pulled up to these stairs, a tall, solidly built black man wearing a superbly tailored pinstriped suit made his appearance in the hatchway. Samuel Forrest Morrison II had experienced enough flying for one day. Since leaving Andrews eleven hours ago, the Special Agent in Charge of the President's Secret Service detail had been confined to the C-17's noisy hold. Except for a single trip to the cockpit to witness one of the two aerial refuelings that they had undergone, this had been the extent of his wanderings, and he couldn't wait to get some fresh air and properly stretch his long legs.

It was only too obvious that summer had arrived in Ukraine, and the hot, humid air outside reminded Morrison of the weather he had just left behind in Washington, D.C. Towering, dark gray cumulus clouds dominated the western horizon, and it appeared that it was only a matter of time before the heavens would open up. The SAIC hoped this shower would hold off until his preparations here were complete, and he glanced down at his watch, noting that he had a little less than two hours before Air Force One arrived.

A short, balding figure dressed in a dark brown suit exited the Zil. It had been nine months since Morrison had last worked with Alexi Kosygin, co-head of the Russian President's security staff. A former Spetsnaz commando, Kosygin was a likable, efficient chap, and the SAIC knew that he was very fortunate to have drawn his services.

"Special Agent Morrison," greeted Kosygin in passable English. "Let me be the first to welcome you to the Rodina."

The SAIC replied after climbing down the stairway and accepting a firm hug and a kiss on each cheek. "It's good to see you again, Comrade."

"I do hope that your flight went well," said Kosygin, his glance drawn to the C-17's tail as its rear loading ramp began opening. "I understand that your Boeing C-17 is a most amazing plane."

Morrison nodded. "They're something special, all right, though not quite up to Air Force One's standards when it comes down to the creature comforts. If we have the time,

I'm certain that the flight crew would be happy to give you a tour."

The deep growl of whining jet engines caused both men to look over at the adjoining runway, where the second C-17 had just touched down. It too stopped well short of the runway's end, prompting the Russian to shake his head in admiration.

"That bird's carrying the limos and our communications van," revealed the SAIC. "We had to fight the temptation to load all of our seven vehicles into one aircraft."

"Why take the chance of carrying all your eggs in one basket when you have the luxury of a backup?" Kosygin mused.

As the newly arrived C-17 headed toward them, a large group of clean-cut men and women dressed in black fatigues climbed down the rear cargo ramp of Morrison's aircraft. They carried black, padded weapons bags at their sides, and the SAIC identified them as members of his Secret Service Counter Assault Team.

While the first of three black Chevrolet Suburbans was driven down the C-17's ramp, Morrison and Kosygin walked over to the nearby hangar, where an operations room had been set up. Waiting for them inside the cavernous structure was Nikolai Zinoviev, security chief of Ukraine's National Police Force. A pencil-thin skeleton of a man, Zinoviev wore a baggy gray suit that hung limply on his gangly frame. Morrison had previously worked with him on a counterfeiting case, and remembered well the skinny Ukrainian's piercing blue eyes and bushy handlebar mustache. He also couldn't forget the man's excellent British-accented English, and his utter embarrassment when Morrison's investigation had revealed the lead counterfeiter to be a senior policeman on Zinoviev's own staff.

After a rather unenthusiastic greeting, Zinoviev escorted them into a vacant conference room. Not bothering to offer any refreshments, he walked over to a display board and pulled back the white sheet that had been draped over it. This revealed a detailed topographic map covering the southern half of the Crimean Peninsula.

"The primary motorcade route that we decided upon remains unchanged," said Zinoviev while using his bony index finger to point out a roadway that was highlighted in red and stretched from Simferopol Airport southeast to the Black Sea coast. "Our public-works personnel worked tirelessly these last few weeks, and I'm proud to report that the road project has been successfully completed. The President of the United States shall have a freshly paved, two-lane highway for his exclusive use, as his motorcade initiates the nineteen-and-a-half-kilometer drive to our President's dacha outside Alushta."

For the past month, Morrison had extensively studied this same route, and even though he knew it almost as well as the way from his home in Chevy Chase to the White House, he approached the map and questioned, "What about the new bridge over the Salgir River? As of three days ago, my survey team indicated that the span was still incomplete."

"It's apparent you haven't spoken with them since," said Zinoviev, trying his best not to boast. "Regardless of the unseasonable late-spring rains, and the worst flooding in a century, your President shall have nothing but new pavement to travel upon during his drive to the coast."

Morrison had yet to contact his preplaced security forces for a final update, and ever hopeful that he now had one less potential problem area to worry about, the SAIC addressed his Russian colleague. "Alexi, I don't suppose that your boss has gone and altered his travel plans any."

"The old man's at sea even as we speak," answered Kosygin. "He left Odessa at daybreak, and at last report, his destroyer was passing Yalta. I can only thank my lucky stars that I wasn't picked to accompany him. After what we went through last fall aboard the *QE2*. I plan to make good my promise never to sail a body of water bigger than my bathtub."

Morrison issued forth a laugh that would have done James Earl Jones proud. "Tell me about it, my friend. I think I would have gone and retired if they had decided to hold this secret negotiating session at sea. I never was a good sailor to begin with, and now I get seasick just driving over the Potomac!"

Zinoviev loudly cleared his throat and once more pointed to the map. "I have two hundred of my best men patrolling the roadway. Our Army has over twice that many soldiers spread out in the forest and hills surrounding the highway. I must admit that, for efficiency's sake, I wish we could have better coordinated their efforts with the numerous Secret Service Counter Assault Teams that are presently covering these same areas."

"Your concerns have already been noted," said Morrison with a grunt. "Our policy has always been to do our work independent of local law enforcement agencies, including our operations inside the United States."

Alexi Kosygin looked at Morrison and nodded. "I'm afraid that not even the Ukraine National Police Force is going to be able to change official U.S. Secret Service policy, Comrade Zinoviev. Now, since our time is extremely limited, I suggest we go over the exact composition of the motorcade."

"I was just about to get to that," said Zinoviev with a hint of resentment. The skinny Ukrainian flipped over the map, revealing a hand-drawn diagram displaying a long column of vehicles. He pointed to the three small vehicles leading the column and began speaking rapidly.

"The motorcade shall be led by three motorcycles driven by a trio of my most decorated patrolmen. They will be followed by a pair of Zil police sedans, the second of which I shall be stationed in. Following me will be a BTR-60 armored personnel carrier, with fourteen heavily armed members of SWAT team Alpha inside. I thought it appropriate that two Secret Service Suburbans should precede the limousines. The other Suburban will follow ahead of the communications van, the ambulance, yet another BTR-60, and a trailing police sedan."

"If you don't mind, I'd like to put those two Suburbans behind the limo carrying Two Putt, with a single Suburban in the lead," said Morrison.

"Two Putt?" Zinoviev repeated.

"Two Putt is the Secret Service code name for the American President, Nikolai," explained Kosygin.

A sharp electronic tone sounded, and Morrison took out a hand-sized two-way radio from his breast pocket. "SAIC here," he said.

Whatever he was hearing caused a scowl to pull ridges across his forehead, and he addressed the two-way oblivious to the curious stares of his audience. "I don't give a damn about any frigging excuses, Special Agent Moreno. This motorcade's not going anywhere if you can't get that ambulance running. Hell, use some initiative, son. Between all those Air Force jet jockeys and our people, there's gotta be someone who can get that frigging engine started. Hell, you drove the damn thing in there, now drive that sucker out, or your frigging ass is history!"

As the SAIC angrily lowered his two-way, Zinoviev met his glance and wryly commented, "Our hospitals may not be as modern as yours in the U.S., but at least our ambulances can get our patients to them."

Vince Kellogg stood on the muddy riverbank, his gaze locked on the swiftly moving waters. The ghostly blanket of fog that had veiled the Eleven Point all morning was at long last lifting. It had been much too long since he had been in such an isolated setting, over a hundred miles away from the nearest sizable city, and Vince scanned the cascading current while filling his lungs with a deep breath of clean Missouri Ozark air.

"Special Agent Kellogg," sounded a voice from behind.

Vince turned and set his eyes on the heavily furrowed, weathered face of the man responsible for this interruption. Ron Wyatt was a native of these woods and, as a thirty-two-year veteran of the U.S. Forest Service, was one of Vince's current hosts.

"I'm sorry to disturb you, Special Agent," said Wyatt, his accent flavored by a slight country drawl. "Ranger Eberly just called. They're climbing out of the springs right now, and should be down here within the next fifteen minutes."

"I sure hope this late start doesn't mean that the VP will miss out on all the good fishing," Vince replied.

"The trophy management area starts a stone's throw downstream from here," said Wyatt. "And this late start don't mean much to those fat lunker trout that live down there. What's gonna make a difference is the Vice President's savvy with a fishin' pole."

"Though I've yet to see him fish, the regulars on his detail swear he's got an almost uncanny knack to catch his fair share of big ones."

"I wonder if it's true that he always releases 'em, like the papers say," pondered Wyatt.

Vince grinned. "What else do you expect from America's number one environmentalist?"

A green Forest Service truck pulling a trailer filled with canoes backed onto the boat ramp and Wyatt excused himself to help unload it. With a practiced glance, Vince surveyed the rest of the site. The immediate area was reserved for official vehicles and security personnel. The general public was confined to the adjoining campground, behind a temporary sawhorse barricade manned by a half-dozen members of the Oregon County Sheriff's Department.

From his vantage point, Vince could see that a crowd of over fifty spectators was gathered in the campground, curiously watching the last-minute preparations. He knew that most of them were waiting for a glimpse of the Vice President. Included in this group was a television news crew from Springfield, Missouri.

To check this crowd for any potential troublemakers, Vince walked over to the barricade. It didn't take him long to spot two of his fellow Secret Service agents, bedecked in shorts and T-shirts, mixed in alongside the motley assortment of tourists and locals. They were working undercover, and appeared to have their attention focused on the current subject of the news crew's cameras.

Without having to cross the barricade himself, Vince

could hear the young, blond reporter as she interviewed an elderly woman wearing a "Give the Eleven Point Back to the People!" sweatshirt. The crowd of tourists and locals offered their encouragement each time the old lady made a pertinent point, often using flowery language that would make most grandmothers blush and keep the news editor busy back at the station.

"To hell with the Vice President and that bunch of outlaws he represents back in Washington!" she ranted, making the best of her moment in the spotlight. "My kin have lived and died on the banks of this river for three generations, and no snotty-nosed bureaucrat is gonna come down here and tell me I've got to sell my land or else the government is gonna take it. This is my home! My parents and grandparents are buried here, and I aim to join 'em, regardless of the intentions of that gang of thieves at the Forest Service."

As part of the crowd issued a boisterous shout of support, Vince carefully scanned their faces. Shortly after he had received this assignment, he'd read a briefing paper covering problems they might encounter during the float trip. The subjects ranged from snakebites to sunburn, and included a short history of the area that explained some of the reasons behind the old-timer's upset.

It was in 1933 that the Forest Service began acquiring lands in the area of the Eleven Point. In 1939 these lands were given National Forest status. Yet it wasn't until 1968, when Congress passed the National Wild and Scenic River Act, and actual private land began to be confiscated, that local resentment of the government reached a boiling point. With the lofty intention of protecting the Eleven Point for generations to come, the Act authorized the Forest Service to forbid all private development along the actual riverway. Scenic easements were required for all property not part of the National Forest system, with the government continuing to pursue an active acquisition process whose goal was one hundred percent ownership of all lands abutting the river.

Government practices such as the enforcement of horse-power restrictions on all watercraft, and the creation of trophy fish management areas limited to artificial lures, further infuriated the locals, who were fiercely independent by their very nature. Forest fires were intentionally set to express their dissatisfaction, with grass-roots political action committees formed in a vain attempt to counter Federal policy. Frustrated when such acts failed to succeed, the remaining landowners had few courses open to them, and the Secret Service feared that one of them might go to the extreme of expressing their displeasure by taking a potshot at the Vice President.

Rumor had it the potential for danger was one reason the President had asked his VP to take this preholiday float trip. Continued policy disagreements between the two politicians was public knowledge, with the more conservative VP accusing his boss of spending too much time on foreign policy matters.

It was shortly after the President informed the Secret Service of his desire to schedule a secret negotiating session in the Crimea that the VP had announced this excursion into the nation's hinterlands. Even though Congress was out of session, the gossipmongers warned that the President wanted the VP as far away from Washington and its summer-starved media as possible.

Regardless of the real reason for their presence here, Vince was delighted when Samuel Morrison had assigned him to head this detail. This was especially the case when the VP stated his decision to host a gala July Fourth charity bash at Branson, Missouri.

Long before the Crimea trip was announced, Vince had hoped to spend the Fourth of July at Branson himself. His in-laws had a condo and boat on nearby Table Rock Lake, and the plan was for the whole family to get together to celebrate Vince and Kelly's twentieth wedding anniversary.

Samuel Morrison knew of Vince's plans, and graciously

offered him this change of assignments. Kelly personally sent the SAIC a box of his favorite Temple Hall cigars upon learning of the transfer. Morrison had been responsible for previously ruining too many holidays for the Kellogg family, yet this reassignment would make up for some of these past disappointments.

A loud metallic clang caused Vince to turn his attention back to the river, where Ron Wyatt and a pair of Forest Service workers were in the process of placing the last of the canoes into the water. The fog had almost completely dissipated, and Vince got his first clear view of the lush forest gracing the far side of the Eleven Point. The oaks and cottonwoods there were in full bloom, with a variety of colorful flowering plants hugging the bank itself.

If all continued to go smoothly, this float trip would be more like a vacation than work. The weather promised to be ideal, and the only thing lacking was the presence of his family. It was comforting to know that Kelly, Joshua, and Kimberly Ellen, the newest addition to the Kellogg family, were currently with Kelly's sister, Julie, in nearby St. Louis. They'd be driving to Branson later in the day, where the anniversary festivities were scheduled to begin in a little less than twenty-four hours.

A Forest Service johnboat, powered by a propeller-free, three-and-a-half-horsepower air-jet engine, approached the ramp from upstream. Special Agent Linda Desiante was perched behind the squared-off, blunt bow of the vessel, a bright orange life preserver tied around her neck.

"How's the water, Linda?" asked Vince as he caught the johnboat's bowline and pulled its bow portion up onto the ramp.

"Cold and incredibly clear," Desiante replied while stepping onto the ramp herself and scanning the operations area. "Where's the VP? I hope he hasn't gone and scrubbed the trip."

Vince shook his head. "His tour of Greer Springs went a little longer than planned. If you had been monitoring the comm net, you would have known that he's on his way back as we speak."

Desiante pulled her two-way out of its waterproof neck pouch and extracted the battery. "The darn thing lost its charge shortly after we got on the other side of the Highway Nineteen bridge."

"I'm almost afraid to ask, but what was your reception like up at the hold site?" Vince questioned while pulling a fresh battery out of his backpack and tossing it to her.

"It wasn't as bad as we anticipated. There were seven canoes in all, at the spot we picked to stop all traffic, with only two of the parties previously unaware that the river would be closed for most of the day. The beer was already flowing, and those not fishing were caught up in a spirited round of Frisbee."

"So much for our feared river insurrection," reflected Vince. "Though there's a crowd of angry locals up in the parking lot that still needs watching."

A green Forest Service truck with a flashing red light on its cab's roof pulled into the campground, prompting Vince to add, "Looks like the show's about to begin. As soon as you get your comm back up, your johnboat will be joining Avila's downstream. I want you close enough to provide an effective point unit, but far enough away that we won't be able to hear your engine. We don't want to go and ruin the man's wilderness experience."

Special Agent Desiante inserted the fresh battery, and as she depressed the two-way's transmit button to ensure that it was operational, the rest of the Vice President's motorcade pulled into the campground. An excited murmur rose from the crowd, and Vince hurried over to the barricade. The VP loved to interact with the public, and even though the president hated to share the media spotlight with him, once he spotted the television news crew, there'd be no stopping him.

One hundred and fifteen miles to the northeast of the Eleven Point's Greer access site, Thomas Kellogg greeted the morning from a town square that could easily belong to another era. Except for the modern vehicles and the clothing worn by the pedestrians, the courthouse he had just emerged from and the classic square that surrounded it were more reminiscent of America at the turn of the century.

Thomas had seen very little of Union when he arrived here in the wee hours of the morning. It had taken him the better part of an hour to get here from the Alcohol, Tobacco and Firearms office in St. Louis. A good portion of the drive followed Old Route 66, with Union lying to the southwest of St. Louis, at the gateway to the Missouri Ozarks.

Thomas had originally been called to St. Louis in early June, when several local Planned Parenthood clinics began receiving threatening letters and phone calls. Three weeks ago, the threats turned violent, when an Improvised Explosive Device exploded inside a clinic reception area. Fortunately, the timer malfunctioned, and the device detonated less than an hour before the clinic would have been filled with patients.

Their luck ran out four days later, after an IED exploded inside a Planned Parenthood laboratory. A technician was partially blinded by the blast, which was repeated the very next day in the adjoining clinic, injuring seven including three patients.

Thomas had spent the rest of the month gathering evidence and running down leads. Because such cases usually took a good deal of time to solve, he was hoping he'd be able to squeeze out a couple of days to join Vince and his family in Branson. It would be a rare opportunity for them to get together outside Washington. An understanding boss and a fortunate set of circumstances had sent Vince packing for southern Missouri. And with Thomas close by in St. Louis, a Kellogg family reunion never looked so promising.

Just when it seemed as if he'd be able to spare the time, another IED detonated inside a dumpster behind the Planned Parenthood clinic in Ballwin, Missouri, a St. Louis suburb. This incident occurred three days ago, and though no one was hurt, an adjoining supermarket was damaged when falling debris set its roof on fire.

Thomas arrived on the scene within sixty minutes of the blast. He was there while the fire department put out the blaze, and was the first one to brave the smoke and climb into the dumpster. His efforts uncovered the most promising piece of evidence so far. It was a still-smoldering, fire-scarred section of cardboard box, originally designed to hold electric detonators.

That very day, Thomas sent the evidence sample to the ATF's National Tracing Center in Falling Water, West Virginia. Experts working there for the Explosives Technology Branch were able to determine that the cardboard container had indeed been part of the IED. By using a laser scanner, they were also able to find out who manufactured the original detonators, along with the all-important date shift code. This alphanumeric series indicated the exact date and plant where the detonators were produced, and provided the vital information needed to complete the trace.

A check of the manufacturer's shipping records indicated that a box of fifty electric detonators had been sent via FedEx to an address in Labadie, Missouri. They were sent on May 28, only a few days before the first threats were issued, with the special-use permit stating that the detonators were to be used for agricultural purposes only.

The small town of Labadie was in Franklin County, only a few miles from the St. Louis County line. A title search showed that the address in question was indeed a farm. Yet when Thomas contacted the owner, he learned that the farmer had long since retired, and had subsequently leased his property to his nephew.

It was as Thomas began investigating this nephew that he knew they had hit pay dirt. Conrad Whitten had a rap sheet longer than Gussie Busch's tax return. A convicted felon and former leader of the Satan's Outlaw motorcycle gang, Whitten appeared to be their man.

With the assistance of the Franklin County Sheriff's Department and the Missouri Highway Patrol, the farmhouse was placed under twenty-four-hour observation. An operations center had just been set up in the Franklin County courthouse, thus necessitating Thomas's trip to Union this morning.

Before they could move in and make an arrest, the ATF had to know exactly what they were up against and who was involved. Was Whitten the bomber, or was he just making the IEDs for someone with an extreme social agenda? The botched raid on the Branch Davidian compound outside Waco, Texas, had taught the ATF many an invaluable lesson in the importance of accumulating proper intelligence, and Thomas found himself preaching this dictum all morning.

After a quick stroll around the square, he was ready to return to the courthouse and complete the stakeout schedule.

An ATF forward observer team was presently providing clandestine surveillance. They would need to be relieved shortly, and Thomas decided to accept the Sheriff's offer to replace them with two members of his elite SWAT team.

Even at this relatively early hour, the temperature was well into the eighties, and his forehead had a light sheen of perspiration on it as he headed inside. Halfway down the brick walkway, he passed a ground crew busy putting up a red, white, and blue banner for the upcoming Fourth of July holiday. A lawn mower growled to a start nearby, and Thomas looked up as the door to the courthouse suddenly swung open. Quick to exit was the Sheriff, with two uniformed highway patrolmen on his heels.

"We've got company down at the site!" he shouted. "One of my deputies just reported seeing three bikers in full colors turn into the driveway leading to the farmhouse, with a large Ryder rental truck following close behind."

Though he would have liked to call in an ATF Special Response Team, Thomas knew they didn't have the time. The Ryder truck most likely meant that Whitten was about to be on the move, and could indicate that the next IED was going to be substantially larger.

"Make certain that your men don't move in until we get there," warned Thomas while they sprinted over to the nearby parking lot. "As planned, we'll meet at the turnoff to the power plant to consolidate our forces."

Thomas accepted a thumbs-up from the Sheriff and climbed behind the wheel of his own car, a well-broken-in ATF Chrysler. With the Sheriff's vehicle leading the way, siren wailing, Thomas stepped on the accelerator to follow him. They had a fifteen-minute drive ahead of them, most of which was on well-paved, two-lane highways.

Once Union was behind them, the road began traversing a series of rolling hills. For the most part, this was farming country. Corn and soybeans were the major crops; an occasional pasture was filled with grazing cattle, pigs, or horses.

Traffic was light, and the Sheriff was able to turn off his siren and travel at a good eighty miles per hour, using only flashing warning lights. Thomas easily kept up with him.

When they turned onto State Highway T, they passed a group of cyclists. It was obvious that the bike riders were making the most of this glorious summer morning, and Thomas couldn't help but envy them. An avid rider himself, he remembered well his last bike trip. It had taken place during the Memorial Day weekend, on his last full day off from work.

Brittany had joined him then for an invigorating, early-morning sprint on the bike path from Alexandria to Mount Vernon. Their continued relationship turned serious last fall, shortly after he returned home from England because of his near brush with death aboard the *QE2*. Brittany felt responsible for forcing him to volunteer for the mission, and upon his safe return, there was an even tighter bond between them. From that moment on, weekends were spent exclusively together.

Lately they had been making plans to move in together, and Thomas was genuinely disappointed when she revealed that she wouldn't be able to join them at the lake for the Fourth. Brittany couldn't tell Thomas the reason that she couldn't come to Branson. She was beginning her last year representing the U.S. Navy as the Military Aide to the President. This was a job of vast responsibility. With an office in the East Wing of the White House, Brittany was one of five officers whose duties included maintaining the President's emergency satchel—the infamous "football." She also provided a liaison between the White House staff and the Navy, and acted as the Commander-in-Chief's aide-de-camp.

As Thomas and the Sheriff continued speeding down Highway T and passed by the village limits of Labadie, the approach of an elementary school on the left side of the road caused the Sheriff to dramatically slow down. He also switched off his warning lights, and after passing through a single-lane, one-way tunnel, he activated his left-turn signal.

Thomas did likewise, and followed the Sheriff's vehicle onto the road leading to the Missouri River and the Labadie power plant.

A trio of police cars was parked across from a quaint country inn, where they drew up a hasty operations plan. Because of time constraints, Thomas knew it was essential that this plan be simple and basic.

He contacted his forward observer team by two-way and learned that the trio of newly arrived bikers had joined Conrad Whitten inside the farmhouse. The Ryder truck had been backed up to the front door. Its driver was a leggy redhead whose short-shorts and skimpy halter top hadn't escaped the notice of the ATF sniper watching her every move from the shelter of the surrounding bushes. Before entering the farmhouse herself, she had unlatched the truck's back door, revealing an empty cargo hold.

"It's obvious that whatever they've got going on inside that farmhouse, they're about to transfer something of significant size into that truck," mused Thomas to the seven men of his raiding team. "My biggest fear from the start of this case was that the bomb maker would try to construct a real attention-grabber, like the ammonium nitrate/fuel oil device that took out the Oklahoma City Federal Building. That Ryder could easily hold such an IED, and we could be getting there right when they're prepping it. So use your weapons only if absolutely necessary, and if you are forced to shoot, pick your targets carefully and don't miss!"

They decided to assault the farmhouse from the woods surrounding the backyard. One of the deputies revealed that he knew of a gravel road that would convey them to these woods without being seen from the main compound. The two highway patrolmen were tasked to block the main driveway near where it intersected Highway T. While they got in position, Thomas climbed into the Sheriff's car, along with the other men of his raiding party, and they sped off for the gravel roadway.

They assembled in an abandoned apple orchard. Before moving in by foot on their objective, Thomas made sure that each of them had his body armor properly fitted. After double-checking their weapons' load, he contacted both the Highway Patrolmen and his forward observer team on the two-way to synchronize their movements. When one of his snipers reported that the bikers had just begun loading the truck with a variety of crates they were carrying from the house, Thomas said a brief, silent prayer, crossed his fingers and gave the assault order.

They moved forward in a modified wedge formation, with Thomas at the forward point of the inverted V. His own weapons were limited to a Winchester Model 12 shotgun, with six 12-gauge rounds in its tubular magazine, and his Glock 17 9mm handgun. His five associates were also armed with a variety of revolvers and shotguns.

He took some solace knowing that his two forward observers were expert marksmen, armed with state-of-the-art Heckler & Koch PSG-1 semiautomatic sniper rifles. They fired specially selected 7.62mm Lapua Winchester match ammunition, put on target by times six magnification telescopes, and pity the poor biker whose wallet-chained ass ended up inside the illuminated crosshairs.

With his greatest worry being that they hadn't had the time to properly rehearse this raid beforehand, Thomas completed his climb of the small rise that lay between the orchard and their objective. Upon sighting the gabled roof of the farmhouse, he immediately signaled the men behind him to halt and kneel. Thomas knelt himself, before lying prone on the weed-filled rocky soil and slowly crawling forward.

The back of the clapboard farmhouse was directly in front of them, at the bottom of a gently sloping hill, a bare one hundred yards distant. He smiled upon noting that the sole window was boarded up, and slowly scanned the thick bushes that extended beyond the left side of the structure.

Somewhere inside this cover, his ghillie-suited snipers were situated, and even though he knew the general area in which they were deployed, Thomas spotted not a trace of them.

Thomas crawled backward, stood, and signaled his party to stand and form a tight line behind him. This would be their assault train, and the strategy now was to rush down the hillside at the back of the house and utilize the cover of their snipers to move forward along the structure's left side. Then, without hesitating, they'd sprint around the corner of the house with weapons raised, and hopefully catch their suspects by complete surprise while attention was still focused on loading the truck.

They initiated their movement and reached the back of the house without giving away their presence. The moment of truth was almost upon them, and as Thomas led the assault train around the structure's left side, misfortune struck when the Sheriff tripped and fell to the ground with such force that his shotgun discharged. The element of surprise now compromised, Thomas had no choice but to lead the rest of his troops around to the front side of the house, where their destinies awaited.

"Federal agents!" he proclaimed to the shocked group of leather-clad longhairs standing alongside the partially filled rental truck.

The smell of marijuana wafted past his nostrils, and Thomas scanned the astounded faces of the four bearded men and one gorgeous woman who stood with jaws agape, staring at the assortment of weapons pointed their way.

"Conrad Whitten, I have a warrant for your arrest," one of the deputies informed him.

"Aw, shit!" cursed the tallest of the bikers, a beer-bellied giant of a man with a full, bushy red beard and long, scraggly hair to match.

While the deputies moved in to frisk their suspects, Thomas peeked inside the back of the truck. A rectangular wooden crate sat within reaching distance, and he thought he could make out a light coating of black powder covering the lid.

"See something of interest in there, Mr. Pig?" asked a deep male voice from behind.

Thomas turned around and found himself staring into the stubby barrel of a chrome revolver. The muscular, tattooed biker who held this weapon had apparently been on the far side of the truck during their initial raid, and he called out loudly so that all could hear him.

"Keep those hands where I can see them, and back away from the truck real nice and slow."

Thomas did as instructed, with the biker jamming the pistol into Thomas's stomach while addressing the others. "Drop those weapons, deputies, or your buddy here is gonna have a new belly button."

The deputies appeared to be momentarily flustered by this unexpected command. They looked to each other for guidance, and when they finally lowered their weapons, Thomas exhaled a long breath of relief.

"Attaboy, Jester," said Whitten, who reached out for one of the deputies' pistols.

Before the redheaded giant could gain possession, the firm voice of the Sheriff broke from the right side of the farmhouse. "Freeze!" he ordered, while chambering a fresh round into his shotgun.

All eyes went to Whitten, who took a second to consider the risks involved before slowly backing away from the deputy and meekly nodding in submission.

"You fucking pussy!" shouted Jester, who roughly pushed Thomas to the ground and went sprinting for the nearest Harley.

The chopper roared alive and peeled off down the gravel driveway, leaving a cloud of exhaust in its wake. Thomas scrambled to his feet and listened as a pair of high-powered rounds exploded from the nearby tree line. A bare second later, the motorcycle went tumbling on its side, its tires shredded by a salvo of expertly aimed bullets.

With his pride bruised more than his body, Jester was pulled out from beneath the bike and led back to the porch. The deputies quickly cuffed him, and reinitiated the frisking process.

Only after he was certain that there were no other bikers who had yet to be discovered did Thomas return to his inspection of the truck. He reexamined the powder-coated crate, and spotted the label CHERRY BOMBS stenciled in red on its side. With the edge of his pocket knife, he cautiously pried open one of the slats. Packed in sawdust inside was a line of bright red, gumball-sized objects with short fuses projecting from them.

"I tell ya, all we're doin' out here is makin' a bunch of fuckin' fireworks!" pleaded Conrad Whitten to the Sheriff. "Sure, we're also smokin' a little skunk, but it's only for personal consumption. And I swear that I was gonna get that fireworks permit as soon as I could afford it."

Thomas found it hard to hide his disappointment as he entered the farmhouse and got a good look at their operation.

"Theresa, I told ya Whitten was nothin' but a pussy," said Jester to the only female in their midst while she was being cuffed.

"Shut the fuck up!" countered Whitten, who now sported his own pair of shiny steel bracelets. "We're in enough trouble as it is, and I'm not gonna take your rap of threatening to shoot a police officer all for a mess of bootleg fireworks."

Thomas had busted an illegal fireworks factory before, and as he stepped inside, everything he saw confirmed that this was what the bikers were doing here. A pair of long wooden tables held a variety of commercial powder presses, cardboard wrapping material, and several boxes of fuses. He also discovered three large barrels of black powder, an invoice made out to St. Alban's Country Club for three dozen high-altitude star clusters, and an assortment of red, white, and blue airburst projectiles.

Although Thomas could take some satisfaction in knowing that a dangerous operation had been shut down, he realized they had failed to apprehend the bomb maker. He shared this disappointing information with his forward observers as they emerged from the bushes in camouflaged ghillie suits. For all effective purposes, they were back at square one, and when his cellular phone began ringing, Thomas supposed that he'd next have to pass on the frustrating news to the Special Agent in charge of the St. Louis field office.

The gravelly voice on the other end of the line was strangely familiar. Yet Thomas still found himself totally caught off guard when the caller finally identified himself.

"Thomas, you old dog. You're harder to track down than the Secretary. It's Ted Callahan. I realize I'm about the last person you expected to hear from today, but I was able to convince Director McShane to divulge your number. I understand from the Director that you've got your hands full with a major investigation, but he gave me the all-clear to ask a little favor of you. Army CID needs your help, good buddy. And I'm willing to forget about those Orioles tickets you promised me last Labor Day and never delivered, for a couple hours of your time down here at Fort Leonard Wood. A mere hundred-mile drive down Route 66 is all it will take to square the account, my friend. So get cracking, before I'm forced to send out the MPs!"

Commander Brittany Cooper had certainly drawn her fair share of unusual duty slots during her career, yet her current assignment was unique in all the military. The flying command post to which she was assigned was officially designated the E-4B and called the National Airborne Operations Center, though it was better known by its code name Nightwatch. The massive Boeing 747 was one of a fleet of four such airplanes, reserved for the National Command Authority, to provide secure command and communication in the event of war.

Though she had toured Nightwatch previously, this was her first real airborne mission, and she was spending much of her time getting better acquainted with the massive aircraft. Most of her duty so far had been confined to the main deck in Operations, and she eagerly took the opportunity to expand her knowledge of the plane by using a coffee break to explore the flight deck.

A spiral stairway led her past a serious-faced, black-beret-clad, armed security man. Halfway up these stairs, she felt the force of clear-air turbulence and had to halt in mid-step and grab onto the railing. The deck vibrated and slightly dipped, so Brittany waited for the shaking to stop completely before continuing into the upper-deck rest area. She headed forward through the flight crew's sleeping quarters and, before entering the open flight deck, was forced to a halt by yet another pocket of rough air.

As she finally stepped into the back of the cockpit, a powdery-blue sky could be seen through the wraparound windshield. First to acknowledge her presence with a smile was the engineer, who was seated to her immediate right, a complicated, instrument-filled console before him.

She nodded in return, remembering him to be First Lieutenant Jake Lasky. A native of Pasadena, California, Lasky had given Brittany her initial tour of Nightwatch back at Andrews, and she enjoyed the curly-haired officer's quick wit and the stories of his adventures on the Santa Monica bike path.

"I tell you, Coach, you're all wrong on this one," proclaimed the copilot, who was seated directly in front of Lasky, his eyes scanning the dozens of digital readouts set into the cockpit around him.

This officer was yet another Californian. Captain Charles "Lucky" Davis lived in Manhattan Beach. His wavy blond hair was almost touching the collar of his flight suit, and Lucky displayed a surfer's good looks and a lean physique to match.

Seated to his left was Major William Foard, or Coach, as he was better known. Their current pilot was from Boston and a Yale graduate. Brittany had conversed with Coach only briefly, but she liked him instantly. He had a blunt, no-nonsense manner, and it was obvious that he had long ago earned his men's respect.

Coach had one gloved hand on the plane's yoke, and he had his attention riveted on making an adjustment to the autopilot. His hazel eyes were hidden behind a pair of wire-rimmed, aviator-style sunglasses, and Brittany was surprised to find him wearing a faded "NO FEAR" baseball cap.

As Brittany stared out the windshield, she realized that it was a gorgeous day for flying. The only clouds visible hugged the northern horizon. From their current altitude of thirty-one thousand feet, the sparkling waters of the Black Sea stretched in all directions, and it was as Brittany caught sight of a single ship below that the copilot finally realized they had a visitor.

Brittany accepted a pair of headphones from the navigator. An intercom patch allowed her to hear Coach as he swiveled around and spoke into his chin-mounted microphone. "Welcome to the flight deck, Commander."

"I hope this isn't a bad time for a visit," she said.

"Not at all," replied Coach.

"In fact, you're the perfect person to prove my point," said Lucky, who pushed back his right headphone and greeted Brittany with the same warm, boyish grin that was responsible for melting the heart of many a beach bunny. "Commander Cooper, we were just having a friendly little discussion about who was the world's most powerful person. Since you're responsible for the football and know what's inside, perhaps you could remind my co-workers that our Commander-in-Chief's the only person in the world who can change our planet's destiny with a single order."

Before she could answer, Coach said, "Destroying the planet is not necessarily what I associate with being the world's most powerful person, Lucky. I'm talking about the consummate mover and shaker, the guy who whispers, and the whole world listens. In my book, the President of the United States just doesn't cut it anymore. He's chained to his politics, with Congress always there to dilute his vision and veto his greatest dreams. That's why my candidate is none other than the Chairman of the Federal Reserve."

"Coach, I agree with your assessment of today's Presidency," added the engineer. "But your choice of the Fed Chairman doesn't quite fill all the requirements. Don't forget that he's still only a government appointee himself, who serves at the bidding of powers that be. One unpopular decision could cost him his job, especially if he starts stepping on the toes of the bankers. Right now, I'm torn between two men, both of whom wield the type of unlimited power that influences each of our lives on a daily basis."

A soft, electronic warning tone caused Lasky to momentarily redirect his attention to the mass of instruments gracing the engineering console. A quick glance was all that was needed for him to reach up with his gloved left hand and reset a tripped circuit breaker. The tone ceased, and, conscious that he still had his audience's complete attention, Lasky slowly turned around and said, "My picks are Michael Eisner and Bill Gates."

"Give me a break, Jake," said Lucky with a laugh. "A mouse and a geek for the world's most powerful? Come on, now."

Lasky was quick to the defense. "You can laugh all you want, Lucky, but think about it. Turn on just about any computer in the world, and I guarantee that you have software compliments of Bill Gates loaded inside. Do the same with your television or radio, and during your next visit to the movies, count the percentage of programs that are produced by Disney, and you'll be staggered. And that doesn't even include Disney's clothing, toy, and book lines. You might laugh, but the mouse and the geek, as you call them, are influencing almost every facet of our lives, as well as those of our children!"

"Jake, my man," interrupted Lucky. "Granted that Eisner and Gates are billionaires leading Fortune 500 companies, but that still doesn't put them in the same league as the President. Commander Cooper will tell you, when they're invited to the White House they still have to get in line with the masses, to pay homage to the man with all the real power."

All eyes went to the female in their midst, and Brittany thoughtfully shook her head and expressed herself. "As far as I'm concerned, none of you is even close. My vote goes to the Pope."

"The Pope?" repeated Lucky like he hadn't heard her properly.

Brittany nodded. "That's right, the old guy with the funny hat who lives in the Vatican. Because if it's supreme power you're concerned with, the Pope is the one with the clout to pull the strings that really count."

Coach rubbed his square jaw and reflected. "Interesting choice, Commander. But there's one thing you're forgetting. Even the Pontiff's at the mercy of a quarter percent drop in the prime. Do you realize how such a minor drop can influence the value of Sunday's collection plate? With a single decision, the Chairman of the Fed could cost the Church billions."

"But can either one of them green-light a ten-million-dollar movie that can bring in a worldwide gross of one hundred times as much, or produce a piece of software that every computer user on the planet can't live without?" countered Jake.

Brittany could see that this argument didn't have a chance of being resolved at this time, and she couldn't help but laugh at the absurdity of it all. Here they were thirty-one thousand feet over the Black Sea, flying in one of the most sophisticated aircraft in the world, and all the flight crew seemed to care about was such an off-the-wall subject matter.

"I understand that Air Force One has landed," she said in an attempt to redirect the course of their conversation.

Coach checked his watch and grunted. "They've been down on the ground for a good fifteen minutes."

"Any of you been to Simferopol before?" she asked.

None of the flight crew had, and Brittany added, "I've got to admit that I didn't even know where it was when the President initially informed us of his desire to travel to the Crimea."

"Scuttlebutt has it that he's down there to finalize the Global Zero Nuclear Alert Treaty with the Russians and the Ukrainians," offered Lucky. "Talk about power. That agreement would change our lives forever, and make a plane like Nightwatch an anachronism."

"I wouldn't go so far as that," said Coach. "Nightwatch would still have its uses in a world without a hair-trigger nuclear response posture." He made a slight adjustment to the throttle before turning to Brittany. "The one thing I've been meaning to ask you, Commander, is how you got stuck with us. Why aren't you down there with the President?"

"It's because of my lousy Russian," she answered directly. "Major Ryan is the Army MILAIDE, and because he majored in Eastern languages back at the Point, he got the main assignment, while I drew backup."

Coach could sense that she had been disappointed by this decision, and he made certain to catch her glance before replying. "Though I can't give you any frequent-flier miles for this trip, or offer you fancy accommodations like on Air Force One, speaking for the crew of Nightwatch, we're honored to have you aboard."

Before Brittany could respond to this gracious statement, a gravelly male voice emanated from the speakers of her headphones. "Nightwatch six-seven-six, this is Spooky Three-nine. Do you copy? Over."

Coach turned a dial on the radio selector and replied into his chin microphone. "Roger that, Spooky Three-nine. This is Nightwatch six-seven-six, reading you loud and clear. Over."

"Nightwatch six-seven-six, be informed that Spooky Three-nine is moving north to patrol sector Avalon at eighteen thousand. Over."

"Roger that, Spooky Three-nine. Don't hesitate to call if we can render any assistance. Out."

Coach turned the radio back to intercom mode and listened as Brittany questioned, "I gather that Spooky Three-nine is our AC-130U?"

"That's affirmative, Commander," Coach answered. "Patrol sector Avalon will put them just off the Crimean coast, should the President dial nine-one-one."

"I'm sure glad Spooky Three-nine is on our side," offered Lucky while looking out the windshield in an effort to spot them. "I got a buddy who flies gunships out of Hurlburt, and from what he tells me, that's one lean, mean fighting machine."

Jake concurred. "In last month's *Airman* magazine, they did a feature on the AC-130U. Did you know they're the only planes in the Air Force that are authorized to display nose art? Most of this art is of various demons, a fitting mascot for a plane armed with a 25mm General Electric Gatling gun capable of eighteen hundred rounds per minute, a 40mm Bofors cannon, and a 105mm howitzer."

"I read that same article, and was impressed by the way all that firepower is delivered on target," said Coach. "An All Light Level Television system, an infrared detection set, and a multi-mode strike radar are all used to help Spooky carry out its main mission of providing surgical firepower or area saturation during extended loiter periods, at night and in adverse weather."

"And then there's their ability to simultaneously engage two different targets with two separate sensors and two different guns," added Jake. "Now that's kicking ass big-time."

"The trouble is," Brittany somberly interjected, "if we do need to call in the gunship to protect the President's motorcade, chances are it will already be too late to make a difference."

Before the flight crew could discuss this assessment, the intercom activated, and Brittany was called back to Operations for a meeting with the E-4B's senior officer, Admiral Trent Warner, the current Chairman of the Joint Chiefs of

Staff. She excused herself and headed aft, down the spiral stairway to the main-deck forward entry area. She returned the nod of the security man and passed by the gallery.

By heading forward, one could access the NCA executive compartment. This was where the Chairman's bunk was located. Brittany proceeded in the opposite direction, passing through the vacant conference room. The long, rectangular table could seat nine, with a projection screen built into the aft bulkhead.

As she ducked through the hatchway, she entered the briefing room. Its eighteen seats were filled with various personnel in the process of receiving a briefing from the officer standing at the compartment's forward lectern. A large-scale map of Europe was projected behind him, and as Brittany crossed through the room, she listened as the briefer discussed the communications frequencies that they would be depending upon during tomorrow's anticipated flight back to Andrews Air Force Base.

Brittany almost forgot that she was flying in an airplane upon entering the next compartment. This was the Operations Area, and it reminded her of the White House military office. A series of twelve computer workstations lined each side of the room. Each of the consoles was fully staffed, with all of the personnel attired in matching green flight suits.

She briefly halted at the second console on the compartment's starboard side. Seated here was Master Sergeant Andrea "Red" Rayburn. The trim, thirty-four-year-old African-American was immersed in a telephone conversation while at the same time entering data into her laptop. Even then, the personable systems analyst managed to flash Brittany a warm smile.

Brittany could only imagine whom she was talking to, and the means by which this conversation was being transmitted. Nightwatch 676 was one of four sites delegated to provide secure command and control of U.S. military forces in support of the NCA. The primary land-based facility was the National Military Command Center, located in the Pentagon, with backups at Site "R" near Fort Ritchie, Maryland, and the Strategic Command underground bunker buried beneath Nebraska's Offut Air Force Base. Of these locations, Nightwatch was the only mobile facility, offering the NCA a survivable, nuclear-war-hardened platform from which they could exercise their national security responsibilities should circumstances warrant. And it was because of this ability to survive a nuclear exchange that Nightwatch was also known as the "doomsday plane."

Trying her best not to further disturb Red, whose nickname was derived from her bright crimson fingernails, Brittany used a key to access the file drawer that had been reserved for her exclusive use. She removed the black leather briefcase that lay inside and joined a group of airmen gathered at the console immediately behind Red. It was here that Brittany sighted the distinguished shock of white hair belonging to Admiral Trent Warner. A former submariner, Warner was a recent replacement for General William Ridgeway, who had surprised the defense community three months ago when he announced his early retirement.

Up until that time, Brittany had had limited contact with Warner. But as Chairman, he had become a frequent White House visitor, and she had made it a point to properly introduce herself. During that initial meeting she learned that Warner had received his first submarine command only after passing the scrutiny of the legendary Hyman Rickover. Like Rickover, Warner made a reputation for himself as a strict disciplinarian. His demands were high, his short fuse notorious.

Brittany would never forget the way Warner's steely-gray gaze had examined her from head to foot. It was like he was holding an inspection, and she found herself feeling uncomfortable, afraid that he'd find a hair out of place or a button unfastened. Several days later, after lunch at the White

House mess, she mentioned this sensation to the Maitre d', a chief petty officer and career submariner. He revealed that one of his best friends had served on one of Warner's submarines, and had experienced a similar degree of discomfort whenever he found himself in his skipper's company.

Now, with each step closer to the Chairman's workstation, Brittany squared back her shoulders, took a deep breath, and mentally prepared herself to be swallowed by Warner's dominant will. She was able to derive some semblance of relief when the knot of male officers gathered around the Chairman let loose a peal of shared laughter. Included in this group was the balding, slim figure of Colonel Lyford Pritchard, the op team's CO.

"And that's the *last* time I ever played golf with our esteemed Commander-in-Chief," said Warner.

Brittany smiled along with the others, even though she'd missed the joke, but her arrival at the workstation generated an immediate change of attitude. The smiles quickly faded, and even the men's postures stiffened. Once again Brittany felt the discriminatory existence of the old boy's network. Some things in the military would never change. She had decided early in her career not to fight it, and pushed onward knowing there were some walls between the sexes that could never be breached.

The Chairman acknowledged her with a nod, and the other officers alertly excused themselves, except for Colonel Pritchard. After Warner made certain that Brittany had brought the briefcase along, he broke the seal of the red file folder he was holding, and reached into the top pocket of his flight suit to remove his reading glasses.

"Commander Cooper," said the Chairman, his voice deep and resonant, "as you most likely know, Air Force One has landed at Simferopol. Per the continuity of government protocol, now that POTUS is on foreign soil, Satchel Bravo is to be deposited in our emergency actions safe. Colonel Pritchard, if you'll be so good as to give the Commander her key."

Lyford Pritchard partially unzipped his flight suit and removed one of two chains that hung from his neck. Both of them held a single key, and he handed one of the chains to Brittany, saying, "Commander Cooper, this key is to be in your possession at all times. It opens one of two locks that ensure the integrity of our emergency actions safe. As op's team leader, I've got possession of the sister key."

Pritchard beckoned toward the compact, bank-vault-type safe that was bolted to the deck beneath the Chairman's workstation. Brittany followed his lead and, with the briefcase at her side, knelt down and watched as Pritchard inserted his key into the top lock. She put her key into the lock below and, on his count of three, simultaneously turned the tumbler. It triggered with a loud click, with Pritchard pulling down on the safe's iron handle.

The interior of the safe was empty, and the briefcase easily fit inside its thick, fireproof walls. Once the case was secure, the door to the safe was shut, and the two keys were once again utilized to lock it inside.

"Let's hope that's the last we see of it until we land back at Andrews tomorrow evening," said Warner, who watched as Brittany draped the chain holding the key around her neck and stood.

Unexpected clear-air turbulence caused the cabin to rattle ominously, and Brittany was forced to reach out and accept the Chairman's steadying hand. His palm was cool and clammy, and she let go of it as soon as she regained her balance, all the while listening as Warner's voice lowered to a bare, conspiratorial whisper.

"Commander Cooper, both you and Colonel Pritchard are now an integral part of the continuity of government protocol. If anything should happen to permanently incapacitate the President while he's in the Crimea, and should Satchel Alpha be compromised, Nightwatch is responsible for relaying the need of a transfer of power to the Vice President or his successor via the FEMA central locator system.

"Yet until the next in line is sworn in, Satchel Bravo will be removed and activated. As the senior NCA representative present, I will be in charge of the nuclear release codes and all SIOP implementation. In the unlikely event that such a tragic turn of events should befall us, our nation is depending upon Nightwatch to not only ensure a peaceful transition of government, but to also orchestrate a timely, effective military response to any enemy that might wish to take advantage of a temporary lapse of executive control. Your cooperation is therefore invaluable, and I'm counting on your support should the unthinkable come to pass."

Another pocket of turbulence shook the fuselage, yet this time Brittany didn't need any assistance to keep her balance. Ignoring the coffee cup that crashed to the deck behind her, she found herself fingering the silver key that hung from her neck, well aware of the great secrets it protected.

Samuel Morrison knew that they were very fortunate to get the motorcade formed and on the road before the rains started. From the backseat of the lead Suburban, the SAIC turned his head to look out the rear window, where the single wiper was doing its best to clear off the copious amounts of rainwater that fell from the stormy heavens. He could just see the headlights belonging to the limousine carrying the President. It was the next vehicle in line, and, in addition to Two Putt, held his National Security Advisor, his Army MI-LAIDE, the Press Secretary, and Special Agent Moreno.

Moreno had more than earned this ride in the so-called "hot seat." He had displayed admirable initiative when he climbed behind the wheel of their ambulance and popped the clutch, while members of the C-17's flight crew pushed the van down the airplane's rear loading ramp. All of them issued a relieved shout as the engine finally turned over.

Without this emergency vehicle running, there would have been no motorcade. The official rules were strict on this point, and as the President's backup physician exited Air Force One and climbed into the ambulance to prepare it for the trip to the coast, little did he know how close they had come to having to call in a local tow truck.

Dr. Charles Kromer was the current doctor on duty. The SAIC knew that he was substituting for Jim Patton, who had asked for this time off to attend the wedding of his son Ricky to Kristin Liu.

As a lightning bolt streaked across the cloud-filled Crimean sky, the SAIC found himself thinking about Ricky, Kristin, and another storm, by the name of Hurricane Marti. The so-called "summit at sea" aboard the *QE2* seemed to have taken place in another lifetime. Yet in reality, ten months had passed since that tragic crossing, which had cost many a good man his life, and almost precipitated World War III.

"Checkmate One, this is Checkmate Two. Over." Special Agent Moreno's voice broke over Morrison's two-way.

"Go ahead, Checkmate Two," said the SAIC into his two-way's transmitter.

"Sir," Moreno replied, the sound of muffled voices audible in the background. "The Press Secretary is having trouble getting a secure line to CONUS."

"Can't she wait until we get to Alushta?" Morrison queried.

"That's a negative, sir," answered Moreno, a single, agitated voice now dominating the background conversation.

Morrison identified it as belonging to the President, and knowing the most likely reason for his anger, the SAIC shook his head and grinned. "Checkmate Two, contact the comm van and have them patch the Secretary's call through Nightwatch. After all, that's what our flying telephone booth in the sky is up there for."

Moreno acknowledged these instructions, and the SAIC lowered his two-way. The rain-soaked outskirts of Simferopol passed in a blur, and Morrison's seatmate voiced himself in Slavic-accented English.

"Do I perceive troubles inside the Presidential limo, Comrade?" questioned Alexi Kosygin.

"I was expecting this," Morrison said with a grunt. "Two Putt is most likely still fuming about that possible press leak to an NPR reporter, and the poor Secretary is trying her best to attempt damage control. I'm afraid, though, that she's too late. That cock-and-bull story they're trying to pass off on the public will never hold up. There are just too many people in the loop whenever the President travels, and a leak is to be anticipated."

"Comrade, you never did say how you were going to explain Air Force One's presence at Simferopol Airport. Even though the aircraft is far away from the main terminal, enough of the local ground personnel have seen it to create a tidal wave of rumors."

"A story was to be circulated saying that the airplane was carrying the President's National Security Advisor, with the President supposedly sequestered in Camp David."

"And the reason for this deception?" Kosygin dared to ask.

"This is just between us, Alexi, but the spin I'm hearing is that Two Putt put this whole thing together so he could surprise the nation with a July Fourth announcement. At that time, he planned to reveal that the Global Zero Nuclear Alert Treaty had been finalized, and after Senate radification, the world would be one step closer to the banning of all nuclear weapons from the face of the planet."

The Russian shook his head and grinned. "I must admit that his timing for such an announcement would be perfect. What a wonderful gift for the American people on their day of national celebration—to be finally independent from the threat of an accidental or unwanted nuclear war."

The Suburban shuddered as it struck a pothole, prompting Morrison to steady himself on the back of the front seat. "So much for the smooth pavement that Comrade Zinoviev promised," he said as the vehicle bounced roughly over a deep rut.

The waves of rain momentarily dissipated, allowing him to see the glowing red taillights and huge rear tires of the armored personnel carrier that they were following. The BTR-60 had a 14.5mm machine gun on its roof, with a helmeted soldier manning the turret. The poor fellow was soaked, and Morrison wondered if they could rely on him, or the fourteen-person SWAT team inside, should they run into any unexpected trouble.

Just as they were leaving the outskirts of the city behind, the SAIC spotted a column of tanks up ahead. The massive tracked vehicles were lined up on a side street, and as Morrison scanned the column with binoculars, his seatmate identified them.

"Those are T-72 main battle tanks, most likely from Ukraine's elite Kirov Guard unit."

"Zinoviev never mentioned anything about having a Guard unit in the area," said Morrison, his amplified glance locked on the long, tapering gun barrel of the lead vehicle. "And our scouting teams certainly didn't report seeing any tanks in the vicinity."

"Perhaps we should contact Zinoviev in his police sedan and find out the reason for their presence," offered Kosygin.

Friday, July 2, 9:10 A.M. C.D.T.

Eleven Point River

The view from the canoe's bow was a spectacular one. Vince plunged his wooden paddle into the cool, clear water, his gaze scanning the thick, wooded hills that surrounded this portion of the river valley. Not a hint of human habitation was visible, the land alive with gnarled oaks, towering cottonwoods, and flowering shrubs displaying a rainbow of vibrant color. Since leaving Greer Crossing, they were able to adjust to their new medium of travel on a relatively calm stretch of water. They had yet to encounter their first rapids, and the float-trip neophytes in their midst took this opportunity to get their balance and learn how best to paddle.

Because of the VP's desire to keep this expedition as small as possible, they had decided to limit the canoe convoy to four vessels. From his vantage point, Vince could see the muscular shoulders of Andrew Montgomery Chapman, seated in the bow of the lead canoe, approximately twenty yards ahead. The VP was wearing a white Harvard polo shirt and khaki shorts, and wasn't afraid to use his paddle to assist Senior Ranger Ben Eberly, who was perched in the stern.

Ron Wyatt was occupying the back end of Vince's vessel. The Forest Service veteran was obviously an expert canoeist, his paddle strokes strong and powerful, and Vince tried his best to keep pace.

The two trailing canoes carried the majority of their camping gear, and were reserved for such emergency functions as communications and first aid. In addition to three Secret Service agents and the VP's Navy physician, they also carried the only true civilian in their midst. Andy Whitworth was a freelance photojournalist representing the major wire services and *Time* magazine. She was smart, tough, and incredibly persistent, Vince having worked with her before when she was assigned to cover the White House.

Andy had already made her presence felt back at Greer Crossing, when she practically took over the impromptu news conference that the inexperienced news anchor from Springfield had initially started. Vince was close by as the VP agreed to give the television crew a brief interview. It rapidly deteriorated into a potentially ugly confrontation between Chapman and the foul-mouthed old lady wearing the "Give the Eleven Point Back to the People!" sweatshirt.

Sensing blood in the water, Andy constantly provoked the old-timer. With miniature tape machine running and 35mm camera constantly clicking away, Andy challenged the woman to defend her antigovernment position. Emotions all too soon got the best of the hotheaded elder, and her irrational diatribes were easily countered by the VP's practiced eloquence. A former captain of the Harvard debating team, Chapman made intellectual mincemeat out of his senile opponent's groundless accusations and paranoid rantings, while she countered by increasing the volume of her voice and the foulness of her rather limited vocabulary.

Things started to get ugly when the locals in the crowd

began voicing their support of the old lady with shouts of encouragement. Vince sensed trouble, and pushing the reporters aside, he intervened to immediately stop the interview before things turned violent.

Now that they were out on the river, Vince knew he had definitely made the right decision. Though the VP was far ahead on debating points, he was in the middle of an argument that he could never hope to win, especially when it came down to a few cleverly selected sound bites on the evening news. Besides, they had traveled to the Missouri Ozarks to enjoy nature and celebrate its preservation, and the gorgeous countryside they were presently passing through would hopefully remind Andy Whitworth of that fact.

"We'll be hitting our first rapids shortly, on the other side of that bend up yonder," revealed Ron Wyatt in a relaxed, southern Missouri drawl.

"Is it anything to batten down the hatches for?" Vince asked, his eyes sweeping the horizon to gauge the distance to this bend, which was formed by the river hitting a lofty limestone bluff.

"As I said before, Special Agent, this section of the river is fairly tame. Other than an occasional root clump or partially submerged boulder, we shouldn't run into anything dangerous until we hit the Class Three rapids at Mary Deckard shoals."

Vince estimated that they wouldn't reach the bend for another five minutes, and he looked to his left, where the Eleven Point branched off into what appeared to be an alternative channel. A good portion of the forest there was cut down, prompting him to query, "What's down there in that clearing?"

"That's Ross Cemetery. There used to be a small settlement in that hollow. In fact, Norma, the old lady the Vice President was arguing with, was born there, some eighty years ago."

"It's hard to believe that people used to live and work on this river," said Vince, his gaze drawn to a red-tailed hawk taking flight from the direction of the cemetery.

"The Eleven Point's just filled with history, Special Agent. And you workin' for Treasury and all should find it 'specially interesting why the folks from Ross called that channel Counterfeit Cove."

"Don't tell me Norma used to print funny money?" Vince asked with a chuckle.

Wyatt held back his response until he spat out a mouthful of tobacco juice. "It was nothin' like that. Back in the twenties, a group of counterfeiters on the run from the law dumped their printing presses and plates into the deep water there. And legend has it that they're still on the bottom of the cove to this day."

"Sounds like it warrants a further investigation by the Secret Service," jested Vince, who could barely hear the sound of crashing water in the distance.

With each paddle stroke, the limestone bluff ahead grew larger, until Vince could practically touch the moss hanging from its steep walls. Several twisted red cedars clung to the rock above, with a family of cliff swallows visible nesting on the limestone ledge close by. The air temperature seemed to suddenly drop several degrees when the canoe was swallowed in the bluff's shadow. At the same time, the crashing sound of agitated water intensified, and Vince got his first view of the obstacle responsible for it.

A massive, partially submerged rock shelf projected from the bottom of the bluff, with white water forming on its exposed surface as the Eleven Point crashed directly into it. A shallow shoal on the opposite bank caused the river to further narrow, the frothing current given additional velocity by a barely recognizable drop in elevation.

Vince watched the Vice President's canoe surge forward in a sudden burst of unexpected speed, and he found his own pulse quickening. They appeared to be headed straight for the shelf, with Andrew Chapman paddling away, seemingly oblivious of any danger.

Professional habit took over, and Vince hastily plotted the manner in which he'd initiate a rescue should the VP's canoe capsize. Though he shuddered at the thought of having to dive into the churning water, he knew that if push came to shove, he'd plunge into the river regardless of any danger to his own person. Protecting the life of Andrew Montgomery Chapman being priority number one.

Less than ten yards from the shelf, Ranger Eberly used his paddle like a rudder to cause the bow of the VP's canoe to move hard aport. With plenty of deep water beneath it, the vessel shot past the bluff like an F-15 on afterburners. And the last Vince saw of Andrew Chapman, before he was forced to concentrate on their own transit of the rapids, was the VP's triumphant fist held high overhead.

"Do you want me to paddle?" screamed Vince, the partially submerged shelf looming menacingly before them.

"Why waste the effort?" Wyatt replied. "Hang on, enjoy the ride, and when I give the word, paddle like hell from the right side."

Vince did as ordered, and couldn't help but find himself invigorated by their own transit of the rapids. His guide displayed superb timing as he dug his paddle into the churning water on the canoe's starboard and angled the blade outward. With a single shout of "Now!" Vince began paddling, and before he knew it, the shelf was past them.

It was on a calm pool on the far side of the bluff that they rendezvoused with the Vice President, to await the other vessels. Andrew Chapman was using binoculars to scan the bluff's craggy summit, and Vince peered out in this direction himself.

"See anything interesting, sir?" he questioned.

"What do you think, Special Agent Kellogg?" said Chapman without lowering his binoculars. "Are they up there? I sure don't see any sign of them."

"Sir, if you're referring to one of my CAT team, they're up on that bluff, all right, as well as every other piece of high ground we'll be passing today. I'd only be disappointed if you did in fact spot them."

Chapman redirected his binoculars to study a pair of large birds circling high above. Vince easily saw these same soaring creatures himself, and he listened as the Vice President identified them.

"Damn, those turkey vultures are tough-looking brutes! That big one's got a mug that would put Speaker of the House Pierce to shame."

Vince laughed, and watched as the VP lowered his binoculars and turned to observe the progress of the other canoes. "I don't know about you, Kellogg, but this place makes me feel one hundred percent alive. Lord, it's good to finally get out from inside the Beltway. You know, there *is* life outside D.C., regardless of what they think on the Hill."

A single quail began crying out from the underbrush nearby, its distinctive "bobwhite" call clearly audible. When another quail answered from the adjoining bank, Vince shook his head in agreement.

"I think I know what you're saying, sir. My pastoral excursions of late have been limited to the backyard of my house in Alexandria. There's nothing like getting out in a real wilderness area to properly feel the pulse of our planet, and to realize how artificial life can be in the city."

"Well said, Kellogg. I'm glad you were able to join my team."

Both of them watched as the canoe carrying Andy Whitworth safely transited the rapids. The journalist celebrated by holding her paddle above her head, and Chapman grunted.

"Part of me wishes they would have capsized, and she would have lost that infernal tape recorder and camera of hers," he offered. "I realize it's important for the American people to get a documented report of the progress we're making out here. But having her around is a corrupting influence. I'm sure you saw the way she was riling up the crowd back at Greer Crossing. Though it's simply the nature of the beast at work, she would have thought nothing of instigating a riot, which leads me to believe that Two Putt had something to do with getting her this assignment."

Vince held his tongue as the canoe carrying the photojournalist made a beeline for them.

"That was wonderful!" exclaimed Worthington, a wide smile on her pinched face. "Mr. Vice President, I'm beginning to see what you find so special on these wilderness jaunts of yours."

For a hopeful moment, both Vince and the VP thought she was actually sincere. But then she pulled out her camera, and while snapping shots of the rapids from this angle, she offhandedly questioned Chapman.

"Mr. Vice President, is it true that the real reason behind this float trip is the President's desire to get you out of the political spotlight at this particular time?" She redirected the aim of her camera to record his reaction and added, "It's well known to all of us covering the White House that the President was upset with your candid remarks regarding the Global Zero Alert Treaty. Since he's obviously negotiating this treaty without you, do you believe the President is fearful that you're in a position to gain more politically if the treaty is to be presented to Congress so close to the upcoming election?"

Andrew Chapman demonstrated remarkable restraint as he answered her. "Ms. Worthington, I am not going to answer any of your questions regarding my relationship with the President. Furthermore, I insist that your story remain focused on this gorgeous river we're privileged to float, and the manner in which our government desires to preserve this great national treasure for generations of Americans to come. If you wanted something different, you should have stayed in Washington!"

The cocksure reporter looked hurt as she lowered her camera, and Vince fought the urge to give the VP a high five. Because of the nature of his work, it was imperative that he remained neutral and detached when it came to political intrigues or the inner motives of pushy journalists. His concerns were of a totally different nature.

As they continued with their float trip, Vince found himself scanning the dense wood line and lush valleys for any signs of his co-workers. The Secret Service had assigned twenty-eight agents to cover the five-mile route that they'd be floating. Most of them were working in two-man teams, concentrating their efforts on the high ground and public-access points.

To augment this rather limited force, the U.S. Forest Service, the Missouri Highway Patrol, and the Oregon County Sheriff's Department were assisting them. Vince had only to activate his two-way to make contact with the nearest land-based team. A network of Forest Service repeater towers allowed for secure communications the entire length of the river they would be traveling.

For additional backup, Marine Two and a Secret Service Blackhawk helicopter were on standby at the Winona Ranger Station. If needed, a heavily armed, airborne assault force could be there to assist them within minutes.

He knew they were very fortunate that the weather forecast remained favorable. The Eleven Point was prone to flash floods, and the only rain anticipated was a spotty summer thunderstorm that could strike later in the afternoon. If all went on schedule, they'd be off the river by then and on their way to Branson, where the VP would be donning black tie and hosting a Party-sponsored charity gala.

Vince shuddered at the thought of having to don a tuxedo in this heat, and he watched as Chapman's canoe floated down the current, the vessel holding Andy Whitworth close beside. The two had obviously made peace, with the VP talking away a mile a minute while the reporter nodded and took notes.

There was no doubt in Vince's mind that Chapman was talking about his favorite subject, the environment, and government's responsibility in preserving it. This was the VP's passion. He had already written a best-selling book on the subject, and made it the cornerstone of his political philosophy.

The Washington image makers had wisely advised the VP that his ability to relate to the land and nature was one of his strongest attributes. His expertise in the matters of pollution control and wilderness preservation polled extremely high, with Americans regarding the Virginia native as if he were a modern-day Teddy Roosevelt.

Instead of a suit and tie, he was most often portrayed in the media wearing jeans, a flannel shirt, and cowboy boots. The great outdoors was his second home, and while the President played golf at exclusive country clubs, Chapman was perceived as someone with down-home, wholesome values, who spent his free time fighting to preserve the planet's fragile ecosystem.

Vince knew that this carefully crafted public image had been years in the making. Andrew Montgomery Chapman was definitely not a simple country boy. The son of Virginia's longest-serving Senator, with a mother who came from one of America's oldest families, Chapman sharpened his vision of the world at Harvard, and in the United Kingdom as a Rhodes scholar. The young man born with the proverbial silver spoon in his mouth soon became the youngest Virginian ever to be elected to the House of Representatives, where he was able to shed his poor-little-rich-boy image by walking the country roads of his district and developing an almost uncanny ability to relate to the common constituent. As Vice President, he was continuing this tradition, with political sights no doubt set on eventually occupying the nation's highest office.

Chapman's current challenge appeared to be convincing Andy Whitworth, and the millions she reported to, that

America had to balance its responsibilities abroad with even vaster needs right at home. And even though he might have been inwardly chomping at the bit to add his two cents worth to such significant international agreements as the Global Zero Alert Treaty, he was wisely backing off to let the President take the spotlight. Far away from the intrigues of foreign summits, he would ignite the passions of the American people right here in the heartland, with a story about how the government saved a river and, in the process, preserved one of the most pristine wilderness areas in the nation.

The hoped-for photo op appeared to arrive shortly after they had transited yet another small rapids. It was at this time that Vince's two-way activated, and Special Agent Linda Desiante excitedly reported in from the next bend.

"Sir, I've been instructed by my Forest Service guide to inform the Vice President that we've got a major mayfly hatch up here. We've got bugs swarming all around us, and I've already seen two big rainbows hit the surface to feed. So I guess he can get out his gear, and maybe we'll get that promised fresh-fish lunch after all."

This was just the sort of report that they had been waiting for, and Vince could already see tomorrow's newspaper headlines, with a picture of the VP's first catch as the most urgent news of the day.

It had taken only a single call to ATF headquarters in Washington for Thomas to learn that Ted Callahan's surprise request for his services indeed had priority over his current investigation. The reassignment had come right from the top, with Director McShane personally getting on the line to inform Thomas that the Special Agent in charge of the St. Louis field office would be taking over the search for the abortion clinic bomber. That left Thomas free to offer Army CID whatever assistance they might need. The Director never did explain the nature of this mysterious case, and Thomas left for his new duty directly from the Labadie raid site.

Fort Leonard Wood was conveniently situated off the four-lane highway he currently traveled. A trip of less than one hundred miles would bring him to the post's front gate, and Thomas spent a good portion of the drive mentally adjusting to the sudden change of venue.

He hated to leave a case unsolved, especially after discovering a promising lead, like the fire-scarred detonator box that he pulled from the trash bin. Would further searching prove that the bikers were making IEDs in addition to their fireworks? And if they weren't, surely someone else in the region had purchased the same lot of detonators, and this was where the piece of cardboard box originated.

It was frustrating to leave these questions unanswered, though Thomas realized that this unexpected reassignment wasn't necessarily such a bad thing. He had been pulled off unsolved cases before, and in almost every instance he returned with a new way of looking at things. Missed clues were rediscovered, and a new perspective often produced amazing insights.

Besides offering a much-needed mental break, to work with Ted Callahan again would be exciting. They hadn't collaborated together since late last summer, when Ted helped him track down yet another bomber in the hills of West Virginia. Callahan's tracing of the C-4 sample was an instrumental part of breaking that case, and Thomas owed him big-time.

An NPR news update redirected his thoughts, and Thomas was surprised by the lead story. It referred to reliable sources confirming the previous rumor that the President had just landed in the Crimea to begin a secret negotiating session with the Presidents of Russia and Ukraine. As the newscaster went on to describe the purpose of this unannounced summit, Thomas remembered well the first time the so-called Global Zero Alert Treaty hit the headlines.

It occurred late last summer, at about the same time he last worked with Ted Callahan. A brainchild of the Russian President, the idea of removing the world's stockpile of nuclear warheads from their delivery systems was initially presented to the United Nations, on the day before the *QE2* set sail for the infamous G-7 summit at sea.

The entire incident had a nightmarish quality to it, and

seemed to have taken place in another lifetime. This was fine with Thomas, who brought home scars of both a physical and an emotional nature. Some doors were better left closed, and that was the way he felt about his experiences aboard the *QE2*.

Except for a private ceremony in the Rose Garden, when the President presented the Kellogg brothers with citations expressing his personal thanks, Thomas had managed to keep out of the public's media-crazed eye. He was content to let the incident at sea fade to oblivion, with the only positive byproduct being a closer relationship with Brittany.

Thoughts of Brittany kept him from losing his temper when a semi pulled in front of him without warning. The impatient trucker was trying to pass a slower-moving competitor, and there was no way he'd be able to complete this move before reaching the steep incline of the next hill. Thusly trapped, Thomas fought back the temptation to sound his horn, and he bided his time thinking instead about Brittany's mysterious whereabouts. It suddenly dawned on him that the reason she couldn't join the Kellogg family in Branson was because she was most likely in the Crimea with the President, on a mission that could very well mean the end of the Cold War's hair-trigger nuclear response posture.

It was as they were leaving the southern outskirts of Simferopol behind that Morrison was able to place a call via the comm van, to determine the identity of the tanks they had spotted earlier.

"Spooky Three-nine," he said into his two-way. "This is Checkmate One. Over."

The crystal-clear response was almost instantaneous. "Roger that, Checkmate One. This is Spooky Three-nine. How can we be of service? Over."

"Spooky Three-nine," he said while studying the detailed topographical map that was spread out on his lap. "I need you to paint a target on map grid Sierra Foxtrot four-two-six-five, seven-three-two-eight. Over."

The pilot of the AC-130U gunship acknowledged the receipt of this request, and less than a minute later, he delivered his answer. "Checkmate One, low-light video shows a formation of seven T-72 main battle tanks occupying map grid Sierra Foxtrot four-two-six-five, seven-three-two-eight.

Infrared scan indicates that vehicles are unmanned, with all propulsion systems inactive. They may be big, ugly, and loaded for bear, but their diesels are cold as ice, Checkmate One. Do you require any additional services from us at this time? Over."

Morrison was relieved by this report, and he looked over at his bald-headed Russian associate and smiled. "That's a negative, Spooky Three-nine. It's good to have you in the neighborhood. Thanks for your help. Out.

"It appears that they produce as advertised," he added to Kosygin while switching off the two-way.

The Russian grunted. "We do not squander our defense dollars. We Russians have learned over centuries to be economical."

Outside, the heavy rains had stopped falling. Even then, dusk came early, and fog began developing as they approached the Salgir River valley.

Samuel Morrison waited until the Suburban's driver was able to switch off the windshield wipers for the final time before pulling out a pair of cigars from his jacket. His seatmate readdressed his own two-way, and Alexi Kosygin looked disappointed as he lowered the radio and turned to Morrison.

"Even with the help of your communications van, I was unable to get through to the destroyer."

"Do you want me to try routing the call via Nightwatch?" offered the SAIC.

"No, my friend, I only wanted a routine SITREP. It can wait. We'll be out of this valley shortly, and then it's but a ten-minute drive over the coastal mountains and down into Alushta."

Morrison handed him a cigar, and the Russian sniffed it like a true connoisseur.

"Cuban?" he asked.

Morrison laughed and shook his head. "I wish. It's a domestic brand that I've gotten fond of, and a recent gift from a special friend. I'm saving mine for later tonight, after I get Two Putt settled into his dacha."

"Then I'll do likewise," Kosygin said, taking a final sniff and stowing it away in his breast pocket.

Morrison put his unlit cigar in the corner of his mouth and unfolded a detailed topographical road map on his lap. He switched on an overhead spotlight, then readjusted the fit of the bifocals that sat precariously perched on the end of his flat nose.

"We're continuing to make damn good time, Alexi. It appears Comrade Zinoviev's road crew has done a fine job after all. Other than that brief patch of rough pavement we came across while leaving town, the ride's been smooth as silk."

"I'll reserve judgment until we reach Alushta," said Kosygin. "The Ukrainians are notorious for starting a project brilliantly, but failing to follow through all the way to the end."

Almost to underscore his comment, the Suburban began bouncing up and down, while the tires started humming slightly.

"We must be crossing the drainage canal bridge," Morrison observed. "It's another quarter of a kilometer to the main bridge spanning the Salgir."

Another rough jolt signaled their passing over the final trestle, and the humming stopped. With the map spread out before him, Morrison looked out the left side window. The fog had further thickened, and he peered over the frames of his bifocals in an effort to spot any familiar landmarks.

Barely visible in the swirling tendrils of mist was the rocky outcrop known as the Salgir highlands. This low-lying, sixty-foot-high plateau was a bane to local farmers, and extended all the way to the river.

By glancing out the window to Kosygin's right, he could see a relatively flat expanse of forested land, filled with thick stands of mature Crimean pines. This ancient woods was all that remained of an immense forest that had once covered most of the peninsula and was now limited to five thousand acres, with many of the trees extending right down to the roadside.

Morrison felt his torso being pulled slightly toward his seatmate when the Suburban followed the road as it turned sharply to the west. It was the Russian who pointed out the ribbon of plowed-up pavement extending farther to the south. A pair of flashing, bright red warning lights could be seen through the fog here, and Kosygin identified them.

"That must be the barricade marking the spot where they closed the old road."

Morrison nodded and looked ahead through the vehicle's windshield. As they completed the turn, the road followed a gently sloping upward gradient, leading them toward a well-lit, steel-girded structure a bare quarter of a kilometer distant.

"And that must be the new bridge," he supposed. "The last report from my survey team mentioned that there was a good week's worth of work left before it would be open to the public. I sure hope the concrete's set."

The fog swallowed the modern superstructure, and Morrison was about to return his gaze to the map when a pair of blinding flashes penetrated the fog at the base of the bridge. This was immediately followed by a pair of deep, resonant booms, and the SAIC's first fear was that there had just been some sort of construction accident up ahead. But then a series of dreaded metallic thuds sounded from the immediate direction of the Suburban's roof and doors, causing Morrison to cry out in horror. "We're taking fire!

"Checkmate Two!" he shouted into his two-way. "Code One! I repeat, Code One! Close ranks and let's get over that friggin' bridge!"

Oblivious to the vehicles ahead of them, the motorcade's Secret Service drivers knew their first priority was to form a defensive shield around the President's limousine. The trailing Suburbans quickly sped up until they were practically hugging the limo's sides, with Morrison's vehicle leading the way from the point of the V, and the trailing limo plugging up the rear.

Like a single entity, the formation shot forward in a burst of high speed. They passed by the BTR-60 armored personnel carrier, which had pulled off on the shoulder, its rooftop gunner laying down a constant barrage of fire toward the high ground on their left. Only a single Zil police sedan could be seen driving ahead of them, a mere ten yards away. They were rapidly closing on it, and Morrison was about to order them out of the way, when the sedan's taillights suddenly disappeared.

"Hit the brakes!" he alertly ordered into the two-way.

Morrison braced himself as his driver followed his instructions, and the Suburban skidded to a halt mere inches from a major break in the pavement.

"My God!" proclaimed his driver. "They blew the ramp. The three motorcyclists, the sedan—they must have driven right off the edge."

"Turn around and head back the way we came!" Morrison ordered.

A round of slugs struck the truck's bulletproof windshield, the sound of the careening shells swallowed by the screech of squealing rubber. Morrison briefly met the worried gaze of his seatmate before finding his torso thrown backward by the force of sudden acceleration. They were headed back to Simferopol now, with the SAIC's vehicle in the trailing position, close on the rear fender of the limousine holding Two Putt.

Hundreds of incoming tracers lit the twilight in ghostly iridescent fingers. Most of the fire originated from the elevated ground of the highlands, which passed now on their right.

"Hang on, we're goin' right through the friggin' killing zone!" Morrison warned.

They sped by the BTR-60's smoking hulk, where the

bloodstained bodies of SWAT team Alpha littered the fog-shrouded ground. An overturned Zil police sedan, its wheels still spinning, lay nearby, and Morrison flinched when a rocket-propelled grenade struck the wrecked car and exploded in a glaring fireball.

"So much for Comrade Zinoviev," whispered Kosygin.

A tight spread of bullets peppered the Suburban's left side, and they could barely see the dark outlines of an infantry assault element emerging from the tree line. Morrison's two-way squawked alive, and the eight surviving vehicles reported in. Seconds later, this number was reduced to seven when a mortar round landed directly on the roof of their ambulance, instantly killing its occupants.

All that really mattered was protecting the integrity of the vehicle directly in front of them, thought Morrison. So far, the President's limo appeared to be untouched. No matter what, it would have to stay that way, and the SAIC desperately peered down at the map, then looked up just as two dazzling bursts of bright light filled the northern horizon.

"They've blown the canal bridge, and there's no way to get over!" the driver of the lead vehicle informed them over the radio.

"Shit!" cursed Morrison, his glance drawn back to the map. For all effective purposes, they were now trapped in a killing zone between two insurmountable bodies of water, and there was absolutely nothing the SAIC could do about it.

"Spooky Three-nine, this is Checkmate One. We have a Code One emergency and request an immediate air strike on map grid coordinates Sierra Lima one-five-four-six, three-seven-two-eight. I repeat, we have a Code One emergency and request an immediate air strike. Do you copy? Over."

Red's initial reaction to hearing this shocking message was pure disbelief. She had been seated at her console routinely monitoring the secure, narrowband voice frequencies, and a Code One, indicating an attempt on the President's life, definitely wasn't the type of broadcast she had been expecting to overhear.

Yet reality sank in when the gunship acknowledged the call for assistance. Red hurriedly verified the code sequences. They were irrefutably legitimate, prompting her to grab the dark blue handset mounted on the lower right edge of the console and punch in a succession of three digits.

"Admiral Warner, this is Master Sergeant Rayburn on the QV-135. I've just picked up what appears to be a distress call from Checkmate One. And, sir, it looks to me that we've got a real live Code One on our hands!"

Friday, July 2, 1801 Zulu

Salgir Highlands

"Damn it, Anderson!" shouted Morrison into his two-way. "I need you to pull that comm van up until you touch the point Suburban's back fender. We need a wall of steel between that high ground and Two Putt."

With no open road to escape on, Morrison's only hope was to "circle the wagons," and make a last-ditch stand at the position he deemed most defensible. They were using the drainage canal to protect their flank, and had the President's limousine surrounded by a V-shaped phalanx. Morrison's Suburban was at the rear of the formation facing the forest, with the spare staff limo sandwiched between his truck and the point vehicle.

Rocket-propelled grenades continued raining down on them from the highlands. A sporadic mortar shell was launched their way, and Morrison knew it was only a matter of time until they got the proper range.

Both Morrison and Kosygin, along with the two Special Agents in the front seat, had just finished prepping their armaments. They had an Uzi and three Heckler & Koch MP5 submachine guns between them, as well as twenty-four spare clips and their individual side arms.

The two-way crackled alive, and all stations reported in, including Moreno from the "hot seat." The President's limo had yet to experience any interior damage, and Moreno signed off just as a phosphorous round hit the side of the communications van.

Dusk became noon in a blinding millisecond. And with this unnatural illumination, Morrison spotted dozens of infantrymen headed straight for them from the cover of the ancient forest's tree line.

"Checkmate Four," he radioed to the point Suburban. "Deploy CAT team and engage troops emerging from position Lima."

Morrison rammed a thirty-round clip into his MP5 and reached for the door handle. "Looks like they're going to need all the help they can get."

"Then whatever are we waiting for?" retorted Kosygin, who chambered a round into his Uzi and joined the SAIC outside.

The air was heavy with the scents of smoke, cordite, and gunpowder. Bullets whined overhead, and Morrison let loose a controlled burst toward the forest before taking cover behind their truck's engine block. From this position, both he and his Russian colleague emptied clip after clip into the human-wave assault force approaching from the trees. Yet they appeared to be unstoppable, their forward progress impeded only when the six-man Secret Service Counter Assault Team charged into their ranks with guns blazing.

The SAIC hadn't seen such a firefight since his service as a Green Beret in Vietnam. The fog-shrouded twilight still lit by the burning phosphorous shell, he watched his men attempt a flanking maneuver. To a staccato barrage of submachine-gun fire, the CAT team rushed forward. Morrison could see the gleam of exploding shells in their black Kevlar helmets and thick safety goggles, their jet-black BDUs all but indistinguishable.

Though badly outnumbered, the CAT team had succeeded in making a totally unexpected assault, and the enemy momentarily halted its advance to repulse them. This was all that Morrison had to see to leave the cover of the truck and rush toward the wood line himself.

The stubby barrel of his weapon was red-hot as he sprayed the enemy with a deadly steel curtain of 9mm slugs. Alexi Kosygin stuck close to his side, and he too emptied clip after clip. It was the Russian who shouted out in warning when a heavily camouflaged attacker sprang up from the tall grass to the SAIC's right. He was only ten yards away at best, and Morrison could clearly see the glowing whites of his eyes as he pumped round after round into the startled soldier's torso.

The CAT team had meanwhile detonated a series of smoke grenades, and was using this cover to mask their flanking movement. The enemy was still unmoving, and appeared confused. Morrison was tempted to call in their last remaining six-man squad to augment this force and assist in a counterattack. He reached for his radio, and only then realized that in all the excitement, he had left it back in the Suburban.

No sooner did he turn for the truck than a high-pitched whistling filled the dusk with dreaded sound.

"Incoming!" warned Kosygin, at the same time knocking Morrison to the ground and covering him with his body.

An earsplitting, bone-rattling explosion temporarily deafened the SAIC. The cool earth shook, and a shower of falling debris rained down onto their backs.

As fate would have it, the mortar round landed squarely in the midst of the CAT team. Each of the six Special Agents was instantly killed, their bodies ripped apart by high explosives and razor-sharp shrapnel.

Morrison's limbs were shaking, and Kosygin had to help

him stand. Together they limped back to the truck, in time to see the enemy assault force renew its attack with increased ferocity.

"Spooky Three-nine, this is Checkmate One. Where the hell are you?" asked Morrison into his two-way. "We desperately need that air strike, and we need it now!"

"Not to worry, Checkmate One," replied a calm voice from the radio's speaker. "This is Spooky Three-nine. Sorry about the little delay getting into position, but we've got a firm visual lock on your position, as well as an excellent infrared reading on the bad guys. Preparing to fire. Over."

Captain Ty "Monzo" Alexander intently studied the green-tinted video screen that was set into the fire control console before him. Regardless of the fact that they were flying at an altitude of over ten thousand feet, and that it was almost pitch-black outside, the monitor was filled with a detailed picture of the ground below.

The gunship's Fire Control Officer easily picked out the V-shaped formation of vehicles belonging to the good guys. He supposed that the elongated limousine in the center of the protective wedge held the President. Though Monzo hadn't voted for the man, he was still Commander-in-Chief, and no crazy terrorists were going to have their way with him if Monzo had anything to say about it.

With the rich strains of Johnny Cash singing "Ghost Riders in the Sky" blaring away in the background of the fire control suite, Monzo isolated the hostile formation moving toward the motorcade on the Infrared sensor system. They were within five hundred meters of the friendlies, which was closer than he would have liked under the circumstances.

"That's your target IR," said Monzo into his chin mike. "Track the northernmost element and sweep south."

"IR's tracking," informed the Staff Sergeant operating the IR system.

"OK, pilot," said Monzo into his mike. "FCO's got IR. Gun one, trainable. Target is thirty-plus dismounts, five hundred meters from the friendlies. FCO is ready!"

"Navigator confirms target, cleared to fire," said the young Lieutenant seated to Monzo's left.

"Pilot's in the sight. Arm number one," ordered the pilot over the intercom.

"Number one is armed," the flight engineer responded.

That was all the IR operator had to hear to mash down on his consent button and rake the enemy formation with three hundred and fifty rounds of high-explosive 25mm projectiles. Monzo noted that the enemy formation was suddenly cut in half, and it was no longer moving toward the motorcade.

"OK, crew, switching to number three gun, trainable on the TV. Prox rounds, same target. FCO's ready."

The crew performed the same series of cross-checks as before. Yet this time the gunners in the back of the aircraft began feeding proximity-fused projectiles into the huge 105mm howitzer protruding from the gunship's left side. These rounds were designed to shower the enemy with razor-sharp shrapnel, and were extremely lethal when used against troops in the open.

It was their TV operator who depressed his firing button, and the entire airplane shook with the recoil of the largest gun ever placed on an aircraft. Ten rounds later, Monzo could see no further movement from the area below.

"Pilot, FCO's got no movement on the western target set. Guidance is shifting east three klicks to the fixed gun emplacements."

They began on the highland's northernmost end. Like a surgeon performing laser surgery, Monzo aligned the crosshairs to isolate the individual bunkers, where the mortars and RPGs were being fired.

"Hold her steady. Guns are armed. FCO's ready. Guns ready. Shoot!"

Once more the gunship violently shook as the howitzer fired. Monzo followed the shell as it descended on target, a streaking, lightning bolt of death from above. Unlike the 25mm ammunition, this shell detonated with a wallop, sending a miniature mushroom-shaped cloud high in the air. In a little more than a minute, this process was repeated ten more times, with ten different targets falling victim to Spooky Three-nine's wrath.

Monzo estimated that he could clear the entire ridge with the howitzer in another five minutes. For variety's sake, he had the boys crank up the 40mm Bofors gun, which had a firing rate of one hundred rounds per minute. After all, the Commander-in-Chief himself was watching this display, and it was time to show the President that those defense dollars were being wisely spent.

Samuel Morrison stood outside his Suburban and watched the incredible display of firepower. He had called down many an air strike while in 'Nam, but none of them came close to matching the amazing precision firepower and area-saturation capabilities of the AC-130U. Like a scene out of Dante's Inferno, the northern end of the Salgir highlands was ablaze in flames, with shells continuing to rain down on the plateau with clockwork regularity.

He had already watched the gunship make mincemeat out of the mysterious ground-assault element that had previously threatened them. From the truck's backseat, he had looked on with awestruck wonder as a wall of deadly lead began descending from the sky. These shells tore into the enemy, and in a matter of mere minutes, the assault force was reduced to a bleeding mass of torn flesh and broken bone.

Before he could cry out in relieved joy, the first shells began to hit the plateau. And since that time, not a single mortar round or RPG had been fired at them. The SAIC knew that they had been extremely fortunate. If it hadn't been for the gunship, they'd surely be either dead or captured. And now was the time to lick their wounds, and get the hell out of this infernal river valley, before their luck ran out.

Since both bridges were out of commission, they had only two options. They could try breaching the barricade and attempt crossing the old bridge, or they could leave the paved road and try to find a drivable pathway through the woods. Neither of these choices sounded particularly appealing to Morrison, and he supposed that if the barricade could be safely circumnavigated, that would provide them the most direct route.

He redirected his glance in an effort to spot the barricade's flashing red lights. And it was as he turned his gaze away from the plateau that he just missed seeing the flame-red plume of a surface-to-air missile, arcing upward into the night sky from the plateau's southernmost tip.

"Strella! Strella, seven o'clock! Break right!" cried the amplified voice of the gunship's pilot over Red's monitor speaker.

There could be no missing the concerned horror in his voice, and an anxious murmur escaped the lips of the knot of personnel gathered around Red's workstation. Included in this distinguished group was Admiral Warner, Colonel Pritchard, and Commander Brittany Cooper.

"So now the bastards not only have an assault element, but a surface-to-air capability as well," fumed Warner. "They've got to be regulars, and not an isolated terrorist group."

All eyes were locked on the console, and when a full minute had passed with no transmission emanating from the wire-mesh speaker, Red dared to address her chin mike. "Spooky Three-nine, this is Nightwatch six-seven-six. Do you read me? Over."

She repeated this same broadcast several more times;

when it failed to garner a response, she shifted frequencies to try a variety of emergency bands. In every instance they received nothing but low-level static, and it was Pritchard who offered the somber assessment.

"I'm afraid Spooky Three-nine didn't make it."

"Master Sergeant Schuster," said Warner to the airman seated at the workstation directly across the aisle from Red. "Are you still in contact with Checkmate Two?"

Schuster pushed back his chin mike and answered, "That's affirmative, sir. The last SATCOM transmission from the motorcade was fifteen seconds ago. They were broadcasting on the backup system, and sent along yet another all-clear."

"At least it appears that the President's still alive," observed Pritchard.

Warner worriedly rubbed his creased brow. "Without the cover of that gunship, who the hell knows how long he'll be able to stay that way. Damn it, I warned him that this whole secret-negotiation business was no good. At the very least, it should have been held on American soil. But no, he had to go and travel to the ends of the earth, and look at the fine mess we're in—a heavily armed, fifteen-vehicle motorcade, now whittled down to five surviving cars, with God knows how many enemy forces still out there, and no way for us to send in reinforcements."

"Surely the Ukrainians will be sending in a rescue force," remarked Brittany.

Warner looked at the MILAIDE and laughed. "Why the hell would they go and do that if they're the ones responsible for this outrageous ambush?"

"I still think it's the Russians," Pritchard interjected. "We all know how the head of the Strategic Rocket Forces reacted to the Global Zero Alert concept. He came out against it from the very beginning, warning that it would needlessly expose Russia to nuclear annihilation."

"Whoever's eventually found responsible," said Warner

with a sigh, "we've still got an incredible mess down there, and I want us ready for any scenario. I want the entire emergency action team assembled in the conference room. At that time, I intend to inform the NMCC of my decision to activate the central locator system, and to launch the TACAMO alert bird. I'm also going to want to know the exact positions of those F-16s I called in from Incirlik. If we're living right, there's always the chance that our Falcons will reach the Crimea in time to save the motorcade."

Almost as an afterthought, the Chairman looked at Brittany, adding, "And, Commander Cooper, I want you close by and within sight at all times. If Satchel Alpha should be compromised, we're going to really have to earn our keep up here."

Friday, July 2, 1823 Zulu

With Checkmate One

Samuel Morrison and the five Secret Service drivers stood huddled next to the President's limo, inside their protective formation near the drainage canal. With the arrival of night, the fog had further thickened, and it was eerily quiet now that the gunship had stopped its incessant firing. Through the cool mist, they could see the fires still burning on the Salgir highlands. The plateau had taken an incredible pounding, yet the amazing aircraft responsible for it was nowhere to be seen. For none of the Special Agents assembled beside the SAIC realized the source of the muffled explosion that had sounded seconds ago, or saw the barely visible flash of light in the sky when Spooky Three-nine exploded in a blazing fireball.

"Then I'll take that as a vote of confidence," said Morrison in reference to the brief tactical debate they had just completed. "Algren, you'll be driving point in the lead Suburban. Because we still don't know the barricade's exact composition, Moreno will be leaving a ten-yard gap between Algren's rear and the limo's front bumper. I'll remain in the trailing Suburban behind the staff limo on the right side of the formation, with Lester's truck all alone on the left. So if there are no more questions, gentlemen, let's get the friggin' hell out of here!"

The SAIC's order was given additional impetus by the RPG round that headed their way from the direction of the highlands. It harmlessly exploded well short of its intended target, though its mere presence meant that their enemy was still very much alive and dangerous.

Morrison barely had time to get settled in the backseat of his vehicle when the formation shot forward in a high-speed burst. This coincided with the arrival of a round of small-arms fire, originating from the nearby pine forest. There was a twanging metallic thud as these rounds ricocheted off the truck's bulletproof, armor-reinforced doors, and Morrison angrily cursed, conscious that the infantry assault-element force had also returned.

A rough, jarring sensation signaled their arrival on the old section of roadway. The drivers slowed down to fifty miles per hour, and as the red, flashing lights of the barricade grew increasingly larger, the lead Suburban accelerated to take a ten-yard lead.

An open radio channel allowed Morrison to keep in simultaneous touch with all five of his drivers, and it was in such a manner that he learned from the point vehicle that the barricade appeared to be made out of wood. Yet before the SAIC could share his relief, the lead Sububan exploded in a column of fire. Seconds later, the Suburban on the formation's left flank also blew up in a billowing fireball, leading Morrison to believe that he knew how these blasts had been triggered.

"Hit the brakes—minefield!" he shouted into the two-way.

The remaining three cars of the formation skidded to a halt, and though the barricade invitingly beckoned less than thirty yards away, the SAIC had no choice but to order the column to carefully back up and return to the new section of pavement. The drivers did a splendid job of retracing their routes, and they made it safely back onto the newly laid asphalt, with the two Suburbans all the while filling their windshields with the glow of flame.

A mortar round detonated close by, and Morrison played the last of his options. With a minimum of ceremony, the President and Major Ryan were transferred into the last surviving Suburban, along with Satchel Alpha, their portable SATCOM phone, and all the ammo that the other agents could spare. As the SAIC climbed into the crowded backseat beside Alexi Kosygin, he flashed Special Agent Moreno, and the other brave men who would be traveling in the limousines, a supportive thumbs-up.

The plan was to try to find an escape route through the forest. Since the four-wheel-drive Suburban had the best chance of surviving such a punishing trip, it would lead the way. The limousines would follow, with the hope that they'd chance upon an old logging road.

A trio of exploding mortar rounds spurred them onward. The Suburban left the road with a jolt, and sped off into the tree line. Because of the great age of these woods, there was a fair amount of open space between the individual trunks. Without letting up on the accelerator, their driver expertly circumnavigated the maze of stately pines, the route made all the more difficult by the ever-present fog.

When he wasn't hanging on for dear life, Morrison was able to turn around from time to time and check on the progress of the limousines. When the fog swallowed the last distant headlight, he contacted them via radio. As expected, they were having a difficult time, often forced to slow down to a virtual crawl because of their bulky size and weight. It was a lack of all-terrain capability that eventually led to their doom.

The SAIC's heart was heavy as he listened to Special

Agent Moreno's latest radio update. The spare limo carrying the President's staff had gotten itself stuck in the bottom of a creek bed. Moreno's vehicle was in the process of backing up to render assistance, and had just come under small-arms fire, when it too found itself trapped in a soggy depression. And the last Morrison ever heard from his colleague was as Moreno signed off, the crackle of gunfire clearly audible in the background.

Though a part of Morrison wanted to go back and help them, a greater responsibility was now his. Considering their predicament, the President was displaying remarkable composure, and had even managed to summon the strength to trade concerned small talk with Alexi Kosygin. When the Suburban wasn't careening over a pothole or bounding over a pile of brush, Major Ryan was able to activate the portable, battery-powered SATCOM phone to pass on an "all clear" Situation Report to Nightwatch. In such a way they were able to inform the NCA that the President was still alive, and that Satchel Alpha hadn't been compromised. They would continue to broadcast these brief SITREPs as long as possible, this being their last means of contact with the world beyond.

"Is that the remains of a road up there on the other side of the clearing?" asked the Special Agent buckled into the passenger seat.

This question immediately caught the attention of the four men gathered in the backseat, as well as the vehicle's driver, who excitedly replied, "I believe it is!"

The SAIC anxiously sat forward and peered out the streaked windshield. He could see little outside but the two bouncing shafts of light coming from their headlights, and as he scanned the clearing ahead of them, an exploding tongue of flame flashed from the blackness. It wasn't until a heavy metallic round bounced off their roof that he identified it as a muzzle flash. They were headed straight for the weapon, and the driver reacted instinctively.

He stomped on the brakes, causing the truck to violently lunge forward, then shifted hard into reverse. He waited to build up traction before hitting the gas, and they shot backward. Only a few feet from the woods, he lifted his foot off the accelerator and whipped the wheel to the left. The Suburban started skidding, and as the President slammed into Morrison's shoulder, the driver jerked the gearshift into forward and once more stepped on the accelerator.

The superbly executed reverse-180-degree turn surely saved their lives, for as they sped off into that portion of woods they had just traveled, a barrage of bullets peppered off the back window. Morrison felt a bit queasy, and as he reached down to pick up the fallen SATCOM device, the driver shouted, "There's that road again!"

The Suburban plowed over a group of saplings, careened over a rough stone-filled draw, and settled onto the remains of an abandoned earthen roadway. It was just wide enough to hold them, and definitely offered the smoothest ride yet experienced.

"We're heading west!" exclaimed the driver after checking the dashboard-mounted compass. "Mr. President, we'll get you out of this bind yet!"

That statement proved to be a bit overly optimistic, for seconds later, they ran over a steel-spike tank trap and punctured the two front tires. The truck nose-dived forward, and the driver alertly hit the brakes.

"Can't you drive on a flat?" asked the SAIC.

"Not with two of them," the driver answered. "But not to worry, sir. We've got a spare and a can of flat fixer. Just give us a sec, and we'll be good to go."

The driver nodded to his seatmate, and both of them exited the vehicle to initiate the repair process. Morrison grabbed his submachine gun and joined them.

It was pitch-black and deathly quiet outside. The swirling fog hugged the floor of the forest, the heavy pine boughs peering down like silent sentinels.

A metallic, scraping sound broke the silence, and Morrison watched his men emerge with the spare. They proceeded to jack up the front end, and went to work replacing the flat right tire.

With his MP5 in hand, the SAIC circled the vehicle, his gaze locked on the tree line. On any other occasion, he would have loved to be in such a forest, where the air was clean and sweet with pine sap. Yet here the scent of death was in the air, and he couldn't wait to be gone from this cursed grove.

"Comrade Morrison," whispered Alexi Kosygin from the barely cracked rear window. "There seems to be a problem getting the SATCOM on line."

Back inside the truck, Morrison took a close look at the briefcase-sized transmitter and found that the rough ride had jarred one of the battery cables loose. He pushed the connectors together and watched as the green "transmit" light began glowing.

"I think I saw something move out there." Major Ryan pointed into the trees in front of them.

Without bothering to switch off the transmitter's open microphone, Morrison looked in the direction that the MI-LAIDE was highlighting, in time to see two brilliant muzzle flashes emanate from the blackness. There were a pair of distinctive pops, and Kosygin dared to stick his head out the window to check the men's progress.

"Dear God, they've both been shot!" he exclaimed.

This was all the SAIC had to hear to dive over into the front seat and grasp for the ignition. "The friggin' keys are gone!"

He madly searched the seat and floorboard, and when this effort failed to produce the keys, he knew he'd have to go out there and get them. "Alexi, Major Ryan, if you'd be so good as to cover me with your weapons."

Morrison readied his submachine gun, took a deep breath, and jerked open the door, ill prepared for the hard wooden butt of the Kalashnikov assault rifle that caught him full on the forehead. He crumpled to the ground at the side of the truck, his vision blurred, on the cusp of unconsciousness. With a nightmare's ponderous pace, he struggled to his knees in time to see a heavily camouflaged soldier materialize at the opposite doorway. This individual's face was covered in green and black greasepaint, and all Morrison could see were the whites of his cruel eyes as he raised his rifle and pointed it into the backseat.

"Who the hell are you, and what do you want?" asked Kosygin, his voice faltering.

An ear-shattering trio of shots rang out, and with Alexi Kosygin silenced for all eternity, the gunman flipped on his laser sight and projected the glowing red beam squarely in the center of the President's forehead. Samuel Morrison fought back a wave of nauseated dizziness to reach for his side arm, all the while fighting to get to his feet and stand.

"For God's sake, I'm the President of the United States. Don't shoot!" implored America's Chief Executive.

The assassin appeared to be relishing this moment of power, and he made certain that the dazed Morrison was still incapable of interfering, before issuing a deep laugh and pulling the trigger. The President's head exploded like a pumpkin, bits of bloody flesh and bone cascading onto the cowering MILAIDE.

Though he held a fully loaded submachine gun in his lap, Major Bob Ryan was in no emotional shape to use it. The assassin knew this, and lowered his rifle to scoot into the backseat himself.

"So now that your President is dead, you're the one," said the assassin in Slavic-accented English.

There was a certain coolness to his tone of voice, and he displayed little emotion as he shoved the President's lifeless body out of the way, tossed aside Ryan's weapon, and directed his glance to the black briefcase that was handcuffed to the MILAIDE's wrist. "And what do we have here?" he asked.

"My name is Major Bob Ryan," the MILAIDE managed to say while he tightly cradled Satchel Alpha snug against his chest. "And my serial number is four-nine-one—"

"No, you fool!" interrupted the assassin. "I don't need your name, only the infamous football that you carry. And don't bother swallowing the key."

Like a zombie, the SAIC continued watching this horrific drama unfold. His severe concussion kept him dazed and comatose; unable to summon the coordination to grasp his pistol, he looked on as the assassin whipped out a razor-sharp K-Bar knife and proceeded to slice through the MILAIDE's wrist. And the last thing Samuel Forrest Morrison II remembered, before the 7.62mm shells exploded from the forest and ripped into his chest to end this nightmare, was the demented screams of Major Bob Ryan.

The occupants of the conference room sat in stunned disbelief as Major Bob Ryan's pained screams sounded from the overhead speaker. This real-time transmission from the backseat of the limousine arrived via the SATCOM's open microphone, along with the series of exploding gunshots that signaled the apparent death of the President.

With forehead cradled in the palms of his hands, Admiral Trent Warner sat at the head of the table, facing a detailed topographical map of the Salgir River valley that was projected on the aft video screen. To his immediate left was Colonel Lyford Pritchard, the CO of the 747's operations team, with Brittany Cooper positioned on Warner's right. The rest of the table's six positions were occupied by select members of the emergency action team. All of them were attired in matching green flight suits, and displayed somber expressions on their weary faces.

The occupants of the conference room collectively flinched when another gunshot sounded, and the demented screams were replaced by the crackle of static. "We've lost the SATCOM feed," advised Red over the speaker.

"Very well, Master Sergeant," replied Pritchard into his chin-mounted mike. "Keep the line open, and let us know the second you get the slightest hint it's still operational."

All of the personnel gathered around the table knew inwardly that it was a lost cause, and all eyes went to the head of the table for an inkling of what to do next. Though they had constantly drilled on many a similar scenario, this was reality of the harshest sort, and the staff of Nightwatch now found themselves leading players in one of the most tragic moments of American history.

Well aware of their great responsibility, the Chairman smoothed back his thick mane of silver hair, sat up ramrod-straight, and scanned the faces of his rapt audience, saying, "It's only too obvious that our country has suffered a great loss this evening. Our Commander-in-Chief has been taken from us in one of the most despicable crimes in history. All of us aboard Nightwatch mourn his passing, but we have no time for tears. Duty calls like never before, and we shall not let our fellow countrymen down.

"Per the continuity of government protocol, as the senior ranking officer of the National Command Authority, I am now assuming supreme control of U.S. strategic forces. Colonel Pritchard, you are to immediately inform your operations team of this fact, and to deactivate Satchel Alpha and activate Satchel Bravo."

Pritchard spoke into his chin mike, and waited less than thirty seconds before verbally relaying the acknowledgment that he received over his headphones. "A multi-frequency scrambled alert has just been broadcast to the NMCC, informing them of your assumption of power, the deactivation of Satchel Alpha, and the activation of the SIOP codes contained inside Satchel Bravo. We are awaiting confirmation and implementation."

While they waited for this all-important reply, Brittany

Cooper found herself subconsciously fingering the key that hung from her neck. Of all those gathered around the table, she had had the closest relationship with the man whose screams of pain had filled the airborne conference room these past couple of minutes. That could very well have been her down there, and Brittany found herself fighting the inner demons of confusion, shock, and fear.

To regain her composure, she began a series of deep, even breaths. Ever afraid that Warner would note her anxiety, she tried her best not to meet his gaze, and she looked instead to the aft bulkhead, where four digital clocks were mounted at the bottom of the projection screen. The glowing red digits of the black, rectangular clock on the upper left showed that it was lunchtime back in Washington, where the Pentagon's NMCC was situated. The clock beneath showed Zulu, or Greenwich Mean Time, while the clock on the upper right displayed local time in the Crimea. The clock below showed : 0. Brittany noted that it suddenly activated and began counting off the seconds, moments before Colonel Pritchard readdressed them.

"We have received a legitimate transfer-of-power acknowledgment from the NMCC. Satchel Alpha has been deactivated. Admiral Warner, you are now the recognized Commander-in-Chief until the Presidential successor relieves you."

Brittany's pulse quickened, her glance pulled to the head of the table and the man destiny had picked to accept this unprecedented transfer of power. No oaths of office had been uttered, with no public inauguration on the steps of the Capitol. Specifically designed for a crisis such as this one, the continuity of government protocol had just inserted an unelected military officer as the acting President of the United States of America.

"Captain Richardson," said the Chairman to the crew-cut Air Force officer seated to Brittany's right. "As our FEMA representative, you are authorized to activate the emergency locator system."

Richardson rapidly attacked the keyboard of his computer, and cleared his voice before replying. "I've already taken the liberty of activating the system, sir. If you'll just bear with me a second, I should be able to transfer the results onto the projection screen."

The map of the Salgir River valley faded from the screen, and as they watched it go blank, the Chairman grabbed one of two white telephones within arm's reach and punched in two numbers. "Major Foard," he said into the handset. "Please be informed that the transfer-of-power protocol that we talked about earlier has been completed. It's time to go home, Major. I'd appreciate it if you'd initiate an immediate course change back to CONUS, with an initial entry point at Andrews."

No sooner did Warner hang up the phone than the 747 began a steeply banked turn. Brittany found herself tightly gripping the edge of the table, and she watched as Colonel Pritchard's half-filled spill-proof coffee mug slid sideways and bounced onto the carpeted deck, along with several unsecured pencils. As an aide scrambled to retrieve the mug, the plane began to level out, and Brittany was able to release her death grip.

"Ah, here it is," said Captain Richardson, in reference to the map of the United States that now filled the projection screen. There was a pair of blinking stars visible, a blue one in the center of the country and a red one on the East Coast, and Richardson went on to reveal their significance.

"As of ten hundred hours Eastern Daylight Time, the blue star indicates the location of Vice President Chapman, with Speaker of the House Pierce highlighted in red."

"Where the hell's the VP? Arkansas?" quizzed Pritchard.

Richardson cleared his throat again before answering. "Actually, sir, he's in the southern Missouri Ozarks on a wilderness float trip."

"Oh, that's just great," Pritchard replied with a disgusted shake of his head. "You would have thought he would have stuck close to Washington like the Speaker, with the President so far out in the field."

"Who knows, with that feud and all, maybe the President didn't even bother to tell Chapman he was leaving the country," offered Major Steve Hewlett, a Marine serving as the op team's SIOP advisor.

"We don't have time for scuttlebutt, Major," scolded Warner. "Nor is it our job to determine the motives of our politicians. Wherever the Vice President may be, we're just going to have to get hold of him and pass on the bad news," he added, with a piercing gaze focused solely on the CO of the aircraft's operations team. "Colonel, all of us knew that if this day ever came, it wouldn't be easy. Because of the unusual circumstances of our loss, the protocol allows us to delay informing the American people until the proper successor is notified, and that's the way I want it."

"I'll have my team get on it at once, sir," said Pritchard, who relayed the order to notify the Vice President via chin mike, and listened as Warner continued.

"Until the successor acknowledges the transfer, we're the ones who will be in charge of determining America's military reaction to this cold-blooded act of murder. We'll be working closely with our intelligence assets to determine if there have been any suspicious strategic moves on the part of the Russians or Ukrainians."

"Sir," interrupted Hewlett, "during a recent Naval War College war game, an OPFOR counterforce strike was initiated with an assassination attempt on the President and select members of the NCA. The theory was that by killing the brain or paralyzing the nervous system, the arms couldn't be properly utilized. The attempt caught our forces by complete surprise. And that's why I think it's only prudent that we change our defense condition to DEFCON Four."

"But we still don't know for certain who was responsible," Pritchard countered. "If we go and threaten the Russians, and find out later it was a Ukrainian operation, we could be losing an important ally in the region."

"I'm not asking to start the countdowns," returned the Marine. "All I'm suggesting is to stir the beast from the annual summer holiday doldrums. And as for possibly insulting an ally, Colonel, our Commander-in-Chief has just been shot down, along with God only knows how many other brave Americans. And when the American people finally learn about it, it's gonna take every bit of restraint we can muster to keep them from demanding a declaration of war!"

The Chairman nodded thoughtfully. "I like the idea of taking us down a notch to DEFCON Four. Colonel Pritchard, inform the NMCC of this change, and get the word out to each of the strategic commands. What's the status of TACAMO?"

Pritchard was already busy relaying this order to his staff, and his aide alertly replied, "Iron Man One is the current alert bird, Admiral. It deployed out of NAS Patuxent five minutes after receiving our initial Code One, with General Lowell Spencer as the senior Emergency Action Officer."

"It's imperative that we keep in close contact with General Spencer, Lieutenant," said Warner to the aide. "If anything should happen to us, we'll be handing off the football to Iron Man One. And speaking of footballs," he added while looking at Brittany, "Commander, are you going to be all right? I know you were close to both the President, his Secret Service detail, and, of course, Major Ryan."

Afraid that her voice might betray her true feelings, Brittany summoned her bravest smile and nodded that she'd be fine. She dared to trade the briefest eye contact with the Chairman. And instead of his usual scrutinizing stare, there was something in Warner's eyes that appeared to be looking within, perhaps to the immense responsibility he had suddenly shouldered.

*   *   *

"Well, gents, it's true, all right," said Jake Lasky as he settled in behind the flight engineer station and buckled his harness. "And not only does it look like the President's been killed, but the football's been compromised as well. Wait till you hear the real-time tape that Red just played for me. It includes the gunshots that took out the President, and ends with his MILAIDE howling away like someone was cutting off his arm."

"Maybe that's how they got the satchel off his wrist," mused Lucky from his copilot position on the right side of the cockpit. "I sure hope the Chairman is putting together one jim-dandy of a retaliatory strike."

"The Admiral and his emergency action team were still meeting in the conference room. But I heard from Red that they were already going down to DEFCON Four," Jake revealed.

"DEFCON Four?" Lucky repeated. "That's all a President, his staff, a National Security Advisor, and an entire Secret Service protection detail are worth nowadays? Hell, if that's not reason to order Cocked Pistol, what is?"

Coach put down the aeronautical chart he had gotten from the navigator and eagerly joined the fray from the pilot's seat. "Did Red say anything about them determining the ones responsible for the slaughter?"

"Come to think of it, she didn't say," answered Jake.

"Then they obviously don't know who it was," Coach inferred. "Which means we can't go launching a full-scale nuclear war without first knowing who the hell did it."

Lucky couldn't believe what he was hearing, and he pushed back his headphones to speak his mind. "Am I missing something? The President flew all the way out here to the Crimea, at the invitation of the Presidents of Russia and Ukraine. Wasn't this to be a secret summit of peace? Obviously not, and there's only two countries to blame. I say hit the both of them, with enough plutonium to put them back into the Stone Age."

"Did you ever stop to think that a third party could be the culprit?" offered Coach. "Maybe it was a bunch of Arab extremists, or a group of international terrorists, who are responsible."

"Coach," interrupted the navigator while pointing to the radar screen, "I believe we've got some company out there."

All eyes went to the rectangular, flashing-green console mounted in the center of the main instrument panel. The digital radar screen displayed the northeastern corner of the Black Sea, with Nightwatch 676 represented by the blinking black star halfway between the Crimean Peninsula and the coast of Romania. Due east of this position, currently passing south of Yalta, was a tight, triangular-shaped formation of three flashing red stars, and it was Coach who made the first attempt at identifying them.

"If I'm not mistaken, they're long-range interceptors, most likely MiG-25 Foxbats. And, Lucky, right now you get my vote for DEFCON One. 'Cause they appear to be headed straight toward us, and if they're carrying air-to-air missiles, we're gonna be in one hell of a fix."

"Base, this is Eberly. Over. Winona Base, this is Ben Eberly. Do you copy?"

Vince could tell from the district ranger's strained tone that he was getting frustrated. For a good five minutes now, Eberly had been trying to reach the Winona Forest Service office on his two-way, with only static for his efforts.

"I don't understand it," said the ranger, his tanned forehead dripping with sweat. "Those new repeater towers usually give us excellent reception."

Vince glanced over to the far side of the sandbar on which they were standing, and saw that the group of agents responsible for deploying the portable COMSAT telephone appeared to be similarly frustrated. Instead of talking on the handset, they focused their efforts on the miniature satellite dish. For as long as Eberly had been trying his two-way, his men had been busy sweeping the skies with the dish, in a vain effort to make contact with the proper satellite.

"It looks like my people aren't having any luck either,"

Vince noted while raising his hand to his brow to shield his eyes from the blazing noon sun, and sweeping his glance to the east. A nine-hundred-foot-tall bluff of solid limestone met his gaze, and Vince didn't have to see any more to know why the efforts of his communications team had been unsuccessful.

"Where exactly did you say we'd find a notch in that bluff?" Vince asked.

"It's immediately downstream from the shoals," replied Eberly. "And you can access it from that sandbar your security team was off to visit in the johnboat."

"Then let's do it, my friend," said Vince. "It's not every day that we receive a partial emergency action alert like that, and it's imperative that we establish a secure SATCOM link with all due haste."

"For expediency's sake, why not load up your SATCOM into one of the johnboats, and we'll run your team down to the access site," Eberly offered. "That way they can set up while we follow in the canoes. It's a ten-minute float through Mary Deckard at best, and that sandbar will be the perfect place to have lunch."

Vince gave his blessings to this plan, and turned to inform the others. He found Vice President Chapman holding court alongside the spot where their canoes and a single johnboat were beached. Chapman was wearing dark green rubber waders and was standing in the water with graphite rod in hand, holding an impromptu fly-fishing clinic. His rapt audience included his physician, Ranger Wyatt, and, of course, Andy Whitworth, who was capturing the entire exhibition on film.

"And by the way," Vince heard Chapman saying as he approached them, "that ten-pound rainbow I hooked upstream was caught with one of these very same cahills that I tied myself on the flight down from Washington. And I would most likely have gone ahead and landed him, too, if I hadn't gone and removed the barb. Sportfishing should be done for the challenge, not for a stuffed trophy to hang on the wall."

Ron Wyatt noted Vince's arrival with a wink, and the leather-faced Missourian stepped aside to spit out a mouthful of tobacco juice before greeting the newcomer in a conspiratorial whisper. "It's obvious he never relied on fishing to feed a hungry family. And because he went and released that trio of four-pounders he did manage to land, we're stuck with peanut butter sandwiches and cold beans for lunch."

Vince smiled, and loudly cleared his throat before speaking up and interrupting the VP's spiel. "Excuse me, Mr. Vice President, but we're going to have to pack up your gear and move downstream."

"Any luck with that uplink, Kellogg?" Chapman asked after taking one last cast and returning to the sandbar.

"That's a negative, sir," returned Vince as discreetly as possible. "And that's why we have to continue downstream, to try another access point."

Andy Whitworth intuitively sensed that something out of the ordinary was coming down, and she brazenly expressed herself. "Excuse me, Special Agent Kellogg, but did something happen within the last half hour or so that can explain why this SATCOM uplink of yours is so darn important all of a sudden? It's obvious that it's not routine, which leads me to believe that someone from the outside contacted you and ordered it. Has there been a threat made on our party? Or is there some other type of danger we should be concerned about?"

Vince was astounded by the reporter's effrontery, and he shook his head, saying, "I can assure you, Miss Whitworth, that the only danger we're facing out here is sunstroke. Now, if you'll please return to your canoe, we'll see if we can give you something to really write about as we prepare to take on Mary Deckard shoals."

The buzz-saw whine of an outboard motor drew Vince's glance to the river. Two of their johnboats were returning upstream from the direction of the shoal. The lead boat approached the sandbar, and Vince walked over to grab the bowline.

"So you survived the legendary Mary Deckard," he said to the stocky brunette seated at the bow.

"Both downstream and up," replied Special Agent Linda Desiante. "It's a wild ride, sir. The boulders are monstrous, and with the water up like it is, there are some treacherous chutes and plenty of nasty snags to watch out for. And that doesn't even include the mini-waterfall located at the far end of the rapids."

"What did the CAT team have to say?" he asked, ever careful to keep his voice low.

"They never showed up. We found the rendezvous site on the sandbar easily enough. There were plenty of footprints, but not a sign of the team—or anyone else, for that matter. We tried to inform you on the two-way, but we couldn't get any of the radios to work."

"We're having the same problem. And speaking of communications, I need you to run the shoals again, this time with Special Agent Lester and our SATCOM. That sandbar you were on should give us a better uplink angle. By the time we run the rapids, you should be well on your way to contacting Milstar and finding out what this mysterious alert is all about."

Desiante's johnboat was soon on its way back down the river, and Vince anxiously waited while the rest of the party climbed back into their canoes. Once more he was teamed up with Ron Wyatt. As they glided out into the current, the canoe carrying the Vice President and Ben Eberly maneuvered in beside them, and Vince listened as the district ranger explained the origins of Mary Deckard shoals.

"It was during the turn-of-the-century lumber boom that a rock dam was placed in the river near the confluence of Hurricane Creek. A good part of this dam was built out of the giant boulders we're about to pass."

"Why go and dam this beautiful river? Was it for flood control?" asked the VP.

"They did it to trap logs," answered Ron Wyatt. "Believe it or not, there used to be a railroad line in these parts running to the river. When the mills in Winona needed wood, all they had to do was send the train to the shoals and load it up with fresh lumber."

The VP scanned the pristine, tree-lined shore and shook his head in wonder. "It's remarkable how quickly the forest reclaimed the land."

"If you think this area is something, wait till you get your first peek at the Irish Wilderness later this afternoon," Eberly proudly added. "The Irish is the largest Federal wilderness area in the Ozarks, and as in all our wilderness areas, development there has been kept to a bare minimum."

The roar of rushing water could be heard in the distance, and Vince peered downstream. The bluffs to their right were getting increasingly steep, and he could just make out a series of huge boulders lying in the white water ahead of them.

The VP's canoe would be first into the shoals, with Vince giving it a twenty-yard head start before they'd enter. The other vessels would follow at twenty-yard intervals.

All but forgetting about his other responsibilities, Vince noted how the current suddenly quickened. The rock obstacles ahead were becoming much larger, and he could see an assortment of tree limbs and other debris projecting from the treacherous shallows. White water was everywhere, and his guide pointed out the first of several wildly spinning whirlpools.

Though it was almost impossible for Vince to pick out the most accessible route, he supposed it would be the channel on the far right. There a group of boulders formed a Z-shaped pattern, with a swiftly moving chute of fairly deep water surging among the rocks.

The roar of the rapids rose to an almost deafening crescendo, and Vince breathlessly watched the VP's canoe penetrate the first chute. Andrew Chapman never stopped paddling, while in the vessel's tapered stern, Ben Eberly seemed content to merely sit back and utilize his paddle like a rudder. After bounding over a fractured rock shelf, the bobbing canoe was steered to the far right-hand side of the channel. A narrow, Z-shaped gauntlet of rock, projecting limbs, and agitated water awaited them there, and only when they passed by the first jagged boulder did Vince note that the VP had wisely pulled in his paddle.

Vince's canoe followed the same route. Astounded by the incredible velocity of the current, he anxiously sat forward when the vessel slipped off the rock shelf signaling the first white-water chute. The canoe dove bow-first into the current, and Vince found himself soaked by an invigorating splash of icy water. He wiped his face dry and felt the canoe turn sharply to the channel's right side as Wyatt used his paddle like a rudder. The first of the boulders loomed ahead, an angry moss-coated monolith with a pike-shaped oak limb projecting from the white water at its base.

They were at the mercy of the current now, and Vince jerked in his paddle as the boulder passed on the right, a mere inch between the projecting oaken spike and the canoe's thin aluminum gunwales. Ahead, the gauntlet of stone awaited, and the canoe cascaded down a narrow chute, the boulders so tightly compressed that they appeared to form a solid wall.

To safely navigate the Z's first turn required a sharp right turn, and Vince's guide would have to apply his rudder/paddle with exacting precision. Otherwise the bow would hang up in the shallows, causing the vessel to be yanked around and then swept through the gauntlet backward. Ron Wyatt readily met the challenge, and when they safely entered the next chute, Vince found himself venting his anxiety with a joyous yell. Unfortunately, his celebration was cut short upon spotting the VP's canoe wedged precariously between the two large boulders forming the next turn. It was extremely close to capsizing, the wildly rushing current only inches from entering the canoe and swamping its passengers.

Vince turned to make certain that his guide knew what was happening up ahead. Wyatt calmly nodded that he saw them, and appeared in total control as he expertly maneuvered the vessel down the chute, nosing their bow right up to the formation that had trapped the VP.

"They're caught up on a snag," Wyatt observed, having to scream to be heard. "I'm gonna try to pull in beside them, and we'll see if we can work them free with our paddles."

Not having any idea how his guide would ever be able to pull off such a maneuver, Vince nodded that he understood the intended strategy. And the next thing he knew, they were snug up against the VP's canoe, with Vince now faced upstream.

"Glad you could join us, Kellogg," yelled the VP, who was obviously enjoying every second of this mini-crisis.

Wyatt was already hard at work, angling the tip of his paddle into the massive snag of tree limbs and roots responsible for this hang-up. Before joining in with his own paddle, Vince found himself wondering how they'd be able to complete their transit of the chute, now that they were facing backward. He supposed that once the VP was free, they'd have to run the rest of the gauntlet with Vince at the rudder position. Such a switch of duties would prove interesting, to say the least, and before he regripped his paddle to assist his associate, he momentarily glanced upstream.

The first thing that caught his attention was an overturned canoe. It was hung up on the projecting shelf of rock at the head of the first chute, with a variety of floating debris visible immediately beside it. Included in this flotsam was what appeared to be a body, lying facedown in the water. Strangely enough, it wasn't moving, and Vince tried his best to scan the river farther upstream, his astounded glance halting on something equally unexpected. Hovering only a few feet above the river at the top of the rapids was a jet-black

Huey helicopter. The bulbous nose of this aircraft seemed to be pointed directly toward Vince, a fact that became terrifyingly clear when a pair of rockets shot out of the twin pods set flush against the Huey's fuselage.

In a terrifying blink of an eye, the missiles struck the roiling water, a mere ten yards upstream from the boulder the men were hidden behind. There was a pair of muted explosions, barely audible over the incessant roar of onrushing current, and Vince found himself soaked by a shower of falling water. The ensuing shock wave caused his canoe to bob slightly upward, and caused the VP's vessel to lift free from the snag. It shot downstream to complete its transit of the gauntlet, its occupants totally unaware of the newly arrived threat from above.

Ron Wyatt learned of the helicopter's presence the moment he looked up to signal Vince they were free to continue downstream themselves. The first look that crossed the ranger's leathery face was puzzlement, then pure horror, as the hovering Huey raised its nose and let loose another rocket. This one detonated near the moss-covered base of the boulder, where seconds ago the VP's canoe had been trapped. Vince barely had time to duck, and there was a stinging sensation on his cheek when he was struck by splintering rock.

A surging underwater shock wave disgorged the canoe from its resting place, and off they went, downstream. To keep them from smashing against the corridor of boulders forming the last portion of the gauntlet, Vince had to hastily redirect his focus on steering the vessel. He let instinct take over, his shocked thoughts still centered on their mysterious attacker.

Somehow they managed to safely transit the final chute, which deposited them in a pool of frothing white water. The current continued to run swift here, and as they kept on going downstream, his guide was able to turn the canoe around so that Vince was once more the bowman.

From this familiar vantage point, Vince spotted the VP's canoe some twenty yards ahead. Chapman and Eberly were halted beside a large, partially submerged snag, examining something in the water. Vince hastily glanced over his shoulder, and failing to spot the helicopter, he dug his paddle into the water to warn Chapman.

"What the blue blazes is goin' on out here, Special Agent?" asked Ron Wyatt, his concerned tone of voice unmistakable.

Vince held back his response, his attention instead riveted on the object of the VP's current inspection. Caught in the snag, her soaked body seemingly crucified in the twisted tree limbs, was the lifeless body of Andy Whitworth. Her tattered clothes were partially torn off, and Vince could soon see that a good portion of her face had been blown away. A paddle and the jagged front half of one of the johnboats were also caught in the snag, and Vince didn't have to see any more to realize the mysterious Huey was responsible for this slaughter.

"Kellogg?" murmured the VP, his eyes wide in shocked horror.

"We've got to get off this river at once!" Vince replied, his words cut short by an ominous shadow.

The sound of its engines still masked by the roar of the rapids, the Huey swept in from the river's western bank. It passed so close above them that they could actually feel the downdraft of its rotor wash, and Vince looked upward in time to see a bearded individual dressed in a green flight suit standing at the open fuselage hatchway. He had a machine gun rigged up in front of him, and upon spotting their canoes, he angled the barrel downward and fired.

The shells tore into the water, stitching a long line of exploding eruptions on the river's surface, a bare inch from the side of the VP's canoe. Both Chapman and District Ranger Eberly didn't have to see any more to know the exact nature of the threat Vince was about to warn them of, and they readily pushed away from the snag, to reenter the main channel. Vince dug his paddle into the water to stay as close as possible, while the Huey began a steeply banked turn to initiate yet another strafing pass.

The sloped banks of the river offered little cover, and Eberly was apparently attempting to make the most of the current to round the next bend, where a steep wall of limestone protectively beckoned. It took a full effort from both Vince and Wyatt to keep up with them. The VP's canoe was establishing a blistering pace, Chapman making the best use of his collegiate rowing experience. Even then, Vince knew that this valiant effort was futile at best. The Huey could easily track them, and he wondered if they'd stand a better chance of surviving the next attack by leaving the canoes and diving into the river.

Vince seriously doubted that even this desperate measure would save them, and he dared to peek over his shoulder to locate the Huey. He spotted it hovering over the river, a good fifty yards farther upstream. Vince wondered if he should stop paddling, so he could reach into the folds of his nylon windbreaker and remove his 9mm Glock from its shoulder harness. This was their last line of defense, and he had the distinct impression that the crew of the Huey was intentionally playing with them.

"Will you just look at that!" exclaimed Ron Wyatt, his excited glance focused downstream. "Here comes the cavalry, my friend!"

Vince broke off eye contact with the Huey, and as he turned back around to see what the ranger was talking about, a formation of two helicopters filled that portion of sky almost directly ahead of them. He knew in an instant that the lead chopper was a specially modified Blackhawk belonging to the Secret Service, with the trailing aircraft sporting the characteristic boxy fuselage and dark-green-and-white paint scheme of Marine Two.

With a minimum of fanfare, the Blackhawk shot forward

to engage the Huey with its chin-mounted machine gun blazing. The Huey blindly shot off a salvo of three air-to-air rockets before breaking sharply to the east.

Vince watched as the Huey's errant rockets streaked by the Blackhawk and harmlessly exploded into a stand of grizzled oaks. Meanwhile, Marine Two further descended. Vince could feel the Sikorsky's powerful downdraft as his canoe glided in beside the VP's. Like a mother hen protecting her chicks, the immense transport helicopter initiated a protective hover above them, while all eyes focused on the Blackhawk's continued pursuit.

Unable to outrun the Blackhawk, the Huey was headed almost due east, at an altitude of six hundred feet. A towering nine-hundred-foot limestone bluff lay immediately ahead. If the Huey didn't gain altitude quickly, it would surely strike the bluff, and sensing that they had their quarry cornered, the Blackhawk let loose another round of machine-gun fire.

A thick column of black smoke began pouring from the Huey's engine, and it was obvious that it'd never generate enough power to get over the bluff. While the VP traded a high five with Ben Eberly, Vince watched the Blackhawk pass through the oily column of smoke, its machine gun blazing away with the coup de grace.

The Huey appeared to be only a few feet away from hitting the bluff, and just missed striking it by initiating a sharp, heavily banked turn to the north. Still immersed in the Huey's trailing cloud of smoke, the Blackhawk fought to turn to the north itself, but in the process clipped the bluff with a rotor tip. For the briefest of moments, the Blackhawk appeared to be suspended in midair. But then the forces of gravity took over, and the helicopter, complete with its five-man CAT team inside, began a spiraling, uncontrolled descent.

It crashed and exploded at the foot of the bluff. From the river, Vince clearly saw the red-hot fireball, and knew in an instant that all aboard were dead. He was sickened with this realization, his grief cut short by the return of the Huey.

Their phantom attacker swept in from the north, only a few feet from the river's surface. Smoke continued to pour from its engine, though that didn't keep it from making its presence known with a pair of spiraling rockets. While one of these missiles exploded in a geyser of water well short of them, the other detonated in the shallows directly amidships of the VP's canoe. A bruising shower of pebbles rained down on both of the canoes. All of them began paddling with renewed intensity, even with Marine Two's sheltering presence above.

As they rounded the next bend and shot over another set of rapids, Vince spotted a clearing ahead on the right bank. There was plenty of limestone cover nearby, and he watched as the district ranger pointed to this same outcrop from the stern of the VP's canoe.

A distance of a good three hundred yards still had to be paddled before they'd reach land, and they redoubled their efforts, taking advantage of the swift current they now found themselves in. The roar of the white water all but swallowed any evidence of Marine Two above, and Vince looked upward to determine its position. The Sikorsky had gained several hundred feet of altitude, and Vince could see one of the Marines bravely standing in the open hatch firing an assault rifle at the Huey, which was headed straight for them from upstream, machine gun blazing.

Vince fought the impulse to pull out his pistol, and he watched Marine Two selflessly position itself between their canoes and the onrushing Huey. The big green Sikorsky had no offensive weapons systems of its own, and displayed remarkable survivability as it took round after round of machine-gun fire originally meant for Vince and his group. In the end, it was a pair of air-to-air missiles that led to Marine Two's demise, and the Sikorsky exploded and plunged nose-first into the river.

A bare one hundred yards now separated them from the protective wall of limestone rocks on the shoreline. The VP's canoe was a boat length ahead, and Vince found himself praying that Andrew Chapman would be able to reach cover before the Huey was able to reposition itself.

A quick glance to his right showed that his prayers would never be answered. A single rocket shot out of the Huey's starboard pod and slammed into the lead canoe. The force of this explosion was enough to split the vessel in half, and Vince looked in horror as Chapman went flying head over heels into the swift-moving waters of the main channel.

Without a moment's hesitation, Vince leaped into the river himself, just missing the rocket that incinerated his own canoe and instantly killed Ranger Ron Wyatt. As he plunged into the icy water, he was suddenly aware of the incredible force of the current. Like a powerful riptide, it sucked him downstream, and Vince fought his way to the surface.

It would be useless to swim, and he rolled over on his back to let the current take him. He shot past a series of large boulders, and was all but oblivious to his sighting of the Huey soaring close overhead, flames and thick smoke pouring from the doomed helicopter's main cabin. Only one thing mattered, and that was locating the man whom Vince had sworn to protect with his life. He found himself issuing the briefest of prayers before lifting his head upward to scan the frothing white water directly downstream. And it was then he spotted the body of Andrew Montgomery Chapman, facedown in the current, and the immense waterfall that he was about to be sucked over.

Thomas picked up a map of the sprawling, 63,000-acre post at the main gate, and his first stop was at the CID field office. They were expecting him, and he was informed that Ted Callahan was waiting for him at Range Thirteen, near Forney Airfield. With directions in hand, Thomas returned to his car and continued south on Constitution Avenue.

This was his first visit to Fort Leonard Wood, and he was immediately impressed. The tree-lined grounds were spotless, the majority of modern buildings that he could see from the road looking more like they belonged on a college campus. The Maneuver Support Center passed on his left, home to the U.S. Army Engineer, Chemical, and Military Police training schools. He went by the veterans hospital, the billeting office, a barracks area, and a large parade ground. Hundreds of BDU-clad soldiers were assembled in formation here, and Thomas could tell from their appearance that they were new recruits, in the early stages of basic training. The Drill Sergeants, in their round campaign hats, looked like they were reading them the riot act, and Thomas noted that a large percentage of the recruits were female.

Two decades had passed since he had experienced his own early military training back at the Air Force Academy. Female cadets were the exception back then. And though it was surely only his imagination at work, most of the recruits, male and female, whom he passed on the way to the airfield looked more like kids who belonged in summer camp rather than people being trained to become soldiers.

The narrow asphalt road leading to the range turned to gravel, and at the third turnoff on the right, he spotted a red pennant flying from a flagpole. Thomas was stopped by a private first class on guard duty, and it took only a brief conversation for his legitimacy to be verified. The road to Range Thirteen further narrowed, leading him through a dense stand of pines and ending at a broad clearing with an earthen berm partially encircling it. Dozens of soldiers could be seen seated in shaded bleachers, facing the shooting range. Yet more soldiers were gathered on the range itself, and they appeared to be in the middle of a demonstration of some sort.

Thomas parked beside a trio of HUMVEEs and a pair of two-and-a-half-ton trucks. The distinctive sound of pistol fire crackled in the distance as he continued by foot to the slightly elevated apron where the shooters were gathered. It was so humid out, Thomas felt like he was pushing his way through a hot sponge.

The targets were a trio combination of paper silhouettes, steel Pepper Poppers resembling the vital areas of a human head and torso, and eight-inch-diameter steel plates. They were spread out in a 180-degree arc, at a variety of distances ranging from fifteen to fifty yards.

Thomas smiled upon spotting the officer who was prepping himself to be the next shooter. Colonel Ted Callahan was attired in BDUs, and was standing in a white, chalk-outlined box, facing downrange and making the final adjustments to his equipment and quick-draw hip holster. He obviously wasn't aware that Thomas had arrived, his attention focused on scanning and mentally rehearsing the target sequence he was about to shoot.

"Special Agent Kellogg," called a man's voice from behind.

Thomas turned and set his eyes on a solidly built, brown-haired officer with movie-star good looks and a warm smile.

"Special Agent, I'm Captain Jay Christian. The Colonel's been expecting you. Shall we tell him you're here?"

"Why don't we let him shoot first?" replied Thomas while accepting a firm handshake. "What's his target and stage scenario?"

"It's a hostage situation, sir. From the first box he will engage the group of Pepper Poppers to his front, which are all bad guys. Once they're downed, the Colonel will move five yards to his right, reload, and enter the next shooting box. There he'll be required to shoot through the open-ended barrel, at a variety of plates, gravity-activated appearing/disappearing targets, and a final array of poppers arranged to protect the hostage taker and his victim."

"Will it end with a tactical neutralization?" Thomas asked, having encountered many a similar scenario on the ATF range.

Captain Christian nodded affirmatively. "The white plate will indicate the no-shoot, the slightly elevated popper behind, the hostage taker. It's a gun-to-the-head situation, and requires a single T-zone shot to be successfully resolved."

Thomas knew that the T-zone referred to the exact center of the forehead, right above the bridge of the nose. By hitting this target, one could take down a subject, instantly severing the nervous system in such a way that the bad guy would never be able to depress the trigger of his own weapon. In a tactical situation, it was one of the most difficult of all shots, and used sparingly.

At the shooting box, Callahan drew out his pistol and inserted a magazine. Still facing downrange, he racked the slide and chambered a round, then replaced the pistol back in its holster, before readjusting the fit of his eye-and-ear protection.

"What kind of weapon is he using?" Thomas questioned.

"It's a Caspian .38 Super with a C-MORE electronic sight that emits a passive red targeting dot," answered Christian. "It's a high-capacity race gun with all the bells and whistles, like the compensator, enlarged mag well, and ambi safeties. All this makes the gun feel good and shoot fast and accurate."

"I haven't had much experience with those electronic sights," admitted Thomas. "How hard is it to acquire the red dot on target after drawing or when you're shooting? Do you actually take the time to find it, or do you do it by feel?"

"As in all shooting, sir, once you get used to your equipment, nearly all of the physical mechanics becomes muscle memory, the gun feeling comfortable and becoming a natural extension of your hand and arm. With practice, not only can you acquire the intended targets more rapidly, but you can also see more and even think faster."

"Are you ready, Colonel?" asked a soldier from the direction of the shooting box as he positioned himself behind Ted Callahan and held up a palm-sized digital timer.

Callahan carefully scanned the targets one more time, then took a deep breath and nodded that he was good to go.

"Shooter ready . . . Stand by . . ."

The timer activated with a loud, piercing tone giving the signal to begin, and Ted Callahan drew his pistol, aimed downrange, and began firing rapidly. In a matter of seconds, the first line of torso-shaped steel poppers fell. It was while running to the next box that he ejected the mostly spent magazine from his gun, and reloaded a full one that he retrieved from his belt. This time his aim was restricted by the steel barrel he was forced to shoot through, the exploding report of bullets striking steel clearly heard as the individual plates and gravity-turning targets were engaged.

Thomas counted off eighteen shots before the next-to-last

popper fell, revealing the final target of the scenario. From his vantage point, Thomas watched Callahan aim the red dot of his pistol to the head of the hostage-taker popper and hesitate the briefest of seconds before squeezing off his final shot. The popper fell with a perfectly centered head shot, and he ejected the magazine, cleared the live round from the chamber, and holstered a safe weapon.

"Hoo-ah!" exclaimed a massed chorus of voices from the bleachers.

"One miss in seventeen-point-five-four seconds, with hostage taker eliminated," reported the official scorekeeper, after sweeping the range with his binoculars.

Another resounding chorus of "Hoo-ah" emanated from the bleachers, and Ted Callahan looked relieved as he removed his ear protection and turned around to acknowledge this cheer of support. And it was only then that he spotted Thomas.

"Hell, if I knew you were watching, Kellogg, I wouldn't have gone and intentionally missed that target," Callahan jested, his smile wide and genuine.

"That's not bad shooting, Colonel, for a desk-bound fast-food junkie," replied Thomas, who accepted his old friend's handshake, and followed him over to a nearby table holding refreshments.

"Seriously, Thomas, it's good to see you again," said Callahan, who toasted his newly arrived guest with a cup of ice water.

Captain Christian was in the process of taking his place in the shooter's box, and Callahan beckoned toward the young officer, saying, "And now we're about to see a real shooter do his thing. Captain Jay Christian is an instructor at the MP school. He was formerly with Delta, and came here from Benning, where he was an award-winning member of the Army Marksmanship Unit."

They watched Christian prepare his weapon, and Callahan's voice lowered to a bare whisper. "I'm sorry I had to pull you off the abortion clinic bombing case, Thomas. But when I called your office at ATF headquarters this morning and learned that you were nearby in Union, I couldn't resist the opportunity of asking Director McShane for your services."

"Your timing couldn't have been better, Ted. In fact, your call reached me just as my latest lead was in the process of fizzling out. It seems for the last month I've been going in circles, and I must admit it's good to get away, clear the old head, and hopefully find some new perspective. Besides, I'm really enjoying being back on an Army post, though with all these young faces around, I'm feeling my age."

"Are you ready?" asked the timer from the shooting box.

Captain Christian nodded that he was, and when the timer's electronic tone sounded, he expertly drew out his pistol and began firing. The first series of shots went downrange like an automatic weapon, and when he sprinted to the next box and reloaded, the entire sequence passed in a blur. Bullets hit steel, the targets fell, and unlike Ted Callahan, Christian didn't hesitate when it came down to the final shot.

"No misses in fourteen-point-four-three seconds, with hostage taker eliminated," noted the official scorekeeper.

"Hoo-ah!" roared the audience from the bleachers.

"Hoo-ah!" repeated Thomas, genuinely impressed by the demonstration he had just witnessed.

A group of soldiers wearing rucksacks emerged on foot from the direction of the gravel road. Ted Callahan caught the attention of the lead figure in this column, and beckoned him over to join them.

"Sergeant Reed," greeted Callahan. "I was beginning to think you were going to forfeit the competition."

Sergeant Sam Reed snapped off a sharp salute and replied, "I'm sorry we're late, Colonel. Our truck broke down and we had to hike in this last klick."

"Sergeant Reed is an instructor in our Sapper Leader course," said Callahan to Thomas. "He's about to take on

Captain Christian's MPs in an action-shooting competition. But before the good Sergeant can show Christian's men why Army engineers lead the way, I'd like you to listen while he shares a little incident he was involved in last night that's indirectly responsible for your presence here this afternoon."

After being properly introduced, Thomas listened while Reed painfully revealed the armed robbery that he and his nine-man Sapper class had been the recent victims of. The incident took place a little over twelve hours ago, in a hollow less than three miles from this very spot. Since Reed was a career soldier who obviously took his duty seriously, Thomas could understand his discomfort as he described the moment when the group of camouflaged strangers emerged from the forest and ordered them to drop their weapons.

When Reed's associate instructor had dared to question this command, he received a shotgun wound in the shoulder for his petulance. Only then did Reed realize the seriousness of their predicament, and he reluctantly instructed his men to do as ordered.

The thieves got away with a virtual smorgasbord of weaponry, and Thomas didn't have to hear any more to know why Ted Callahan had asked for his services. Included in this haul was an M60 machine gun, a pair of M249 Squad Automatic Weapons, two M4 carbines with M203 grenade launchers attached, four M16A2 assault rifles, twenty pounds of C-4, a box of detonators, a roll of detonation cord, three tactical radios, four AN/PVS-7D advanced Night Vision Goggles, and an assortment of flares and artillery projectile ground-burst simulators.

Sergeant Reed's voice was cracking with embarrassment upon describing the final act of humiliation that the thieves inflicted on them. For as they gathered up the weapons, they ordered the Sappers to remove their BDUs, and the engineers soon found themselves stripped to their underwear and bound up with duct tape.

"And chances are that we'd still be out there at the mercy

of the mosquitoes if it hadn't been for one of my men driving out there two hours later in the water truck," bitterly concluded the senior enlisted man, who waited until Thomas ended a perfunctory question session before discreetly putting a pinch of chewing tobacco behind his lower lip.

Poor lighting conditions and heavy camouflage face paint kept Reed and his men from being able to further describe their assailants. And the last they saw of them was as they silently disappeared back into the tree line, with both their weapons and their BDUs in tow.

Before Ted Callahan excused Reed, Thomas was able to schedule a proper interrogation session with the Sapper Leader course instructor for later in the afternoon, in the CID field office. As they watched him join his men beside the first shooting box, Ted revealed that both CID and a squad of MPs were currently combing the woods where the robbery took place for evidence. He also offered to personally convey Thomas to the site.

Storm clouds were gathering in the western sky, and Thomas accepted this invitation on the condition that they proceed out there at once, before the threatening thunder showers washed away any promising clues. It was while rummaging through a carton of MREs for a field lunch that Thomas vented something that had been bothering him.

"I can appreciate the Army's desire to nail the thieves, Ted, but why do you need my help specifically? And why call you out from D.C.?"

"Because last night's robbery wasn't the first to strike Fort Leonard Wood with the same MO."

Callahan sniffed at the tuna and noodle pack he'd been stuck with, while Thomas had dug out the only spaghetti. He continued his story while leading Thomas to his HUMVEE to eat.

"I was originally called out here last week, after a group of Special Forces engineers were robbed in almost exactly the same manner when working the Demo range. The take was over a hundred pounds of C-4, more detonators, and several cases of Eastern Bloc mines that had been confiscated in Bosnia and were being detonated to see how they functioned."

"Mines?" repeated Thomas, his expression tightening in horror.

"Tell me about it, Special Agent. I realize that we in the CID and the ATF have enough on our hands tracking down all the automatic weapons, ammo, and high explosives being lost from our bases. But mines bring us into a shadowy new area, almost too terrifying to even think about.

"The devices included in the heist were fully armed and equipped with fuses, detonators, and explosives. They included toe poppers, claymores, antipersonnel, frags, trip wires, and anti-armor—a full gamut of mine hardware that could wreak unimaginable havoc if they were to get in the wrong hands."

"And you really think the same individuals are responsible for both robberies, Ted?"

Callahan halted at the driver's door of the HUMVEE. "Like last night's robbery, the mine heist took place at night, with our Special Forces squad caught totally off guard. They too were ordered to take off their clothes by a group of heavily camouflaged assailants, who subsequently tied our Green Berets up with duct tape. And because it was all taking place in a driving thunderstorm, the clues were all but washed away by the time CID got out there late the next day."

"Could it be an inside job?" questioned Thomas. "I mean, who better than another soldier to sneak up and rob a group of Green Berets?"

"Whoever it was had *muchos cajones*, and a thorough knowledge of these woods and the approaches that lead into them."

"How about the locals?" Thomas continued. "Any recent militia activity in the area?"

Callahan snickered. "This is the heart of the Ozarks, Thomas. I don't have to remind you, of all people, that some of the most virulent antigovernment groups in the country are based in these parts. Remember a few years back, when we traced down that stolen crate of Browning Automatic Weapons to our old friends in the Covenant, Sword, and Arm of the Lord? We found them buried in the Mark Twain National Forest, just south of here."

The muted boom of thunder rumbled in the distance, and Thomas found his attention drawn back to the shooting range, where Captain Christian was approaching them at a full sprint.

"Colonel Callahan!" he shouted between heaving breaths. "The post has just gone on full strategic alert, and the CG wants you down in the Emergency Operations Center on the double, sir!"

The red command flags hanging outside Hoge Hall in the Maneuver Support Center indicated three general officers in the building—a pair of one-star Brigadier Generals, and the two stars belonging to Major General Levering Atwater, the post CG. Thomas followed Ted Callahan inside, past a pair of smartly attired MPs armed with holstered side arms. Yet another MP, this one an attractive female, was stationed beside the reception desk, and she greeted them with a crisp salute.

"Colonel Callahan, I'm Sergeant First Class Joanna Blair, and I'll be escorting you down to the EOC." Looking at Thomas, she added, "I don't believe we were expecting a civilian, sir."

"Special Agent Kellogg is with the Bureau of Alcohol, Tobacco and Firearms, and I'll personally vouch for him, Sergeant."

SFC Blair didn't dare challenge this endorsement, and she led the way down a wide stairway. The modern glass, steel, and polished wood interior could easily pass for the headquarters of a Fortune 500 company. Great expense had been dedicated to its design and construction, a factor no doubt reflected by the Engineering Center that was housed here.

At the bottom of the stairs, their escort conveyed them down a long, carpeted corridor. The pictures on the walls showed various scenes depicting the history of the Corps of Engineers. It was a rich legacy that went all the way back to the Revolutionary War, and continued on to Desert Storm and beyond.

Beside a stylized painting of today's engineers at work on the modern battlefield was an adjoining hallway into which the MP led them. The walls here were lined with sound-absorbent tile, and Thomas noted the open entryway was protected by a thick, steel, blast-proof door.

The muffled sound of voices signaled their arrival in the EOC. It was a large, ten-thousand-square-foot room, with a theater-style briefing area that faced a series of seven computer workstations, with four consoles currently manned. A podium was positioned to the side, and three immense projection screens dominated the room's forward wall.

The first four rows of seats in the briefing area were completely filled with officers of Major rank or above. All were dressed in BDUs, and Thomas felt conspicuous in his khakis, polo shirt, and lightweight ATF windbreaker.

No sooner did Thomas join Ted in the vacant fifth row than the overhead lights dimmed. The middle projection screen flickered alive with a rich royal blue background surrounding the official crest of the Chairman of the Joint Chiefs of Staff. This backdrop faded, to be replaced by the Chairman himself. Admiral Trent Warner was standing behind a podium, dressed in a green flight suit. The silver-haired flag officer appeared uncharacteristically tense as he stared into the camera and began speaking.

"My fellow Americans and members of the Armed

Forces, I am coming to you live from the National Airborne Operations Center, high above Eastern Europe. This unprecedented alert brief has been generated by a tragedy of immense proportions that started off several hours ago, when our President landed in the Crimea for what was to be a secret nuclear-arms negotiating session with the leaders of Russia and Ukraine.

"I regret to inform you that our Commander-in-Chief never made it to that summit. Approximately one hour ago, while transiting Ukrainian soil, the President's motorcade was attacked, and he was unmercifully gunned down by yet unknown assailants. Rest assured, this cold-blooded murder will not go unavenged!"

The Chairman paused, and a murmur of shocked disbelief filled the EOC. Thomas found himself too stunned to talk, and he traded astounded glances with Ted Callahan, who incredulously whispered, "I don't believe what I'm hearing!"

Thomas found himself thinking about the other government personnel in the President's motorcade. His brother, Vince, had been previously assigned to the same detail, and he listened as the Chairman continued.

"Per the continuity of government protocol, I have assumed supreme leadership of America's Armed Forces. I have also activated the alternative codes to our strategic arsenal, and have ordered these forces to an alert stage of DEFCON Four.

"The very fact that I'm addressing you now speaks well for our continued command and control capabilities. This broadcast is being simultaneously transmitted to U.S. military command posts worldwide, but not the general public so as to avoid needless panic. Until the Vice President, or his successor, has been duly sworn into office as President, I will continue to fulfill my sworn duty as senior ranking military officer of the National Command Authority.

"With your continued support, cooperation, and assistance, we shall prevail in this hour of darkness. Our great nation has undergone many great hardships in a little over two hundred years of existence, and this one, too, shall test the fabric of Lady Liberty's will to prevail. It is up to the proud men and women of the United States military to take up the torch of liberty, to ease the nation's fears, and to give our people hope for a brave new tomorrow. America's best days are yet to come. God bless . . ."

Before the Chairman could complete this time-honored affirmation, the floor beneath him suddenly bucked steeply to the left, then dove sharply downward. He grabbed onto the shaking podium as a water glass tumbled off it. And for a sobering moment, Thomas saw fear in Warner's steely gaze as the Chairman looked to the still-rocking, tripod-mounted camera for one last second before the picture went unceremoniously blank.

"Break left! Break left! Incoming missile!"

Coach listened to his copilot's shout of warning, and immediately turned the yoke hard aport. The 747 reacted almost instantaneously, and in the center of the instrument panel, the Altitude Director Indicator rolled hard in the direction that the plane was now turning. Coach could feel the strain on his shoulder harness, and he listened as Lucky anxiously cried out:

"Radar shows a single air-to-air missile headed our way, compliments of that Red bastard in the lead MiG. It's gonna be close, gents!"

Nightwatch was still in the midst of its steeply banked turn when the cockpit filled with a resounding explosive crack. This was accompanied by a blinding streak of white-hot light that shot past them at supersonic velocity, a mere one hundred yards away from their right wing tip. In the blink of an eye, the eastern horizon lit up with a blazing fireball, and Coach and his copilot found themselves diverting their glances to keep their night vision intact.

"American military 747," intoned a Slavic-accented voice over the radio. "This is Colonel Anatoly Dubrinski of the Ukrainian Air Force in Foxbat One. You are hereby ordered to return at once to Simferopol Airfield, to answer to the charges of crimes of treason against the Ukrainian people. And be forewarned, next time I won't intentionally miss!"

"What in the blazes is he talking about?" quizzed Coach, ever hesitant to return to the eastern heading that they had previously been traveling. "Lucky, get Colonel Pritchard on the horn. Inform him of the situation, and find out how in hell he wants us to respond to this threat."

"Don't forget to remind him that we've got no defensive countermeasures," interjected Jake Lasky, clearly shaken by the near miss. "And that we're a virtual sitting duck up here!"

Lucky's call caught Colonel Pritchard in the briefing room. The compartment was filled with fallen debris, including two airmen who had been thrown to the deck during the unexpected turn.

"Captain Davis," said Pritchard into an intercom headset. "Hold our present course, and I'll get back to you."

The Operations team CO ripped off his headphones and met Trent Warner's icy stare. "Sir, the air-to-air missile responsible for that evasive maneuver originated from the lead Foxbat. A Colonel Dubrinski of the Ukrainian Air Force has just ordered us to return to Simferopol, to answer to charges of treason. And if we don't, he's threatened to shoot at us again, and this time he says he won't miss."

"What?" screamed the Chairman, his face red with rage. "Like hell we're going to return to the Crimea! And to answer to charges of treason? The nerve of those spineless Ukrainian cowards!"

"But are we in a position to challenge them, sir?" asked

Pritchard. "Must I remind you that Nightwatch has no offensive or defensive capabilities?"

The Chairman paused for a moment to consider their dilemma, and was suddenly aware of the stares of the other personnel in the briefing room. "Colonel," he said in a calm, reassuring manner, "until this situation is resolved, I feel it's prudent to hand off the football to Iron Man One. You are to immediately transfer all strategic authority to General Spencer aboard TACAMO. You are to emphasize that this is on a temporary basis only, and that their own version of Satchel Bravo shall be accessed only if the United States should come under actual attack. And then I think it's best if you got the Ukrainian Defense Minister on the line. It's time to remind him that before he gives us a reason to bomb his homeland to oblivion, he'd better take pause to consider the consequences of their actions."

The waterfall was steeper and more powerful than Vince had expected, and he found himself being pulled over the brink, his body somersaulting through the spray like a soaked rag doll. It seemed to take an eternity to hit the pool below, and when he finally struck solid water, he was sucked into the mouth of a swirling whirlpool. No matter how hard he kicked or stroked with his arms, he was powerless to escape the maelstrom, and he would most likely have drowned if the river hadn't freed him on its own volition.

He broke the surface, desperately gasping for air. After momentarily gagging on all the river water he had swallowed, he cleared his lungs, and only then did he remember his duty.

His search of the pool was blessedly brief, for he located the Vice President on his very first sweep. Andrew Chapman was floating facedown beside a sandy portion of riverbank. He wasn't moving, and Vince sprinted over to assist him, using an overhead-crawl swimming stroke.

The first thing he did was turn Chapman over. The VP's face was ghostly pale, his lips were blue, and he didn't appear to be breathing. The water was shallow enough for Vince to stand, and he began CPR right there in the river.

Because hypothermia was also a concern, Vince slowly worked his way over to the bank, all the while continuing the resuscitation effort. He stopped only long enough to drag the VP's body up onto dry land, then redoubled his efforts with renewed intensity. He blew breath after breath between Chapman's frigid lips, and when this failed to get him breathing, Vince rolled the VP over and pushed down hard on his lower rib cage. Water streamed out of Chapman's mouth, and Vince rolled him over onto his back and reinitiated CPR, this time halting every sixth breath to massage his patient's heart.

"Come on," he urged between breaths. "Nobody dies on my watch!"

This declaration was seemingly answered by Chapman when his stomach muscles began to spasm. His lungs heaved upward, and after vomiting an incredible amount of fluid, the Vice President of the United States began breathing on his own.

Vince fought the temptation to hug the man, and instead focused his attention on getting him as warm as possible. A massive cottonwood currently shaded them. Noting that the clearing faced the southwest, Vince realized that all they needed to do was relocate a few feet away, to be directly in the sun's powerful rays while still benefiting from the cover of the cottonwood's branches. He didn't know who else could be out there.

He helped Chapman sit up before dragging him over the sand and propping him up against the cottonwood trunk. The sunlight's effect was instantaneous, and Vince felt his own chill dissipate.

"Damn it, Kellogg," the VP managed to say while regaining his strength. "Who the hell is trying to kill us?"

Vince was thinking about this very same thing, and already focusing on security concerns, he plunged his hand beneath his windbreaker, then cursed upon finding his holster empty.

"I must have lost my weapon after following you over the waterfall," Vince noted, pulling out a soggy cigar from his breast pocket.

"Don't you know that smoking is hazardous to your health, Special Agent?" said the VP, his usual sharp wit already on the rebound.

Vince took a fond look at the wet stogie and reluctantly flung it into the underbrush. "Our esteemed SAIC gave it to me, to celebrate my anniversary."

"I wonder what Samuel Morrison the second would make of our current predicament," Chapman said. "Didn't any of our party make it?"

Vince surveyed the river and somberly shook his head. "It sure doesn't look that way. And what scares the hell out of me is that our ground-based CAT teams have also apparently been eliminated. It was nothing short of a damn slaughter!"

"I never realized the true extent of the resentment that the locals must have built up against the Federal government," said the VP. "But where did they get that helicopter?"

Vince's reply was cut short by a sudden rustling noise in the underbrush. He put his finger to his lips for silence, and reached down to grab a broken tree limb, the only available weapon.

"Drop it, Bubba, and down on your knees!" ordered a strong male voice.

Five shotgun-toting individuals emerged from the surrounding cover. Each of them wore camouflaged coveralls, with faces colored in green, brown, and black greasepaint.

"Are you deaf, Bubba? I said drop it and kneel!" repeated the stranger, who backed up this command with a deafening burst of his 12-gauge.

It was shortly after the Chairman's video image abruptly faded from the EOC's projection screen that Thomas was introduced to Major General Levering Atwater. The post's CG turned out to be a short, stocky, square-jawed individual with a salt-and-pepper crew cut. Together with his steely-eyed Judge Advocate, Atwater escorted both Thomas and Ted Callahan to the front of the room. They appeared to already know who Thomas's employer was, and after the CG conveyed a request to one of the soldiers manning a computer workstation, the left-hand projection screen filled with a detailed map of south-central Missouri.

"This is indeed a dark day for our country, gentlemen," said Atwater, his voice deep, his words crisply spoken. "We find ourselves dealing not only with the assassination of our Commander-in-Chief, but also with a problem of a more immediate nature. We've just been contacted by the Director of the Secret Service. It appears they've been unable to contact Vice President Chapman and inform him of the tragedy in the Crimea."

"Is it a communications glitch?" Callahan asked.

Atwater chose his words carefully. "That was their first assumption. But then the FEMA central locator system was activated. This system was specifically designed to track down the Presidential successors wherever they may be. It relies on a broad spectrum of arrays, including radio, cellular, and satellites, to offer instantaneous, secure communications worldwide." Utilizing an electronic cursor, he addressed the map, highlighting a large, light-green-colored segment in the southeastern corner. "As you well know, the VP is supposed to be in the midst of a float trip here, on the Eleven Point River. Though the initial alert was received by his party, there's been no response. Local efforts at contacting them have been equally fruitless, with the entire U.S. Forest Service radio grid inexplicably inoperative."

"Surely the Secret Service CAT teams in the area can contact them?" offered Thomas, well aware that Vince was the acting SAIC of the VP's detail.

The Judge Advocate answered, "The Secret Service has been unable to make contact with these land-based assets. This includes the efforts of Marine Two and the CAT team Blackhawk, with both helicopters reporting shots fired before mysteriously breaking radio contact and seeming to disappear into thin air."

"Shots fired?" Thomas repeated, his stomach suddenly tightening with concern.

"Gentlemen, we've obviously got a serious situation down there," observed Major General Atwater, who used the cursor to highlight Fort Leonard Wood's location on the upper portion of the map segment. "As the crow flies, it's approximately seventy-five miles from this EOC to the spot on the Eleven Point where the VP's party was last heard from. We've just been tasked to send a platoon-sized element down into the Mark Twain National Forest to seek out Andrew Chapman and determine his ability to assume the Presidency. Time is therefore critical, and since the Secret

Service and the FBI will be unable to get personnel to the area until later this evening, we've drawn the assignment."

"Special Agent Kellogg," interjected the Judge Advocate, "as both you and Colonel Callahan know, it is highly unusual for us to receive tasking from a government organization other than the DOD. This is especially the case when this tasking concerns an operation on American soil. Title Eighteen of the United States Code, Section 1385, severely limits the manner in which the military can operate under such circumstances."

"The Posse Comitatus Act," added Ted Callahan.

"Precisely," said the Judge Advocate. "And to legally overcome these restrictions, we intend to invoke House Joint Resolution 1292, which directs all departments of the government, upon the request of the Secret Service, to assist that service in carrying out its statutory protective duties."

Major General Atwater quickly chimed in. "I've already called together a Search and Rescue force, comprised of a squad of combat Sappers and the post's MP Special Response Team. They're currently gathering their gear, and will be ready for a helicopter airlift to the Eleven Point within the half hour, with a mechanized unit to follow by road."

"Special Agent Kellogg, to ensure that our men don't infringe on Posse Comitatus restrictions, we'd feel a lot better if you'd consider accompanying them," posited the Judge Advocate.

"And Colonel Callahan," added Atwater. "You'd also be an asset in this regard."

Thomas replied without a moment's hesitation. "I'd be honored to go along, especially since my brother, Vince, is the Special Agent in Charge of the VP's security detail down on the Eleven Point."

"You can count me in," agreed Ted Callahan.

"Excellent," replied Atwater. "I've taken the liberty of putting together some gear for both of you. So good luck, and good hunting!"

"American military 747, this is my last warning. You are to immediately return with me to Simferopol Airport or suffer the consequences."

Coach's frustration was obvious as he pushed back his chin mike and spoke to his copilot. "Lucky, whatever it takes, stall him. I'll get the good Colonel on the horn, and get a definitive answer on how the hell they want us to handle this mess."

Lucky flashed Coach a "why me?" stare, and paused for a moment before addressing the radio. "Come again, Foxbat leader? Your last transmission was incomplete. I suggest that you switch frequencies to NATO band . . ."

Ever appreciative of his copilot's ingenuity, Coach activated the intercom. "Colonel Pritchard, it's Major Foard. Unless you have any better ideas, I'm afraid we're gonna have to change our flight plan from Andrews to Simferopol."

"Can't you stall them just a little bit longer?" Pritchard's amplified voice sounded pleading. "The Chairman's still trying to get in touch with the Ukrainian Defense Minister. And we're having one hell of a time making contact, because it appears they're in the middle of some kind of coup down there!"

"Sir," countered Coach, "coup or no coup, we're about to get an AA-6 air-to-air missile up our keister. As air crew commander, I say it would be more prudent if we sorted this whole thing out down on the tarmac at Simferopol."

"He's not buying it, Coach!" interrupted Lucky. "He says he's gonna shoot!"

Coach abruptly ended his intercom conversation to concentrate on the crisis at hand. "What's our lead Foxbat's range?"

"Twelve and a half miles and holding steady, sir," replied the navigator from the rear of the cockpit.

"That's well within the AA-6's IR envelope," informed Jake Lasky. "With an approach speed of Mach 4.5, we'll be toast before we know what hit us."

"American military 747," the radio boomed, "unless you turn at once for Simferopol, I have no choice but to take you out. Be informed that I'm initiating armament sequence and launch countdown."

"At least we can't say he didn't give us plenty of warning," noted Coach, who found himself without options. "It's time to turn this big lady around for some Ukrainian cooking."

As Coach reached out to deactivate the autopilot, Lucky readjusted the scan of the instrument panel's radar screen. He requested maximum range, and had to do a double take upon spotting a formation of four new contacts, rapidly approaching from the south.

"We've got some more company coming!" he excitedly revealed.

Coach looked at the radar screen, and a smile lit up his face as the three MiGs suddenly broke off their pursuit and turned back to the north.

"Looks like Comrade Dubrinski has had a sudden change of heart," observed the grinning pilot.

"Nightwatch six-seven-six," broke in a crisp voice over the radio. "This is Captain Brantley Williams, your Fighting Falcon leader. How can we be of service this evening? Over."

Back in the 747's Operations Team Area, the arrival of the U.S. Air Force F-16s was met with shouts of relieved joy. Nightwatch was now free to continue on the long flight back to Andrews, and as it initiated a wide-banked turn to the west, Brittany Cooper had to reach out and steady herself on the side of the workstation she was standing next to. On the other hand, the woman seated behind this console didn't appear to be the least bit fazed by the sudden turn. Oblivious to her straining seat harness, Red continued to attack her keyboard, her glance locked on the assortment of data filling the console's flashing monitor screen.

"Iron Man One," she said into her chin mike. "This is Nightwatch six-seven-six. I have a Priority One transmission. Over."

Brittany knew that this call was being directed to yet another U.S. military airborne command post. Iron Man One was their current TACAMO alert aircraft. While Nightwatch was a U.S. Air Force platform, TACAMO belonged to the Navy. Its original mission was to offer survivable communications to the strategic submarine fleet. For over three decades, and using several types of aircraft, TACAMO had proved itself an invaluable asset, utilizing a five-mile-long antenna to transmit VLF broadcasts to submarines deep beneath their patrol zones.

With the addition of a new state-of-the-art airframe, TACAMO had recently expanded its mission. Iron Man One was the first TACAMO platform to be outfitted with the so-called "Looking Glass" operations suite. Looking Glass was originally an Air Force program, run by the Strategic Air Command, that offered survivable command and control of nuclear-armed ICBMs and land-based bombers.

Aboard Iron Man One, the normal TACAMO communications personnel were joined by a command battle staff. This emergency action team was responsible for transmitting Emergency Action Messages, the unlock codes for America's nuclear warheads. In addition to releasing these codes, the battle staff had the capability of actually launching an ICBM from the air, should ground-based command and control be compromised.

"Admiral Warner," said Red into her mike, "I have General Spencer on the line."

The moment the two senior officers began conversing, Red cut off the verbal feed, and she looked up to address Brittany. "That should keep him out of my hair for a couple of minutes. Now what's all this about those MiGs hightailing it back home?"

"It seems that our saviors are a group of F-16 Fighting Falcons out of Incirlik," Brittany told her. "They were originally scrambled to assist Checkmate One, and arrived seconds before that lead Foxbat was threatening to blow us out of the skies."

"I'm sure glad we weren't forced to land at Simferopol, Commander. From what I could tell from the Ukrainian Defense Ministry, they're in the midst of a military insurrection of some sort, and now it looks like the Russians are involved."

"The President's assassination may have been an instigating factor, or part of the plan so as to disenable us from reaching and perhaps siding against the coup's leadership," mused Brittany.

"Though I caught only a portion of the Chairman's conversation with the Defense Minister, it actually sounded as if the Ukrainians were blaming *us* for both the attack on the motorcade, as well as the coup attempt that followed. And that's why they sent up those MiGs."

A loud electronic tone sounded from Red's computer, and she immediately broke off her conversation with Brittany, typed a flurry of commands into her keyboard, and spoke into her chin mike. "Yes, Admiral . . . I understand, sir . . . I'll see what I can do about it, sir."

Red cut off her mike, and, still able to hear the audio feed over her lightweight headphones, she began attacking the keyboard. "Damn static," she cursed, more in annoyance than in anger. "You'd think that with all the big bucks we spend on this high-tech gear, the least we could get is a clear telephone conversation."

Brittany sensed her frustration, yet realized that establishing secure communications via satellite between two airplanes—one flying over the Black Sea, the other off America's East Coast—was no easy feat to begin with.

"Admiral Warner, keep your cool, dude," mumbled Red to herself, in reference to the conversation she was continuing to overhear. "Even if you are Chairman, the man's still a General."

Brittany didn't have the foggiest notion what Red was referring to. She watched her complete the final filtering process before removing her headset and looking up at Brittany, a mischievous look in her eye.

"Though I could get a court-martial for sharing this with you, it seems our esteemed Chairman just read General Spencer the riot act."

"Whatever for?" asked Brittany, her curiosity piqued.

Red's voice lowered to a conspiratorial whisper. "With your clearance, you'd probably find out anyway. But promise me you'll keep it between us."

"My lips are sealed, Sergeant."

Red eagerly continued. "I entered the conversation just as the football was being transferred back to Nightwatch. And it was then that Warner went ballistic. It seems Spencer played a SIOP option. He had Iron Man One transmit an EAM to one of our Tridents, authorizing a limited nuclear strike against Ukraine, should Nightwatch have been downed. And all he wanted to do was properly revenge our deaths, and Warner goes and cuts his head off!"

Commander Benjamin Kram sat alone in his stateroom, the nautical strains of Richard Rodgers's "Victory at Sea" playing on his CD player. Though his small, fold-down desk was loaded with paperwork, his complete attention was riveted on a single document. He had read it over and over since receiving it in Norfolk a little over two weeks ago.

Kram had had an intuitive feeling about what lay inside the sealed envelope from COMSUBLANT, and he'd waited until Hampton Roads was well behind before opening it. Inside was a single sheet of paper, instructing him that, starting this fall, he was to be transferred to the Pentagon to work for the Director of the Submarine Warfare Division. Career-wise, this was an excellent move. Yet it was devastating on an emotional level.

For all he knew, this current patrol could be his last. Command at sea was the reason he had decided to join the Navy over two decades ago. He had dedicated twenty-seven years of his life, endured countless extended watches, and missed too many of his kids' birthdays, all to earn the coveted title of "skipper." And now he would be packing his sea bag for the final time, to join the ranks of those forlorn sailors who would sail the oceans no more.

His wife, Donna, would certainly be thrilled with this new assignment, as would his twin sons, Michael and Andrew. They would be getting a full-time husband and father back, while he would be losing another family, the existence of which his wife and kids never really comprehended. He had yet to inform the crew of his new orders, and he supposed he should first share the news with Dan Calhoun, his Executive Officer. Then he'd inform Master Chief Inboden, the *Polk*'s affable Chief of the Boat.

Sharing the news would put him one step closer to stepping off the submarine's gangway for that final time. And once the rest of the crew got wind that the "Old Man" was leaving, he'd be like a baseball player announcing his retirement, and then making the last round of ballparks to share his glory days with the fans. Reveling in the past was certainly not the way he wanted to spend his last days on the *Polk,* and Kram decided to delay sharing his new orders for the immediate future.

The growl of the intercom diverted his musings, and he reached under the lip of the desk to grab the nearest handset. "Captain here."

The anxious voice on the other end was the boat's radio officer, reporting that he believed he knew the reason that the exercise they were supposed to be in the midst of had been suddenly canceled. Kram cut short his introspection and notified the young officer that he was on his way to radio to get these findings firsthand.

He hid his transfer orders under the latest "Naval Submarine League Review" and, before leaving the stateroom, changed into a fresh set of blue coveralls, or poopy suit, as it was known to the submariner. After a quick splash of cold water on his face from his Pullman-style washbasin, he strode out into the passageway, turned to the right, and had to walk but a few steps toward the aft portion of the boat in order to reach the radio room.

He found the officer in charge seated at a workstation reserved for cryptograph analysis. This newly installed encryption system was designed by the National Security Agency, and incorporated into the sub's communications shack to secure the integrity of all message traffic. In 1985, the Walker family spy ring taught the Navy the utter importance of ensuring secure cryptography. During the years since, new equipment and procedures had come on line to rectify such security breaches.

Operating these complicated systems was a new generation of computer-savvy sailors. It was in the high-technology end of his business that Kram felt his age. Men like his current radio officer were incredibly competent technicians. Young and bright, they were the faces of the new Navy, a fighting force designed around microchips and high-tensile steel.

"What have you got for me, Lieutenant Ritter?"

Lieutenant Michael Ritter had been reading a complex message on his monitor screen, and Kram's question caused him to flinch nervously. "I'm sorry, sir. You caught me deep in cryptospace. In fact, I was just completing the decoding sequence of the VLF TACAMO transmission responsible for the exercise's abrupt cancellation."

Kram peered over his subordinate's shoulder, and found himself unable to decipher the computerese visible on Ritter's monitor screen. "I would have hated to see that message before you decoded it," he sarcastically quipped. "What's it say?"

"It looks to me like an EAM, sir."

"The receipt of an Emergency Action Message would certainly override an exercise," reflected Kram, still trying his best to make sense out of the screen's scrambled contents. "Why don't you contact them on Gertrude and get a verification? I'll be in Sonar, and you can reach me there when you get an answer."

Ritter was already reaching for the underwater telephone as Kram exited the radio room. Directly across the narrow passageway was a closed hatch, with the words SOUND SHACK printed above it. The state-of-the-art sonar equipment inside provided their ears to the underwater realm in which they sailed, and Kram heard for himself the sounds of the sea beyond, the moment he entered the cramped, dimly lit compartment.

The familiar cries of a pod of whales emanated from the overhead speakers. It was a mournful, ethereal symphony, made up of long-drawn-out bellows, and gentle, catlike mewings, interspersed with rumbling bass trills. Kram identified the faint, high-pitched wavering sound in the background as belonging to a large freighter that had passed almost directly over them earlier, and which the sonar watch team had designated Sierra Eleven.

This team was comprised of three individuals who were huddled over their consoles, totally unaware of their newly arrived visitor. Kram smiled upon noting that the current sonar watch supervisor, or "Sup," as he was known to his men, was Petty Officer First Class Brad Bodzin. Bodzin was the *Polk*'s senior enlisted sonarman. A grizzled veteran at the age of twenty-eight, the Houston, Texas, native was known for his rather remarkable intuitive abilities and easy-going, hands-on management style. He was presently standing behind his seated associates, and Kram listened as he shared his unique expertise.

"Because humpbacks sing in long, repetitive phrases, it's possible to time our sprint-and-drift sequences to coincide with the portion of whale song that's most conducive to masking our signature."

"I certainly never learned that one at the Naval War College," remarked Kram, who stepped forward and greeted Bodzin with a fond pat on the shoulder.

Bodzin's face blushed with embarrassment. "I never meant to infer that such a tactic was part of our official operational doctrine, Captain. But you've got to admit that taking advantage of the natural sounds of the sea makes good sense."

Kram replied while scanning the waterfall displays of the BQ-7 conformal array and the BQ-21 broadband unit. "I do believe I once read a Norwegian Navy white paper that promoted the use of naturally existing marine biologics for submarine operations in the littorals, and in theory, it's not that crazy an idea."

"Especially with the increase of the world's marine mammal stocks," added Bodzin, excited to have his CO's feedback. "The end of unrestricted whaling has led to an amazing turnaround of whale populations. We're monitoring them in ever-increasing numbers, with the Navy even using SOSUS to prove this point."

One of the humpbacks projected a deep, sonorous bellow, and Kram watched the signature of this cry display itself on the BQ-21 as a thick white line. "It's almost ironic," he said with a grunt. "But as the whale population increases, the number of blue-water, nuclear submarines has gone in the opposite direction."

"Quantity isn't everything, sir," Bodzin reminded him. "The number of nuclear-powered submarines might be down, but you've got to admit that those new boats are awesome. Seawolf is one mean, quiet dude. And even with all their military cutbacks, the Russians are still managing to put to sea an entire new generation of sophisticated attack subs."

"Sup, I've got Sierra One again!" interjected S1C James "Jaffers" Echoles, the broad-shouldered black man responsible for monitoring the series of low-frequency, passive hydrophones mounted around the *Polk*'s bow. "Bearing zero-four-zero, with a relative rough range of twelve thousand yards."

Both Kram and Bodzin noted a slight flutter on the

BQ-7's waterfall display. The sound line continued to develop, and Bodzin reached up into the overhead air duct and removed a can of Dr Pepper and a Mars bar.

"Jaffers, my man, you win again," said Bodzin while handing over the cherished prize, accepting a high five, and returning his glance to the green-tinted display screen. "We must have been in their baffles the whole time," he added wondrously. "That boomer is one quiet big lady."

Kram accepted a call on the intercom, and he wasted little time sharing its contents. "Mr. Bodzin, it's time for the *Polk* to go back into the Anti-Submarine Warfare business. Radio just got the word that the *Rhode Island* has received an EAM, which means we go from a special ops platform to keeping any unwelcome strangers off their tail."

"Does this mean that today's transfer of the SEALs by mini-sub is scrubbed, sir?" asked Bodzin.

"That depends on the EAM," answered Kram while turning to exit. "If it's canceled, Captain Lockwood wants to reschedule the transfer for later this afternoon. Now I'd better inform Commander Gilbert."

Kram left Sonar and continued aft, to the control room. He found the Chief of the Boat standing behind the ship control station. Chief Roth, his usual unlit cigar clenched between his teeth, was seated in front of COB. At his sides were the planesman and the helmsman, their hands tightly gripping aircraft-style steering yokes.

A single, practiced glance at the variety of readouts and gauges mounted into the bulkhead before them showed Kram that they were currently traveling on a northerly heading, at a depth of five-hundred and seventy feet and a speed of sixteen knots. He didn't have to go over to the nearby navigation station to know that they were due east of Florida, and approximately twelve hours away from the *Rhode Island*'s home port of King's Bay, Georgia.

"COB, I believe we now know why the transfer exercise was canceled," announced Kram.

"Don't tell me, Captain," retorted COB, a boyish grin on his heavily furrowed face. "I bet Captain Lockwood finally realized he was gonna be stuck with our SEALs for an entire twelve hours."

Kram snickered. "If I know Lockwood, that probably crossed his mind. But the only thing that got him off the hook this time was the receipt of an EAM."

This revelation caught the attention of Chief Roth, who looked up and matter-of-factly voiced himself without taking the cigar out of his mouth. "Is it another exercise, sir?"

"I sure hope it is," said Kram. "The most I could get out of Radio was that the *Rhode Island* was notified of an alert change to DEFCON Four."

"The Russian President must have gotten another cold," quipped COB. "Or maybe the Chinese have gone and hijacked another ocean liner."

This comment caused Roth to playfully grimace, and Kram snapped back, "I'm sure the alert is only routine, and chances are it will be rescinded shortly, with Lockwood wanting to attempt another transfer later this afternoon. I was on my way to share the news with Commander Gilbert. I gather he's still down in the rec room."

"Last I heard, he'd called for a full debrief. Shall we go see?" offered COB.

Kram beckoned aft, past the drawn curtains of the periscope pedestal and the vacant fire control console. With COB leading the way, they left the control room and passed through an elongated, narrow compartment with two long consoles lining each bulkhead. Here the members of their SEAL team would coordinate the activation of the dry-deck shelter and the launching of the new Mark VII mini-sub.

A sharp left took them beyond the space where the Ships Inertial Navigation System was stowed. A hatchway set into the after bulkhead conveyed them into the cavernous space, formerly reserved for the *Polk*'s missile magazine. Though the tubes were still here—sixteen in all, positioned in two parallel rows of eight—the missiles themselves had long since been removed. Today they were used to stow the voluminous amount of equipment needed by the SEALs, with tube six providing access to the dry-deck shelter and the mini-sub.

A lattice-steel catwalk encircled the magazine. It was often used as a jogging track, with sixteen and a half laps equaling a mile. Kram therefore wasn't surprised to see one of his men jog around the aft end of the magazine and head down the catwalk toward them. He was attired in a bright blue T-shirt and matching shorts, and it was COB who identified him.

"Either I'm seein' things, or that's Chief Mallott!"

CPO Howard Mallott was the *Polk*'s head cook. His exclusive domain was Jimmy's Buffet—the name of the ship's galley—where Mallott ran his department like a virtual fiefdom. Not the most physical of specimens, Mallott had a bulging waistline, gold-wire-rimmed glasses, and a spiky crew cut that were familiar to all. Yet this was the first time that either Kram or COB had seen the personable cook with a sheen of exercise-induced sweat on his forehead.

"Hello, Captain! Afternoon, COB!" Mallott grunted between heaving breaths, a good twenty yards separating them.

Kram couldn't miss noting his leaden stride, and he flashed the portly cook a supportive thumbs-up.

"Gotta keep fit, sir," Mallott added, with ten yards still between them.

"Don't go droppin' from a cardiac on us, Mallott," teased COB.

"I might be a few pounds overweight," Mallott retorted, his labored breaths clearly audible. "But my good cholesterol far outnumbers the bad."

"Love the new bison burgers, Chief," commented COB, trying his best to keep a straight face. "It's a refreshing change from all that turkey."

Mallot's pace seemed to quicken, and as he prepared to pass them, he made certain to meet Kram's admiring glance. "I'm serving bison chili at midrats, sir. I'll make certain to save you a bowl."

"Thank you, Chief," said Kram, who watched Mallott strike COB's open palm with his right hand before continuing his labored run around the catwalk.

Kram led the way down a nearby stairwell to Three Deck, where a short passageway conveyed them into the relatively large compartment usually reserved for the crew's activity space. This afternoon it was being used as the special operations briefing room.

There were a good number of officers and enlisted men gathered here, with a mix of *Polk* crew members and SEALs. As usual, the SEALs occupied the right side of the room, where they had their laptops set up on three tables, one behind the other.

Commander Doug Gilbert, the wiry, silver-haired CO of SEAL Delivery Vehicle Team Two, stood at the front of the room, facing a cross-section diagram of the new Mark VII mini-sub. It was apparent that he hadn't seen the two newcomers in their midst, and Kram didn't dare interrupt him.

"So you see, ladies," continued Gilbert while highlighting the circular transfer skirt on the bottom of the diagram with a pointer, "the ability to transfer both personnel and equipment from sub to sub gives us an entirely new mission. And if the unlikely day should ever come when treaty obligations indeed require that submarines such as the *Rhode Island* go to sea without their missile warheads, we can provide the all-important backup delivery service. 'Cause as I told you before, ladies, this SEAL trusts no one!"

"The day the politicians order us to remove those warheads from our missiles and bombs is the day I start digging a fucking fallout shelter!" proclaimed the SEAL XO from the front table. "It's our nukes that have kept us free for the last five decades!"

His associates voiced their support with a spirited round of applause, shouts, and whistles. Gilbert turned around to face them, and only then noted Kram's presence in the back of the room.

"Pipe down, ladies!" Gilbert ordered. "Captain's here, and we certainly don't want him to think we're holding a damn political rally."

"I've got to admit that you'd get my vote," said Kram, who had to wait for another raucous chorus of applause to die down before adding, "I thought you'd like to know that it was the *Rhode Island*'s receipt of an Emergency Action Message that led to the cancellation of our exercise. Captain Lockwood hopes to reschedule the transfer, which could take place as soon as later this afternoon."

"An Emergency Action Message," repeated the SEAL team XO. "To hell with that Global Zero Alert Treaty. Maybe we're at war!"

"Commander Gilbert, sir," the team's meteorologist dared to interject. "If we can't complete the exercise today, does that mean we won't be home as planned for July Fourth?"

"Well, excuse me, Chief Murray," returned the senior SEAL with an inflection that would have made Jackie Gleason proud. "Did you hear that, ladies? Mr. Sunshine is worried about missing fireworks with his old lady. Hell's bells, Chief. If you wanted holidays with the family, you should have joined the fucking Air Force!"

Vince estimated that they had been traveling for a good hour since their initial capture. They had been immediately blind-folded, hog-tied around the waist, and led on foot like a dog on a leash through the thick forest. After they'd been ordered not to talk, the mysterious trio who had captured them be-came eerily quiet too. All Vince could hear from that group was an occasional grunt or swear word, the heavy sound of breathing, and the thud of footsteps, rustling leaves, and snapping twigs underfoot.

The route they were following led away from the river. There didn't appear to be a developed path, and shortly after the roar of the rapids faded, they began their way up a steep incline.

Vince tried his best to remain orientated, and he initiated a rough pace count, presuming they were headed in a northerly direction. The heat and humidity were intense. His clothes were soaked in sweat, his mouth bone-dry. Because of the tight blindfold, he was the victim of numerous painful encounters with projecting limbs. Thorns tore into his sun-burned skin, and several times he was forced to a halt after colliding with a sapling, boulder, or root clump. No sooner did he regain his footing than he'd feel a rough jerk on the rope that was tied around his waist. This rope was also connected to Andrew Chapman, who followed several feet behind.

At first Vince toyed with the idea of directly challenging the trio and asking for mercy. Yet he was unable to forget their forceful order for silence, and he decided instead to hold his tongue for the moment. One good thing was that they hadn't immediately executed them. He supposed they were in league with the personnel aboard the black Huey, and that both Vince and the Vice President were going to be held hostage. In such situations, discretion was most often the best policy, and Vince could only hope that they'd eventually get a chance to plead their case with the ringleader of this mysterious group.

With this hope in mind, Vince tried his best to remain as calm as possible. He would need a level head to talk their way out of this fix, and he attempted to soothe his anxieties by focusing on the soothing sounds and scents of the encircling forest. He could hear the warm wind blowing through the thick, leaf-filled boughs above, and the creaking of swaying limbs. The hum of cicadas was ever-present and all-powerful, with buzzing insects and singing birds adding their voices to this pastoral symphony.

The clean, moist scent of the woods was the fragrance of life itself. It was in vast contrast to the sour odor exuding from the men who had captured them. They could use a good wash, stinking as they did of sweat, tobacco, and red meat. Back in Vietnam, Vince had learned that such a distinctive smell would often give away an American soldier long before he was seen or heard. That was one of the primary reasons the Green Berets had adopted a native diet whenever possible.

Knowing full well that he'd have to tap many of the lessons learned in combat in order to persevere in this situation, Vince was forced to a sudden halt by a tug on the rope behind him, accompanied by the loud rustling of underbrush and a frustrated curse from the lips of Andrew Chapman.

"For God's sake, I'm caught up in a damned thorn bush! Will somebody help me?" pleaded the VP.

"Shut your trap, Bubba, and quit whining!" ordered one of the hostage takers from the back of the line. "If you'd just hold still a sec, I'll cut you loose."

Vince fought the urge to share an encouraging word with the VP, and he listened to the distinctive click of a folding knife being snapped open, followed by the sounds of limbs being sawed. Fifteen anxious seconds later, a rough pull on the rope around his waist signaled Vince that it was time to continue moving forward once again.

It took fifty-seven more painful paces to complete their climb. This put them on a relatively flat ridge, which they followed to the east for another sixty paces before heading down into a steep ravine.

A barking dog greeted them as they reached the bottom of the hollow. The heavy scent of smoke was in the air, and Vince knew they were approaching a campsite of some sort upon hearing a barely audible, static-filled version of Rush Limbaugh's radio show.

An earthen path conveyed them up a short rise and into the wide mouth of a cave. The air temperature noticeably dropped, and Vince dared to shorten his stride and bend over, ever fearful of striking his head on a projecting obstacle.

As he heard the hollow sound of dripping water nearby, the overpowering stench of putrid, rotting flesh enveloped him. The air temperature further plunged, and Vince had the distinct impression that they had just stepped into a subterranean meat locker of some sort.

"Sit, wait, and keep your big traps shut!" directed one of their escorts.

They did as ordered, seating themselves on a cool, moist shelf of rock, that one of their captors led them to. Vince began shivering, and he fought back the urge to wretch, so powerful was the scent of death that continued to fill the air here.

A good ten minutes passed before the echoes of a barking dog signaled the arrival of a newcomer. This individual announced his presence with a loud, commanding voice, which was initially directed at his snarling canine companion.

"Satan, shut the fuck up!"

"Look what we pulled outta the river, Pa," said one of the hostage takers with obvious pride.

"I can't see much of anything, Junior, with those damn blindfolds covering their faces. Remove the dang things."

There was a blinding cone of white light as Vince's blindfold was yanked off, and he found himself staring into the beam of a powerful flashlight. He could see only the outlines of a group of men standing before him and the VP, though he was able to confirm that they were indeed deep in a cave. Stalactites hung from the jagged roof, and Vince soon tracked down the source of the putrid stench—a pair of partially butchered deer carcasses hanging from a nearby crossbeam.

Out of the corner of his eye Vince could see Andrew Chapman, perched on the ledge behind him. Except for a nasty cut on his cheek, the VP appeared to be in one piece, and Vince expressed his relief with a long sigh.

"Junior, you son of a bitch!" shouted the booming voice of the newcomer, who was more astonished than angry. "Do you realize who that is?"

"Ain't it two Feds, Pa?"

"That's just not any Fed, boy. That's fucking Andrew Chapman, the Vice President."

Vince squinted in a vain effort to see beyond the blinding light, and he noted that the beam had begun shaking wildly.

"C.J., I told you there was somethin' special about these two!"

"That you did, Junior," replied a hoarse, high-pitched voice.

"Well, Amos," said another voice, this one deep and resonant, "you always did say that if you ever met this goddamn tree hugger face-to-face, you'd put a bullet through his head."

The crisp, metallic sound of a rifle bolt chambering a round was heard, followed once more by the individual with the deep, resonant voice. "Here's my thirty-thirty, old man. Fire away!"

They had been in the air a little less than thirty minutes when Thomas noted a sudden change in pitch of the Chinook's twin 2,850hp engines. The throaty roar deepened, and he anxiously peered outside the helicopter's forward hatchway. Since leaving Fort Leonard Wood behind, they had been flying over a seemingly solid expanse of rolling, tree-filled hills. This forest was still visible outside, and as the Chinook began to lose altitude, Thomas spotted a portion of a two-lane roadway down below, and the first of several single-story structures belonging to the small Ozark town of Winona.

Thomas looked to his right, and flashed Ted Callahan a thumbs-up. Both of them were now dressed in BDUs, and except for a lack of unit insignias, they were attired identically to the eighteen soldiers who sat alongside them on the nylon-webbed bench.

Rucksacks, rifles, and other equipment were stored further aft, near the Chinook's rear ramp. The giant twinrotored helicopter could easily handle twice their number, and Thomas knew they were fortunate that this Wisconsin National Guard platform had been in the middle of summer exercises at Leonard Wood when their alert came down.

He felt his body pulled forward and to the right as the Chinook began a steeply banked turn. A fenced-in compound could be seen below, with an American flag flying alongside the largest structure, a one-story wooden building with a gabled forest-green roof.

"I sure hope there's enough room down there for this big lady," shouted Ted Callahan, who had to practically scream to be heard over the clattering engines.

They descended rapidly but touched down with barely a jolt on an open portion of driveway in the compound's rear. With rotors grinding away unabated, the rear ramp was lowered, and Thomas followed Ted Callahan, Captain Jay Christian, and Sergeant Sam Reed outside onto the asphalt parking lot.

A group of Forest Service personnel waved them over to the nearest structure. Here they were greeted by a pert brunette, decked out in a light green U.S. Forest Service blouse and brown slacks.

"Hi, I'm Jody Glickman, the district naturalist, and I'll be your guide down the Eleven Point. How many are in your party?"

"There are twenty of us," replied Ted Callahan, who went on to introduce his associates.

"I'm afraid I was only able to get five jet boats down to the Greer access site," she added. "I don't suppose we'd be able to squeeze a couple more inside your helicopter."

"Ranger Glickman," said Sam Reed, "we could probably fit a full dozen of 'em inside that monster and still have room to stretch our legs."

"Then we'll pull a couple of boats off our lot and take them with us," she offered. "Per General Atwater, the river downstream from Greer remains closed to the public. And by the way, we still haven't heard from the members of our team who were sent along to accompany the Vice President's party."

"Any luck getting your communications back, Ranger?" asked Jay Christian.

Glickman somberly shook her head. "The entire grid's still down, and from the reports that are starting to come in, it looks like someone went and intentionally destroyed our network of repeater towers."

Thomas looked at Ted Callahan. With this shocking revelation, their Search and Rescue mission suddenly took on an additional sense of urgency.

"Stable. Ready. Contact!"

Brittany anxiously listened to Lucky relay this all-important status update from the cockpit's jump seat. She couldn't believe how calmly it was delivered, considering there was a Boeing KC-135R aircraft directly in front of them, speeds matched perfectly at nearly 450 mph, its underside so close that she could actually see the face of the tanker's wing boom operator staring down at them. This individual was responsible for "flying" the refueling boom, which extended from the tanker's aft belly, and whose tip just penetrated Nightwatch through the slipway doors, located directly above the cockpit.

"We've got fuel flow," observed Jake Lasky.

"Commander Cooper," said Coach, while tightly gripping the yoke and trying his best to keep them flying in tandem with the tanker. "See that series of three lights on the 135's belly? The blue one means ready, green indicates contact, and the orange light behind it will illuminate the moment we have a disconnect."

"What's the purpose of those red and blue lights farther up on the fuselage?" she asked.

"The row on the left is for elevation, and the one on the right is for telescoping," Coach explained. "They're used during the initial approach, with red telling me where to position my nose, and blue directing our fore and aft movement."

"It looks incredibly difficult," she commented. "How do you keep from colliding?"

Coach made a lightning-quick adjustment to the yoke before answering. "It's a game of patience, honed by hundreds of hours of practice. The secret to the approach is all in the glide path and a steady tanker platform. Then, once contact has been made, you learn how to gauge the amount of sky showing between the trailing edges of the tanker's wings, and to force one's eyes back and forth between engines to keep them lined up properly, using the tanker as your Altitude Direction Indicator, or ADI."

Though Brittany had experienced other aerial refuelings, never before had she had such an incredible vantage point. The mere thought of these two immense aircraft a mere stone's throw away from each other, mated in this manner to download thousands of gallons of volatile JP-8 fuel, was mind-boggling. Of course, she couldn't fail to note the tenser-than-normal atmosphere that prevailed inside the cockpit during this entire sequence. This was dangerous, complicated work, requiring every ounce of skill that both aircrews could muster.

"Commander Cooper, I have that chart of our tentative flight plan," said the navigator from his station behind her.

Brittany swiveled around and glanced at the chart, while the navigator highlighted the way points. "As you can see, our refueling is taking place here, twenty-three thousand feet above the northern Adriatic. We'll continue on a westerly heading, crossing over Italy, the Swiss Alps, central France, and then begin our great circle route over the Atlantic to Andrews."

"We've got us a flasher!" cried Lucky.

Brittany hurriedly turned around to see what the copilot was referring to, and her glance was immediately drawn to the underside of the tanker, and the window where the boom operator was positioned. His illuminated face had been replaced by a sign, drawn in Day-Glow paint. It read: PLZ CALL WIFE! 810-558-8214. 927 ARW WILL BE HOME ON 4TH!

"They don't call us the flying telephone booth for nothing," Lucky reflected.

"I doubt if Admiral Warner would appreciate any personal calls, especially with all that's been coming down these last couple of hours," said Brittany.

"Speaking of the devil," said Coach, after making the barest of adjustments to the throttle with his gloved right hand. "Scuttlebutt has it that the good Chairman traded a few choice words with the CG aboard TACAMO."

Brittany shook her head. "The gossip on this plane is worse than on a ship."

"Then it's true?" Coach persisted.

She chose the words of her response with the utmost care. "From what I heard, it seems Admiral Warner and his counterpart on TACAMO had a little procedural disagreement. It supposedly involves a certain EAM that TACAMO transmitted during their run with the football."

Before anyone could respond to this news, the cockpit vibrated and there was a sudden rolling motion.

"Nightwatch six-seven-six, breakaway! Breakaway!" the firm voice of the tanker's boom operator screamed over the intercom.

With this warning, the floor seemed to drop out beneath them as the giant Boeing 747 plunged like a rock to the bottom of the air-refueling altitude block. Brittany found herself grabbing onto the edges of her jump seat while experiencing the first hint of airsickness.

"That's flying for you," Coach managed to remark, the steering yoke firm in his grasp. "Hours of boredom, interrupted by moments of sheer terror!"

After the longest ten seconds of his life passed and a rifle was yet to be fired, Vince knew that now was the time for him to intercede. "In the name of God, please don't do anything that you'll be sorry for later on!" he pleaded.

"Mister, I'd rather you kept the Lord outta this," replied the man who had answered to the name of Amos.

"Amos, you're nothin' but a pussy," remarked the deep, resonant voice of his associate. "Give me my thirty-thirty back, and I'll do it for ya."

The dog began barking once more, prompting Amos to yell, "Damn it, Satan, shut up!"

"At the very least, will you tell us what it is that you're so angry about?" asked the Vice President. "What possibly motivated you to attack my party like you did? You slaughtered many a brave individual this afternoon."

"What the hell are you talkin' about?" Amos retorted. "It would take me the rest of the day to list all the reasons why I always dreamed of killing you. But who said anything about me goin' and attackin' your party this afternoon?"

Again Satan let loose a series of excited yelps, this time inspired by the approach of yet another person.

"Pa!" greeted a female with great enthusiasm. "You'll never believe what all that shootin' was about. It was the black helicopter again, and it tore into a bunch of float trippers down near Mary Deckard with a vengeance."

Vince spoke up, frustrated that he still couldn't see the faces of the people who held them captive. "That was our float trip that was attacked! And you mean to say you didn't have anything to do with it?"

"Why in the hell would we be in cahoots with the United Nations scum inside that infernal black chopper?" Amos replied sincerely. "That's the trouble with you Feds. Always jumpin' to conclusions, without takin' the time to get your facts straight."

United Nations troops inside America and mysterious black helicopters—Vince was no stranger to the conspiracy freaks who actually believed there was a clandestine plot to take control of the U.S. government by imagined One World interests, and he probed most carefully. "Look, I happened to see that chopper right before it went down. If you're really telling the truth, what do you say if I was to lead you to the crash site? Then all of us could find out the true identities of the ones responsible for this act of cold-blooded murder. And if it turns out to be a United Nations operation, you've got my word I'll be right there to serve the warrant that will close their doors forever."

Friday, July 2, 2358 Zulu

U.S.S. James K. Polk

The first hint that something extraordinary was occurring outside the hull was a slight flutter on the BQ-7's waterfall display. Jaffers immediately pointed it out to Brad Bodzin, who hesitated only long enough to confirm that it wasn't an anomaly, before grabbing the overhead handset to warn the control room.

"Conn, Sonar. We have a submerged contact, bearing zero-four-three. Designate Sierra Twelve, possible hostile submarine!"

As Control acknowledged this warning, Bodzin readjusted the fit of his headphones, and hurriedly addressed the auxiliary keyboard to isolate the narrowband processor. He filtered out the static as best he could, and had to increase the volume tenfold to hear a barely audible throbbing sound that caused his pulse to suddenly quicken.

"It appears to be headed on a direct collision course with the *Rhode Island!*" he shouted.

The unexpected, earsplitting ping of an active sonar pulse

filled his headphones, and Bodzin reached forward to turn down the volume, all the while cursing in pain. "Who the fuck lashed us?"

"I believe that was Sierra One's collision-avoidance sonar, Sup," offered Jaffers, also a victim of the excruciating lashing.

This observation was confirmed when an extended series of sonorous pings sounded from the direction of the *Rhode Island*. Bodzin dared to turn up the volume again, and he breathlessly listened as the active scan continuously quickened to such a degree that the hollow succession of individual pings sounded like a single entity.

"Damn it, they're gonna hit!" Bodzin exclaimed.

The raw, grinding sound of metal on metal filled the seas, and Bodzin yanked back his headphones and addressed the intercom. "Conn, Sonar. Sierra One has collided with Sierra Twelve! Initiating damage control, signature analysis."

Brittany was in the galley, drinking a club soda to ease her queasy stomach, when she first learned that an American Trident submarine had been the victim of an underwater collision with a yet-unknown vessel, somewhere off the coast of Florida. It was only after rushing back into the Operations Team Area that she learned this Trident was the U.S.S. *Rhode Island*.

The *Rhode Island* was their Atlantic basin alert platform, armed with a lethal load of twenty-four Trident II D-5 missiles, each capable of carrying up to seven 300-kiloton Maneuverable Reentry Vehicle warheads. Because of the *Rhode Island*'s forward patrol area, it had been the same submarine that Iron Man One had passed an EAM to earlier, and the loss of this capable platform could drastically affect America's strategic posture.

Brittany arrived in Operations just as the Chairman stormed in from the aft end of the 747, with Colonel Pritchard and Major Hewlett on his heels. Warner appeared to be furious, and he vented his anger and frustration beside Red's workstation.

"This whole fucking situation is getting totally out of control. Colonel, I need you to keep that line open with COMSUBLANT. I want to know the second that we get a SITREP on the *Rhode Island*. And where the hell's General Spencer?"

Red looked up from her console and efficiently answered, "Admiral Warner, I've got the General for you on line seven."

As the Chairman strode over to the adjoining console and grabbed the red handset, Brittany met Red's glance. They traded conspiratorial winks, while listening to Warner refocus his rage on Iron Man One's CG.

"Absolutely not, Lowell! Until all the facts are in, I feel a move to DEFCON Three is totally unwarranted . . . Lowell, I'm well aware that she's our Atlantic basin alert platform. But until we hear otherwise, we've got to presume that the *Rhode Island*'s still operational . . . I'll keep that in mind, General . . . Very well. Out."

The Chairman hung up the handset, and forcefully addressed his SIOP advisor. "Major Hewlett, be informed that General Spencer recommends an immediate alert change to DEFCON Three. He's substantiating this with the assumption that the *Rhode Island* was intentionally struck by a Russian attack sub. Since we still don't know this fact for certain, I can't in all good conscience agree to this provocative move, which could very well incite the very war we're trying so hard to avoid."

"And if we indeed learn that the Russians are responsible for this collision, sir?" asked the Marine, well aware that the entire Operations team was riveted on their conversation.

Warner paused in thought, and without bothering to issue a reply, he spoke instead to Red. "Sergeant, it's time to take the bull by the horns. Get me a secure line with the Russian Defense Ministry in the Kremlin. If anyone can get to the bottom of this mess, it's General Alexi Zhukov."

"If I was a betting man," said First Sergeant Sam Reed while kneeling down beside the assortment of footprints imprinted in the sandbar, "I'd say that they definitely stopped here for a fishing break. These tracks are still fresh. I doubt if they're more than four hours old."

"Since we're at the southern end of the trophy trout management area, such a stop wouldn't be out of the question," said Jody Glickman.

Both Thomas Kellogg and Ted Callahan stood at the ranger's side, and together they watched the efforts of the rest of their team. The seven johnboats that had brought them down from the Greer access site were pulled up on the sand, with the Sappers exploring the woods on this side of the river and the MPs roaming the opposite bank.

"And here I always thought that Washington's humidity was bad," said Callahan, after wiping his soaked forehead with the back of his hand. "If they're out in that forest, I sure hope they've got plenty of shade and water."

"My brother spent a couple of unforgettable years in Vietnam's Rung Sat Special Zone," revealed Thomas. "Vince was able to survive that tropical hell, making the Ozarks a walk in the park."

"Commander One, this is Commander Two. Over," broke in Captain Jay Christian's amplified voice over Callahan's two-way.

"Commander Two, this is Commander One. Over," Callahan replied into his radio's transmitter.

"Commander One," said Christian in a whisper. "We've stumbled upon a path that I believe you'll be interested in seeing. It's loaded with fresh prints, which are headed due north into the deep woods. They could very well belong to some of our people. Over."

A bare mile farther downstream, where the sound of the outside world was masked by the constant, thunderous roar of Mary Deckard shoals, Vince Kellogg broke from the underbrush, getting his first view of the river since his capture. They were upstream at the head of the shoals, and he barely noticed it when Miriam Stoddard and her brother, Junior, joined him on the scrub-filled clearing. Now that his blindfold had been removed, Vince was at long last able to see his hostage takers, and subsequently size them up.

With Andrew Chapman still held hostage back in the cave, Vince found himself with an opportunity to win their freedom. He would do so most carefully, initiating this process by first earning the trust of the two individuals who accompanied him.

Of the pair, Junior appeared to be the most unstable. He was a skinny, shaggy-haired, hotheaded teenager, with a penchant for tattered coveralls and chewing tobacco. Vince doubted that he had any formal schooling, and it was evident that he was the victim of an overbearing father. Because of this, there was always the possibility that Junior would express his independence by taking his aggressions out on Vince. He would have to be watched carefully.

On the other hand, his sister, Miriam, was in almost every way his opposite. Vince liked her straight off. Also in her teens, she reminded him of a redheaded version of the country singer Leanne Rimes. Her denim cutoffs and sleeveless flannel shirt were worn yet clean, and Vince couldn't believe she was able to get around on this rough terrain without shoes. Unlike her brother, she wasn't afraid to look Vince straight in the eye, and he sensed that she could be a potential ally, for she exuded a refreshing natural innocence, in vast contrast to her brother's inherent mistrust.

"Is that one of your canoes caught in the snag by the first of the big boulders?" asked Miriam while pointing downstream.

Vince looked toward the Z-shaped chute, and somberly nodded upon spotting the overturned U.S. Forest Service canoe. Yet more debris littered the shore, and he identified several torn seat cushions, the lid of a Styrofoam cooler, and a partially submerged first-aid kit.

"Bubba," said Junior, making it a point to aim the barrel of his 12-gauge at Vince, "I thought you said we'd find the black helicopter down here."

Vince continued staring downstream to orient himself. He spotted the high bluff where the CAT team's Blackhawk had gone down, and pointed toward the opposite bank, at the far end of the shoals.

"The last time I saw it, the helicopter was headed toward that clearing at the bend of the river. I was about to go over the falls at the time, and it flew right over me, with thick smoke pouring from the cabin."

"What do ya think, Miriam?" asked Junior. "Should we cross here or down by the falls?"

Miriam answered her brother by stepping off the bank and beginning her way directly across the river. Vince looked at Junior before following, and the teenager directed Vince onward with the barrel of his shotgun.

The water was icy cold, the current swift and the slippery footing treacherous. Vince tried his best to follow Miriam's exact route, and at the center of the channel the water covered his knees, hitting him mid-thigh at the deepest point. His lower extremities were numb by the time he climbed up onto the opposite bank, where Miriam was waiting with a wide grin on her face.

"Who needs fancy air-conditioning when you've got the Eleven Point to cool you off?" she said with a pleasant smile.

Before Vince could reply, her brother climbed onto the bank. Junior didn't look happy to have been subjected to the frigid soaking, and he roughly prodded his prisoner forward with the barrel of his shotgun.

They continued downstream, following the narrowest of earthen tracks. The chute passed to their left, the deafening roar of its cascading waters overwhelming all other sounds. Vince easily located the boulder where the VP's canoe had gotten itself stuck, and his curiosity turned to horror upon spotting the bloated body of one of his agents caught in the same rocky snag. A smashed Forest Service johnboat lay floating on the other side of the snag, along with an assortment of fishing gear and torn clothing.

Vince found himself mentally re-creating the terrifying moment when he had first spotted the black Huey. This imagined drama became chillingly real once again as they passed the crucified corpse of Andy Whitworth, and spotted the floating body of yet another agent. And just when Vince thought he could leave both the chute and the nightmare behind, there was the partially submerged, torn hulk of Marine Two, awash in the center of the channel like a lifeless Leviathan.

More tragedy awaited around the next bend, where an overturned johnboat had snagged itself on the shoreline. The bullet-ridden body of Special Agent Linda Desiante lay nearby on the sandy shoreline, and Vince redirected his grief upon setting eyes on the briefcase-sized metallic container that sat on dry sand just out of Desiante's outstretched reach. It was their SATCOM unit—the device that could provide them contact with the outside world—and amazingly enough, it appeared to be intact!

The raised clenched fist of their point man caused Thomas to halt in mid-step. They had been following the narrow, earthen track where the footprints had been discovered for the better part of a kilometer. The throaty roar of the river had long since faded, to be replaced by the rustling sounds of the wind coursing through the oak limbs and the hypnotic grinding cries of the cicadas.

From his position in the middle of the file formation, Thomas watched Captain Christian cautiously approach the point man. The senior MP's stare appeared to be focused on the ground below, and both soldiers were soon in a crouch position, examining something on the path itself. Thomas supposed that they had discovered yet more footprints, and he was genuinely surprised when Christian signaled him forward, all the while pointing out the barely visible, fine nylon trip wire that was stretched across the trail at ankle level.

Together they traced the nylon wire as it disappeared into the underbrush at the far side of the trail, and it was Thomas who identified the device to which it was tied. The green cardboard cylinder was an artillery projectile ground-burst simulator, approximately seven inches long and one and three-quarters inches in diameter. Activated by a pull-friction fuse lighter, the device would emit a piercing whistle before detonating with a loud burst.

Unlike a Claymore, it was not an offensive weapon, and it was almost certainly placed here to warn of the approach of unwanted trespassers. Christian nevertheless asked and received permission from Ted Callahan for his troops to load live rounds into their weapons, and it was in such a manner that they continued up the trail, ever vigilant for booby traps of a more lethal nature.

"As long as you're willing to haul it, I don't see any harm in taking it along. It's your back that's gonna suffer," said Junior after opening the SATCOM's carrying case and inspecting the contents.

Vince resealed the case and picked up the thirty-five-pound unit by its padded handle. The alien weight pulled on his arm and shoulder, yet he carried this new burden without complaint, grateful to have the device in his possession.

"Now I thought you said that we'd find the helicopter in this clearing," Junior muttered, his impatience most obvious. "You'd better not be yankin' my chain, Bubba."

Vince could clearly hear the roar of the waterfall that had almost swept both him and the Vice President to their deaths, and he tried his best to re-create the black helicopter's last-known flight path. He seriously doubted that the badly damaged aircraft could have cleared the limestone bluff on the far side of the bank on which they stood, and it was toward this feature that Vince pointed.

"Well, for your sake, you'd better hope that's where we'll find it," said Junior, who then poked Vince forward with the barrel of his shotgun.

Miriam took off for the bluff in a sprint, and as soon as she disappeared over a low ledge of rock, Junior shoved the gun barrel into Vince's back once more. Vince fought the urge to turn and wrest the gun out of Junior's grasp. He supposed it wouldn't be that hard to push aside the barrel, and as he sized up the risks involved, Miriam's voice redirected his thoughts.

"Junior, over here!"

They found her standing on a limestone clearing at the base of the bluff, with the twisted, burned-out fuselage of a helicopter lying at her feet. Black, oily smoke continued to pour from the cabin, and as Vince stepped over one of the fractured rotor blades, he had no doubt whatsoever that this was the Huey that had attacked them.

"Do you believe it, little sister?" said Junior while examining the wreckage. "We finally got one of the black bastards!"

Miriam pointed into the fire-scarred cabin. "There's a body in there!"

Vince spotted the charred remains and somberly noted, "I'm afraid no one lived through that crash."

Almost to underscore this observation, a low-groaning moan sounded behind them. Vince turned to trace its source, and spotted a booted foot extending from a nearby thorn bush. He carefully pushed aside the brambles, revealing a bearded bear of a man sprawled out on his back and dressed in a torn green flight suit. His breaths were quick and shallow, and when his eyes momentarily fluttered open, Vince gasped in astonishment. Lying before him was a man he hadn't seen in over three decades!

The last time he had seen Chief Warrant Officer Lewis Marvin, the big-boned Green Beret was headed on a secret mission deep into the heart of Cambodia. Marvin and his Studies and Observation Group fire team never returned, and had been officially listed as missing in action. Vince couldn't even begin to imagine how Marvin had made his way back, let alone what his new mission might be.

"Take cover, sniper!"

The dreaded warning sounded a bare second after the first round exploded from the surrounding forest. Thomas dove to the ground, and as he pressed his body into the damp soil in a desperate attempt to gain cover, another bullet ricocheted close overhead.

From the rear of their formation, an M16 returned fire,

and Thomas rolled over into the same shallow culvert that also sheltered Ted Callahan. Yet more sniper rounds whined overhead, and Thomas listened to Callahan as he urgently addressed his two-way.

"Commander Three, this is Commander One. We are taking live fire, and request immediate assistance. Over."

The order calling Coach down to the conference room arrived just as the lights of Brest, France, were visible in the night sky thirty-two thousand feet beneath them. Taking his place at the pilot console was his backup, Major Owen Lassiter. Lassiter was short and wiry, with a spiky crew cut that did little to cover up his rather large, protruding ears. The Ross Perot lookalike took his flying seriously and didn't care for idle chatter in his cockpit, a fact that both Lucky and Jake were painfully aware of.

While Lucky was in the process of giving Lassiter a weather update, Coach excused himself, taking a moment to stretch his cramped limbs in the vacant upper-deck rest area. His bunk invitingly beckoned, yet he turned instead for the stairway that conveyed him down to the main deck. At the base of the stairs, he passed the ever-present, dour-faced security guard, and grabbed a mug of black coffee at the galley, before continuing forward into the conference room.

There were six individuals seated there. At his usual

place at the head of the table was Admiral Warner, with Colonel Pritchard, Major Hewlett, Captain Richardson, Brittany, and Red seated alongside the Chairman. Each of them had their eyes locked on the rear projection screen, where a real-time video conference with General Lowell Spencer was being held.

As quietly as possible, Coach took the vacant seat next to Brittany, all the while listening to TACAMO's distinguished, silver-haired EAO describe the tense situation currently taking place beneath the Atlantic.

". . . and that's the extent of the damages," continued Spencer, his deep blue eyes showing little hint of outward emotion. "I'm confident that the *Rhode Island* can complete the repairs from their position on the continental shelf, and that they'll still be able to fulfill their alert platform duty should they be called upon to do so."

The Chairman leaned forward and addressed the microphone that was placed in the center of the table. "I appreciate the update, Lowell. It sounds like Captain Lockwood and his men are doing one hell of a fine job down there. Any word on the vessel that struck them?"

Spencer shook his head. "We're relying on the *Polk* to track it down. But so far, the Red bastard has eluded us."

"We still don't have any proof that it was a Russian submarine, Lowell," reminded the Chairman.

A pained expression crossed Spencer's face, and he dared to counter. "I don't want to get into another argument with you, Mr. Chairman, but as far as I'm concerned, it's only too obvious who's responsible for this flagrant act of undersea aggression. Regardless of what General Zhukov told you, how can we trust a nation that can't even tell us who's in charge of its nuclear arsenal?"

"The Russian Defense Minister gave me his word that their nuclear release codes haven't in any way been compromised during the current power struggle," stated Warner. "And I have no reason to doubt him."

"Then why can't we speak to their President directly, and get his personal guarantee that the codes are still under his direct control?" Spencer countered.

The Chairman looked at Red. The systems analyst wore headphones and a chin mike, and after inputting a flurry of data into her laptop's keyboard, she indicated with a despondent shake of the head that she still had no luck getting in touch with the Russian President.

"It appears the President remains at sea, unreachable," the Chairman said in a bare whisper.

"It's another goddamn coup attempt!" exclaimed Spencer. "The spineless sons of bitches killed our President, and now they want to take over the goddamn world. Where the hell's Vice President Chapman? This country needs its Commander-in-Chief!"

Coach couldn't believe Spencer's audacity, and he watched the Chairman's face redden with rage. Trent Warner wasn't the type of man who liked to have his authority challenged, and he angrily scanned the faces of those gathered around the table, finally halting on Captain Richardson.

"Can FEMA provide an answer for the good General?" he asked impatiently.

Richardson double-checked his laptop's display screen before answering. "The central locator system indicates that we've yet to make contact with the Vice President or his party. The Speaker of the House is on his way to Missouri's Fort Leonard Wood to personally coordinate the Search and Rescue effort and to be immediately available to take the oath of office should the Vice President be deceased, while Senator Brennan, the next in line for the Presidency after the Speaker, is standing by on Capitol Hill."

Spencer appeared to be somewhat appeased by this information, and he waited for a pocket of air turbulence to pass before expressing himself with a sober seriousness. "I gather that you're still headed for Washington?"

Coach was the next to be swallowed by the Chairman's

icy glance, and he took this as a prompt to answer the General. "Nightwatch is just passing over the coast of Brittany. Our ETA at Andrews is 0735 Zulu."

Yet more turbulence shook TACAMO, and Spencer could be seen grabbing the edge of his padded command chair. Worry crossed his face, and Coach noted that the decorated veteran suddenly looked every one of his sixty-three years and then some.

"Damn it, Ted. The way they've got us pinned down, we'll never get out of this ditch alive."

Yet another 7.62mm round whined overhead, and Ted Callahan dared to look up and meet Thomas's glance. "Hang in there, Kellogg. Sergeant Reed and his Sappers should be arriving on the scene any second now."

From his prone position beside Callahan, Thomas expressed his number one fear. "If these are indeed the guys who snatched the VP and my brother's Secret Service team, I wonder what in hell they're trying to pull off. They might be able to keep us temporarily at bay, but it's only a matter of time until we bring down enough reinforcements to take them out."

"I'm just concerned that these are the same skunks who've been stealing weapons from Leonard Wood. If they're locals, they'll have a thorough knowledge of these woods, making tracking them down difficult."

A series of three closely grouped sniper rounds rained

down on them. One of the rounds ricocheted off a boulder, embedding itself in a tree trunk only a few feet behind them. Thomas instinctively ducked, and as he pressed his head into the ground, he inadvertently swallowed a mouthful of wet dirt. He spat out the mud, and his companion laughed.

"We finally made a mud eater out of you, Kellogg."

"I'll never complain about an MRE again," promised Thomas, who managed a nervous smile himself.

An intense outburst of automatic-weapons fire sounded in the distance. It had a vastly different pitch from the fire previously directed upon them, and Callahan glanced at his watch and matter-of-factly commented:

"If I'm not mistaken, that should be Sergeant Reed and his boys completing their flanking maneuver."

No sooner were these words spoken than Callahan's two-way activated, and the sound of gunfire faded. "Commander One, this is Commander Three. Over," broke in a breathless voice from the speaker.

"Commander Three, this is Commander One. What did you find up there, Sapper leader?" asked Callahan.

"Commander One, the opposition has been neutralized. And, sir, you'll never believe what these rascals were up to."

"Have you located the Vice President?" Callahan asked hopefully.

"We're still checking, sir. If you proceed about half a klick up the path, you can't miss us."

"Roger that, Commander Three. We're on our way. Over."

Callahan informed the MPs of the all-clear. They emerged from cover, and with Captain Christian leading the way to check for booby traps, they continued up the trail.

Thomas was last in line. He was relieved to be on the move once more. Ever hopeful that his brother would be found safe and sound close by, he easily kept up with the formation, which proceeded forward with a new sense of urgency.

It was as they neared a large open clearing that he

smelled the distinctive odor of ammonia. A group of Sappers were in the process of examining a ramshackle Airstream trailer that was positioned at the clearing's western edge. Two men with their hands restrained behind their backs were spread out on their stomachs nearby, with a Sapper keeping watch over them with an M-16. They were dressed in camouflage fatigues, and had their long hair tied in ponytails.

Sergeant Reed emerged from behind the trailer, carrying a pair of hunting rifles with scopes on them. Ranger Glickman accompanied him, and when she spotted Thomas, a wide grin lit up her face.

"Special Agent, I believe you'll be especially interested in what we found back there."

"I assume that it's not the Vice President."

"I'm afraid there's no sign of him," replied the Ranger. "Though at long last we've managed to catch a pair of notorious methamphetamine bootleggers who have been plaguing the forest. Their lab is right out there in the woods, and we caught them using stolen anhydrous ammonia fertilzer to convert ephedrine into meth."

Thomas found it hard to hide his disappointment, and he looked at Ted Callahan and vented his frustration. "Where the hell's Vice President Chapman and Vince?"

"I believe the answer to that question lies further down the river, my friend," offered Callahan stoically.

They used an improvised field stretcher constructed out of salvaged canoe paddles and fishing line to carry Lewis Marvin from the crash site. Vince noted the severe burns that covered Marvin's backside as they pulled him from the underbrush. The rear portion of his flight suit was burned away, revealing raw, burned skin, and when they initially moved him, he howled in pain and slipped into unconsciousness.

He remained unconscious for the entire hike into the hollow. Vince suspected he was in shock and that, in addition to the burns, he had severe internal injuries as well. Marvin would need immediate medical attention. Yet because of their isolated location and the hostile nature of their escorts, getting him to a doctor was doubtful. All that Vince could do was keep him as comfortable as possible, and try to attend to his wounds once they were at the campsite.

Junior was particularly anxious to have his father question their new prisoner. Marvin was apparently the first solid evidence proving the existence of the dreaded UN-sponsored, One World/Black Helicopter conspiracy. Vince's previous acquaintance with Marvin only served to fuel Junior's paranoia, and Vince could only hope that he'd get a chance to clarify their relationship. Of course, he was equally interested in learning all about Marvin's involvement with the ambush.

One of Vince's greatest fears was how Andrew Chapman had fared during their hike to the river. He was afraid that the VP might have further incurred the wrath of his captors and had been subsequently shot. He was thus pleasantly surprised when they entered the campsite and found Chapman alive and well, in the midst of a spirited game of checkers with Amos Stoddard.

The checker players were seated on the wooden porch of a small, ramshackle cabin. There was an open Mason jar filled with a clear liquid substance beside them, with Satan snuggled up alongside Andrew Chapman's outstretched feet.

Just as Vince and his party emerged from the forest with Marvin in tow, Amos completed an eagerly anticipated triple jump, wiping the last of the VP's checkers from the board.

"You might be a devious politician," shouted Amos in triumph, "but you sure are a lousy checkers player."

Satan began barking to announce the newcomers, prompting Tiny to exit the cabin. The tall, potbellied redhead with the inappropriate name carried a shotgun, and he called out to Junior in a deep, resonant voice.

"Who are ya carryin' in that stretcher, Junior? Don't tell me you went and snagged the President?"

Junior ignored this facetious remark, and instead excitedly addressed his father. "Pa, it's a United Nations storm trooper! We practically pulled him right out of his black helicopter on the banks of the Eleven Point."

They lowered the stretcher onto the porch, and both Amos, Tiny, and Andrew Chapman examined the ashen-faced man whom it carried. Marvin remained unconscious, and his quick, shallow breaths and cold, clammy skin didn't bode well for his continued survival.

"Could someone please get him some water?" Vince pleaded.

Miriam put down the SATCOM to fulfill this request, while Junior said, "Our Fed knows him, Pa. They're most likely in cahoots together."

"His name's Lewis Marvin," Vince interjected. "We served together in Vietnam. The last time I saw him was some thirty years ago. He was on his way into Cambodia for a Search and Rescue mission. Not a single member of his unit ever came back, with Marvin himself listed as missing in action."

Amos snickered. "SAR mission, my ass. He was no doubt part of the CIA's secret war, and they purposely listed him MIA to use him for other clandestine operations, like the one he's currently involved with."

"Though I was too young to serve in Vietnam," interrupted Andrew Chapman, "I got a chance to serve on a Senate Intelligence committee during my stint in Congress that was tasked with investigating the CIA's involvement in the war. I have no doubt that they were indeed involved in some activities that were never reported to the American people."

"Yeah, like selling opium on the streets of America to finance their One World agenda," Amos retorted.

"I never saw any proof that such a thing ever occurred," replied Chapman.

"That's 'cause you're either a fellow conspirator or dumb enough to believe their doublespeak," said Amos. "You politicians are all alike. You've sold out to other interests, forgetting that your true purpose is to serve the people."

"I beg to differ with you," countered Chapman. "You're making an unfair generalization."

Amos spat at Chapman's feet. "Like hell I am! You're nothing but a bunch of self-serving crooks. It's time to clean out Washington, and tar and feather the whole lot of you."

"You can do that with your vote," said the VP.

Vince didn't like the direction this argument was taking, and he cringed when Amos Stoddard began laughing wickedly.

"Like this country has ever seen a fair election," said Amos, looking directly at the VP. "We might be poor, but we ain't stupid. The only candidate who wins is the one that best serves the corporate, One World interest. Us folks at the bottom of the economy don't have any real say in the government. We're too busy fighting to survive, and 'cause we never had the time for a decent education, the system has passed us right by. The trouble with you politicians is that you've lost touch with the American heartland, and deserve to be shot for your inattention."

Tiny alertly rammed a shell into the barrel of his shotgun and offered it to Amos, saying, "Come on, old man. It's time to back up those bold words of yours with some action. Let's shoot the Federal bastards."

"Yeah, Pa," Junior put in. "Now's our chance to really make a difference."

Vince knew it was time to intercede and defuse this volatile situation, and as he was mentally formulating a strategy to do so, Lewis Marvin began to stir. He issued a low moan, and when his eyes opened, Vince took advantage of his return to consciousness to divert attention from the VP.

"Lewis, it's Vince Kellogg from A Company, First Battalion, Third Group."

Marvin's bloodshot eyes slowly focused on Vince, and he didn't appear to display the least hint of recognition, prompting Vince to add, "Our teams were assigned to the Rung Sat Special Zone together, under Colonel Sharp."

"That bastard," cursed Marvin, his hoarse voice but a whisper. "It were pencil-dicked sons of bitches like Sharp who lost the war for us. Jesus, Kellogg, it looks like I really screwed the pooch this time. What the hell are you doing out here in these infernal woods?"

"I was all set to ask you the same question, Lewis. I was part of the canoe convoy you attacked."

Marvin winced in pain, and as he struggled to scan the faces of those gathered around him, his stare finally halted on Andrew Chapman.

"So you were hanging out with the likes of him," he said, his vehement hatred of the Vice President most obvious.

"I'm working for the Secret Service now, Lewis, and for the most part, it was my team that you managed to slaughter."

Miriam arrived with some water, and Marvin took a drink and began coughing violently. Vince waited for this spell to pass before continuing.

"I'm almost afraid to ask, but what did you hope to prove with this act of cold-blooded murder?"

Marvin redirected his gaze back to Vince. "I call it fulfilling my sworn duty to God and country. I see that you're still part of the problem, Kellogg. If I remember correctly, you always were the type of gung-ho soldier who truly believed in the legitimacy of your orders. I was privileged to learn otherwise.

"It's no different today, and I'm proud of the movement I serve. Your boss and the administration he represents are the real enemies, Kellogg. They're in the process of selling us out, with the Union at risk like never before."

Marvin hesitated for a moment to catch his breath, then said, "It's not too late to join us, Kellogg. But don't tarry, for the time to act is now. Someday the patriots gathered beneath Freeman shall be likened to Washington's men at Valley Forge. Though this time our mortal enemy stands elected amongst us."

Marvin pointed directly at Andrew Chapman, and tapping his last reservoir of strength, he struggled to sit up, all the while reaching out toward the astounded VP with his outstretched arm.

"Damn you!" he cursed, his voice quivering with rage.

"Because of you, the greatest nation ever to grace God's good earth shall be no more!"

Another coughing fit possessed him, and before Vince could assist him, blood started to flow from his nose and mouth.

"Eternal vigilance is the price of our freedom!" he managed, before his body began convulsing in the first throes of death.

It took several minutes for him to die, and it was Vince who shut his eyelids for the final time.

"What in the world was he talking about?" asked Andrew Chapman, clearly traumatized by this confusing encounter.

"It appears that someone else is aware of your traitorous ways," observed Amos. "Because now it looks like you have stolen not only our land, but the rest of the nation along with it."

"Cut the crap!" Chapman protested. "There's no damned conspiracy!"

"I don't suppose any of you can explain what Marvin was referring to when he mentioned the patriots gathered beneath Freeman?" Vince questioned, ignoring the VP's outburst. "Is Freeman a local landmark of some sort?"

"Freeman Hollow is located just south of here, in the heart of the Irish Wilderness," Miriam told him.

"The Tater Hill swamp lights!" exclaimed Junior. "Pa, that's where you saw the UFO."

Amos shut his son up with a single menacing stare. The damage already done, Amos looked at Vince and explained what Junior was talking about.

"We suspected that the black helicopters could be operating out of Freeman Hollow for some time now."

Vince sensed the legitimacy of this revelation, and he tried his best to voice himself with sincerity. "I realize that I'm asking a lot, but if you can just take me to this hollow, I'll do my best to determine if a clandestine military group is really operating out there."

"And if there is?" asked Amos, his tone noticeably softening.

"Then you've got my word that I'll do everything within my power to halt its operation, and after exposing it to the authorities of your choice, I'll be right there to wipe it out," promised Vince, who sensed that a deal was already in the making.

Saturday, July 3, 0115 Zulu

Iron Man One

"General Spencer, we're receiving flash traffic from Cheyenne Mountain."

Lowell Spencer received this intercom page while stealing a spare moment to eat a pasta salad in the crew's rest area, immediately behind TACAMO's flight deck. He pushed away the partially consumed meal, scooted out from the fold-down table, and headed aft into the next compartment, where his five-person battle staff was stationed.

Spencer's vacant console occupied the forward right-hand position. His SIOP and Air Launch Control System advisors were already seated beside it, with his team chief, senior NCO, and Airborne Communications Officer positioned on the other side of the compartment. As Spencer buckled himself into his padded command chair and put on his headset, his ACO addressed him.

"Sir, NORAD reports a confirmed missile launch from the Russian ICBM base in Tyuratam."

Spencer hastily read the data that began filling his display screen. It was a copy of the original warning order that was broadcast from NORAD's missile-warning center, situated beneath Cheyenne Mountain, Colorado. The data indicated that approximately ninety seconds ago, the sensors of a Code 647 Defense Support Program satellite known as DSP East had picked up the hot plume of a single ICBM leaving the lower atmosphere. If this missile was armed with a nuclear warhead and headed for the continental United States, it could reach its target in less than thirty minutes, and Spencer reacted accordingly.

"Major Childress," he said to his SIOP advisor, "what do we know about the launch site?"

"It's an active ICBM field, sir, that reportedly houses thirty-six long-range SS-18s and a dozen SS-11s."

"I don't suppose the Russians announced any prescheduled missile tests for today?" continued Spencer.

Childress alertly answered, "That's a negative, sir."

Lowell Spencer was a thirty-year Air Force veteran who had begun his career flying B-52s for Curtis LeMay's Strategic Air Command. An active participant in the Cold War, he had shared in many similar alerts, though none with circumstances quite like this one.

"Considering that this is indeed a belligerent launch, Major, why only a single missile?" Spencer asked.

Childress thought for a moment before responding. "I'd say that it's all part of a carefully orchestrated counterforce strike, sir. Since they've already eliminated our Commander-in-Chief, and attempted to take out our Trident alert platform, all they'd need to do is hit us with a high-altitude nuclear burst to create enough Electro-Magnetic Pulse to negate our command and control ability."

"General," interrupted the ACO. "NORAD reports that the Russian ICBM has completed its post-boost phase and is initiating a polar trajectory."

"That gives us twenty-five minutes at best to respond, sir," Major Childress reminded him. "I advise sending an immediate EAM to the *Rhode Island,* and ordering our strategic forces to DEFCON Two."

"Unfortunately, that decision is not ours to make, Major," said Spencer. "It's time to contact Nightwatch. They've got the ball, and it's our esteemed Chairman who's going to be calling the plays."

Saturday, July 3, 0118 Zulu

Nightwatch 676

It was Red who fielded the urgent call from Iron Man One. News of the Russian missile launch had already reached Nightwatch, and the Chairman readily listened to General Spencer's somber assessment of the situation.

"I agree wholeheartedly, Lowell," said Warner into a handset. "Under the circumstances, it's only prudent to change our alert status to DEFCON Two. Though for the life of me, I still can't believe this is really a legitimate Russian attack. You also have my permission to convey an EAM to the *Rhode Island*. If we are forced to retaliate, that should give Captain Lockwood enough time to wrap up repairs and spin up his missiles."

There could be no mistaking the solemn expression that graced Warner's face when he hung up the phone and addressed Red. "Sergeant, get Colonel Pritchard and Commander Cooper down here on the double, and have them meet me at the emergency action safe. And where the hell is that secure line to General Zhukov that I asked for?"

Barely a minute after General Spencer had completed his conversation with Nightwatch, TACAMO prepared to contact the *Rhode Island*. From the state-of-the-art glass cockpit, the flight crew got a clear view of the sparkling waters of the Atlantic below. No surface vessels of any sort were visible, the platform they were tasked to communicate with lying deep below the ocean's surface.

"Orbit entry checklist complete," said the pilot into his chin mike. "Okay, Reels, you have access."

"Roger," answered the reel operator from his console at the rear of the aircraft. "Short wire's on its way."

In order for their radio signal to penetrate the ocean depths, a pair of thin wire antennas had to be extended from TACAMO's belly. The short wire extended five thousand feet from the tail, and over two hundred thousand watts were needed to power it.

"Long wire's on its way," the reel operator next reported. This antenna was over twenty-five thousand feet long, and was pulled from a huge spool that was stored just aft of the reel operator's position. It formed a giant dipole with the shorter "hot" wire, and produced the actual VLF waveform.

"Both wires are out and parked," reported the reel operator. "Flight, you have access."

"Roger," acknowledged the pilot, who guided the aircraft into a steeply banked, racetrack orbit, so that the drogue-stabilized long wire would point toward the ocean's surface. "It's all yours, Comm," he added into his chin mike.

"Roger; bring up the Power Amplifier," instructed the ACO from his V-shaped console located aft of Spencer's battle-staff compartment.

"PA's coming up," the flight technician reported. "Full power, two hundred."

"Roger. Send it!" ordered the ACO.

"Conn, Radio. We're receiving flash traffic, Emergency Action Message! Recommend Alert One!"

Captain Terence McNeil Lockwood listened to this excited intercom page from his command position inside the submarine's control room. He had only just returned from Sonar, where most of the damage from their recent collision was confined, and upon hearing this dreaded announcement, he raced toward the radio room.

It was at the OPCON—a cramped compartment featuring a small three-person booth and a console topped with a trio of locked safes labeled TOP SECRET—that Lockwood was joined by his XO and his radio officer. They held the telegram-sized EAM, which had just been torn off the radio console's printer.

"Sir," said the XO, "we have a properly formatted Emergency Action Message from the National Command Authority, for strategic missile launch."

"I concur, sir," said the radio officer.

"Captain, request permission to authenticate," stated the XO.

"Permission granted," returned Lockwood.

The sealed packet holding the authenticator card was removed from the largest of the three safes. The XO tore open the packet, removed the card, and held it up against the EAM.

"Alpha, Tango, Alpha, Charlie, Echo, Echo, Bravo," read the XO.

The radio officer checked the authenticator card himself and repeated this sequence, prompting the XO to report, "The message is authentic, Captain."

"I agree," said the radio officer.

Lockwood was the picture of composure as he double-checked the EAM and reached up for the nearest intercom handset to address the crew over the 1MC.

"Men of the *Rhode Island*, this is your Captain. The release of nuclear weapons has been authorized. Man battle stations for strategic missile launch. Spin up all missiles."

Friday, July 2, 6:25 P.M. C.D.T.

Eleven Point River

Thomas had been anticipating the worse, but nothing prepared him for the shocking scene that awaited them at Mary Deckard shoals. As their jet-powered johnboats began transiting the Z-shaped gauntlet of boulders forming the initial rapids, the first overturned canoe was encountered. The partially sunken vessel was hung up alongside a rock shelf, and strangely enough, it was riddled with dozens of bullet holes.

Thomas found his stomach tightening with dread, and his worst fears were realized when a pair of bodies were discovered in a nearby snag. The water-soaked corpses were also punctured with bullet wounds, and it was Ranger Glickman who identified one of the unfortunate victims as a fellow U.S. Forest Service employee, assigned to the Van Buren field office.

With the roar of the rapids a constant companion, they continued downstream. The boat carrying Thomas, Ted Callahan, and Captain Christian was the first to complete transiting the shoals. Along the way, the twisted wreckage of four more boats was discovered, along with seven bodies. One of these corpses belonged to Andrea Whitworth. The journalist was found hung up inside a tangled snag of twisted branches, with half of her familiar face blown away.

While a shocked group of Sappers and MPs began solemnly collecting the corpses, Thomas and his party continued down the river. They passed the partially submerged, twisted remains of Marine Two, and realized that an intense battle of some sort must have taken place out here.

It took another thirty minutes to complete a thorough sweep of the area, and a total of thirteen bodies was eventually picked from the river. Amongst the dead were the VP's physician and two more U.S. Forest Service rangers, whom Jody Glickman tearfully identified as Ben Eberly and Ron Wyatt.

The only consolation Thomas could derive was that the bodies of Andrew Chapman and Vince weren't among the victims. With the barest of hope that they were still alive, the parties renewed their search, with Ted Callahan coordinating the effort from a sandy clearing situated near the base of a steep waterfall.

Fresh human tracks led Sergeant Reed and his Sappers to the still-smoking, burned-out hulk of a Huey helicopter. Meanwhile, Captain Christian and his MPs completed the somber task of pulling as much evidence as possible from the river. This left Thomas and Ranger Glickman free to portage the waterfall and begin their way farther downstream.

Alongside a large pool at the waterfall's base, Thomas spotted some fresh footprints imprinted on the sloping bank. Yet more footprints were found on an adjoining clearing, and Jody Glickman discovered the soggy remains of a discarded cigar.

"What do you make of this, Special Agent?" she asked while carefully picking up the cigar and handing it to Thomas.

The cigar itself had yet to be smoked, and Thomas noted the familiar brown band that encircled its base, with the label TEMPLE HALL imprinted on it.

"This is my brother's brand!" he exclaimed, all the while searching the surrounding clearing for any more clues. And it was then he spotted a narrow earthen trail, and an assortment of footprints headed up into the thick forest filling this side of the Eleven Point.

"NORAD reports that the Russian missile continues on its polar trajectory," informed Master Sergeant Schuster from his comm console in the 747's Op area. "Estimated time of arrival over the CONUS in seventeen minutes and counting."

"Iron Man One indicates that the *Rhode Island* has acknowledged receipt of the EAM. Missiles are spinning up," added Red from her own adjoining console.

Brittany Cooper was amongst the group of concerned senior officers gathered close by. She found it hard to hide her nervousness, especially now that the briefcase she was responsible for carrying lay open on the counter beside Red. The thick crimson file folder that it held was now in the hands of Admiral Warner. With bifocals perched on the tip of his nose, the Chairman completed his study of the document before handing it to his SIOP advisor.

"If we're forced to order a retaliatory launch, which target package do you like, Major?" asked Warner.

Hewlett answered while reading the top page. "Unless we want a full-scale exchange, our only option is to answer this attack in kind, with counterforce package Zulu Tango. By ordering the *Rhode Island* to launch such a three-shot salvo, we can hit them with a high-altitude pin-down blast, followed by a strike against those Strategic Rocket Forces command and control facilities that are farthest away from any major civilian population centers."

Warner appeared distracted as he looked to Red and questioned, "Any luck reaching Zhukov?"

Red pushed back her chin mike and shook her head no.

"Sir," interrupted Hewlett, "I advise contacting Iron Man One at once, and getting them to pass on target package Zulu Tango to the *Rhode Island*. Time is critical."

The Chairman appeared to ignore this urgent advice and instead turned to address Captain Richardson. "What are the results of the latest central locator query regarding the Vice President?"

"They're still negative, sir. With our move to DEFCON Two, FEMA is implementing a Level One evacuation of the Capitol."

"And the location of the Speaker?" queried Warner.

"Sir, he remains in air transit to Leonard Wood."

"I guess there are worse places to be in the event of a nuclear detonation," mumbled Warner, who glanced back at his SIOP advisor. "Under the circumstances, it appears that we have no option but to be prepared for a worst-case scenario. It's time to instruct Iron Man One to relay Zulu Tango to the *Rhode Island*. Sergeant Rayburn, if you'll be so good as to reconnect me with General Spencer."

Red failed to react to this request, her attention focused on the unexpected arrival of a superhigh-frequency radio message. Brittany and her fellow officers watched Red's face lighten with renewed hope as she looked up to address the Chairman.

"Sir, it's the Russian Defense Ministry calling for you!"

"It's about time," said Warner. He grabbed the nearest red handset and shouted into the transmitter. "Alexi, what the hell is going on down there?"

Brittany breathlessly listened to the Chairman initiate a spirited conversation filled with choice curse words and long pauses. It was during the course of this long dialogue that Sergeant Schuster's excited voice filled the compartment.

"NORAD reports that the Russian missile has dropped off its radar screens with a splashdown in the East Siberian Sea!"

"So I understand, Comrade," continued Warner into the handset. "Get back to work, and don't hesitate to contact me should the situation warrant."

The Chairman hung up the phone, a relieved grin on his tired face. "Sergeant Rayburn, contact Iron Man One and relay the code sequence to terminate the alert. And I want an immediate status change back to DEFCON Four. That was no belligerent launch on the part of the Russians. It was only their Defense Ministry's way of showing the world that they still have control of their nuclear forces."

"We'll stop up yonder by that spring," Amos Stoddard told the six individuals who closely followed him.

Vince was third in line, behind Andrew Chapman, and he watched the VP briefly turn around with this news, a relieved grin on his sweat-stained face. They had been traveling nonstop for a good two hours. From the very start, Amos had established a blistering pace that led them almost due south through some of the most rugged and breathtaking forestland Vince had ever experienced.

During this entire hike, not another human being was encountered. For the most part, they followed a narrow trail that appeared to be little more than an animal track. No roads, pathways, or habitations of any sort were sighted, with nothing but thick woods stretching for as far as the eye could see.

They passed through a succession of steep valleys. These hollows were thick with trees, and Vince identified several varieties of oak including scarlet, blackjack, and white.

Gnarled red cedars clung to the edges of the steep bluffs, while sour gum, walnut, hickory, and maple found a foothold on the rocky slopes.

In the course of their journey they encountered a multitude of wildlife, such as dozens of gray squirrels, several foxes, a raccoon, and an abundance of birds ranging from robins and blue jays to cliff swallows and a flock of noisy turkeys. Bobwhite quail softly called from the underbrush; red-shouldered hawks angrily screeched from above.

Under different circumstances, Vince would have truly enjoyed this wilderness hike. But he found it hard to relax knowing there were three armed men following close on his heels. Both Junior, Tiny, and a scraggly-haired associate named C.J. all carried shotguns. Somewhere in their ranks was Miriam. She appeared to be unarmed, and the last Vince saw of the good-natured redhead, she was collecting blackberries.

Vince was hungry, tired, and thirsty, and the SATCOM he had decided to lug along didn't help matters any. He could feel the added strain of the thirty-plus-pound case on his upper arms, shoulders, and back, and several times when they were climbing up a particularly steep ridge, he considered abandoning it.

It was thus with great relief that Vince halted beside the stream that Amos and his dog, Satan, were already drinking from. Vince thought better of joining them, and he watched as the old-timer's son, daughter, Tiny, and C.J. also knelt to drink from the brook.

Andrew Chapman looked longingly at Vince, licked his parched lips, and beckoned toward the clear, gurgling water.

"Sir, I really wouldn't if I were you," warned Vince.

"Don't be scared of the water. This here's a fresh spring, and I promise that you won't get sick from it," offered Miriam.

She scooped up a handful of water and poured it into her open mouth. Vince swallowed heavily, his mouth bone-dry. But even then he stubbornly refused to relent.

After ascertaining that the brook appeared to be emerging from a fracture in the solid rock wall of an overhanging bluff, Andrew Chapman gave in to temptation and bent down to test the water. He dipped his cupped hands into the spring and sniffed it, oblivious to Vince's continued cautionary words.

"Sir, I was warned by the Forest Service that the fresh water in these parts was unfit to drink."

"Balderdash!" countered Amos after slaking his thirst and sitting down on a flat boulder. "I sure hope you don't believe everything the government tells you. I've been drinking from this spring since I was a young pup, and I've yet to get sick from it."

The VP dared to dip his cupped hands into the water once more, and this time he took a tentative sip. He must have liked what he tasted, because he followed this sip with a healthy gulp.

"Come on, Kellogg," he urged. "It's time to start living dangerously. Besides, it's better than dying from dehydration."

Vince watched him kneel beside the brook and properly satisfy his thirst. As the VP gratefully soaked his face in the stream, Vince reluctantly succumbed to temptation. The water was cool and smelled fresh, and once he started drinking, it was hard to stop.

"That's the spirit," said Amos, who pulled a sausage from his backpack and began slicing off thick pieces with a pocketknife. "Anyone hungry?" he asked between bites.

Both Vince and the VP hadn't eaten a thing since an early breakfast. They were ravenous, and after drinking their fill, they readily accepted the old-timer's offer.

Vince found the sausage extremely tasty. It was moist and mildly spiced, with a sweet aftertaste. He ate three slices, and Chapman did likewise.

"Does that make them lawbreakers, Pa?" asked Junior, who watched them eat with a mischievous sparkle in his eye.

"What do you mean by that remark?" asked the VP.

Amos laughed. "Junior was referring to the deer meat that

made up your sausage. If you want to go and get technical, you just ate an animal harvested out of hunting season."

"You mean to say you poached it," clarified Vince.

Amos offered Vince another slice of sausage, and when he refused it with a disgusted shake of his head, the old-timer fed it to Satan, saying, "You might call it poaching, but we call it survival. If you haven't already noticed, there ain't no grocery stores out here. And even if there were, we wouldn't have the money to do any shopping. If we want to eat, we have to gather our food right here in the forest."

"I'm truly sorry that times are so tough for you," offered the VP. "But if everyone went into the forest to live off the land as they pleased, we'd kill off all the game and use up the resources in a matter of days. We're forced to create hunting seasons and game limits to control and preserve the number of animals in wilderness areas such as this one. Why, back in the 1920s, this entire region was an ecological disaster zone. An out-of-control lumber industry stripped these hills bare, while overgrazing, unrestrained hunting, and the use of slash-and-burn techniques for weed control all combined to make this area one of the poorest during the Depression."

"And even with all your Federal legislation since that time, ain't we just as poor today as we were back then?" countered Amos. "It's not natural for folks who aren't from these parts to come down here and take our property, while telling us that we no longer can live off the land like our ancestors did. I bet you didn't know that my pappy once owned a three-hundred-acre tract right off the Eleven Point near Greer Springs. It was prime real estate, and he spent his last dime to create a small canoe-rental business there. Me and my kids would be running it today if it wasn't for the Feds who came down here uninvited and stole our land for pennies on the dollar. That land was all we had, and when it was gone, we had no place to go but these woods."

"That land was needed to preserve the Eleven Point for generations to come," replied the VP.

"But what about preserving the rights of me and my family today?" Amos argued. "As far as I'm concerned, it was the Federal government that illegally chased us off our property, and I've got the full right to take all the deer, fish, and other wildlife I might need to keep on living."

Vince didn't like the direction that this conversation was headed in, and he tried his diplomatic best to change the subject. "Will we be able to reach Freeman Hollow by dark?"

"What do ya mean reach, Bubba?" answered Junior. "We're there."

Vince scanned the forest surrounding them with renewed interest. Thick stands of red oak made viewing difficult, and he dared to bring up a subject that had caught his ear earlier.

"When you were talking about this hollow back at your campsite, what did you mean by the Tater Hill swamp lights? And what sort of UFO was sighted out here?"

Amos looked at his son and disgustedly shook his head. "Since you're the one who went and opened up his big mouth, why don't you answer the man, Son?"

Junior knelt on the ground opposite his father, and Satan ran to his side. It was while picking the burrs and ticks from the dog's black fur that he began speaking, hesitantly at first.

"This hollow has always been home to strange lights and other weird activity. Rumor has it that Freeman once housed a top-secret, subterranean government installation where a captured UFO was stored in the early sixties. It was way back then that Pa and Gramps actually saw this craft, hovering over the forest, shining a light that turned night into day."

Amos nervously chuckled. "Now, we know this weren't an alien spaceship at all, but the first of the UN helicopters arriving to stake out their claim."

"Then how do you explain the strange green lights that me and Satan saw over by Tater Hill last Halloween?" asked Miriam. "I still think it's an Indian burial ground that's responsible, and that this hollow is haunted with their spirits."

"Was the spot where you saw this UFO near Tater Hill?" Vince asked Amos.

The elder Stoddard shook his head that it was, prompting Vince to surmise, "Then I bet that's the spot where Marvin's Huey was based. How far is it from here?"

"It's a fifteen-minute hike at best," Amos answered. "Junior, why don't you and Tiny escort the Special Agent down to Tater? I'll wait up here with the Vice President, along with your sister and C.J."

"Can't I go too, Pa?" requested Miriam. "I can show them the exact spot where I saw the spook lights."

"I suppose it won't hurt any," Amos replied. "Just don't get yourselves captured by whatever the hell is out there."

Satan accompanied them down into the hollow. It was a difficult hike. There was no trail of any sort to follow, and the footing was treacherous. Overhanging limbs slowed their progress, and at one point Vince stepped into a spiderweb and needed Miriam's help to pick the sticky web off his back and shoulders.

Even though there was a good hour of summer sun left in the day, dusk came early to Freeman Hollow. A steep ridge to the west had already swallowed the sun, yet the heat and humidity persisted. Vince's clothes were thoroughly soaked, and his shoulder still ached from the SATCOM unit, which he had left behind with the Vice President.

To a chorus of crickets and cicadas, they reached the hollow's floor. Thorn bushes and thick scrub replaced the oaks and cedars. The very air here was thick and heavy, and even Satan appeared to miss the fresh breezes that had accompanied them on the ridgeline. At a crossroads of sorts, the dog was having difficulty choosing between two faint trails, so Junior revealed which of these paths he'd like them to follow.

"We'll take the one on the left. It'll bring us to the overlook where Pa got his first glimpse of the UFO."

"The other trail is the one leading to the swamp lights," said Miriam. "If there's a secret base out here, that's where we'll find it."

Her brother stubbornly shook his head. "I disagree, Sis. The overlook offers the best view of Tater. It should also provide us with easy access to the base of the hill, where the installation is most likely positioned."

"Then why are the swamp lights on the other side?" protested Miriam. "I say we check them out before heading to the overlook."

Vince sensed a serious deadlock, and he offered a compromise. "Miriam, why don't I go with you to the place where you saw the lights? Then we can meet up with your brother at the overlook and compare notes."

The siblings accepted these terms, and Vince followed Miriam and Satan up the trail to the right. They cautiously picked their way through a briar patch, then began a short downhill climb into a stunted pine forest. The setting sun was all but blotted out from the sky, with mist beginning to form at the base of the twisted pine trunks. It was eerily quiet, a single owl hooting mournfully in the distance.

Satan stuck close to Miriam's side, and Vince couldn't shake the sensation that they were being watched. It was easy to see how an overactive imagination could play tricks with one's head in such a place. He could readily conjure up the spirits of the Osage Indians who had once lived in these parts. What he wasn't prepared for, though, was the green-faced men who suddenly materialized out of the mist, capturing them so quickly that even Satan wasn't able to let out a single yelp.

"I know this place," said Ranger Glickman as the trail they had been following led into a small clearing. "A family of poachers named Stoddard have been living here without Forest Service authorization. Our law enforcement officer thought they had moved on."

"Well, obviously someone's been living here," said Ted Callahan, in reference to the wash that still hung from a clothesline, and the checkerboard that lay on the porch of the crude, one-room cabin.

"Do the Stoddards have any militia ties?" Thomas questioned. "Or could they be part of a local movement against a Federal presence in these parts?"

"I can't answer the first question, Special Agent Kellogg," said Glickman. "Though I believe that the family patriarch, Amos Stoddard, could very well harbor a legitimate resentment against the Federal government. If I remember correctly, his father owned quite a bit of riverfront property near Greer Springs. That land was absorbed by the Forest

Service against the family's wishes. Like many others who lost their property at that time, they griped that the price paid was substantially below the fair market value."

Behind them, the Sappers and the MPs were busy sweeping the campsite for any clues. Captain Christian's men reported the discovery of several fresh deer carcasses in a nearby cave. An assortment of beaver, opossum, and mink pelts were also found there, along with several barrels of what appeared to be moonshine.

Sergeant Reed's Sappers were responsible for uncovering the most promising evidence—a set of fresh footprints, headed to the southeast. Ranger Glickman pulled out a detailed topographic map of the area, highlighted their current location, and drew an imaginary line to the southeast.

"It appears that they're most likely headed into the Irish Wilderness," she said.

"Could they have another campsite in there?" Ted Callahan queried.

"The entire wilderness is set aside as a minimal-use area," she answered. "There are no roads or habitations of any sort. In fact, the only real facility remaining down there is a long-abandoned underground shelter, originally designed by the Strategic Air Command to offer survivable command and control in the event of a nuclear war."

This unexpected revelation caught Thomas by complete surprise, and he pointed toward the map and asked, "And where is this shelter located?"

Glickman turned the map so Thomas could see her point to the Irish Wilderness; then, when her finger reached the feature labeled Freeman Hollow, she said, "Buried beneath one of the most inaccessible spots of the entire wilderness."

"Skipper, the trespassers have been locked up in detention. Should I begin the interrogation?"

Thusly called from his deep, meditative trance, Dick Mariano responded to this request from the shadows of his darkened study, his powerful voice but a hoarse whisper. "I'll handle it myself, Richy. I need you out on the perimeter with Doc."

"Aye, aye, sir."

Alone once again, Mariano completed another series of deep breaths, then closed his session with a silent prayer. He would need divine guidance to see him through the next couple of hours, a period of time that could very well be the most important in American history.

As he stood up from the rattan mat on which he had been seated, Mariano stretched his solid, muscular, six-foot frame. The blood rushed into his numbed limbs, and the ponytailed veteran attacked the shadows with a lightning-quick series of complex karate blows. This physical activity served to awaken him completely, and he stopped briefly at the adjoining head to relieve himself and wash up.

The reflection staring back at him from the bathroom mirror was that of a stranger. The full salt-and-pepper beard that covered most of his face was less than a month old. He hadn't worn his hair this long in years, and it felt odd lying against the middle of his back.

Of course, there could be no mistaking his rather large, flat nose, which had been broken too many times to set properly. Familiar dark brown eyes stared back at him beneath thick, bushy brows, and even though his grandmother had warned of bad luck, he allowed them to merge at the bridge of his nose. His late wife, Carmen, had always said that he reminded her of a muscular version of Charles Manson whenever he let his hair and beard grow. How very ironic it was to favor a mass murderer, when in reality he was only putting on yet another disguise for his occupation as a paid, government hit man.

Still serving his country at an age when most men would be counting the days to retirement, Mariano could escape the ravages of age by the strength of his convictions. There were serious affairs of state to attend to, and he would somehow channel his energies to keep his worn body going. After all, final victory would soon be theirs, and there'd be plenty of time for rest in the halcyon days to come.

With this hope in mind, he exited his quarters and headed for the detention block. The rock-hewn passageway was lit in red, and Mariano's eyes needed time to adjust to the dim conditions. With brisk, clipped steps, he passed by Operations, where a trio of technicians were seated at their workstations, needle-shaped stalactites hanging from the irregular ceiling above them.

The cavernous rock-walled room in which they worked had been built by the Defense Department in 1963. It was one of seven so-called Delta Operations sites, secretly constructed beneath the United States to offer top military brass safe haven during a nuclear conflict.

The Freeman site was within easy driving distance to the Whiteman Air Force Base ICBM fields. Government architects had taken advantage of a naturally occurring limestone cavern to create a self-sufficient, blast-proof command post. An ample supply of prestocked foodstuffs, auxiliary power generators, and an unlimited source of fresh water from its own underground river guaranteed the site's survival should the unthinkable come to pass. In the event of war, select VIPs and their families would be evacuated to the cavern city, to ride out the attack and wait for the fallout to settle.

Along with billions of dollars of obsolete weapons systems, the Delta sites had been retired in the early '70's. Today, few in the Pentagon even knew they existed, and it was because of this anonymity that Mariano and his forces were able to clandestinely base their operations here.

The advent of computers and satellite communications allowed them to work with a minimal staff. Supplies were stored in bulk, and except for an occasional visit by one of their helicopters, the locals had no reason to suspect that this subterranean complex existed.

As site Commander, Mariano had many responsibilities, security among them. When the hand of fate, and a well-placed insider on the White House staff, conveyed Andrew Chapman practically into their backyard, Mariano's forces expanded their duties. The elimination of the Vice President was his top priority, and until he received concrete proof that Chapman was dead, he couldn't rest—so important was this to their mission's ultimate success.

In a cramped cavern offshoot that previously had held radiation-detection gear, they had built a detention cell. Except for the incarceration of an occasional drunk co-worker, this was the first time it had been officially put to use.

Mariano silently slipped into the darkened passageway outside this cell, and peered through the steel bars of the

locked entryway. There were two individuals confined inside. The redheaded female appeared to be in her early
twenties, and was dressed in tattered blue jeans and a
skimpy halter top. She looked like a local, and he focused
his attention instead on her companion.

Mariano guessed his age to be about fifty. He was attired
in wrinkled khakis and a dark blue polo shirt, with an empty
leather holster clipped to his belt. He was in superb shape,
and it was while studying his face that a relieved smile
crossed Mariano's bearded face. Somehow his men had succeeded in capturing one of the very men he had been so desperately seeking these past couple of hours.

"First Sergeant Vincent Kellogg, if I'm not mistaken,"
greeted Mariano from the shadows. "Or should I say Special
Agent?"

The shocked look on his prisoner's face was all the confirmation that Mariano needed to see, and he stepped toward
the bars and added, "It's been much too long, Kellogg. I believe the last time I saw you was back at Long Thanh, when
my team was headed in-country and you on your way
on the gravy train back to the States."

Mariano grabbed the cold steel bars, where there was just
enough light for his prisoner to see the face of the man who
was addressing him.

"Chief Mariano?" Vince spoke like a man seeing a ghost.

"That's me, Sergeant Spit and Polish. You know, there's
one thing I always wanted to ask you. Why would a Special
Forces soldier of your caliber turn down an opportunity to
join SOG and command his own team?"

Vince wasted little time replying. "I guess I couldn't
stomach the idea of earning my rice bowel being a cold-
blooded assassin."

Mariano grunted. "You're still a fucking geek, Kellogg.
You swallowed the company philosophy hook, line and
sinker, didn't you, my fine cunt-eating friend. It never did
get through that thick skull of yours that it's impossible to

win the game unless you're playing on a level playing field."

"Since you two obviously know each other, would you mind releasing us from this place? You have no right locking us up like this," protested Miriam. "And who are you, anyway?"

Mariano laughed. "Let's just say I'm a ghost from the past, sent here to torment your Boy Scout companion."

"Listen to the girl, Mariano," urged Vince. "I don't know what you're up to, but you certainly don't have the right to lock us up like this."

"You're going to lecture me on human rights, Kellogg? That's a laugher, coming from one who serves the great deceiver himself."

Mariano halted for a moment to regain his composure, and when he continued, he did so with a contained calmness. "We've been fated to meet again, my friend, and you might as well make the best of it. You've stumbled into a real goat fuck this time, Kellogg. But you don't know how lucky you are.

"I don't know what candles you're burning, but you were spared a certain death in the Crimea. Our mutual friend, ole spit and polish himself, Sam Morrison, took your bullet, Kellogg, as did our esteemed Commander-in-Chief and the rest of his pencil-pushing, butt-fucking entourage."

"Hold on a minute, Mariano. The President's been assassinated? And you're responsible?" Stunned, Vince suddenly remembered the partial alert they had fielded just before the black helicopter attacked.

"I warned you that it was a real goat fuck, Kellogg. And you still don't know the half of it. The only reason I'm even sharing this with you is that I need your help to complete my mission. I'm gambling that there's an ounce of unadulterated patriotism left in you, and that you'll listen to me with an open mind.

"The movement to which I've dedicated my life seeks to

redirect priorities, and put our beloved country back on the path to greatness. Only a total fool could believe that America is headed in the right direction. The country has turned its back on God, selling out for a quick, self-serving buck. We're spiritually bankrupt, and you have only to look to the top to see that ethics and morality are no longer a prerequisite for leadership.

"Like a malignant cancer, outside forces are at work undermining the foundations of Lady Liberty. For the first time in our history, foreign officers in the service of the United Nations, are leading American troops into battle. A so-called World Court attempts to order one of our states not to execute a convicted rapist and murderer, while the World Bank is busy redistributing our hard-earned wealth to undeserving nations far from our shores. We've lost our way, and have forgotten the last words of Founding Father John Adams, who went to meet his Maker proclaiming, 'Independence forever!'

"By the good grace of God, a group of patriots has gathered together to save America in its hour of need. I'm proud to be a part of this movement, whose ranks include dozens of high-placed government officials, military officers, and select civilians. With a nerve center here beneath America's heartland, we've taken that all-important first step in a second revolution. And even though many brave citizens have already died for the cause, their blood shall nourish America's rebirth."

"If I'm hearing you right," interrupted Vince, "you're talking about a coup d'etat. What could possibly motivate you to go to such an extreme?"

Mariano tightened his grip on the cell's steel bars, and his powerful voice rose in response. "To tell you the truth, we could have lived with the encroachment of One World interests and the moral corruption of our leaders. But the one thing that spurred us into action was the proposed Global Zero Alert treaty. With America's military might already decimated by foolish budget cuts and shortsighted planning, the treaty would have left us wide open to another Pearl Harbor-type sneak attack. A truly determined enemy wouldn't think twice before breaking the agreement, no matter how strict its tenets are. And hell, it's the threat of a nuclear war that's kept the peace for the past five decades!

"We urged the President not to support this dangerous experiment in arms control. But he wouldn't listen. So we were forced to intervene, by utilizing an assault force in the Crimea, to terminate his command and redirect the ship of state from a certain catastrophic collision." He paused, slowly smiling. "We thought it would be difficult to arrange, you know. But you can buy anything in Russia these days."

"What's a Global Zero Alert treaty?" asked Miriam, perplexed by the exchange.

Vince answered her. "It's an idea first proposed by the President of Russia, to prevent an accidental nuclear war by removing the explosive warheads from all the various delivery systems."

"Could you really sleep soundly at night knowing that our nuclear forces would be unable to immediately retaliate in the event of a surprise attack, Kellogg?" asked Mariano.

"It doesn't matter what I think as an individual," Vince replied. "If such a treaty were to be ratified by our Congress and signed by the President, I guess I'd learn to live with it."

A look of disgust filled Mariano's face. "Spoken like the good sheep that you are, Kellogg. Thank goodness there are others who see this treaty as the dangerous folly that it is, and have dared to act on their convictions."

"I still can't believe that any high-ranking military men would ever go to the extreme of actively supporting such a cause," remarked Vince.

Mariano grinned. "You'd be surprised, my friend. Our leadership comes right from the very top, and extends all the way down to the individual unit level."

"Certainly you're not talking about the Joint Chiefs?" Vince said.

"No. Their *Chairman*," returned Mariano, a twinkle in his dark eyes. "And not only does Admiral Trent Warner bring his years of experience to our movement, but also his own flying command post—Nightwatch.

"Now that the President has been eliminated, the Chairman has control of the nuclear football, making him the temporary head of state until the next in line is sworn in as Commander-in-Chief."

"But that's the Vice President!" blurted Vince.

"Precisely," Mariano retorted. "We know you're the Special Agent in Charge of Andrew Chapman's security detail. And as such, surely you can tell us where we can find him."

Now that Vince was aware of the favor Mariano wanted from him, he reacted instinctively. "You really think I'd tell you, after you sent Lewis Marvin and one of your teams to blow us out of the water?"

"Damn it, Kellogg! You always were a stubborn, pig-headed asshole. I'll give you fifteen minutes to reconsider. Then we'll kill the girl, with you to follow."

Mariano disappeared into the shadows, and Vince looked at Miriam, sensing both her fear and her confusion.

"Who was that guy, and what on earth was he talking about?" she questioned, tears clouding her big green eyes.

Vince hugged her. "He's a man I served with during the Vietnam War, and he's talking about taking over the United States government."

"I guess Pa was right, and the enemy really does have a base beneath Freeman Hollow," she remarked, unwilling to break Vince's protective embrace. "Was he serious about killing us?"

Vince checked his watch, and answered while scanning

the cell's interior. "I imagine we'll find out in about fourteen minutes. But instead of just waiting around until then, I say let's see if we can break out of this joint."

A hurried inventory found a filthy mattress rolled up in a corner, and a rusty bucket—their toilet facilities. A shelf had been carved into the rock beside the bucket, and they were somewhat surprised to find a half-filled plastic soda bottle on it, along with a brown plastic packet that Vince identified as an MRE.

"Are you hungry?" he asked while using his teeth to tear open the book-sized packet.

"Mister, I'm so nervous I can't even think about food. Don't tell me you're gonna eat?"

Vince emptied the MRE onto the floor and began sorting through its contents. "Let's see now, we've got a packet of beef stew, some apple jelly, Tabasco sauce, cherry-flavored beverage powder, a slice of pound cake . . . and here's some spearmint gum." He tossed Miriam this last item, and while she removed a piece, he pulled out a clear plastic envelope and eagerly tore it open.

"What in the world is that?" she said, referring to the four-by-five-inch, thin gray wafer he proceeded to remove and hold up like it was a precious gemstone.

"My dear, this MRE heater could be our ticket out of this dungeon," he whispered triumphantly.

Vince checked the cell's locking mechanism before unscrewing the half-filled bottle of soda and sniffing the contents. "It's flat and warm, but I guess it should do the trick. Give me a piece of that gum, and do me a favor and chew up the rest of the pack."

Miriam did as ordered and, after chewing three more pieces, handed over the entire wad. Vince added his piece to this collection, rolled the sticky wad into a ball, and stuck it to the side of the plastic soda bottle.

"Now go and unroll that mattress, pull it in the far corner, and get behind it," he instructed.

Vince began crumbling the gray wafer, and he deposited the broken-up pieces into the bottle. He then shook the bottle, and as soon as all of the gray chemical residue had dissolved, he tightly capped it. As expected, the plastic started to get hot from the reaction that was occurring inside, and Vince stuck the bottle directly on top of the cell's locking mechanism, then took off to join Miriam.

No sooner did he duck behind the mattress than a loud explosion sounded. A cloud of fetid smoke filled the cell, and they had to wait for it to dissipate before seeing if the lock had triggered.

At first glance, it appeared that the explosion had failed. The door remained in place, and Vince found it hard to hide his disappointment. He went up to the entryway, grabbed the steel bars, and when he yanked them toward him, the door swung open with a loud click. They were free to go, and both of them didn't tarry.

No alarms sounded as they began their way down a dark passageway. The rough limestone walls were solid, and Vince guessed that they had absorbed much of the blast's report.

Blind luck brought them to a long passageway where a cool draft of moist air invitingly beckoned. They headed directly into the breeze, and they heard the sound of rushing water long before seeing the current responsible for it. The stream itself was a narrow, quick-moving ribbon of white water, a good quarter the width of the Eleven Point. It snaked off in both directions, through a smooth limestone tunnel, and Vince supposed that it could just fit one of the three dark green fiberglass canoes he spotted sitting on an adjoining ledge.

Because of the rote nature of submarine duty, meals were something to look forward to. Of all the submarines in the fleet, the *Polk* featured an award-winning dining facility, with the best food service beneath the seven seas.

Brad Bodzin and Jaffers were certainly looking forward to their meal as they arrived in the mess, got in line for the steam table, and picked up their trays. They were scheduled to take the next sonar watch, and a full belly would keep the hunger pangs at bay throughout this six-hour shift. Both of the sonarmen filled their trays to nearly overflowing with hamburgers, baked beans, corn on the cob, onion rings, and French fries.

The only one of the twelve elongated, picnic-style tables that had two vacant places left was the one usually reserved for the Chiefs. COB was already seated there, along with the senior radio technician, Chief "Shorty" Hassler, and one of the boat's SEALs.

"Can we join you, COB?" Bodzin asked.

"Make yourselves at home," COB answered.

They wasted little time setting their trays on the red-and-white-checkered tablecloth, and they dug into their food like they hadn't eaten in a week. They were well into their respective meals when Mallott came over, wearing his customery khakis and royal blue polo shirt, complete with a crest displaying a palm tree and a colorful parrot, with JIMMY'S BUFFET embossed in gold below.

"Well, gents, how do you like your chow?" Mallott queried.

"I'm not complaining any, Howard," said COB. "But whatever happened to that low-fat, reduced-cholesterol menu you were promoting? Why, we haven't had turkey in a whole three days."

"Who said anything about abandoning my low-fat menu, COB?" replied Mallott with a wide grin. "Those are lean bison burgers you're scarfing down, with those rings and fries cooked in pure canola oil. Why, even your shakes are made of reduced-fat ice cream. Inside Jimmy's Buffet, you eat good and healthy at the very same time."

Mallott excused himself, leaving the diners to sip their shakes and reflect on their full bellies.

"Any luck tagging the bogey that struck the *Rhode Island*, Mr. Bodzin?" asked COB.

"Negative, sir. The current watch team hasn't heard a peep out of them. While I was in my rack, I played the tape of the collision over and over. Whatever the *Rhode Island* hit, it came out of a black hole, and returned there afterward."

"Maybe they struck a whale, or a submerged wreck," offered Shorty.

"I seriously doubt that, Chief," Bodzin replied. "The only thing that could have caused all that damage to the *Rhode Island*'s sonar dome was another submarine."

COB directed his next inquiry to their senior radio technician. "Hey, Shorty, what's the skinny on that latest salvo of EAMs? Are they legit, or just another drill?"

Shorty made certain that he had the undivided attention of all those present before replying. "The latest news is that this last alert was generated by a Russian test launch that was mistakenly thought to be the first wave of a full-scale nuclear attack. Lieutenant Ritter says our boomer was actually spinning up its missiles, and was less than ten minutes away from a launch when the termination order came down from TACAMO."

COB finished his milkshake and grunted. "Yet another reason to give some serious thought to that Global Zero Nuclear Alert Treaty that's been making the headlines lately. With our hair-trigger nuclear response, we've been very fortunate all these years that we haven't been the victim of an accidental war. Even if we have a legitimate crisis, at least if it took a while to marry up the warheads with the delivery bodies, there'd be some time for cooler heads to prevail."

"Bullshit!" replied the SEAL. "That fucking treaty is a one-way ticket to certain destruction. If such an agreement was signed, do you really think the Russkies or the Chinks won't keep a few nukes stashed away for safekeeping? Then if they got a hair up their ass, they could hit us with a surprise attack, and we'd never have the capability to retaliate. Hell's bells, they'd think nothing of blowing us to kingdom come, and we'd be down here stroking our cocks while our loved ones back home were being incinerated."

Both Vince and Miriam shouted out in relief when the underground river they had been following dumped them and their canoe unceremoniously into the Eleven Point. It had been a wild ride, which reminded Vince of an amusement-park log flume attraction.

With practically no direct lighting of any sort to illumine their way, they had been at the complete mercy of the narrow, swiftly moving subterranean spring. Vince steered from the aft position, and they somehow circumnavigated a twisting series of tight turns that ended with an incredibly sharp drop-off. They couldn't begin to count the number of times that the keel of their canoe scraped rock, and the gunwale had a nasty dent in it after they crashed into a protruding boulder. But they had survived their ordeal, soaked and chilled but none the worse for wear, and Vince's main priority now was to make certain they weren't captured again.

"Where are we, Miriam?" he asked from the rear of the canoe.

Twilight had arrived at this portion of the Eleven Point, and Miriam scanned the riverbank, where a low-lying veil of mist was beginning to form. "It appears that we're just upstream from Greenbriar Hollow."

A chorus of bullfrogs and cicadas sounded over the gentle rush of the water. Vince swatted at a pesky mosquito, and ducked when a small, brown bat flew close overhead. "Which way to the spot where we left your father?"

"Freeman is just north of here, upstream a mile or so."

Vince peered upstream. Except for the spot where the spring joined the river, the water was slack, and Vince wondered out loud, "If we could paddle up there, it would sure be easier than traipsing through the underbrush. Any rapids to speak of upstream?"

Miriam shook her head that there weren't, and Vince dipped his paddle into the clear water. With Miriam's help they made excellent progress, even with the added security precaution of hugging the bank whenever possible and proceeding with a minimum of noise. They spooked a doe and her fawn drinking from the river, and got an excellent view of a wicked-looking horned owl perched on a cottonwood limb.

With the advent of dusk, their night vision sharpened. Miriam didn't appear the least bit afraid of traveling on the river at night, and after rounding a wide bend lined with red cedars, she pointed toward an adjoining slough and whispered, "If we head up that backwater, we can pull up the canoe and go on foot to the Freeman overlook, where my Pa is hopefully still waiting for us."

They made landfall in a muddy swamp, and Miriam had to help Vince make his way onto dry land. She knew exactly where they were, and decided upon a route that would convey them to the overlook but keep them well away from the spot where they had been captured. Vince followed closely on her heels, this time being extra vigilant for booby traps.

After passing over a scrub-filled clearing, they began

their way up a steep ridge. Trees hugged the rocky soil, and the dusky sky was all but obliterated by the overhanging limbs, making visibility difficult. He tried to apply his Army training to make the best of his night vision. But even then he was unable to escape several painful lashings from projecting limbs and razor-sharp brambles.

Near the crest of the ridge, Miriam halted, cupped her hands around her mouth, and began softly cooing, like a turtledove. Less than a minute passed before an almost identical bird call answered from the ridge top, generating a broad smile on Miriam's dirty face.

"It's Pa!" she excitedly whispered.

The reunion that followed was a joyful one. While Amos Stoddard hugged his daughter, and Junior, Tiny, and C.J. waited their turns, Vince traded a warm handshake with Andrew Chapman.

"Sir," he said, "you don't know how good it is to see you."

Before Vince could continue, Miriam could be heard addressing her father. "Pa," said she, relishing the spotlight, "we almost got killed out there."

"When you failed to show up at the overlook to meet your brother, I thought the worse had happened," admitted Amos. "If anyone harmed a single hair on your pretty head, they're gonna hafta answer to me. Who captured you? Was it those damn foreign storm troopers?"

"It wasn't exactly the United Nations," said Vince to Amos and the Vice President in particular. "But I've got to admit that you were right, Mr. Stoddard. There is an unlawful, clandestine organization based beneath Freeman Hollow, and I just happen to know one of them personally. He's an ex-SEAL by the name of Dick Mariano. He was a bad seed when I served with him back in 'Nam, and the years haven't changed him any." He added, "I guess he and Lewis Marvin met there also."

"You did say living *beneath* the hollow?" questioned Amos.

"It's a regular underground city, just like Meramec Caverns, Pa," Miriam told him. "We were held in a cell with steel bars, and with Special Agent Kellogg's help, we escaped on an underground river, which brought us to the Eleven Point right near Greenbriar float camp."

"I bet that was Graveyard Springs," remarked Junior. "A couple of years ago, we followed it up from the river. It appeared to go for some distance, with plenty of clearance. And we would have explored it further till Tiny here thought he saw a ghost and we skedaddled."

"Hey, man, I swear I saw something weird in that tunnel," said Tiny. "Besides, the place gave me the creeps."

"Well, the spring goes a good distance beneath this hollow, all right, and we had us one whopper of a float to get to the Eleven Point," said Miriam.

"Kellogg," interrupted Andrew Chapman, "you never did say what this fellow Mariano's agenda was."

"Sir, if what he told us is true, we've got one hell of a predicament on our hands," Vince cautiously replied. "Mariano professes to being part of a revolutionary movement, comprised of high-ranking military and government insiders who are attempting a coup d'etat. Remember that partial alert we received right before the Huey attacked? Well, what's really disturbing is that Mariano admitted that their forces had already initiated the coup by assassinating the President in the Crimea."

Chapman appeared to be stunned by this revelation. The blood drained from his face, and he gazed blankly at Vince. "Did he give you any concrete proof of this?"

Vince somberly shook his head. "Mariano might be a few cards short of a full deck, but I don't think he's a liar. He says that the Chairman of the Joint Chiefs of Staff is the ringleader, and that he's orchestrating the coup from Nightwatch."

Chapman's expression suddenly changed to one of introspection. "That son of a bitch! No wonder they want me out of the way. Warner wants to take over himself. I should have seen it coming—the incredible hostility he's shown to our defense-budget proposals these last couple of months, and his abhorrence of SALT Two, the Global Zero Alert Treaty, and any other arms-reduction agreement with the Russians." Pausing for a moment to massage his forehead, he added, "A coup d'etat, of all things. But what can we do about it?"

Vince beckoned to the case holding the SATCOM, then looked up to meet the curious gaze of Amos Stoddard. "First off," said Vince with urgent firmness, "we're going to need your trust and support. I realize that you have some legitimate gripes against some of the people in Washington, but I know down deep that you love the country itself."

"Bringing back my baby safely showed a lot of moxie," Amos acknowledged. "And I guess all government employees aren't that bad. I owe you one, Kellogg, so how can we help?"

Vince gestured toward the SATCOM unit, and asked, "Can we deploy it?"

Amos glanced at his son and his two associates, then turned his gaze back to Vince and nodded. Vince immediately knelt beside the case, unsnapped the lid, and anxiously switched on the battery pack. He allowed himself a brief smile when a green light began glowing from the "ready to transmit" port.

"Now I need someone to climb that cedar behind me and place the satellite dish on the topmost accessible limb, pointing to the southwestern horizon," he instructed.

When no volunteers stepped forward, Amos looked at his son, and Junior meekly nodded. "I'll do it, mister."

It was while Junior began his climb that Vince turned to the Vice President and said, "Now the million-dollar question is, who do we call?"

"The only person I trust in Washington is my dog," remarked Chapman. "And since the finger of blame appears to be pointed directly at our esteemed Chairman, I say we go right to the source."

"You want to contact Nightwatch?" Vince asked, his surprise most obvious.

"Though I don't think it's prudent to talk with Admiral Warner, I do know someone on board who's a trusted friend. I went to high school with Major William Foard, the plane's pilot, and if anyone can unravel this mystery, Coach is the one."

Since most of the communications traffic aboard Night-watch was generated to and from the operations staff, Red was a bit surprised when a High Frequency, satellite-relayed call arrived for the 747's senior pilot. She connected it directly to the cockpit, and had all but forgotten about the call until Coach contacted her several minutes later and discreetly asked her to meet him in the upper-deck rest area.

After temporarily transferring her duties to Sergeant Schuster, Red excused herself for a rest-room break and headed straight upstairs. Waiting for her in the flight crew's lounge area was not only Coach, but Commander Cooper as well. Both of them looked worried, and Coach addressed Red in a conspiratorial whisper.

"I don't suppose it's possible to trace that call I just received, to determine both its point of origin and its legitimacy?" asked Coach.

"Did you get a breather?" This light remark didn't break the barest of smiles, and Red added in all seriousness,

"Though I'm unable to trace the call's exact origin, I can tell you that it arrived on a Level One encrypted line, usually reserved for NCA personnel working out of the White House or Executive Office Building."

"Would that include the Vice President?" Coach queried.

"Most definitely," Red answered.

Coach looked at Brittany and then back to Red. "Strange as this might seem, that call supposedly originated from a Secret Service SATCOM unit situated deep in the Missouri Ozarks, with the caller himself none other than Andrew Chapman."

"That's wonderful news!" Red exclaimed. "Does either the Chairman or Captain Richardson know this? FEMA has been going absolutely crazy trying to locate the VP."

Coach put his right index finger to his lips to remind Red to keep her voice low, and he worriedly shook his head. "I think it's wise if we keep this news to ourselves at the moment."

"But why?" Red countered. "If the VP's still alive, that means we have a Presidential successor to swear into office, and that we can finally transfer the reigns of power from Nightwatch."

"Red," said Coach, after accepting a solemn nod from Brittany, "I realize I'm taking a chance sharing this with you. But you've always been a trusted ally, and both Commander Cooper and I are going to need your unique expertise in a matter of the gravest importance to our nation's survival. Andrew Chapman just informed me that he too has been the recent victim of an assassination attempt. He swears that the individuals behind this attempt are the same ones who killed the President, and that they've taken this extreme course of action in order to take over the United States government."

"Is it the Russians?" Red questioned.

Coach shook his head that it wasn't, adding, "Here's the kicker, Sergeant. The Vice President seems to think that the coup is being orchestrated from this aircraft, and that our esteemed Chairman is the ringleader!"

A look of utter disbelief filled Red's face, and Brittany quickly chimed in. "I know just how you're feeling, Red. Coach shared this with me seconds before you arrived up here, and I'm still stunned."

"Without us knowing?" Red managed to say, her voice filled with skepticism.

"I have no doubt whatsoever that the man I talked with was Andrew Chapman," offered Coach. "We went to high school together, and we had a chance to get reacquainted last summer, when I piloted Air Force Two during his trip to India."

"And I happen to know the Secret Service agent who originally fielded this SATCOM call on the VP's behalf," Brittany revealed. "Special Agent Vince Kellogg is a personal friend. In fact, his wife, Kelly, is closer to me than my own sister, and I'm even dating Vince's brother, Thomas. Vince Kellogg is not the type of man who can be easily fooled, and if he says there's trouble aboard Nightwatch, then we'd better take serious note."

"Do you think anyone else is involved? Do you think . . . even Colonel Pritchard?"

Coach tried his best to ease her fears. "The Colonel might very well be, Red, though Andrew Chapman didn't mention him by name. At the moment, the only thing we can do is to proceed as if everyone aboard this aircraft is suspect."

The cabin began shaking in the grasp of a sudden pocket of outside turbulence, and Coach alertly grabbed the nearest handset when the intercom activated with a loud chime.

"Foard here . . . I felt it, Lucky. Go ahead and hit the seatbelt warning sign. And don't bother to wake up Major Lassiter. I'll be back up there in two shakes of a stick."

"Did the Vice President mention what his immediate plans were, or suggest what we can do to help rectify the situation?" asked Brittany as Coach hung up the handset.

"The VP and Special Agent Kellogg were planning to remain incommunicado, investigating the plot from their end," replied Coach. "They're depending upon us to determine the true extent of the Chairman's involvement."

"And if he's indeed the ringleader?" Brittany dared to say.

Yet another pocket of turbulence shook the cabin, and Coach answered while grabbing an overhead handhold. "We'll address that when and if we have to. Right now, there are too many unanswered accusations, and we need some solid evidence. I'm going to get back to the flight deck before my associates get suspicious, and I'm relying on the two of you to see what you can come up with back in Operations."

"What can I do?" Red inquired.

"For starters," replied Coach, "how about compiling a list of all the Chairman's outside telephone conversations? He can't run a successful coup without being in constant contact with his supporters back in the CONUS."

"That shouldn't be too difficult to come up with," said Red.

"I'm going to take a closer look at the Admiral's tactical log," said Brittany. "The strategic considerations in a plot of this magnitude are considerable, and if the Chairman is really attempting a military-backed coup d'etat, it should show up in his SIOP folder."

"Sounds good for starters, ladies," said Coach, who momentarily lost his footing when the fuselage canted hard to the right. "Now I'd better go find us some stable air. Be careful. And remember, trust no one."

Thomas Kellogg stepped over the fallen oak trunk without breaking his stride. Considering the dwindling-light conditions, the nine-man Sapper squad that he was following was moving with an incredible swiftness, and it was taking a full effort on his part to keep up. The Sappers had been given the lead position, with Sergeant Reed walking point. They were moving in a modified wedge formation, an eight-meter interval between soldiers.

Twenty-five meters behind, also moving in a wedge, were Ted Callahan and the MPs. Ranger Glickman was included in this group, which was heavily armed with M16s, SAWs, and M60s. Since their encounter with the meth bootleggers, they were extra cautious to be on the lookout for booby traps, but this still didn't keep them from moving at a blistering pace.

Thomas was starting to feel the fifty-five-pound rucksack that he wore on his back. The heat and humidity were fierce, and to slake his ever-present thirst, he took cautious sips on the plastic tube of the Camelbak water bladder that was stored in his ruck.

The sun had long since set, the fading hues of the midsummer twilight barely visible through the tree limbs. In the forest a gray darkness prevailed, and as his night vision sharpened, Thomas attempted to put to use some of the limited-visibility techniques he had learned in the Air Force. Even then, he stumbled over too many fallen branches to count, while saplings slapped his face, and sharp thorns tore at the rip-stop cloth of his camouflaged BDU pants.

He was ever thankful for the protective goggles the Sappers had given him, and as he wondered when he'd have time to utilize the NVGs that were stashed on his back, the soldiers in front of him raised their open palms overhead. The squad halted, and from the center of the wedge the PL could be seen slapping the cargo pocket of his BDUs.

Thomas moved forward to participate in the map check. He knelt beside the PL, and they were joined by both the compass men and the pace men, as well as the veteran walking point. Sergeant Reed was the consummate professional soldier. As the senior Sapper leader course instructor, he was an expert at his unique craft, and Thomas could sense the respect that his fellow soldiers afforded him.

"If you didn't know any better, you'd think we were back home at Leonard Wood," commented Reed, who spat out a torrent of tobacco juice and pulled out a red-tinted flashlight to illuminate the PL's map.

While they tried to decipher the detailed topographical map, the sound of footsteps foreshadowed the arrival of Ted Callahan, Captain Christian, and their U.S. Forest Service representative.

"Looks like that's it for the last light of dusk," was Callahan's greeting. "Anyone know the moon phase?"

"It's a day away from the first quarter," Reed answered. "Since the sky is clear, and is forecast to remain that way throughout the night, we should have plenty of natural, ambient illumination."

Thomas noted that Jody Glickman was carrying a full rucksack herself, and he watched her kneel beside the small knot of soldiers gathered around the map.

"We should be right about there," she said, pointing to a quadrant near the center portion of the wilderness area. "We've already passed Fiddler Spring, which puts us on the northern slope of Slash Bay Hollow, with Freeman the next hollow to the south."

"How are you doing reading the trail, Sergeant?" asked Callahan.

Reed spat out more tobacco juice before answering. "Right now, I'm following the dog tracks. There's still seven individuals in the party, with one of them either a woman or a large child. Because the soil's getting increasingly rocky, and since it hasn't rained in these parts for a while, with nightfall and all, it could get difficult."

"Well, we don't have much farther to go, since it's obvious they're headed into Freeman," said Callahan. "Sergeant Reed, you and your Sappers will continue to lead the way. Per our OPORD, I think it's best if we move in a file formation from here on in and slow down the pace a bit. And for those who've got them, it's time to deploy the NVGs. The army that can fight at night is the army that wins."

Friday, July 2, 9:03 P.M. C.D.T.

Freeman Hollow

"The more I think about it, the more I fear that Coach didn't believe my warning," said Andrew Chapman.

Vince was seated on the same fallen oak trunk as the VP, and he replied while gazing up at the ever-darkening portion of sky visible from this portion of the overlook. "You've got to admit it was an earful, sir. It's only natural for him to be cautious at first. And if he's really the outstanding officer that you say, he'll get over his initial skepticism and begin looking into the matter."

"I'm beginning to have second thoughts myself," mumbled Chapman, strain and frustration clearly visible on his tanned face.

From the other side of the clearing, Miriam could be heard talking with her father. "Pa, I think I'll go down and see if I can help Junior find Satan."

"Absolutely not, young lady!" retorted Amos, who had been passing the time whittling a maple branch. "I told your lamebrained brother that we're gonna skedaddle from these parts once night falls, and if he doesn't hurry and get back up here, he, Tiny, and C.J. are gonna be traveling solo."

"I sure hope they're staying far away from Tater Hill," offered Vince. "Those boys don't have any idea what they're up against out there. Mariano's a skilled tracker who's specially trained to hunt down and kill his fellow humans."

Amos peered across the clearing, and made it a point to slice off a thick piece of wood before responding to this warning. "My boy might be a little short in the brains department, but one thing he can do is survive in the woods. Shit, I taught him myself, and Junior was stalking deer when most boys his age were still on the breast."

A booming explosion sounded nearby, seemingly punctuating this bold comment, and after flinching, the occupants of the clearing nervously stood. They stared into the blackened hollow, vainly trying to see any visual aftereffects of this resonant blast, which Vince attributed to either a grenade or a mine.

"Junior!" exclaimed the worried parent, who dropped his knife and went sprinting into the woods, toward the direction of Tater Hill.

Miriam followed her father, and Vince cried out, "Damn it, Miriam, come back!"

She didn't, and Vince listened as the VP beckoned toward the woods, saying, "We can't go and abandon them now that there's trouble afoot, Kellogg. Besides, one of those boys might be hurt, and could use our help."

Vince could hardly believe his eyes when Chapman brazenly pursued Miriam into the forest, leaving him no alternative but to curse angrily and follow.

"Sounded to me like a claymore," Sergeant Reed told Thomas and the other Sappers gathered at the head of the formation. "And best guess is it blew a couple of klicks due south of here, smack in the heart of Freeman Hollow."

Thomas nodded in agreement, listening carefully as the senior Sapper instructor began detailing the manner in which they'd proceed, now that yet another threat had to be contended with.

Red somewhat halfheartedly prepared to initiate her computerized scan of the phone logs, unable to give this project her complete enthusiasm. Though she had a sincere respect for Coach, the bizarre warning that he had shared with both her and Commander Cooper sounded more like the disturbed rantings of a paranoid conspiracy buff. Of course, this was definitely not the type of behavior that one would expect from the senior pilot of one of the Air Force's most important aircraft. She knew that Coach and his fellow flight crew members were subject to frequent, intensive physical examinations that included a comprehensive psychological evaluation. There was no way that he'd be allowed to command Nightwatch unless he passed these tests with flying colors, and Red supposed that a mental ailment was most likely out of the question.

Coach therefore deserved her support, and she felt a bit embarrassed for questioning his sanity. After all, it took immense courage on his part to even share this warning, and for him to pick Red showed how much he trusted her. To properly investigate an unthinkable event of this magnitude, an open mind was needed, and she decided to hold back further judgment until the facts were on the table.

To access the proper phone log, she needed to input the Chairman's personal key number. Each crew member aboard Nightwatch had one of these numbers, which had to be fed into the computer before initiating either a telephone, radio, or data transmission. Because she was responsible for placing the majority of Warner's calls, Red was most familiar with his key number, and she inputted the sequence 4-6-1-3-3 into her keyboard.

Before initiating her query, she looked up from the monitor and took a moment to scan the Operations Team Area to see which senior officers were present. She felt like a conspirator herself upon determining that neither the Chairman nor any members of his immediate staff were in the compartment. Across the aisle, Sergeant Schuster was busy with a systems diagnostic, with Colonel Pritchard last reported to be aft in Technical Control. If she was going to proceed without being caught, now was the time to do so, and she took a series of deep, calming breaths before readdressing her keyboard.

She began her search on 2 July, at seventeen hundred hours. This was the approximate time that Air Force One had landed in Simferopol, and if a coup were being attempted, this time segment would be all-important.

A list of over one hundred transmission transactions filled her screen. Most of these were individual phone calls, dialed on the Chairman's behalf by either herself or Sergeant Schuster. The majority of the numbers were in the 703 area code, with the most frequent party being the Pentagon's NMCC. Another frequently dialed number was STRAT-COM operations, located outside Omaha, Nebraska.

It was hard not to miss the dozens of calls to the Russian Defense Ministry. Most of these Red had dialed, and though she knew the supposed reason they had been made, she couldn't help but wonder if General Alexi Zhukov was part of the plot.

Iron Man One was yet another frequent contact point. General Spencer would be an ideal individual for the Chairman to be working with if a coup were being attempted, though Red was unable to forget the caustic nature of their conversations. Most of them were characterized by intense arguments, not the type of cooperation one would expect from fellow co-conspirators.

She came across a long series of calls that had apparently been dialed for the Chairman by Sergeant Schuster. They corresponded to a variety of military installations located throughout the United States, and Red recognized the numbers to COMSUBLANT, NORAD, SOCOM, COMSUB-PAC, and a number of Air Force and Army installations, ranging from Andrews Air Force Base in Maryland to Georgia's Fort Benning. Several calls to individual combat units had also been made, leading Red to wonder why the Chairman would bother taking the time for such conversations when his subordinates could surely handle them for him.

She was in the process of scanning the most recent series of calls when she looked up momentarily from the monitor, in time to see Major Hewlett headed her way from the direction of the briefing room. She immediately hit the keyboard's escape button, the screen going blank just as the serious-faced Marine passed by her workstation. Red couldn't fail to miss the way he seemed to intentionally turn his head in an effort to see what she was working on. She met his inquisitive gaze with her best smile, and the SIOP advisor redirected his glance to the rear of the compartment without acknowledging that she even existed.

Disturbed by this encounter, Red wondered if Hewlett had been sent to spy on them. Could he be part of the coup? Hewlett was a new addition to the Chairman's battle staff, and as SIOP advisor, he would be an all-important ally if a coup effort were to succeed. Red supposed that his phone log could provide them with a wealth of information, and it was while wondering how she could get his access code that a sudden thought hit her. What proof did she really have that a coup d'etat was really being attempted?

Other than the wild tale that Coach had shared with them, she had yet to come across any solid evidence to support the Vice President's bizarre accusations. All of the phone calls that Warner had made these past couple of hours could be attributed to his routine duties as Chairman of the Joint Chiefs of Staff. Surely she was only letting her imagination run wild, and becoming overly paranoid herself.

After another series of deep breaths, Red decided to exit the phone log and reassess her participation in this foolish, time-wasting effort. To close the program, she had to reaccess the activity screen, and as the log reappeared on the monitor, her eyes were drawn to the very last entry. It referred to a phone number that had been placed sometime within the past minute from the Chairman's personal stateroom.

Since it was out of the ordinary for Warner to make such a call on his own, Red took a closer look at the number he had dialed. The area code 573 was an unfamiliar one, and she fumbled through her directory in an attempt to identify it. When this effort failed, she debated whether or not she should contact an associate in the NMCC and have her look up the number.

Discretion overrode expediency, and Red decided to do the detective work herself. She addressed her keyboard, and accessed the INMARSAT communications satellite serving this portion of the mid-Atlantic. It was in this manner that she reached a computerized information operator back in the United States.

"What area of the CONUS does the area code five-seven-three correspond to?" she queried via her keyboard.

Only a few seconds passed before her screen filled with the data—SOUTH-CENTRAL MISSOURI.

Red was unable to forget that Vice President Chapman's SATCOM warning was supposedly broadcast from this same location, leading her to wonder who it was in the Missouri Ozarks that Admiral Trent Warner had just gotten off the phone with.

While Red was in the process of taking a closer look at the Chairman's phone log, Brittany was seated in the briefing room, her open laptop before her. Now that Major Hewlett had left the compartment to join Colonel Pritchard in Technical Control, she was free to reinitiate her investigation into the possibility that a coup was being conducted from Nightwatch.

As it turned out, the Chairman's SIOP advisor had just instructed Brittany to document in detail their reaction to the Russian missile launch that had occurred earlier in the day. This gave her the perfect opportunity to access the battle staff's tactical log and look for any suspicious deviations.

It was a joint staff decision that had brought them to DEFCON Two shortly after the initial warning from NORAD had arrived. Brittany also couldn't find fault with the decision to implement Counterforce package Zulu Tango in the event that the Russian missile had turned out to be an ICBM headed for the CONUS.

She noted with interest that the log stated that this was one of the rare instances, during these past couple of hours, when General Spencer aboard Iron Man One actually concurred with the Chairman. Normally the two commanders would be reading from the same page, and for a difference of opinion to be part of the official record was most unusual, as was the sealed folder she came upon at the end of the log. It contained their current SIOP options, and Brittany tried several different passwords to unlock it.

Knowing full well the Chairman's penchant for using football slang for his passwords, she tried every such term she could think of. She typed in "pigskin," "gridiron," and "quarterback sneak," along with dozens of other words and phrases, all to no avail. Since golf terminology was another one of his favorites, she was about to try this avenue of approach when the term "audible" popped into her head. She tried it, and the folder miraculously opened.

The targets listed were the exclusive responsibility of their Atlantic alert platform, the U.S.S. *Rhode Island*. Brittany needed an atlas to identify the corresponding longitude and latitude coordinates that the Trident warheads would be headed to in the event of war. Most of the targets were situated in central Russia and Siberia, with another scenario featuring a limited strike inside the People's Republic of China.

The final scenario possibility demanded but two of the *Rhode Island*'s Tridents. Code-named Yankee Hotel, the targeting coordinates were vastly different from the previous strikes. Once again Brittany needed the atlas to determine that one of the submarine's nuclear-tipped warheads was targeted at the airspace off the coast of Georgia, while strangely enough, the other was directed squarely at the Ozarks region of south-central Missouri.

Vince was able to catch up with the Vice President just as Chapman was in the process of reaching the bottom of the hollow. Frantic voices sounded ahead, the encroaching night veiling all but the trees and scrub that immediately encircled them.

"Mr. Vice President, you've got to slow down and think about what you're doing," warned Vince. "If that blast was a mine, it means that Mariano's men will also be drawn there."

"To hell with Mariano!" cursed Chapman, who was vainly attempting to extract his foot from a tangled snare of twisted branches. "Those poor folks need our help, and I'm not going to abandon them."

Vince realized it would be fruitless to argue his point further. He merely knelt, pulled the branches apart, and as Chapman pulled out his foot, Vince had time to deliver one more passionate plea. "At the very least, let me lead the way. If there are mines out here, I'll be the one to trigger them. Keep a good five paces behind, and try to step only where I do."

They proceeded in such a manner, Vince trying his best to navigate a safe course toward the voices that continued to sound in the distance. Though he failed to uncover a single trip wire or booby trap, they were unable to escape the overhanging tree limbs that scratched their faces and threatened to gouge out their eyes, the thorn bushes that grabbed at their clothes and skin like barbed wire, and the ankle-twisting, rock-filled potholes.

"Oh, sweet Jesus, Pa, ain't there nothin' we can do for him?" sounded Miriam's pleading voice from nearby.

Vince carefully scanned the forest in the direction of her voice. Because of the lack of direct light and the abundance of vegetation, it was all but impossible for him to see more than a few feet ahead. Andrew Chapman was practically standing on his heels, and Vince turned around and whispered, "They appear to be on the other side of this scrub. Please follow my every step, sir, and try to keep your distance."

To reach the others, they had to tear their way through a bramble patch, step over a succession of fallen timber, and circumnavigate an immense limestone boulder. This put them in what appeared to be a clearing of some sort. Stars could be seen twinkling from above, where the last light of dusk illuminated a scene that Vince would not soon forget.

Huddled in the center of the clearing were Amos, Miriam, and Tiny. C.J. lay in a bloody heap at their feet, his skull cracked open and his intestines hanging out of the large hole that had been blown in his lower abdomen. Junior was kneeling close to his fallen friend's side, his face covered in blood, the stiff corpse of Satan held tightly in his grasp.

"When I catch the bastards responsible for this slaughter, there's gonna be hell to pay!" warned Amos, who watched C.J.'s body issue a frenzied spasm before surrendering to the final throes of death.

"Not only did they set that trap, Pa, but they went and cut

Satan's throat," the still-sobbing Junior managed to mutter. "They're nothin' but a spineless bunch of cowards!"

While Andrew Chapman moved in to comfort the bereaved, Vince pleaded for them to keep their voices down. Then he surveyed the clearing in which they stood. It didn't take him long to discover the piece of nylon fishing line that had served as the trip wire, and the jagged piece of green plastic proving a claymore mine was responsible for killing C.J. The claymore was a favorite weapon of SOG, and Vince scanned the surrounding woods, knowing full well that Mariano's forces were surely close by.

"I think it's best if we got out of this hollow with all due haste," Vince advised. "Mr. Vice President, I insist that we get moving this moment. Either you come with me voluntarily, or I'll carry you out of here by force if necessary."

Andrew Chapman was comforting Miriam. He had his arm draped over her shoulders, and as Vince moved in to enforce his ultimatum, a pair of green-faced, ghillie-suited individuals dropped out of the overhanging trees. At the same time, three heavily armed, BDU-clad commandos emerged from the woods, and though Tiny bravely charged into their ranks, Vince knew in an instant that resistance was futile.

". . . which leads me to believe that they plan to target both General Spencer aboard Iron Man One and the Vice President in the Ozarks."

Coach and Red breathlessly listened to Brittany's chilling words of warning from the hushed confines of the upper-deck rest area. Their worst fears were now realized, and they struggled to put the entire situation into perspective.

"Whomever the Chairman called in the Ozarks, they'd better have one hell of a fallout shelter if Yankee Hotel is ever implemented," Coach said with a worried shake of his head. "With both the VP and Iron Man One out of the way, Warner will have effectively wiped out the opposition."

"With the individual military units that he contacted standing by, should any unexpected obstacles be encountered," added Red.

"I still can't believe he really thinks he can get away with it," said Brittany. "And what could his motives possibly be?"

"Megalomania, delusions of grandeur, or some infantile

shortcoming that he never fulfilled—it really doesn't matter at the moment," replied Coach. "The one thing we have to focus on is how we're going to stop him."

"If only we could get the Vice President to address the American people," suggested Red. "Once they see him alive, and he's sworn in as the new President, Warner's forces won't stand a chance."

The cabin shook slightly, and Coach replied while steadying himself on the edge of the table he was standing beside. "The question remains, how can we help the VP in the meantime?"

"I think it's only obvious that we have to share our findings with General Spencer," offered Brittany. "As the EAO aboard Iron Man One, he's the second most powerful man in the country until the next President's sworn in, and with TACAMO at his disposal, he's in the best position to directly challenge Warner."

"You don't feel that Spencer could be part of the coup?" asked Coach, carefully testing the waters.

"At some point we've got to trust someone in a position of real power, and the General appears to be our only safe bet," answered Brittany.

"I agree," concurred Red. "I can't forget the way Spencer took on the Chairman earlier. They were arguing away like a bunch of schoolboys, and even if it does turn out that Spencer's a coup insider, he can't be a happy camper."

"Then we'd better be giving the good General a call," said Coach, who removed the "NO FEAR" ball cap he was wearing, and smoothed back his full head of wavy black hair. "As aircraft commander, I'll shoulder the responsibility of passing on the bad news. Now all I need is a secure line to Iron Man One."

Red flashed him a thumbs-up, and less than five minutes later, Coach was sitting alone in the upper-deck rest area, sharing his suspicions of the impending coup with General Lowell Spencer.

* * *

"Sir, we've got a security compromise—upper flight deck rest area, unauthorized SATCOM transmission."

Trent Warner had been dozing on his stateroom's cot when this call arrived. He snapped awake instantly upon hearing the gravelly voice of his SIOP advisor, his mind already considering the manner in which they'd react to this serious infraction.

"Who's the call directed to?" he queried.

"Iron Man One," answered Hewlett.

"Shit!" cursed the Chairman. "Major, tap the call, and quietly assemble the security team. We'll meet at the forward entry area. And let's pray that someone up there is only schmoozing with an old friend on Uncle Sam's dime."

". . . I'll try to get that information to you, General . . . So I understand, sir. I'd rather not reveal their names at the moment, but rest assured that they're trusted members of the battle staff . . ."

Coach got the impression that Spencer appeared to be genuinely stunned by their accusations, and if he was in fact a coup insider, he was certainly doing a superb job of expressing his shock. The General was in the process of relaying his own suspicions regarding the Chairman's actions of late when Coach noticed a newcomer at the head of the upper-deck stairway. One glimpse at the pistol this individual carried in his right hand was all Coach needed to abruptly disconnect the line. He was just hanging up the handset when the head of the airplane's security team emerged from the stairs, followed by Major Hewlett and the Chairman.

"Sergeant, arrest that man!" ordered the Chairman, pointing at the stunned pilot.

Coach tried his best to control his pounding pulse, and he

raised his hands overhead and addressed Admiral Warner in his most innocent manner. "Excuse me, sir. Did I do something wrong?"

"How about treason for starters!" replied the Chairman, who beckoned toward Coach and spoke to the security man. "Sergeant, handcuff the Major and hold him in protective custody in my stateroom until further notice."

"Sergeant," countered Coach, "it's Admiral Warner who's to be arrested. As aircraft commander, I officially charge the Chairman with complicity to carry out a coup against the government of the United States of America."

A look of confusion momentarily crossed the Sergeant's face, and the Chairman alertly retorted, "Sergeant, I said to handcuff Major Foard and to detain him in my stateroom. The man's delirious, his paranoid rantings the byproduct of Russian misinformation."

The barrel-chested security man had no choice but to carry out the Chairman's instructions, so he handcuffed the pilot's wrists behind his back and prepared to escort him down the stairway. Coach knew that it would be a waste of energy to further resist, and he looked at the Chairman and shook his head.

"Admiral, why don't you admit to yourself that the game is over? I know all about your involvement with the assassination of the President and the attempted murder of Andrew Chapman. You might lock me away, but rest assured that I'm not the only one in a position of power who knows about your misdirected coup attempt."

"From what little I've heard already, it appears that you've already managed to pass on quite an earful to General Spencer," revealed the Chairman, an icy coolness to his glance. "I'm certain that the good General will be fascinated to hear all about your nervous breakdown, Major. Do you promise to go quietly, or must we incapacitate you with a narcotic?"

Coach reluctantly bowed his head, signaling his wish to

proceed without further resistance. As he was led down the stairway, the Chairman looked at his SIOP advisor and discreetly whispered:

"Major, before I attempt damage control with the good General, I think it's time to contact the U.S.S. *Truman*. Under the circumstances, I feel it's only prudent that both Nightwatch and Iron Man One have a proper escort, and a flight of Tomcats should be sufficient. Then we'd better get Lassiter to take Foard's place inside the flight deck, and find out who the hell the Major's been working with inside this airplane."

Thirty years of military service had done little to prepare
Lowell Spencer for the perplexing situation that he currently
faced. He had just completed the second of two bizarre
phone calls, both of which had originated from Nightwatch
676.

The first of these calls was made by the 747's senior
pilot. Spencer knew Major William Foard personally. He
was a likable young man, with a propensity for wire-rimmed
sunglasses and unauthorized headgear. Both of them had
been B-52 commanders in the earlier stages of their careers.
Although the General had never flown with Foard, for the
Yale graduate to go from nuclear-armed bombers to an important assignment such as Nightwatch spoke well for his
many talents.

With such vast responsibilities to shoulder, Foard
wouldn't be the type of person prone to baseless accusations. That was only one of the reasons Spencer had listened
closely to the wild tale he had hurriedly related—a story

purporting that Admiral Trent Warner was currently attempting to orchestrate a coup d'etat. According to Foard, it was the Chairman who was responsible for killing the President and attempting to assassinate the Vice President, who was still alive in the Missouri Ozarks and running for his very life.

Foard had also stated that he had solid proof that the Chairman had recently contacted his fellow coup forces in the Ozarks, and had also alerted various military units throughout the CONUS. And to take this wild tale one step further, he claimed that Warner had also created an SIOP file, in which both the Ozarks and the airspace above Iron Man One's patrol sector off the coast of Georgia were to be targeted by a pair of the U.S.S. *Rhode Island*'s Tridents.

Before he could learn the grounds for Foard's accusations, the pilot had abruptly signed off, leaving Spencer seated at his console inside TACAMO's battle-staff compartment, scratching his head in pure bewilderment. There was always the possibility that Foard was telling the truth—that his facts were accurate—and that a coup was indeed being orchestrated by Warner aboard Nightwatch. Coach could also be the victim of misinformation. Or he could have snapped.

It was this latter condition that Trent Warner had just called to warn him about. During the course of this curt, one-sided conversation, the Chairman revealed his reluctant decision to have Foard placed in protective custody because of a complete nervous breakdown.

Spencer cautiously acknowledged the receipt of a recent phone call from Foard. He also admitted that the pilot had made some pretty wild accusations. To appease the Chairman, he readily accepted his apology for Foard's aberrant behavior, and they signed off without further mention of the entire incident.

In his thirty years of Air Force service, he had certainly seen his fair share of men who had taken the sudden, unexpected plunge into insanity. No matter the stringent, psychological tests that all pilots had to pass both before and after they received their wings, the pressures of the Cold War had broken many a bomber pilot's spirit. Perfectly sane one moment, completely deranged the next, they suffered the cost of doing business under stress levels that no man was impervious to.

Foard could very well have succumbed to the enormous pressures of his job, and this breakdown could have generated the paranoid delusions he had so passionately warned about. Yet what if he hadn't gone insane and the coup was real? Was Trent Warner trying to pull the wool over his adversary's eyes?

Spencer couldn't forget how unwilling the Chairman had been to place the blame on the Russians for assassinating the President. He had even balked at accusing the Russians of colliding with the U.S.S. *Rhode Island*, and had subsequently resisted altering the nation's alert status in the face of these belligerent acts. Was the reason for his hesitance based on an unwillingness to go to war with Russia for acts that his own forces were responsible for? Spencer hated the idea of having to even consider such a distasteful scenario, though he'd be negligent for ignoring it completely.

"Comm," he said to his communications officer, who was seated in the aft portion of the battle-staff compartment. "Now that Nightwatch six-seven-six has got its feet wet, keep me informed of any alert traffic that it might attempt to transmit on its own."

Almost as an afterthought, he personally contacted the headquarters of the 1st Air Force in Langley, Virginia, and ordered a flight of F-15 Eagles skyward, to escort Nightwatch as it approached U.S. airspace.

"So you came back after all, Sergeant Spit and Polish. And just look who you brought along. Good evening, Mr. Vice President. Welcome to your worst nightmare!"

Vince, Andrew Chapman, the Stoddards, and Tiny stood in the darkened corner of an immense cavern. From their vantage point, their surroundings indeed looked like they belonged in a bad dream. Stiletto-shaped stalactites hung from the jagged rock ceiling, with thick gray stalagmites forming much of the cave's floor.

Dick Mariano orchestrated this nightmare from the center of the dimly lit chamber. The ex-SEAL was dressed in black VC pajamas and leather thongs. He held a Colt M4 carbine loosely at his side, and relishing this moment of triumph, he bowed in further greeting, a wide grin visible on his bearded face.

"You made me proud constructing that IED like you did, Sergeant Spit and Polish. And now you're back here, just liked I planned. By the way, your fifteen minutes are up. Are you ready to die, Kellogg?"

Mariano inserted a fresh magazine into his rifle, and Andrew Chapman dared to intercede. "What could possibly be so important as to warrant taking another man's life?"

"I believe you're more than qualified to answer your own question," said Mariano. "After all, that's what you do every time you send a soldier into battle for another one of your worthless, no-account, good-for-nothing causes."

With polished expertise, the ex-SEAL rammed a bullet into the rifle's chamber, clicked off the safety, and waved the barrel of the weapon toward them. "I want all of you to step backward and put your big butts against the wall. It's time to complete this cocksucking mission by putting the entire lot of you out of your fucking misery."

Vince sensed that Mariano wasn't bluffing, and that he intended to execute them right here in the cavern. As he joined the VP and the others up against the cold rock wall, he spoke out in a desperate attempt to stall for time.

"The very least you owe us is an explanation, Mariano. What did we do to warrant your wrath?"

"Goddamn it, Sergeant Spit and Polish! I've already gone over that with you. I'm tired, bored, and horny as all hell, and I want out of this infernal shit hole. So the sooner I take you geeks down, the better."

Junior was still seething with anger from the deaths of C.J. and Satan, and he brazenly rushed forward, oblivious to the rifle barrel that was soon pointed his way.

"Junior, no!" warned Amos, too late to stop the deafening burst of gunfire that filled the cavern with ear-shattering sound.

Bullets whined overhead, and Vince yanked the VP to the smooth rock floor and covered Chapman's body with his own. A ricocheting round careened off a stalagmite and passed inches overhead, so close that Vince could practically feel it shoot past his ear.

The firing stopped, and Vince looked up. Mariano stood before them laughing. Junior lay sprawled out on the ground, blood pouring from his right leg. His father and sister were already rushing to his side, and Tiny was close by, pointing at the ex-SEAL and boldly taunting.

"You think you're a big, tough guy, don't ya, mister. Well, I think you're nothin' but a lowlife coward, shootin' unarmed boys and cuttin' the throats of defenseless dogs. I dare ya to put down the rifle and fight me like a man."

Mariano laughed. "What do you think this is, a schoolyard? Some redneck bar? You want some of me, fine." And before Tiny could even flinch, Mariano took two quick steps forward and slammed the butt of his carbine into Tiny's forehead. Tiny went down like a bag of wet sand.

Vince found himself anxiously balling up his fists, thinking about taking Mariano while he was distracted. He passed the Stoddards and noted that the Vice President was attempting to tie an improvised tourniquet around Junior's bullet-ridden leg, and was already covered in the youngster's blood.

"Skipper!" yelled an excited voice from the other side of the cavern.

Vince halted in mid-step, and watched a green-faced, BDU-clad commando join Mariano in the center of the room. Though Vince couldn't hear what this newcomer proceeded to whisper into Mariano's ear, he clearly heard the ex-SEAL's surprised response.

"He *what*?" shouted Mariano. "Why, that pencil-pushing asshole! Didn't he think we could carry out this gravy-train mission?" He waved the muzzle of his rifle at the prisoners. "Lock up our friends here, and this time there'll be no MREs intentionally left behind. I've got to get on the horn with the man, and straighten out this cocksucking mess before all of us get butt-fucked."

They set up their tentative ORP inside the clearing where they had discovered the bodies of the young man and the German shepherd dog. Jody Glickman identified the unfortunate victim as a local named C.J. He'd been a close friend of the Stoddard family, and Thomas could only hope that Vince and the Vice President hadn't shared his fate.

Captain Christian's MPs discovered signs of a struggle, and a trail covered with footprints leading farther down into the hollow. They also found the green plastic claymore fragment that had most likely cut down C.J. Thus when they began their way down this promising new trail, it was with the utmost caution.

Thomas volunteered to be part of the point unit, a five-person Sapper team that would be conducting the initial route-sweeping operation. His responsibility was security, and he stayed right on the heels of their RTO, Sergeant Reed, and the two mine-detector operators.

Their NVGs lit up the night with a ghostly green tint. Thomas fought back the natural urge to hold his breath as they slowly inched their way forward. It was eerily quiet, with not even the barest of breezes present to rustle the limbs of the overhanging oaks.

While one of the mine-detector operators checked the trail for trip wires with a grappling hook that had fifty feet of rope attached to it, his co-worker crawled forth on his stomach, poking the earth with a ten-inch-long, stiff plastic probe. It was slow, tedious work, and just when Thomas began wondering if it was worth all the bother, the grappling hook snagged the first trip wire.

The taut nylon wire was all but invisible to the naked eye. It was set up to be triggered by either a foot or an ankle, and Sergeant Reed carefully followed it into the brush by the side of the trail.

Thomas was surprised when Reed beckoned him and pointed toward the device to which the trip wire was tied. "What do you make of it, Special Agent?"

Illuminated in the red-tinted beam of Reed's flashlight was a fist-sized metallic object, anchored into the ground on a wooden stake. It looked much like a large hand grenade, with the trip wire attached to a firing pin that was set into the top portion of the device. It definitely wasn't a claymore, and the doughnut-shaped rings that encircled the object's body, were unlike anything that Thomas had ever seen before.

"Perhaps Colonel Callahan can help us identify it," he suggested.

Ted Callahan had been following in the next team, and it didn't take him long to join them. Only a single glance on his part caused him to audibly gasp, and when he spoke, it was with shocked reverence.

"That, my friends, is a Yugoslavian Type PMR-2A antipersonnel mine. It's got a kill radius of fifteen meters, and is designed to kill and maim by fragmentation. Our units in Bosnia were the first to encounter it, and, I'm afraid to say, it appears we've finally found one of the mines that were stolen from Leonard Wood."

"Well, I think someone should go down there and check on his condition," said Lucky from the copilot's seat. "It's not like Coach to go and get sick like that."

Major Owen Lassiter was seated beside Lucky, and the pallid-faced backup pilot voiced himself while reaching up to make a minor adjustment to the navigation display. "None of us are immune to food poisoning, Captain. It can strike without warning, and take down the most healthy of individuals. I'll never forget my honeymoon in Acapulco, when I came down with the worst bout of diarrhea of my life. Poor Peggy, 'cause I didn't leave the toilet for three whole days."

"Ole Montezuma's revenge," mused Jake Lasky, their current flight engineer. "Yes, I know it well."

"That's only to be expected when eating in Mexico," countered Lucky as he pushed back his chin mike. "But all of us ate the same chow this evening, and none of us got sick."

"Look, Captain, I'm only passing on what the Op chief

told me," Lassiter retorted, a caustic edge to his voice. "And the initial prognosis was that Major Foard has come down with food poisoning, and that he's resting in the Chairman's stateroom."

"Come to think of it, Lucky," offered Jake, "Coach did order his club sandwich without bacon. I bet it was made especially for him, and that's why none of us hog eaters came down with the runs. It only further proves my case that health diets are nothing but dangerous fads, and that a body needs a variety of nutrients."

Lucky adamantly shook his head. "I wouldn't go that far, Jake. There are some foods that are—"

"Gentlemen," interrupted Lassiter, "would you mind piping down and keeping the idle chatter to a minimum? A guy can't get a moment's peace up here."

No sooner were these words spoken, than the nasally voice of the ACO broke over the intercom. "Flight, prepare for wire-out and the transmission of flash traffic."

"Roger, Comm," replied Lassiter into his chin mike. "Initiating orbit entry checklist."

Nowhere was the order to prepare for wire-out and the transmission of flash traffic met with more dread than in the 747's forward entry area. It was here beside the galley, in a small private nook reserved for the Operations staff, that Brittany and Red had gathered, on the pretense of taking a coffee break.

"I tell you, Red, I feel totally out of the loop," revealed Brittany, a mug of steaming black coffee cradled in her hands. "The Chairman and Major Hewlett have been playing their cards extremely close to their vests. They won't even include me in the standard SIOP briefings, and I'm afraid they suspect something."

"Don't feel alone, Commander," replied Red as she finished stirring her hot chocolate. "For the first time in the entire flight, neither I nor Sergeant Schuster is being allowed to place the Chairman's phone calls. From what I understand, Major Hewlett is making them personally, leading me to believe that our SIOP advisor is an inside player."

"If only Coach were here with us. He'd know what to do next," Brittany said worriedly.

"Food poisoning, indeed," retorted Red with a disgusted shake of her head. "That has to be one of the lamest excuses I've ever heard. He looked perfectly fine the last time we saw him. And what's this I hear about Coach being allowed to recuperate in the Chairman's stateroom?"

Brittany sighed. "Before meeting you here, I took a stroll by Warner's quarters. Coach appears to be in there, all right, along with an armed sentry outside and a DO NOT DISTURB sign posted on the closed door. They must have caught him red-handed talking with General Spencer, and then placed him in detention."

Red's troubled expression suddenly brightened, and she put down her drink, bent forward, and whispered, "You know, there's a way to get into that stateroom without going through the front door. The majority of my transmitters are located in the forward lower equipment area, directly below us. Behind the SHF SATCOM transponder is an access shaft, utilized both for ventilation and to hold power conduit. It's designed to fit a single individual, with iron footholds extending up the shaft, which extends right past the Chairman's stateroom, before terminating behind the flight deck."

"That's certainly good to know, Red. But before we're forced to go to such a dangerous extreme, I'll see if I can get some additional information on the nature of this flash traffic we're about to send. If it's indeed Yankee Hotel, our first priority should be to warn General Spencer."

Both of them had to reach out and grab their mugs when the aircraft suddenly initiated a steeply banked turn, this extreme maneuver but a precursor to the tight racetrack orbit that was next on their flight plan.

*   *   *

"Orbit entry checklist complete," came Owen Lassiter's flat voice over the conference room's intercom. "Wire-out in three minutes and counting."

The Chairman expectantly met the glance of his SIOP advisor, who was seated to his right, a laptop computer open on the table in front of him. "So the moment of truth is almost upon us, Major. When we originally made the difficult decision to support the movement, we knew there was the possibility that this dark hour would come. Brave Americans have already died, and now it looks like many more are about to join them. But such is the steep price of our continued liberty."

The sharp angle of the airplane's canted deck further steepened, and the Chairman alertly reached out and grabbed his fountain pen before it slid off the table. "Let's get on with it," he said with a heavy sigh. "Bring up Yankee Hotel on your screen. I want to take another look at that warhead selection."

Hewlett addressed his keyboard, and the monitor filled with a complicated targeting graphic, with the heading YANKEE HOTEL emblazoned in red at the top of the page. To better see it, the Chairman slipped off his bifocals, then scanned the screen, thoughtfully rubbing his temples.

"I realize it appears to be a major overkill just to eliminate a single individual," remarked Hewlett. "But now that we're certain Chapman is contained inside the wilderness area, we're going to need, at the very least, three 100kt MIRVs (Multiple Independently targetable Reentry Vehicles) to ensure complete saturation."

"And the number again on the estimated civilian casualties?" asked the Chairman.

"If we strike sometime within the next couple of hours, we can take advantage of favorable meteorological conditions to guarantee minimal fallout drift. The last weather report showed continued high pressure over the target area, with light, westerly winds prevailing."

Hewlett looked up from the screen, and made certain to directly meet the Chairman's gaze before adding, "Since St. Louis and Memphis are at the extreme edges of the fallout envelope, I believe the number of immediate fatalities can be kept below five thousand, with long-term radiation exposure limited to the towns of Poplar Bluff, Sikeston, Paducah, Bowling Green, and Memphis."

"That's a hell of a price to pay for one man," commented the Chairman. "But at the moment, we have no other options. If we don't get back on schedule, this entire operation is threatened, and until we get positive confirmation that Chapman's dead, we need this strike to be one hundred percent certain. Now, what's the word from FEMA?"

"Sir, the Director is prepared to issue an immediate press release blaming the blast on an explosion at an experimental nuclear reactor site located at a heretofore-top-secret Department of Energy research facility buried beneath the Mark Twain National Forest. The Secretary of Energy will support this claim, and will issue her own press release shortly after General Clayton at NORAD announces news of the test of a high-altitude, Star Wars-type antimissile weapon off the coast of Georgia and the subsequent crash of Iron Man One. He'll note that all other details must, of course, remain classified."

"To think that such a tragic accident will be responsible for taking the life of that esteemed hero of the Cold War, General Lowell Spencer," mused the Chairman, whose further comments were cut short by an unexpected knock on the conference room door.

Brittany poked her head inside and nervously cleared her throat. "Excuse me, sir," she said before entering the room.

"What the hell do you want, Commander?" barked the Chairman. "Can't you see that we're up to our necks with work in here?"

"That's just it, sir," returned Brittany, holding a legal pad and a pair of pens in her hand. "I understand that we're about to transmit an EAM, and as part of the SIOP team, I was wondering what I can do to assist you."

The Chairman shook his head in disgust. "Your services aren't needed at the moment, Commander. So get out of here, and shut that door behind you."

Brittany had already noted that Hewlett's laptop was activated, though from this distance she was unable to get a clear look at the flickering screen. Well aware of the steeply canted deck, and determined to secure a closer look at the monitor's contents, she "accidentally" dropped her pens. As calculated, they rolled down the slick linoleum floor, passing beneath both the Chairman's and Hewlett's outstretched feet.

Both of them bent over to retrieve the fallen writing instruments, giving Brittany the opportunity to take several quick steps forward and hurriedly scan the screen. She was able to make out only the two words emblazoned in crimson type at the head of the page before Hewlett emerged with her pens. Stunned by that which she had seen, she mumbled apologies, excused herself, and headed at once to Red's console in Operations.

Brittany's startling findings in the conference room gave Red no choice but to risk contacting General Spencer. She accessed a Milstar relay satellite to reach Iron Man One as it was flying over the Atlantic, some two hundred and fifty miles off the coast of southern Georgia.

As it turned out, Spencer was anxiously awaiting her call, and Red was able to confidently relate the strange facts regarding Coach's detention, and the alarming nature of the EAM that Nightwatch was preparing to send. Spencer was particularly interested in the EAM's contents, and one mention by Red that it concerned Yankee Hotel, and was about to be transmitted to the U.S.S. *Rhode Island*, was enough to cause the General to ask for additional details.

Red's reply was cut short by the hard barrel of a pistol shoved painfully into the back of her ribs. At the same time, the line with TACAMO went dead, and Red anticipated the worst, when Hewlett's gravelly voice urgently whispered into her ear.

"Sergeant, I think you know what this is all about. So either you can come with me quietly and no one else has to see this pistol, or you can resist and be shot. The choice is yours, ma'am, but please make it quickly."

Saturday, July 3, 0317 Zulu

Iron Man One

General Lowell Spencer sat dumbfounded before his console in the battle-staff compartment, the abbreviated Milstar transmission from Nightwatch still ringing in his ears. Though he never thought he'd be relying on an unknown master sergeant to deliver a strategic briefing of this importance, this entire situation was unprecedented. It was also extremely disturbing, and Spencer couldn't help but feel that it had an almost surreal quality to it. Yet reality struck home when the voice of the ACO sounded from his headphones.

"General, I've just monitored a rather puzzling VLF transmission from the U.S.S. *Rhode Island*, acknowledging the receipt of a properly formatted EAM. Since it didn't originate from us, and because we're the only TACAMO presently working the Atlantic, it must have come from Nightwatch."

Spencer ingested this news and fought the impulse to pound his fist into the overhead console. As shocking as it might appear, the threatened coup that he had been warned about appeared to be yet one step closer to fruition. It was completely against NCA protocol for Nightwatch to instigate an EAM without first informing either Iron Man One or the NMCC. And Spencer was beginning to wonder if Trent Warner was still in control of his faculties.

Once more his headphones activated, this time with the voice of their pilot. "We have some company headed our way, General. Radar shows a pair of high-performance jet fighters approaching our sector. They appear to be Tomcats, range a hundred miles and rapidly closing."

Spencer's stomach tightened; he was well aware that he knew nothing about any such fighter escort. Was it just a routine intercept by a pair of bored jet jockeys, or could there be a nefarious reason for their sudden presence, with Warner the one responsible?

He was unable to forget that the airspace directly above them was one of the supposed targets of attack scenario Yankee Hotel. Ever fearful that the F-14s had been sent in by the coup supporters to ensure that Iron Man One wouldn't interfere with the launch by challenging the EAM, Spencer knew that he'd have to act quickly.

"Flight, prepare for an immediate wire-out," he commanded into his chin mike.

It didn't take long for Iron Man One to begin a tight racetrack orbit. While the VLF antenna was deployed from the tail of the plane and the amplifiers powered up, he mentally formulated the EAM that he planned to send personally.

Standard nuclear-alert protocol would make it a waste of time to attempt contacting the U.S.S. *Rhode Island*. Captain Lockwood and his crew had been trained to ignore any alternative flash traffic not originating from the EAM's original source—in this instance, Nightwatch.

He thus had no choice but to direct his warning to Captain Benjamin Kram aboard the U.S.S. *James K. Polk*. Spencer would have to relay, in no uncertain terms, the shocking details behind Yankee Hotel, and then pray that Kram would believe him and move in to intercede.

The *Polk*'s SEAL team would have to be relied upon to use their mini-sub to board the *Rhode Island*, preferably while the Trident remained on the floor of the continental shelf, completing repairs. It would then be up to these SEALs to convince Lockwood that the EAM from Nightwatch was unauthorized, and that their missiles were in fact targeted on their own homeland.

There were ever so many additional details that remained to be worked out, and Spencer was spurred into action when the flight technician informed him that the power amplifier was up full.

"General," said the ACO, "we're ready to transmit."

Spencer attacked the keyboard. The system's analyzer automatically formatted his message into code, his efforts given new urgency by the amplified voice of the pilot.

"Tomcats continue to approach. They've yet to reply to our comms, though we've just been painted by their attack radar."

Spencer cursed his leaden fingers. Sweat began to form on his forehead, and his pulse quickened with the pilot's next update.

"We've just been instructed by the lead Tomcat to halt all VLF transmissions and reel in our wire. General Spencer, how do you want me to reply?"

Spencer ignored this question, trying instead to focus his complete attention on completing the EAM.

"Sir," cut in his SIOP advisor from the console to Spencer's right. "What the hell is going on out there, and why is that F-14 ordering us to quit transmitting?"

"Major Childress," Spencer anxiously replied, "I need just a couple more minutes to complete this EAM; then I promise I'll explain everything."

"General Spencer, sir!" exclaimed the pilot's frantic, amplified voice. "The Tomcats have threatened to attack unless we reel in our wire at once. Sir, I believe they're serious."

"Stall 'em, Captain!" Spencer ordered into his chin mike.

"Sir," interrupted his ACO from his console on the opposite side of the passageway. "For whatever reason, the threat from those Tomcats appears to be real. I recommend immediately ceasing VLF transmission, bringing in the reel, and sorting this thing out before it gets completely out of hand."

"I concur, sir," said the SIOP advisor.

Spencer was in the process of detailing the manner in which the *Polk*'s SEALS could convince the *Rhode Island* to terminate its launch. He had all but completed inputting this passage, when the intercom filled with the frantic voice of his pilot.

"Incoming rounds!"

This urgent warning was followed by a series of sharp, crackling explosions. The cabin began vibrating so violently that Spencer's hands slid off the keyboard. There was a sickening feeling in his gut as the aircraft abruptly broke out of its orbit and experienced a sudden loss of altitude. Alarms started going off, and thick, caustic smoke began filling the battle-staff compartment.

Spencer struggled to reach up and put on his oxygen mask, and he had to hold on for dear life as Iron Man One canted over hard on its right side, caught in the grasp of a heart-stopping death spiral.

"They've shot off our damned wire!" exclaimed the pilot while fighting to keep them in the air.

Saturday, July 3, 0326 Zulu

U.S.S. *James K. Polk*

Captain Benjamin Kram was informed of the Priority One transmission from TACAMO while in the midst of a routine inspection of the engine room. He quickly left Polk Power and Light behind, and headed forward to the radio room. He was met there by his XO, and together they read and reread General Spencer's rather complex, strangely compressed EAM. Neither officer had ever received such a peculiar message, which Kram conveyed to his stateroom so that they could discuss it in private.

"What do you think, Skipper?" asked the XO as he sat down on the stateroom's only chair. "Do you really think Admiral Warner could be responsible for orchestrating a coup and authorizing the release of nukes against our own citizens? Not to mention assassinating the President and attempting to kill the VP. It sounds to me like General Spencer has gone off the deep end."

Kram sat down heavily on the edge of his bunk, the dispatch still held tightly in his hands. "I've got to admit that it's a wild accusation, but General Lowell Spencer is one of the most levelheaded individuals I've ever met, and he's definitely not prone to paranoid delusions or outlandish exaggeration. I served with him for a short time while I was assigned to STRATCOM, and I got a chance to know both the General and his wife. Believe me, Dan, they don't come much better."

"Then if he's telling the truth, do you think that Trent Warner is capable of such heinous behavior? I mean, the Admiral's a fellow submariner, Skipper, and one of our proudest days was when he was named Chairman."

"I realize that, Dan. But what do any of us really know about the man?"

"Graduated at the head of his class at Annapolis, one of the few submariners to see combat during Korea and Vietnam, personally selected by Rickover to command one of the first Tridents, a tireless proponent of continued submarine development in the post-Cold War Navy—I believe his résumé is pretty much a matter of public record, Skipper."

"I'm well aware of that, Dan. But beyond his professional accomplishments, what kind of *man* is Trent Warner. What are his personal beliefs, frustrations, fears? Have you ever worked directly for him?"

The XO shook his head, and Kram added, "Well, neither have I, though I have several colleagues who served with him as recently as last year, during his short stint as CNO. From what I gathered from them, the Admiral was a difficult man to serve under, much like Hyman Rickover. Like Rick, Warner is incredibly intelligent, prone to fits of rage should his subordinates fail to meet his high standards. I also heard him described as hard-driving, a perfectionist, with an enigmatic dark side to his personality."

"Did you say dark side, Skipper, as in evil?"

"I wouldn't go that far, XO. What I'm referring to is a conversation I remember having with a neighbor of mine who served on one of Warner's submarines as weapons officer. I'll never forget his detailed descriptions of then Captain Warner's infamous wardroom chats. It seems Warner liked to use his wardroom as a bully pulpit.

"He demanded that his officers remain at table after dinner in particular, so he could preach to them on his favorite subjects—the dangers of American involvement with organizations such as the United Nations, the World Bank, the IMF, and the G-Seven. He had a particular abhorrence of strategic-arms-control treaties with the Russians, and constantly preached about the dangers of SALT Two."

"Then I can imagine what the Chairman thought about the President's support of the Global Zero Nuclear Alert agreement," the XO interjected.

Kram met his XO's stare, his eyes wide with sudden enlightenment. "You could be onto something, Dan. The grapevine had it that the President was on his way to the Crimea, preparing to sign that very same treaty. What an opportune time for a coup formed by opponents of this treaty to remove him from office."

"But why go and launch an attack using American nuclear warheads against our own people?" the XO countered.

"It's apparent that there's somebody at ground zero whom they've got to eliminate, and that they'll go to any extreme to do so," said Kram, who knew then that it was imperative for him to act on General Spencer's request with all due haste. "I see no harm in launching the mini-sub and sending the SEALs over to the *Rhode Island*. We're not in a state of war, and with their underwater telephone out of commission because of the collision, sending in Gilbert and his men is the only way we're going to get to Captain Lockwood and stop those nukes from being launched."

Kram stood up to implement this order, and his XO also rose, leaving him with one last question. "Even if we do manage to get over to the *Rhode Island*, why should he believe the SEALs? Wouldn't he consider them a possible enemy diversion, a bunch of spies he should lock up or shoot on sight? What's to keep Lockwood from meeting our boys with force, following his original EAM, and launching?"

"To guarantee that they'll take a moment's pause and listen to our argument, XO, I'm going to accompany SEAL Team Two myself!"

"It's true, all right," said Brad Bodzin to the members of his sonar watch team, after hanging up the intercom and shaking his head in wonder. "I just heard it from Mallott, who got the word from COB, who spoke directly with one of the SEALs—the Skipper's in that mini-sub even as we speak, and the XO's got the Jimmy K until Captain Kram returns from his visit to the *Rhode Island*."

"Speaking of the mini-sub," said Jaffers, headphones covering his ears, eyes glued to the BQ-7 waterfall display, "Sierra Three is purring away like a kitten, its course straight and true. ETA *Rhode Island* in twelve and a half minutes."

"Did Mallott say why the Captain's hanging with the SEALs?" asked Seaman Wilford from the BQ-21 broadband display.

"If I know our hands-on Skipper, he probably wants to be part of the first routine underwater transfer of personnel from an attack sub to a boomer," offered Bodzin, his practiced glance scanning the glowing CRT screens. "And then there's always the possibility that he's going along just to make certain that Gilbert and his gang behave themselves."

"I've got a contact, Sup," reported Wilford, in reference to the thick white line that had suddenly popped up on the left side of his sonar display. "Designate Sierra Six, biologic."

Bodzin checked this screen himself, and isolated the frequency that the screen was displaying on his headphones. The familiar crackling sound of shrimp met his ears, and he picked up the intercom handset that hung from the ceiling.

"Conn, Sonar. We have a new contact, bearing zero-six-one. Designate Sierra Six, biologic."

"Sonar, Conn. Designate Sierra Six, biologic. Aye, Sonar," returned a voice from the overhead speaker.

"What's the latest on Sierra One, Jaffers?" Bodzin questioned.

The broad-shouldered black man addressed the joystick that was situated on his console, and studied the pattern of vertical lines that filled the BQ-7's waterfall display. "Still not a peep out of them, Sup. They haven't stirred off the bottom, meaning that the big lady is still completing repairs to their dome."

"At least we're around to provide their ears, and their launch ability wasn't compromised during the collision," said Bodzin.

"Sup, I think you'd better take a look at this," interrupted Seaman Wilford, a definite edge to his tone.

Bodzin anxiously peered over his shoulder, quickly spotting the peculiar flutter in the BQ-21 display. It wasn't another biologic, a fact that Jaffers confirmed with an excited discovery of his own.

"I have a narrowband contact, bearing one-four-zero. Sounds like it just popped out of the thermocline, and it could be another submarine, Sup!"

Bodzin hurriedly fitted on his headphones. He utilized the auxiliary console to isolate the narrowband processor, and a deafening blast of static caused him to wince in pain. He turned down the volume feed, engaged the graphic equalizer, and the static faded, to be replaced by a barely audible throbbing sound that caused him to gasp in instant recognition.

"Conn, Sonar!" he shouted into the intercom. "We have a submerged contact, bearing one-four-zero. Designate Sierra Seven, possible hostile submarine!"

Dan Calhoun was in the narrow, elongated compartment just aft of the control room, talking with the SEALs who were responsible for launching their mini-sub, when the frantic warning from Sonar arrived. The XO dashed into Control, which was dimly lit in red to protect the men's night vision, and joined COB behind the two seated helmsmen.

"I had a bad feeling we hadn't seen the last of that damned bogey," whispered COB as his eyes scanned the various digital indicators showing that the *Polk* was currently traveling on a northwesterly heading, at a depth of four hundred and seventeen feet, with a forward speed of five knots.

"The Skipper knew the risks, and now it's up to us to keep Sierra Seven off our mini-sub's back," said the XO, suddenly aware of the heavy burden of his new command. "How soon until they reach the *Rhode Island*?"

COB glanced up at the bulkhead-mounted clock and answered, "Another ten minutes and eighteen seconds, sir."

The XO reached overhead for the nearest intercom handset. "Sonar, Conn. Do you have anything else on Sierra Seven?"

"Conn, Sonar," answered Bodzin's amplified voice. "I'm afraid not, sir. We're barely picking up a signature, though from all initial indications, there's a high-percentage probability that it's another submarine."

"Sonar, Conn. As soon as it's available, get me Sierra Seven's exact bearing and range. I've got to know if it's headed toward Sierra Three."

"Conn, Sonar. Aye, sir. We'll do our best."

The XO lowered the handset and solemnly addressed COB. "Something bad is going on out there, COB. I can feel it in my gut, and we've got to be prepared for the worst."

"We can always determine Sierra Seven's intentions by going active," suggested COB.

"Before we let them know that we're aware of their presence, we'd better be ready to rock and roll," said the XO, who raised the handset to his lips and addressed the entire crew over the 1MC. "Man battle stations torpedo! This is not a drill!"

Saturday, July 3, 0328 Zulu

Nightwatch 676

Brittany found the access shaft behind the SHF SATCOM transponder, just like Red had said. Once the rumor had begun circulating that Red had been incapacitated by the same intestinal ailment that had stricken Coach, Brittany knew in an instant the real reason for her abrupt disappearance. With both of her allies in detention, she had a choice of attempting this daring rescue or trying to stop the Chairman on her own. Now that the EAM had been sent, and Yankee Hotel was one step closer to being implemented, time was of the essence, and Brittany knew that whatever she did, it would have to be done quickly.

What Red had neglected to pass on was that a screwdriver was needed to remove the cover panel. Brittany found one in the flight avionics bay, an equipment-packed compartment that adjoined the forward lower equipment area. Brittany wasn't comfortable with tools, and it took a bit of doing to remove the screws and pry off the panel.

The narrow shaft inside was pitch-black, and she had to

return to the avionics bay to get a flashlight. This would hopefully be the last item she would need to initiate the dangerous task at hand, and she knelt before the now-open shaft and prepared to enter it.

It was at this inopportune moment that an airman entered the compartment. She had no choice but to duck inside the shaft, and her pulse was madly throbbing as she reached out and did her best to cover the open portal with the cover panel. From the black confines of the shaft, she cautiously peeked outside and watched the airman begin working on the VLF transmitter, which was positioned at the aft end of the room. He seemed to take forever to complete his work, yet Brittany didn't dare continue until he had finished.

When he finally completed the job and left, Brittany moved forward. The shaft was just wide enough to fit her shoulders, with thick cables running along the walls. The iron rungs were hard to grip, her progress further slowed by the constantly vibrating fuselage. She supposed that most of the maintenance work performed in this portion of the airplane would occur when Nightwatch was on the ground, and she continued the difficult climb as quickly as possible.

The sound of muffled voices signaled her arrival at the deck above. She halted to catch her breath, and was able to hear the distinctive chatter of people talking. One of these voices was female and could belong to Red, and Brittany prayed that the Admiral's stateroom was nearby, though there was no sign of any vent opening.

She swept the shaft with her flashlight, and discovered the outline of an access panel that appeared to be identical to the one she had originally climbed through. The voices seemed to be coming from the other side, though the screws holding this panel were nowhere to be seen. Fearful they could be removed only from the other side, she began probing the shaft's surface with the pointed tip of the screwdriver, and in this manner uncovered a layer of stiff, rubberized insulation that she quickly pried free.

A familiar pattern of screw heads was soon exposed. She hesitated briefly before removing them, well aware that, other than Red's cursory description earlier, she didn't know which portion of the airplane this cover panel would open up to. And even if it turned out to be the Chairman's stateroom, were the prisoners there with no sentries or any of the coup supporters present?

A woman's voice could be heard once again from the other side of the panel, and Brittany took several deep breaths before deciding that the gamble was worth taking. Her hand was badly shaking as she raised the screwdriver to the head of the first screw. It took a concentrated effort to remove it, and as she went to work on the second screw, Nightwatch suddenly lost altitude, causing the entire shaft to suddenly pitch forward.

The screwdriver slipped from her grasp, and as it began dropping into the black void below, she blindly kicked her leg out and was just able to trap the tool between her thighs. She reached down to grab it, and no sooner did she secure it in her grasp than air turbulence caused the shaft to begin wildly vibrating. All but forgetting about the immediate task at hand, she found herself hanging on for dear life.

By the time Nightwatch finally leveled out and found smooth air again, her nerves were all but shot. She fought the temptation to give up, and resolutely regripped the screwdriver to get back to work. Except for one stripped screw that needed her every last bit of strength to budge, the rest of her effort went smoothly, and with a great sense of relief, she put the palms of her hands onto the center of the panel and pushed. It opened with a dull pop, and she could barely contain herself to see Red's smiling face appear in the aperture.

"It's about time, Commander. What took you so long?" said Red.

Clearing a safe lane for the unit was proving to be a nerve-racking, time-consuming process, now that antipersonnel mines had been discovered buried alongside the trip-wire-activated booby traps. This was the first time Thomas had ever seen Army Sappers clear such a field, and he was impressed with their expertise, patience, and thoroughness.

A hand probe had uncovered the first Yugoslavian, pressure-activated mine. Thomas was close by as the Sappers carefully extracted the cleverly constructed device, crafted out of molded plastic. Ted Callahan pointed out that this type of mine had no metal content, making it impervious to discovery by a magnetic mine detector. It could be neutralized only by hand, mine plow, or a line charge.

Seven similar mines had since been discovered buried in the track-laden footpath. Instead of digging them up, the Sappers marked them with Cyalume chemical lightsticks, or chem-lites, as they were better known, their wrappers partially torn off in such a manner that only the advancing unit could see them.

Thomas was continuing to travel with the point Sapper unit, with much of their progress measured in mere inches. He had adapted well to his Night Vision Goggles, and was trying his best to ignore the ever-present mosquitoes and other biting pests.

"Special Agent Kellogg," whispered Sergeant Reed from the head of the formation, "check this out."

Thomas crawled forward and looked farther down the trail, in the direction that the Sapper instructor was pointing.

"Do you see those cylinder-shaped objects on the left side of the path, some ten yards ahead of us?" Reed questioned.

With the assistance of his NVGs, Thomas spotted what appeared to be a sizable grouping of thick, five-inch-long firecrackers scattered on the ground. "Are they M80s?" he asked.

"They're much more lethal than that," replied Reed. "Those devils are what we call toe poppers. They're activated by pressure, and are designed to mutilate by blowing off a foot."

Thomas made certain to give the toe poppers plenty of leeway when it came time to pass them by. He made it a point to hug the trail's far right side, a decision that almost had tragic consequences.

"Special Agent, stop in your tracks!" ordered Sergeant Reed, who was now following him.

Thomas had to hear no more to freeze in mid-step. He carefully placed his foot back on what he thought to be solid ground, and the earth gave way, causing him to lose his balance and fall forward into some sort of newly exposed depression. He felt a firm hand grab his shoulder and yank him back on his feet. It was Sergeant Reed who proved to be his savior, and Thomas found himself staring down into a shallow pit filled with a wicked-looking group of very sharp stakes.

"Punji sticks," said Reed with a grunt. "And odds are they're covered with excrement. Somebody out here certainly knows his business, Special Agent. And that means if the VP and his party passed over this trail without triggering any of these pitfalls, you can rest assured that the folks who set them are the ones leading their way."

Dick Mariano anxiously paced back and forth like a caged animal. The other occupants of the subterranean Operations Center were trying their best to give the ex-SEAL a wide berth, ever afraid of further aggravating his rotten mood, and triggering yet another invective-filled outburst.

"Damn it, Richy!" yelled Mariano to his green-faced associate, who was seated at a vacant communications console sorting through an MRE. "How can you even think of chow at a fucking time like this?"

Richy held back his reply until pulling a miniature bottle of Tabasco sauce out of the plastic packet and downing its contents in a single gulp. "I was only looking for a pick-me-up, Skipper," he said, after licking his lips and tossing the packet aside.

"That Cajun rotgut's gonna eat a hole right through that belly of yours, bro," Mariano remarked, before venting his rage on the beard-stubbled, BDU-clad technician responsible for monitoring their SATCOM unit. "Are you certain that the motherfucking receiver is even working, Chief? Surely we should have heard from that cocksucker Pierce by now."

The technician somewhat nervously beckoned toward the series of green lights that lit his console, saying, "All systems are up and operational, sir. If you'd like, I can run another systems check."

"Do it!" ordered Mariano, who looked at Richy and shook his head. "Ain't this the ultimate goat fuck? How much longer is that pencil-pushing government asshole going to keep us waiting? His plane should have landed at Leonard Wood by now, and besides, don't those flying palaces of theirs have phones in them? Hell, here we are standing around at ground zero with our dicks in our hands, all primed to pass on the news he's been waiting for all day, and that motherfucker has forgotten that we even exist. It's just like fucking 'Nam. Those self-important government pricks haven't changed in the least, and if we didn't need them for funding, we'd do better to eliminate them all and let the military run the show."

"How 'bout the prisoners, Skipper? I still say shoot them, and kick ass getting as far away from this place as possible before those warheads fly," offered Richy.

"The safest place to ride out that storm is right here, bro. And as for our distinguished prisoners, regardless of what the Speaker has to say, their time's a-comin', never fear."

"Where in the blazes did that sucker disappear to?" queried Brad Bodzin, in reference to the sonar signature that had unexpectedly faded from their waterfall display. "Jaffers, run me a quick systems analysis, to see if the problem isn't with our sensors."

"My money says it isn't, Sup. But it's your call."

While Jaffers attacked his keyboard, Bodzin addressed the blond-haired sailor seated beside him. "I hope to God we haven't lost Sierra Three, Wilford."

"That we haven't, Sup," remarked the easygoing Tampa native while pushing back one of his headphones. "The signature of our mini-sub is coming in loud and clear. ETA *Rhode Island* in two minutes, fifty-eight seconds."

"Sonar, Conn," a deep, amplified voice broke in over the PA. "What's the status of Sierra Seven?"

Bodzin recognized this concerned voice as belonging to the XO, and he answered him as honestly as possible. "Conn, Sonar. I can't really say, sir. We never did have a firm lock on them, and sometime within the last two minutes, our sensors lost them altogether."

"Sup," said Wilford, his tone urgent, "I think Sierra Seven could be back."

"It's them, all right!" exclaimed Jaffers, a thick white vertical line forming on the right side of his CRT screen. "Approximate rough range twelve thousand yards, bearing zero-eight-five."

Bodzin hurriedly addressed his keyboard to isolate this contact on his headphones. And as he was in the process of putting the intercom handset to his lips, a dreaded, growling, buzz-saw whine sounded from the direction of Sierra Seven.

"Conn, Sonar. Torpedo in the water!" he shouted into the handset. "Sierra Seven has reappeared on bearing zero-eight-five, and sensors indicate a confirmed torpedo launch. Relative rough range is eleven thousand five hundred yards and quickly closing, with Sierra Three a possible target!"

Saturday, July 3, 0402 Zulu

Sierra Three

A garbled warning came from Dan Calhoun, courtesy of the *Polk*'s underwater telephone: "Sierra Three, torpedo continues its approach. Range down to eleven thousand yards, and we have a definite confirmation that you're the target!"

From his position in the mini-sub's copilot seat, Benjamin Kram curtly spoke into his chin mike and acknowledged the transmission, then turned his attention back to isolating the oncoming threat on sonar.

"ETA *Rhode Island* in two minutes, eleven seconds," informed the pilot, who was seated to Kram's immediate right, his hands tightly gripping two black plastic joysticks. "Can we make it, sir?"

Dozens of gauges and digital readouts were mounted into the cramped bulkhead before them, and Kram isolated the green-tinted CRT screen that monitored the mini-sub's passive sonar array. He was able to make out both the signature of the advancing torpedo and that of the *Polk* as it steadily picked up speed, with neither readings lightening his spirits any.

"I'm afraid it's just not worth chancing, Commander," replied Kram glumly. "That torpedo has us in its crosshairs, and we can't risk drawing it any closer to our boomer. Come around hard on course one-nine-zero, and let's see if she's as fast as the contractor says she is."

With a flick of the left joystick, the pilot was able to guide the mini-sub into a tight turn. Kram felt his restraint harness bite into his shoulders, and he could hear the grinding whirl of the boat's single-screw, battery-powered propeller bite into the surrounding water. Even with this all-out speed, the digital knot indicator never budged over eight, and with the torpedo coming in at over ten times that speed, the prognosis wasn't favorable.

"What are you trying to do, Captain, outrun the damn thing?" asked Doug Gilbert from the adjoining passenger module.

The SEAL team leader was seated there alongside a wet-suit-clad associate. Four additional SEALs sat shoulder to shoulder in rows of two behind them, with a full load of weapons and other equipment stuffed into the cramped, elongated compartment as well.

"Sierra Three, torpedo has broken the ten-thousand-yard threshold," reported the *Polk*'s XO, his garbled voice barely recognizable over the mini-sub's PA speakers. "Please state your intentions. Over."

Kram relayed their new course change, and he listened to his XO's firm reply. "Sierra Three, we intend to get between you and Sierra Seven. On my mark, please initiate wipe-off procedure. Five . . . four . . . three . . . two . . . one . . . Mark!"

Impressed with Dan Calhoun's bravado and tactical ingenuity, Kram didn't dare challenge his decision, and he ordered the pilot to immediately deactivate the mini-sub's power train. As they powered back to zero, the digital knot indicator dropped accordingly, as did the constant whirring grind of the boat's sole propeller shaft.

"What the hell are you doing up there?" quizzed Gilbert

as the mini-sub began silently drifting. "We're nothing but a sitting duck out here, and without any propulsion, we don't stand a chance."

His fellow SEALs supported him with a chorus of concerned chatter, and Kram interceded to ease their anxieties the best he could.

"Gentlemen, we all knew the great risks we were taking when we started this mission without first addressing the threat of that unidentified submarine out there. Now that it's taken a cheap potshot at us, the *Polk* is attempting to readdress the situation by getting between us and the torpedo. By powering down and going silent, we've essentially gone invisible to any probing passive sensors, including the sonar that's directing that wire-guided torpedo."

"If that's the case, how's the Jimmy K gonna shake that fish off its tail?" asked one of the SEALs from the back of the passenger module.

Kram replied while worriedly rubbing his forehead. "I guess we'll all know the answer to that one about sixty seconds from now."

Kram reached out to the console and set the digital timer to sixty seconds. He somberly watched the seconds begin counting down, all the while fitting on his headphones to listen to the frantic underwater battle that continued to develop outside their fragile hull.

In the cold depths almost due north of them, a warship he was still personally responsible for was selflessly positioning itself to draw away the ever-approaching torpedo. He knew that it would be the ultimate travesty to end his long career at sea by losing the *Polk*, and the one hundred and forty-seven men who remained on board, while he cheated death.

"Torpedo has lost us and reacquired the *Polk*," informed the pilot, his own gaze locked on the target acquisition sonar. "I make the new range to target five thousand yards and closing."

This almost matter-of-fact revelation generated no joyous outburst from the mini-sub's occupants. In their minds, they collectively knew that though they might be out of harm's way for the moment, their co-workers on the *Polk* were now in a relentless race with oblivion.

The deep, guttural roar of the *Polk*'s nuclear reactor powering up for flank speed sounded in Kram's headphones. With a distinctive cavitational hiss, the *Polk*'s propeller could be heard biting into the sea, and he could imagine the huge vessel gathering momentum, the eyes of the control room crew centered on the diving console, frantically urging the knot indicator forward.

"Range to new target, forty-five hundred yards and continuing to close," came the rote voice of the pilot.

Kram breathlessly listened to the grinding report of the *Polk*'s noisemakers being launched. These diversionary simulators were designed to divert the torpedo, and the cacophony of sounds that soon met his ears seemed to meld together in a single, macabre symphony.

It was as the digital timer hit the ten-second mark that Kram yanked off his headphones, and he flinched when a rumbling explosion sounded clearly in the distance. The mini-sub's sonar was rendered all but inoperable by this deafening underwater blast, whose ensuing shock wave tossed the vessel violently from side to side. The lights failed, and in the impenetrable blackness that followed, Benjamin Kram's thoughts refocused themselves from forlorn mourning to selfish prayers for his own survival.

"Well, how about it, Jake? Are we going to need that additional pit stop before landing at Andrews?"

The E-4B's flight engineer held back his answer until he double-checked his latest fuel calculations. "Don't bother with it, Lucky. Even with our brief wire-out, the lack of head winds is gonna put us in a good fifty minutes early."

Lucky turned to address the officer seated to his left. "If it's okay with you, Major, I'd like to abort our last scheduled aerial refueling."

Owen Lassiter stifled a yawn and unenthusiastically replied, "Very well."

"I can't help but wonder what's going to be waiting for us back in Washington," offered Jake from his workstation directly behind the copilot.

This remark hit a nerve, and Lassiter readily chimed in. "One thing you can be certain of is that the President's death is going to put a damper on the July Fourth festivities. And here Peg's sister and four kids are visiting from Tacoma, and we planned to take them to the Capitol Mall to enjoy the fireworks and music."

"From the somber mood of the Chairman and his staff of late, I'm just hoping we won't be at war come the Fourth," said Lucky.

"Tell me about it," Jake muttered. "I heard from a sergeant on Captain Richardson's staff that FEMA still hasn't made contact with the VP. Now that's certainly strange, as was that unscheduled EAM we just finished transmitting. Do you think the rumors are true, and that our Atlantic alert platform was intentionally rammed by a Russian attack sub?"

"That's enough of your groundless scuttlebutt, Lieutenant," ordered Lassiter. "Next you'll be telling us that Coach really has the Ebola virus."

"I can personally attest that's not true," cut in a familiar deep voice from the back of the flight deck. Fresh from climbing out of the open hatchway on the floor of the upper-deck rest area, Coach nodded in greeting, with Brittany and Red joining him in quick succession.

"Look who's back from the dead," Jake fondly greeted him.

"Are you finally feeling better, Coach?" inquired Lucky.

"If I were you, Major, I wouldn't rush things," suggested Lassiter. "As I was telling the boys, I suffered from the runs myself, during my honeymoon. And just when I thought I had them licked, I couldn't get to that infernal toilet quick enough."

Coach had all but forgotten the fictitious excuse that the Chairman had circulated to explain his incarceration. Yet before he could set the facts straight, the collision-avoidance radar began loudly chiming. It took only a quick glance at the center console for him to determine that the radar scan was set on maximum range. And it was Lucky who pointed out the two flashing blips visible on the outer perimeter of the blue-tinted radar screen.

"Since they're coming out of the west, the smart money says they're ours," added Lucky.

This fact was verified seconds later, when the intercom filled with the sharp voice of one of these newcomers. "Nightwatch six-seven-six, this is Eagle One. Good morning. Please be advised that per the express orders of General Lowell Spencer aboard Iron Man One, you've been diverted to Langley, and we'll be accompanying you. Over."

Confusion filled Lassiter's face as he pushed away his chin mike and addressed his copilot. "What the hell is this all about? Captain Davis, get the Chairman on the horn, and inform him of General Spencer's request to alter our flight plan."

"Lucky, if you'll just hang loose a sec," interjected Coach, who beckoned both Brittany and Red to join him on the flight deck, before instructing them to shut the cockpit door, and then sharing with the flight crew the real reason for their presence amongst them.

It was at a temporary ORP at the side of the trail that Ted Callahan called together Thomas, Sergeant Reed, Captain Christian, and Ranger Glickman. They convened beneath the protective cover of a camouflaged tarp. With Reed illuminating a detailed U.S. Forest Service map of the Irish Wilderness with his red-lensed flashlight, Jody Glickman pointed out their current position.

"Tater Hill is right over the next rise," she whispered, her right index finger circling the corresponding topographical feature on the map. "It's another kilometer at most, and it's here that we'll find the entrance to the Defense Department's underground facility."

"Surely it can't be accessed by the general public," remarked Callahan.

"There's a barbed-wire-topped, chain-link fence and an iron barricade protecting the entrance, which most hikers mistake for the opening of a collapsed cavern," Glickman said.

"Since it's apparent that's where the footprints we've been following are headed, why not bypass this booby-trapped trail altogether?" Thomas suggested. "It would certainly speed things up."

"Not really," objected Reed, who had just put a pinch of tobacco in his mouth. "My R&S team reports that the surrounding woods are saturated with freshly placed claymores. The footpath might seem slow, but it's safer in the long run. At least we know where to look."

"I wish we had time to call in some of that mechanized equipment from the Alton staging area," said Jay Christian. "A Grizzly could clear us a safe lane to Tater in a matter of minutes."

"Though we don't have a Grizzly, my Sappers are carrying bangalore tube charges," Reed revealed with a grin. "They might be noisy as all heck, but I guarantee that we can clear us a lane to that cave entrance without taking the time to probe by hand."

Less than a meter away from the five individuals gathered beneath the tarp, Doc Martin peeked out of the heavily camouflaged slit trench in which he was buried. He was so close to the intruders he could almost reach out and touch them, and the ex-SEAL fought the temptation to take all of them out with a single frag grenade.

His mission and that of his three-man unit was R&S, with strict rules-of-engagement limitations imposed on them by Dick Mariano. This was fine with Doc, who got just as much satisfaction from tracking a man down as from cutting his throat.

He had been taught this forgotten skill by some of the best trackers on the face of the earth—Vietnam's Montagnards, or Yards, as the members of SOG preferred to call them. The Yards were Vietnam's largest minority, their culture organized along tribal lines much like the American Indians. They were nomadic hunters and foragers who still used the crossbow, and had taught Doc that the real art of camouflage was blending one's spirit into the forest as well as one's own body.

He had also learned from the Yards how to sharpen his senses through meditation. Through a variety of self-realization techniques such as deep breathing and chanting, he discovered that one could smell an enemy long before he could be seen or heard.

Nowhere was this more evident than from Doc's current vantage point, where the distinctive scents of the five intruders overpowered his sensitive nostrils. Without having to even hear her voice, he knew that one of them was female. Yet another chewed tobacco, while all of them were most likely meat eaters.

Of course, masking their own body odors through eating a native diet was only one of the tricks that this group of neophytes needed to master in order to survive. They made too much noise, and wasted valuable time fidgeting with their high-tech NVGs. They also needed to better utilize listening halts to become more aware of their surroundings, while their R&S teams had to learn to slow down and quit trying to cover so much territory on their sweeps.

It was only too apparent that these soldiers had never seen battle. They were most likely instructors from nearby Fort Leonard Wood, whose combat was limited to organizing war games. Doc had been there himself, and knew they'd get a sobering dose of reality the moment Mariano inevitably changed their rules of engagement.

For Captain Terence McNeil Lockwood, his duty was perfectly clear—he'd continue the repair efforts on his sonar and communications systems, while at the same time prepare to execute the EAM that the Chairman of the Joint Chiefs of Staff had personally conveyed to them via Nightwatch. Only a few minutes ago, a rumbling explosion had sounded outside their hull, and Lockwood feared they'd be unable to fulfill this sworn obligation.

He assumed that the most likely source for the blast was a torpedo exchange between the phantom submarine that had collided with them earlier and the U.S.S. *Polk*. Because they still didn't know this fact for certain, or whom the victor was if this exchange had indeed come to pass, he could only pray that they'd get the all-clear from the *Polk* by 0500, the preappointed time for the first Trident to fly.

To ensure that this launch went off without a hitch, Lockwood exited the control room, where he had been coordinating the repair effort, and headed aft. This brought him to the upper deck of the missile compartment. Other than the engineering spaces, which occupied the after end of the boat, the missile magazine was the largest single compartment on the *Rhode Island.*

He paused for a moment to survey the twenty-four launch canisters. They were positioned twelve to a side, and painted an orange-tinted red. Each one of them held a nuclear-warhead-tipped Trident missile. Only a pair of these Tridents would be needed to fulfill their current duty, and Lockwood headed down to the magazine's second level to check their status.

He found his weapons officer, or weps, as he was better known, in the missile control center. Weps was seated in front of the main launch console, his complete attention focused on the twenty-four rows of digit-sized buttons that occupied the center part of the console. At the moment, only the buttons labeled 1 and 24 were illuminated, as were the four buttons beside them marked 1SQ, DENOTE, PREPARE, and AWAY.

1SQ referred to the state of readiness needed to precipitate a launch. It was a compilation of factors including the state of each missile's three-stage, solid-fueled propulsion system. Of equal importance was a spinning up of the latest targeting data.

In order to hit a target thousands of miles away, the missile had to know the coordinates of the target and the precise location of the submarine at launch. The *Rhode Island's* twin MK-2, MOD 7 Ship's Inertial Navigation System, would provide the exact point of missile release, through a complex array of electrostatically supplied gyroscopes, accelerometers, and computers.

The target coordinates were relayed in the EAM, and were automatically fed into the system so that the crew would never know a warhead's exact destination. That way, a crew member with relatives living in Moscow wouldn't have to live with the knowledge that one of their Tridents was targeted on the Russian capital, or on any other location that might have personal significance.

"How much longer until we have 1SQ on those two birds, Weps?" asked Lockwood in greeting, a heavy weariness to his voice.

Weps replied without taking his eyes off the console. "Another fifteen minutes and we'll be good to go, Captain. Sorry about the continued delay. That collision did a lot more damage than we had originally thought, but I promise we'll be ready when it's time for launch."

"Let's continue to pray that sometime within the next fifty minutes the geopolitical situation will change for the better, and we'll be ordered to stand down," remarked Lockwood.

"From that commotion outside our hull, it sounds to me that whatever mess we're in is only heating up," said Weps. "I don't suppose you have any additional info on the source of that explosion, or have since heard from the *Polk*?"

Lockwood reached out to innocently massage Weps's shoulders. "Right now, I know just as much as you or any other member of the crew. I have COB's personal assurance that by the time we're ready to ascend to launch depth, he'll have sonar up and Gertrude functioning. That way, if our phantom submarine is still around, at least we'll be able to tag them, and talk to the *Polk* if we need to."

The 1SQ button to missile number one began blinking, generating a frustrated curse from Weps. It was as he initiated a diagnostic to trace the problem that Lockwood's XO paged him.

"Skipper, the folks in Engineering are reporting a strange scraping sound. It seems to be originating from outside our upper hull, at the forward end of the engine room."

"I've got the yellow stripe," reported Benjamin Kram, his eyes riveted on the real-time scene visible on the control panel's video monitor. "Forward ten meters, starboard three."

The video picture was compliments of a miniature camera set into the mini-sub's lower hull. The bright yellow stripe it was focused on was painted alongside the *Rhode Island*'s aft, upper-deck accessway. In order to mate the mini-sub's transfer skirt directly onto this accessway, the pilot expertly manipulated his joysticks, causing the thrusters to propel them slightly forward and to the right.

"There are the crosshairs!" Kram proclaimed. "Down one."

There was a distinctive, clamorous clanging noise as the mini-sub settled down onto the *Rhode Island*. Kram had to utilize yet another video camera to finalize the alignment, and it was with great relief that he gave the order to attach the transfer skirt and pressurize.

"Commander Gilbert," he added to SEAL Team Two's

mustached CO, "if it's all right with you, I'd like to join your men when they unseal the hatch."

"Me and my ladies would be honored for your company during this historic, first operational transfer," Gilbert proudly replied.

To extract himself from his cramped command chair, Kram had to grasp the overhead handholds and scoot backward into the passenger compartment. Together with Gilbert, they hunched over and continued farther aft into the transfer module, a circular compartment with a round hatch cut into its deck.

They made certain that the pressure was equalized before kneeling to undog this hatch, which noisily squealed as they yanked it toward them. Exposed below was the dark gray outer skin of the *Rhode Island*'s upper hull. Portions of the bright yellow decal that Kram had been watching on the monitor were also visible, and they had to call upon two muscular SEALs to deploy the heavy iron tool needed to actually crack open the Trident's hatch. It too opened with a grating squeal, and there was a popping sensation, followed by a cool draft of polythylene-scented air.

Kram peered anxiously into the open accessway. The glowing lights of the Trident's aft, upper-level missile magazine invitingly beckoned down below. A steep, iron-rung ladder was anchored into the side of the hatch, and Kram readily accepted Gilbert's offer to lead the way.

The descent went quickly, and as he dropped onto the deck below, Kram looked up to see which of the SEALs was following. It was at this exact moment that a camera triggered from inside the mini-sub, temporarily blinding him.

He gently rubbed his eyes, his sight returning in time for him to view the strange reception committee that waited for him inside the missile magazine. Gathered in a tight, protective phalanx was a group of helmeted sailors wearing full-body armor, a lethal combination of combat shotguns and pistols trained his way.

It was from the wire operator, of all people, that Trent Warner learned about the other aircraft flying in close formation off their tail. After getting a confirmation that the object the startled airman saw out the window of his wire port was indeed another airplane, the Chairman flew into a rage.

"Has the flight crew forgotten that I'm supposed to be the first to know about any other planes we might encounter?" he shouted to no one in particular, then made a beeline straight for the stairway leading to the flight deck.

"Major Lassiter!" he exclaimed as he stormed into the cockpit. "Are you asleep on the job up here? Why didn't you tell me that we've picked up an escort? Is it one of my Tomcats?"

The Chairman's eyes opened wide with disbelief when the individual seated in the pilot's position calmly turned around, exposing the grinning face of Coach.

"Sir," came a woman's firm voice from behind, "if you'll

please keep your hands where we can see them, and back out of the cockpit."

Shocked horror filled Warner's face upon learning that the speaker of these words was none other than Commander Brittany Cooper. The President's military aide held a flare gun in her determined grasp, with Sergeant Rayburn close at her side.

"What's the meaning of this outrageous act of insubordination, Commander? Put down that damned pistol before someone gets hurt! Have you lost your senses, woman?"

Brittany coolly answered him. "It appears that you're the one who needs a long rest, sir."

"And how about starting with early retirement at Leavenworth?" Red put in.

"So the conspiracy nuts have escaped, and now they're spreading their dangerous, paranoid fantasies to the rest of my flight crew," said the Chairman to Lucky, Jake, and Owen Lassiter, who had taken the navigator's position behind Coach. "What did they tell you, gentlemen? Don't tell me it's that coup d'etat crap again?"

The collision-avoidance radar began chiming, and Lucky leaned forward to inspect the screen. "We've got more company headed our way, gents. There're three of them this time, approaching on a direct intercept course from the north."

All eyes went to the wraparound cockpit window, where the flashing red and green strobe lights of the lead F-15 Eagle that had already joined them took up a defensive position in the black sky ahead.

"Nightwatch six-seven-six, this is Strike Eagle Leader," announced a clipped voice from the overhead intercom speakers. "Please be advised that I show a flight of three bogeys coming in on zero-one-five. Eagle Two will remain in your six o'clock. Over."

"Strike Eagle Leader, this is Nightwatch six-seven-six," replied Coach into his chin mike. "We've got the bogeys on radar. Thanks for your concern. Over."

"So our escort this early morning is compliments of the Air Force," stated the Chairman with a bitter laugh. "I hope they've got some fight in them for a change, 'cause my Toms fly with an attitude."

"Admiral, enough!" warned Red, who had had her fill of the Chairman's intimidating head games. "Back out of that cockpit, and keep that trap of yours shut!"

"Sergeant," interrupted Major Steve Hewlett's deep voice from the top of the stairway, "is that any way to speak to the Chairman of the Joint Chiefs of Staff?"

The broad-shouldered Marine SIOP advisor stood there with a 9mm pistol in his right hand, and he pointed the barrel at Brittany. "Drop it, Commander!"

Hewlett took a tentative step forward, and he directed his next remark to the silver-haired individual standing in the back of the cockpit. "Are you okay, Admiral?"

"I am now, Major. Arrest them all, and throw the whole lot of them in detention."

Hewlett took another step forward, and Red beckoned toward the gun that Brittany still had trained on the Chairman. "One more step, Gomer, and Commander Cooper is gonna put another hole up the old man's ass!"

"Major Hewlett, don't listen to the darned fool," commanded Warner. "And besides, do any of you think it makes any real difference if I live or die? Our movement will continue regardless!"

"Nightwatch six-seven-six," a male voice with a slight Southern drawl to it broke in over the cockpit's intercom. "This is Tomcat Leader, from aggressor squadron Baron, based on the *Harry S. Truman*. Be advised that your escorts have arrived for door-to-door service all the way to Andrews."

"Nightwatch six-seven-six, this is Strike Eagle Leader. You are to disregard that offer. Eagle Flight will be your escort to Langley as ordered."

"Strike Eagle, this is Tomcat Leader. On whose authority do you base your orders, sir?"

"Tomcat Leader, this is Strike Eagle, and my orders come directly from General Lowell Spencer, Deputy Commander of the U.S. Strategic Command. Please move out of our airspace so we can proceed to Langley. Over."

There was a noticeable pause as the Tomcat Leader appeared to be mulling over this request, and the Chairman defiantly grabbed the auxiliary radio headset that was hanging beside Jake. "Tomcat Leader, this is Admiral Trent Warner calling from Nightwatch six-seven-six. You are to ignore the instructions of Strike Eagle and provide escort to Andrews as I originally requested. Over."

Jake reached up and ripped the Chairman's headset plug out of the radio socket. At the same time, Coach spoke into his own chin mike.

"Strike Eagle Leader, this is Major Foard, Nightwatch six-seven-six's commander. I realize there are some contravening orders this morning, but be advised that I'm personally requesting escort to Langley, per the authority of General Spencer aboard Iron Man One. Over."

"Major Foard, this is Strike Eagle Leader. Roger that, sir. My wingman in Eagle Two will be joining me off your nose for the flight to Langley. Over."

Seconds later, the red and green strobes of the F-15 that had been trailing them could be seen through the cockpit window, taking up a position to the right of Eagle One. No further radio transmissions emanated from the overhead speakers, the only sound that filled the flight deck being a new outburst of warning tones from the collision-avoidance radar.

"The Tomcats are continuing their approach," noted Lucky. "Those idiots appear to be painting us with their attack radar!"

"Surely they wouldn't shoot at us," Jake said uncertainly.

"I warned you that they had an attitude," the Chairman reminded them, a sly grin on his face. "Commander Cooper, put down that damned flare gun, and I'll act to defuse this ridiculous situation before it gets further out of control."

"Don't listen to him, Brittany," Red urged.

Hewlett racked his pistol's slide, chambered a round, and diverted his aim to include Red before returning to Brittany. "You make one threatening move toward the Chairman, and I swear I'll blow the two of you away."

The collision-avoidance radar continued chiming, and Lucky was the first to spot the flashing strobe lights of the flight of three swiftly approaching U.S. Navy F-14 Tomcats. "Oh, shit!" he cursed, as two of the swept-wing jet fighters flared out to take up an outer position beside the F-15s, and the remaining Tomcat initiated an incredibly tight arcing turn to position itself directly ahead of them.

"Nightwatch six-seven-six, this is Tomcat Leader. I've just been informed by the *Truman* that Strike Eagle's orders are unauthorized. You are to immediately come around to course three-zero-four, at an altitude of three-zero-one-five-zero feet. Over."

"Tomcat Leader, this is Major Foard aboard Nightwatch six-seven-six. Be advised that I don't intend to alter our current flight plan. You are to break formation and clear our airspace. Over."

"Nightwatch six-seven-six, this is Tomcat Leader. I have been authorized to use any means at my disposal to get you to alter course to Andrews. Do you copy? Over."

Foard was tiring of this foolish game of chicken, and there was a definite tone of finality to his voice as he spoke into his chin mike. "Tomcat Leader, this is Nightwatch six-seven-six. I intend to land this aircraft at Langley Air Force Base, as ordered by General Spencer, and that's final. Over."

The line went dead, and all the occupants of the flight deck watched as the three Tomcats abruptly broke formation and roared off into the night, the red-hot plume of their afterburners clearly visible in the crystal-clear black sky. While Lucky tried his best to follow them on radar, Jake vented his nerves with a long sigh of relief.

"Thank goodness that's over with," he remarked, a thin

sheen of perspiration gathered on his brow. "I mean, it's not like they were gonna shoot us down for not changing our destination airfield."

"Don't be so sure of that, son," said the Chairman heavily.

"Major Hewlett," said Brittany, after transferring the flare gun to her left hand, "it's time to end this impasse as well. I'll lower my weapon if you do likewise. I'm certain that we can come to some sort of mutual understanding for the remainder of this flight."

The Marine nodded in agreement, and both of them tentatively lowered their pistols. A sense of relief was shared by all, and Coach addressed them collectively.

"There will be plenty of time to sort this whole mess out once we're on the ground. If the winds continue to cooperate, that will be in approximately ninety minutes. So please, keep those guns stashed away, and try to get along until then."

"Coach," interrupted Lucky, "we're not out of the woods just yet. The Tomcats have broken formation, and we've been once more painted by their attack radars."

This tense revelation was followed by the unexpected arrival of a blinding volley of tracer rounds that streaked past the cockpit, parting the narrow void between Nightwatch and its F-15 escort.

"Are those guys nuts?" screamed Lucky, who couldn't believe that the Tomcats had the audacity to shoot at them.

"Tomcat Leader!" Coach forcefully exclaimed into his chin mike. "You are to refrain from further firing at once! Do you read me, Tomcat Leader?"

There was an ominous silence, broken only by the urgent chiming of the collision-avoidance radar. "Incoming bogey directly ahead of us!" warned Lucky. "Break left, Coach! Break left!"

Without a moment's hesitation, Coach turned his steering yoke hard to the left, and the sudden, steeply banked turn that followed caused the four occupants of the flight deck who were not restrained by seat belts to go crashing to the floor. Coach had no time to worry about them, his attention focused instead on the F-14 Tomcat that appeared to be headed toward them on a direct collision course.

He ignored the bite of his shoulder harness, and with the yoke still fully engaged, he looked on with horror as the Tomcat soared directly over the cockpit, so close that he feared the afterburners might have scorched the E-4B's upper fuselage.

"That crazy son of a bitch!" cursed Coach, trying his best to pull out of the turn as smoothly as possible.

He ignored a frantic intercom page from Colonel Pritchard, who wanted to know the reason for this sudden turn, and reached up to activate the seat-belt warning sign.

"The Tomcats appear to be coming around for another intercept," said his badly shaken copilot. "We're a damned sitting duck up here!"

"Major Foard!" shouted Red from the upper-deck rest area. "Major Hewlett has just grabbed the Chairman, and they're headed down the stairway!"

"Let them go!" Coach replied, his eyes riveted on the Primary Flight Display.

The fixed bar representing the plane's wings gradually evened itself out against the green-tinted artificial-horizon display representing the earth's surface. This indicated level flight, and before Coach could express his relief, the Tomcats returned—this time with tragic consequences.

The F-14s were attempting to divert the Eagles with a crossing pattern, with two fighters coming in from the right and one from the left. The startled occupants of the E-4B's cockpit were seated at center stage, and looked on with shocked horror as the trailing Tomcat appeared to clip the wing of Eagle Two. There was a blinding fireball as both aircraft exploded, with only a single parachute spotted amongst the fiery debris that proceeded to shower from the skies.

"Goddamn it!" Coach cursed, jerking the yoke hard to the right to miss striking the remnants of the two doomed aircraft. "I knew this was going to get totally out of control."

They watched the remaining F-15 peel off to engage the unlikely enemy that was responsible for taking out its wingman, and seconds later, the E-4B's radio crackled alive.

"Nightwatch six-seven-six, this is Tomcat Leader, and I'm smack on your tail. Now come around to course three-zero-four, at an altitude of three-zero-one-five-zero, or next time you'll be the one going down!"

"Somebody sure wants this plane either on the ground, at Andrews, or blown out of the fucking sky," said Jake.

"Which means they probably intend to continue orchestrating their coup from Nightwatch once we return home," Coach surmised.

Lucky looked at Coach, his frustration obvious. "We've got to get that fucking Tom off our tail."

Coach returned his copilot's supportive glance, and he flashed the slightest of grins as an idea suddenly came to mind. "Wire operator!" he shouted into his chin mike. "I need you to initiate an immediate wire-out."

"But, sir," countered the amplified voice of the perplexed airman manning the antenna operator's station behind the aft lower equipment area, "there's another aircraft directly behind us."

"Son," retorted Coach, "deploy the goddamn wire!"

"Wire is deploying," Jake reported. "Ten feet . . . twenty feet . . . thirty feet . . ."

"Nightwatch six-seven-six, this is Tomcat Leader. You've got ten seconds to change your course as ordered before I begin shooting. Ten . . . nine . . . eight . . ."

Coach breathlessly waited until the countdown reached five, then grabbed for the emergency wire cutaway lever, which was positioned on the far left portion of the flight control console. "Tomcat Leader, up yours!" he cried into his chin mike, engaged the lever, and called out, "Wire away!"

The horrified wire operator provided the blow-by-blow commentary that followed. From the glass-enclosed confines of the wire port, he described how over seventy-five feet of drifting wire antenna got ingested into one of the Tomcat's GE-400, augmented turbofan engines. There was an explosive flash, and the last thing he reported seeing was the F-14's canopy being jettisoned, the pilot's frantic attempt to bail out.

There were no celebratory high fives traded inside the E-4B's cockpit, the crew instead refocusing their attention on the furious air battle that was taking place in the skies to their right. Fiery tracers and eerily glowing missile contrails indicated that the sole remaining Tomcat and the last of the Eagles were engaged in a winner-takes-all battle between fellow countrymen. It was a bizarre sight to behold—this initial engagement of America's second civil war, fought not with huge armies, but with a couple of high-performance jet fighters over the mid-Atlantic.

"Coach," warned Red from the upper-deck rest area, "we've got Major Hewlett and a security team headed up the stairway!"

"Shit!" cursed Coach. "They're not going to be happy until all of us are dead. Lower the fire door at the top of the stairs, Sergeant. And then you'd better reseal that accessway we crawled out of earlier."

The collision-avoidance radar began chiming once more, but nothing was showing up on the screen. Puzzled, Lucky scanned the skies, in the direction where the air battle was still taking place. And then he saw the oncoming contrail, and the pinprick, fiery plume of a single, misdirected Sidewinder air-to-air missile, headed directly toward them out of the pitch-black sky.

"Break left! Break left! Incoming missile!" he shouted.

Coach once more yanked the yoke hard aport. Unlike Air Force One, Nightwatch had no chaff dispensers, or any other defensive countermeasures, and all he could do was get them as far away as possible from the oncoming missile.

Just as the restraint harness began biting into his upper torso, indicating that Nightwatch was in the midst of the turn, the Sidewinder detonated. A massive shock wave caused the entire aircraft to violently shudder, with the majority of the blast directed to the plane's underside. Thousands of pieces of shrapnel pierced the lower fuselage, the damages immediately indicated on the flight panel displays.

"I'm showing power anomalies in engines one and three!" Jake informed them. "Hydraulic pressure is dropping across the line, and we're rapidly losing fuel from the main bladder. Initiating emergency fuel crossover procedures."

Alarms were sounding throughout the cockpit, and both Coach and Lucky summoned their every last bit of strength to pull back on their yokes in a desperate effort to counter the rapidly falling altimeter. The lights flickered, and when smoke began pouring into the flight deck, Coach realized that his command had taken a lethal hit.

"Hang on!" he cried. "We're going down!"

Vince pounded the bars in frustration, and Andrew Chapman grabbed his bruised fist and kept him from inflicting further punishment upon himself.

"Easy does it, Kellogg. Since it's apparent that you'll never smash your way through those bars, chill out, and quit blaming yourself for our predicament."

"The more I think about it, the more it makes sense," whispered Vince bitterly. "Those bastards intentionally left that MRE in here so I'd have an opportunity to escape, and lead them right to you."

The VP shook his head in disagreement. "Look, Kellogg, it was my decision alone to reenter the hollow when we heard that claymore detonate, and whatever happens, that's something I can live with."

"But what about them?" said Vince, referring to their four cellmates, who were huddled on the floor behind them. "That boy is gonna bleed to death unless we get him some medical attention, and I should never have allowed them back into the hollow after learning what kind of animals we were up against."

At the rear of the cell, Junior was sprawled out on his back, fading in and out of consciousness. His father and sister were doing their best to attend to the tourniquet that Chapman had helped rig up. Tiny was nearby, his pride hurting more than his bruised skull.

It had been nearly an hour since one of their captors had checked on them. This was only a cursory visit, and the green-faced commando refused their urgent request for water and medical supplies. It appeared that they had been abandoned altogether, and just as they were about to give up hope of ever getting any help, a pair of BDU-clad men holding M16s and ammo-laden LBEs rushed past the detention cell.

"Hey, stop!" pleaded Vince. "We need a first-aid kit!"

They disappeared into the cavern's black recesses without so much as a flicker of recognition, and once again Vince pounded his fist into the iron bars.

"You know, it looks like some kind of alert is coming down," remarked the VP. "Perhaps our rescuers are on their way even as we speak."

Vince greeted this hopeful comment with a pessimistic grunt, and he listened as Chapman added, "This Mariano character seems to be a bit of a psychopath. If he's indicative of the type of individuals the leaders of this supposed coup are relying on, they don't stand much of a chance."

"A soldier like Mariano has his place, sir," returned Vince. "Every army needs its trained assassins, and as for Mariano's psychopathic personality, it's the nature of the beast. After all, we created and trained his type to fight a guerrilla war that we never intended to win. And now we have to learn to live with the consequences."

"The latest diagnostic indicates that it definitely isn't our equipment that's at fault," reported the technician, ever

afraid that this news would generate yet another angry outburst from the bearded veteran anxiously pacing the floor of
the Op Center behind him.

Dick Mariano accepted this revelation with a disappointed shake of his head, and there was an uncharacteristic
timidity in his voice as he glanced at the overhead clock and
calmly replied, "Then there's nothing we can do but continue to wait for his call. Why don't you try another digital
page, Chief? I'm beginning to wonder if something bad
hasn't happened to the man, and I'm tempted to give ole
spit-and-polish Warner a buzz to get the skinny."

Mariano's two-way activated with a burst of static, and he
readjusted his cranial headset and spoke into the miniature
chin mike. "Mariano . . . I expected as much, Doc. Pass on
a 'Job well done' to the boys, and get your keisters back to
the inner perimeter. I want you sealed up inside the compound in ten minutes' time. 'Cause at midnight, all hell's
gonna rain from the sky, and those pussy-eating Sappers will
be nothin' but overdone barbecue."

"Captain, the weapons system is at 1SQ. Missiles number one and twenty-four are ready to launch."

The amplified intercom announcement echoed through the missile magazine, and Benjamin Kram and the five SEALs gathered at his side looked out pleadingly to the armed group of sailors who continued to face them. Captain Terence McNeil Lockwood appeared to ignore the intruders as he reached up for the nearest intercom handset.

"COB, I want that sonar up within the next two minutes, at which time I intend to ascend to launch depth."

Lockwood lowered the mike and listened as Kram reinitiated his argument. "At the very least, ask your weapons officer to access the target coordinates from the EAM. I realize it's a breach of the protocol, but this situation is unlike any other that we've ever faced."

"Damn it, Kram," replied Lockwood, his disgust obvious. "We've been going over this for the last half hour, and it just won't sink into that thick skull of yours. We received a properly formatted, duly authorized EAM from the Chairman of the Joint Chiefs of Staff. I don't know about you, but I've been trained to consider such an EAM as gospel, and nothing you say can convince me otherwise."

"But I'm not doubting the EAM's legitimacy, Terence," Kram retorted. "What I'm questioning is its validity. General Spencer was absolutely convinced that, for whatever reason, Nightwatch intentionally conveyed to you an EAM ordering a surgical nuclear strike against a target inside the continental United States. It's not our responsibility to determine the reason behind this unprecedented occurrence, only to ensure that such an unthinkable event doesn't come to pass."

"Captain," interjected the relieved voice of the *Rhode Island*'s COB over the intercom. "Sonar is up and fully operational."

Lockwood immediately put the intercom handset to his lips. "Conn, this is the Captain. Ascend to one-five-zero feet, and prepare to launch as ordered."

The sound of venting ballast indicated that this order was in the process of being implemented, and Kram attempted one last, desperate plea. "We're not at war, Terence. You can't launch!"

"Then how do you explain the explosion that sounded outside our hull?" countered Lockwood. "And what in the hell has happened to the *Polk?* For all we know, your command could have been taken out by that Russian bastard, and he could just be waiting to do the same to us the moment we open our missile hatches."

"Please, Terence, I'm begging you, as one officer to another. Break the protocol, and ask your weapons officer to check the targeting coordinates. Do that for me, and I swear to you that I'll rest my case."

The surging roar of venting ballast was briefly overridden by a renting, scraping noise, caused by the now-lightened Trident lifting off its stationary perch on the continental shelf. The hull rolled, and Lockwood reached out to steady himself on the side of the nearest missile launch tube.

"Damn it, Kram," he said, more in frustration than in anger. "Here you go and compromise our alert security by barging in like this, and then you expect me to ignore a properly formatted EAM from the Chairman, who's a former boomer skipper himself."

"I realize your dilemma, Terence. Just verify those targeting coordinates, please. If I'm wrong, fire away. But if Spencer is right . . ."

"Damn it," repeated Lockwood before once more addressing the handset. "Weps, this is the Captain. Key up the EAM and pull the targeting coordinates out of Yankee Hotel. And yes, I realize it's a violation of the protocol, but I'll take personal responsibility for breaching it."

Kram's relief was cut short by the amplified voice of the *Rhode Island*'s sonar operator. "Captain, we've got an unidentified submerged contact. Bearing one-one-five, range fifty-five hundred yards. Classify Sierra One, possible hostile submarine."

"Man battle stations torpedo!" ordered Lockwood over the 1MC.

The alarm sounded, and Lockwood beckoned his security team to lower their weapons. "Commander Gilbert, as long as you promise that your SEALs will behave, I see no further need for keeping those weapons trained on them. Hell, if it turns out that there's a Russian sub out there waiting to turn us into fish food, we'll share the same fate regardless. And, Kram, how about accompanying me to the missile control room? It's time to put this matter to rest once and for all."

Kram gave Doug Gilbert and his SEALs a hopeful thumbs-up, then readily went with Lockwood into the adjoining compartment. As they entered, the *Rhode Island*'s weapons officer glanced up from his button-filled console, an expression of pure bewilderment on his smooth-shaven face.

"Sir, you're not gonna believe it, but that coordinate analysis shows that Trident number one is being targeted on the airspace off Georgia, while number twenty-four's three MIRV'd warheads are being directed on what appears to be the south-central portion of the state of Missouri. Sir, my family lives in nearby Arkansas, and I'd like to know, why have we been ordered to launch three 150-kiloton nuclear warheads on the Ozarks?"

With astounded eyes, Lockwood scanned the display screen to verify this information, and only then did he look up to meet Benjamin Kram's resolute stare. "Good Lord, Ben, what in hell does Trent Warner think he's doing up there?"

Lockwood proceeded to terminate the launch, and immediately afterward, the report arrived from Sonar that made Kram's long day complete.

"Captain, we have a positive ID on Sierra One. It's the *Polk,* sir, and the Jimmy K's riding shotgun off our starboard beam, just where they're supposed to be."

Both Coach and Lucky found themselves pinned to their seats, unable to pull Nightwatch out of its uncontrolled descent. They were falling now at over fifteen thousand feet per minute, with the airframe and wings subject to five times the force of gravity, more than twice the aircraft's original design limit. The E-4B had already lost large portions of its horizontal stabilizer, along with sections of the outboard elevator and all of its HF antennas, and had even had the auxiliary power unit sucked out of the wildly vibrating tail.

The terror took on an added dimension when Nightwatch actually flipped onto its back, rolled over, and began a horrifying, disorientating spiral dive. It was all Coach could do to catch sight of the rapidly dropping altimeter, and as they passed the eleven-thousand-foot mark, he realized they would plunge into the Atlantic in less than forty seconds.

The plane shuddered violently, and he breathlessly listened as yet another alarm began chiming, followed by the panic-filled voice of Lucky. "The landing-gear latches have failed, and I show that all four bogeys have deployed!"

Nightwatch had four separate landing-gear bogeys, one on each wing and a pair on the main body. Each of these massive structures had four wheels apiece, and hoping that their activation would provide some additional stability, Coach summoned his last ounce of strength to yank back on his steering yoke. He could hardly believe it when this frantic effort actually managed to pull up the plane's nose slightly, and with the additional assistance of Lucky, they broke out of the dive and achieved level flight, less than two thousand feet above the pitch-black ocean.

There were no shouts of celebration as they nursed Nightwatch back into the heavens. The airplane was handling sluggishly, and with alarms still continuing to chime in the background, Coach dared to ask Jake for a preliminary damage-control report.

"We're losing hydraulic systems one, three, and four," he somberly reported. "I'm going to try to switch off the air-driven pumps, and depressurize the engine-driven system."

Hydraulic pressure was the big jet's lifeblood, and when the system continued to lose pressure, Jake solemnly added, "Coach, I'm permanently shutting down hydraulic systems one, three, and four, leaving only two operational."

"Without one and four available, how are we going to raise the trailing edge flaps?" asked Lucky.

"We can raise them using the secondary electrical system," offered Owen Lassiter, who remained tightly buckled in behind the navigator's console.

"And the landing gear, gents?" Lucky continued.

"Speaking of the landing bogeys," said Jake, scanning the flashing lights of his console, "I hate to be the bearer of additional bad news, but I'm afraid that the two body gears have been ripped off their hinges."

Coach turned his head and addressed Jake directly. "We

certainly don't need any additional bad news, Lasky, and I hope that's the end of it."

"Actually, sir, it's not," said Jake with an uneasy grimace. "We've also lost our primary and secondary braking systems. But at least we're still in the air."

"I'm very grateful for that fact, Lieutenant," replied Coach before briefly scanning the faces of the flight deck's other occupants. "And now I have only a single question for each one of you. Where in the world can we possibly land this big lady with half of our landing gear ripped off, a minimum of hydraulic power, severely damaged flying controls, no primary or secondary braking systems, and a crazed group of maniacs in the back who want nothing less than to kill us and overthrow our elected government?"

"Fire in the hole!"

Thomas wasted little time reacting to Sergeant Reed's warning, and he alertly ducked down behind a shoulder-high, elongated limestone shelf, alongside Ted Callahan, Ranger Glickman, and Captain Christian.

There was a deafening, gut-wrenching blast as the last of the bangalores detonated. Even though they were a good three hundred yards from the blast itself, debris still peppered off the pockmarked face of the ledge they hid behind.

"All clear!" yelled Reed, this being all Thomas and the others had to hear to leave their shelter and head toward the blast site.

As expected, the bangalore had cleared the last of the obstacles leading to the cave—a hastily emplaced, double-coiled strand of extremely sharp concertina wire, which had been booby-trapped with claymores. Sergeant Reed had already picked his way through the breach, and they joined him in front of a section of locked, chain-link fence.

"And that's where our trail of footprints is headed," he told them, pointing to the fence's far side.

The oval-shaped entrance of the cave could be seen from here. A protective barrier of iron bars extended from the irregular limestone ceiling to the rock floor. Several feet beyond this barrier, blocking the entrance itself, was a sealed doorway constructed of tempered steel.

"We can cut through this fence with wire cutters and use plastic explosives to penetrate the bars," said Reed, who scanned the remaining barrier with his flashlight. "That inner vault, though, could be the showstopper. Our best bet appears to be to hit those side hinges with our remaining hundred pounds of C-4."

"You know, there's a secondary entrance to this cave system," remarked Jody Glickman. "It's on the other side of the hill, and we use it to count the cavern's population of endangered Indiana bats."

"Then you've actually seen the abandoned underground command post?" asked Thomas.

Glickman answered while shaking her head no. "The cave system beneath Tater is immense, and my explorations have been limited to the cavern where the main bat population is located. But I'm almost sure we'll be able to access the portion of the cave where the government facility was supposedly situated."

"Ranger, me and my MPs would be willing to join you there to learn this fact for certain," offered Jay Christian.

"And you can count me in," Thomas added.

"I'll stay here with Sergeant Reed and his Sappers," said Callahan, who looked at his watch and added an urgent, "Let's do it!"

Saturday, July 3, 12:37 A.M. C.D.T.

Beneath Freeman Hollow

"Hell's fucking bells, Chief. Do you mean to say there's still no answer to our page?"

There was fear in the communications specialist's eyes as he met the intense gaze of Dick Mariano and curtly replied, "That's affirmative, sir."

"That sniveling, ass-licking beaurocrat!" exclaimed Mariano, who allowed himself one last look at the Op Center's digital clock before venting his anger on the five BDU-clad, green-faced commandos standing beside him.

"It's another goat fuck, compadres. A goddamn, motherfucking goat fuck! You'd think we'd know better than to trust another pencil-dicked politician. But no, we allowed ourselves to be stroked by Admiral Spit and Polish Warner, and swallowed the line of the kingpin bureaucrat of them all—that smooth-talking, sniveling idiot Pierce!"

"Maybe there's been some unexpected delay in getting Yankee Hotel implemented, Skipper, and that's why the warheads have yet to fall," offered Doc, who had a much better understanding of nature than of the complicated world of man.

"No, Doc," said Mariano. "I bet Yankee Hotel was nothing but a scam, most probably to light a fire under our asses to track down the VP for them, and now we're the fucking shills."

"I say let's complete the job we've been sent here to do, and kill Chapman," suggested Richy. "We can still access the river, and those faggot Sappers will never know where the hell we disappeared to."

Mariano looked at Richy, and nodded supportively. "Compadre, I believe we'll do just that. Since it's obvious we've been cut out of the loop, it's time to cut our losses and run while we still have our dicks."

A reverberating explosion sounded in the near distance. Doc looked out into the cavern's dark recesses and queried hopefully, "Could that be Yankee Hotel?"

Mariano's two-way activated, and the frantic voice of their sentry broke from the speaker. "It's the Sappers, Skipper! They've breached the outer perimeter, and it looks like they're coming in!"

"Damn those pesky geeks!" cursed Mariano. "Doc, take your boys and see what you can do about denying them further access. And, Richy, you come with me. It's time to pay our prisoners a visit, and then get the hell outta this stinking hole."

Trent Warner had been in the forward entry area, at the base of the stairway leading to the flight deck, when Nightwatch unexpectedly fell from the sky and began its harrowing, out-of-control spiral dive into oblivion. He found himself violently flung forward, and a tenuous hold on a secured food-service cart kept him from being thrown to the deck like the others in his party.

During the terrifying free fall that followed, his entire life seemed to pass before his horrified eyes: those exciting days of his early Navy career, his first submarine ride while only a midshipman, his initial meeting with the legendary Hyman Rickover. Then to have sacrificed the best years of his life helping to win the Cold War, only to die with his lifework so close to fruition, was the ultimate tragedy.

Yet, as if he were a condemned man with a last-minute pardon, destiny had another fate in store for him, which came to pass when Nightwatch miraculously pulled out of its dive and achieved level flight. Warner ignored the spilled food that stained his flight suit; and, ever thankful to still be alive, he made his way back to Operations to assess the damages.

He found it in shambles. Overturned equipment and fallen personnel lay scattered everywhere, with the compartment itself lit eerily in the dim red emergency lighting.

The first priority had been to attend to the many injured. A makeshift triage was set up in the aft technical control area. The majority of injuries were cuts and bruises, with several fractures and four concussions, the most severe of which had knocked out their wire operator. Yet there were no fatalities so far, an astounding fact considering the severe damages they had incurred.

Once the wounded were tended to, it was time to get on with the task of assessing these damages. The Chairman then called a meeting in the conference room, and the first person to report in was Colonel Pritchard.

The balding Op team leader refused to sit down, preferring instead to deliver his brief standing, with several ceiling panels conspicuously absent above him. After revealing that over half of his team had been injured in some manner, he made it a point to complain that his every effort at contacting the flight deck had been unsuccessful.

"I'm beginning to think it's a communications glitch," he added, a certain nervousness in his voice. "And when I sent Maintenance to check it out, they found the fire door sealed shut at the top of the stairway."

"Colonel Pritchard," interrupted the Chairman after briefly meeting his SIOP advisor's steady glance, "I realize the great concern that you have for your staff, and I'm sure the flight crew will contact us in time. But right now, I desperately need a comprehensive list of all the damages done to our communications systems. Do I still have a workable command post, or must I transfer my responsibilities to the NMCC?"

Pritchard seemed a bit embarrassed as he answered the

Chairman. "I'm sorry, sir. For the moment, the only system that's completely inoperable is our high-frequency radio. I've got Sergeant Schuster doing a complete diagnostic on the state of our other equipment, but as long as we can stay in the air, the damages suffered shouldn't prevent you from carrying out your duties."

"Captain Richardson," said the Chairman to the seated FEMA representative, "does the loss of HF capability affect your monitoring of the central locator system?"

"It shouldn't, sir," answered the crew-cut Air Force officer. "I've been routing my priority comms through Milstar. In fact, the latest transmission arrived barely five minutes ago, and indicated that Vice President Chapman's whereabouts continue to be unknown."

The Chairman looked genuinely upset with this news, and he made it a point to scan the faces of all those present while voicing himself. "It appears that Andrew Chapman might very well have met the same unfortunate fate as our President. What does the locator say about the next in line, Captain?"

"Sir," said Richardson, "the plane carrying the Speaker of the House has safely landed at Fort Leonard Wood, Missouri, where he'll be standing by to assume the Presidency should Vice President Chapman be unable to do so."

This was the vital news that the Chairman had been waiting for, and he abruptly cut short the briefing, and called aside his SIOP advisor.

"Major, I find it a bit disturbing that Richardson had nothing to say about any FEMA reports of a nuclear accident in southern Missouri."

"Perhaps the news hasn't reached them as yet," offered Hewlett.

The Chairman grunted. "Or just maybe Yankee Hotel was never fully implemented. Either way, we must continue on, ever ready to meet every possible contingency."

"How do you want to deal with that bunch up on the

flight deck?" Hewlett questioned. "It's only too apparent that Pritchard hasn't figured it out yet, and with them sequestered up there, the possibilities are good that it will remain that way."

The Chairman responded in a bare whisper. "And that's the way I want to keep it. From what I understand, short of using an explosive device, the maintenance crew will never be able to budge that fire door from this side of the forward entry area. Major Foard and his cohorts will surely keep it sealed until we're on the ground, and that's when we must strike, to wipe out the entire lot of them before they share their suspicions with the others."

"I've got it!" proclaimed Owen Lassiter, who tightly grasped one of the dozens of FAA landing-facility charts he had been anxiously sorting through. "How does a halogen-lit, fifteen-thousand-foot-long, three-hundred-foot-wide, reinforced concrete runway, with a thousand-foot soft-soil/concrete overrun sound?"

From the adjoining upper-deck rest area, Brittany and Red couldn't help but overhear Lassiter's promising news, and they poked their heads into the cockpit just as Coach was in the process of replying.

"Owen, if we're going to have any chance of getting this baby safely on terra firma, that's just the kind of facility we'll need. So where in the hell is this dream of a runway?"

"It's the Shuttle Landing Facility at Cape Canaveral," Lassiter excitedly replied. "And at our current speed, we can be there in just under two hours."

Saturday, July 3, 1:01 A.M. C.D.T.

Beneath Freeman Hollow

The cave entrance that Jody Glickman led them to was little more than a narrow fracture in the face of a huge limestone bluff. The MPs had to take off their equipment in order to squeeze their way through, and Thomas was the last member of the eleven-person party to crawl inside the tight opening. He found himself hunching over to keep from hitting his head on the low rock ceiling, and needed to use his red-lensed flashlight to illuminate a long, downward-sloping tunnel that the others were already traversing.

He picked up his pace so that he wouldn't be left behind, and noted that the air temperature was dropping quickly, and was a good twenty degrees lower than that of the hot summer night outside. It almost felt as if he had just stepped into an air-conditioned room, the temperature continuing to drop as the tunnel opened up into a large cavern. There was a bitter, musty scent to the air here, and Thomas joined their U.S. Forest Service guide and Jay Christian at the head of the column.

"See those brownish-white splotches that cover the

ground?" said Glickman while scanning the cavern's interior with her red-tinted flashlight. "That's bat guano. And those small, rust-colored objects that are hanging from the ceiling are none other than the critters who make this cavern their home."

"I thought bats feed at night," Christian remarked.

"They do," replied the naturalist. "Those little fellows up there are the young, old, or sickly, and you'd definitely know the difference when the entire colony is present."

The soothing, hollow sound of dripping water could be heard nearby, and Thomas searched the cavern's dark recesses with his flashlight. "How much further is that underground river?" he asked.

"It's a half kilometer at the most," answered Glickman. "And just wait until you see the magnificent chamber that we have to pass through to reach it. It alone is worth the trip."

Ted Callahan had experienced his fair share of explosions in his lifetime, but nothing could compare with the simultaneous detonation of a hundred pounds of C-4. The very earth below seemed to shake, and even with ear protection and his eyes closed, the flash penetrated his eyelids, and his ears still rung from the deafening roar.

Though there had been some initial doubt whether the blast would be sufficient to penetrate the tempered steel hinges of the inner vault, when Ted finally gathered the nerve to leave cover, he found the entrance to the cave wide open. Sergeant Reed wasted little time gathering together his Sappers, and they entered in a tight line formation, with Callahan second from the rear.

Because of the complete lack of ambient light, their NVGs were all but useless. Red-tinted flashlights illuminated their way, and Callahan made certain to keep close on the heels of his Sapper buddy in front of him.

For the first one hundred and fifty yards or so, they followed a good-sized tunnel. Its limestone walls appeared to have been bored out by machine. The ceiling had a good eight feet of clearance, and one could easily drive a large vehicle along the tunnel's smooth rock floor.

Ever on the lookout for any trip wires or toe poppers, they reached the end of the tunnel without incident. Before transiting the bend of a blind curve, Reed ordered them to form an assault train. This tightly knit formation would allow them to move forward like a single entity, and was a technique that was utilized in the MOUT environment.

From his position near the end of the train, Callahan readied his weapon, a Colt M4 carbine, with an M203 grenade launcher attached beneath the barrel. Because he hadn't seen real combat since the Persian Gulf War, and then only on a very limited scale, the mere act of chambering a live round and flicking off the safety caused his pulse to quicken.

It was only too obvious that their enemy was an experienced one, armed with weapons stolen from Uncle Sam's very own arsenal. Since the Vice President was most likely in its custody, they couldn't go in with guns blazing, and had to proceed with the utmost caution—ever ready to defend themselves, but always on the lookout for a potential hostage situation.

Callahan was in the midst of a series of deep, calming breaths when the assault train began moving forward with quick, shuffling steps. He adjusted his footsteps accordingly, the soles of his combat boots slapping against the limestone pavement in exact cadence with his fellow soldiers.

He was so close to the Sapper in front of him that he could actually smell his sweat, the reflective white cat eyes on the back of his BDU cap practically touching Callahan's forehead. They were moving quickly now, and as they snaked around the bend, two of the Sappers in front of the train peeled off to sweep the blackened shadows with the barrels of their M16s. The train kept moving onward without them, with the next two point men peeling off at the next bend.

It was as they were in the process of rounding the next blind curve that their progress was abruptly halted by the ear-shattering blast of a stun grenade. This was followed by a deafening volley of exploding rifle rounds, which sent Callahan diving to the ground for cover.

"Sappers, return fire!" ordered Sergeant Reed.

Ted Callahan needed no more prompting to train his carbine's barrel toward the tunnel up ahead and begin squeezing off rounds. The now nine-man Sapper squad did likewise, and together they poured a devastating curtain of lead into the black void where the ambush had originated.

"Sounds like Doc and his boys are havin' one hoot of a time out there," said Dick Mariano, referring to the almost constant outpouring of gunfire that could be clearly heard in the distance. "Doesn't the sound of an M16 on full automatic bring back fond memories, Sergeant Spit and Polish?"

From his position standing inside the detention cell, Vince Kellogg didn't bother dignifying this remark with a reply; his thoughts were focused on the source of these unexpected gunshots. Beside him, Andrew Chapman was having similar thoughts, with any hopes of a last-minute rescue dashed when Mariano pulled out a .45 Colt pistol from his waistband and pointed it at them.

"How very frustrating it must be for the two of you," said Mariano as he racked the pistol's slide and chambered a fresh round. "To have to die with your rescuers practically knocking on your cell's door. But such are the ironies of war, compadres."

From the rear of the cell, Junior howled out in renewed pain, oblivious to the administrations of his father and sister.

This anguished cry served to further infuriate Tiny, who charged the cell's iron bars and hollered:

"You might be a big man out there with that gun, but I know that without it, you're nothing but a spineless coward!"

"Such a brave man," Mariano said, "yet one without any capacity for learning." He displayed a remarkable lack of emotion as he pointed the pistol at Tiny and squeezed off a single round. The bullet penetrated Tiny's left thigh, and he collapsed onto the floor, blood gushing from the wound in such copious amounts that both Amos and Miriam abandoned their patient to rush to his side.

"That should keep the big hick's mouth shut," said Mariano, who smirked and pointed the gun at Andrew Chapman. "I feel generous, Kellogg. You make the call. A shot to the head, or one to the heart?"

"Damn it, Mariano! This isn't war, it's an execution!"

Renewed gunfire sounded in the distance, and before the bearded ex-SEAL could respond to Vince's outburst, Richy entered the tunnel at a full run.

"Skipper," he managed to say between heaving breaths, "we've got us a major incursion. It's a full squad at least, and Doc's been hit, along with Traveler and Old Dog."

"So the gates are wide open, and here comes the cavalry," calmly observed Mariano. He readjusted the aim of his pistol to target Vince before returning the barrel to the VP. "It would be a shame to waste a bullet on you two now, especially with help so near."

Richy was utterly confused by this comment, and he urgently expressed himself. "Tap 'em, Skipper, and we can still make the river before the others reach us!"

Mariano appeared to ignore his associate's suggestion, and instead pulled a key out of the pocket of his black pajamas. He proceeded to unlock the cell door, then beckoned for Vince and Andrew Chapman to join them outside.

"What in the hell do you think you're doin', Skipper?" quizzed Richy.

Mariano answered while roughly grabbing the VP from behind and shoving his pistol into Chapman's neck. "Richy, you don't get paid to think, remember? Now, be so good as to escort Sergeant Spit and Polish here, and we'll take off for the river, along with the ultimate insurance policy."

Owen Lassiter was the first to notice that Coach had nodded off behind the controls. The backup pilot tapped Lucky on the left shoulder and beckoned toward the sleeping officer.

"Hey, Coach," said Lucky firmly.

Foard's eyes snapped open, and Lucky discreetly added, "Why don't you let Major Lassiter spell you and take five?"

"I'm doing just fine, Lucky," protested Coach with a partial yawn.

Lucky couldn't fail to spot the uncharacteristic dark pouches beneath the senior pilot's eyes, and he remarked in his most diplomatic manner, "We're gonna need you bright-eyed and bushy-tailed for that approach into Canaveral, sir."

"Quit being so stubborn, and listen to Captain Davis, Major," Lassiter interjected. "You're way overdue for a break, and I can handle things here while you freshen up for the landing."

Coach stifled yet another yawn, and realized they were right. He unbuckled his harness, scooted out of his command chair, and stood behind the flight engineer console as Lassiter took his place.

"How's it look, Jake?" he asked their engineer while stretching his cramped limbs.

Jake pointed to the gauge of hydraulic pressure system number two. "So far, so good, sir. Pressure's holding just above the critical range. Ever land an E-4B without a primary or secondary braking system?"

"Who has?" returned Coach, then scanned the console's various displays and grunted. "I'll make you a deal, Lieutenant. You give me one good hydraulic system all the way to Florida, and I'll buy the tickets to Disneyworld."

"You're on," responded Jake before sealing the bargain with a handshake.

Coach left the cockpit, and as he entered the upper-deck rest area, he spotted Brittany in the galley, making a fresh pot of coffee.

"That's just what the doctor ordered," he greeted her with a tired smile.

"Be forewarned that it's brewed Navy style," returned Brittany. "With two parts coffee to every one of water."

"Pour on," Coach instructed.

He initiated a series of stretching exercises while the coffee brewed. He then accepted a mug from Brittany, and joined her in the adjoining booth.

"How are you holding up, Commander?" he asked after taking a tentative sip of the piping-hot brew.

The cabin roughly vibrated, and Brittany held back her reply until the shaking ceased. "To tell you the truth, I'm scared, confused, and stressed out to the max."

"Don't feel alone," said Coach sincerely.

Again the cabin rattled, this time so violently that the pilot's coffee spilled over his mug's ceramic rim.

"How much longer can this plane hold together?" asked Brittany, her voice strained on the edge of full panic.

Coach reached out and supportively grasped her hand.

"Hang in there, my friend. The Boeing 747 is the greatest aircraft ever built, and this one's no different. They're designed to take a remarkable amount of punishment, with the human component more prone to failure than the mechanical systems."

Brittany managed a brave smile, and she squeezed his palm, then pulled her hand free and picked up her coffee mug.

"Speaking of the human component," she said between sips, "what do you think the Chairman's up to, and why hasn't he tried to retake the flight deck?"

"Right now, I'd say he's busy getting the comm systems back on line, and consolidating his forces. It's not in his best interest to interfere with our operations up here. Admiral Warner might be a political deviant, but he's no fool. He knows that this airplane has taken a beating, and my best guess is that he won't try to pay us another visit until we're on the ground."

"Oh, for Pete's sake, not again!" protested Red from the aft portion of the compartment.

Both Coach and Brittany turned around to see what was bothering her, and they watched as Red tore off her headset and stood.

"What's the matter, Sergeant? Having more transmission problems?" Coach questioned.

Red walked over to their booth to explain the reason for her frustration. "I'm getting a clear line out, all right, sir. But the problem lies with the party I'm trying to reach. After querying Lord only knows how many directory assistance operators, I finally got the number to the Shuttle Landing Facility. And would you believe, all I get is an answering machine saying that when there are no shuttle flights in progress, the tower closes at ten p.m. and won't reopen until eight in the morning."

"Can we land without those runway lights?" Brittany asked.

Coach momentarily ignored this question and addressed Red instead. "Sergeant, try getting hold of the Air Force range control center at the Cape. They're surely manned around the clock, and we'll rely on our boys in blue to get those NASA folks out of bed and have that shuttle runway lit up for us. 'Cause we're gonna need all the help we can get, and then some."

Shortly after they left the cavern holding the bats, Thomas began having serious second doubts about their rather rash decision to follow Ranger Glickman. A narrow rock ledge conveyed them deeper into the deathly quiet underground realm. It was a steep, twisting, circuitous route, made all the more treacherous because of the slick rock they were forced to tread upon.

They were using up valuable time, with no guarantee that their efforts would succeed in locating a back entrance to the government facility. Thomas wondered how Ted Callahan and the Sappers were progressing. Surely their explosives had breached the main entryway by now, and they must be well on their way into the cavern themselves.

Thomas took yet another look at the luminescent dial of his wristwatch, and decided to wait until half past the hour before calling a halt to reconsider their options. They were currently transiting a narrow tunnel that was covered with several inches of water. He had to be careful not to hit his head on the projecting rock, and twice he almost fell after losing his footing on a slick spot.

The black expanse seemed to go on forever, and he was somewhat surprised when it suddenly opened up into a larger room. They halted here on an elevated overlook, and their escort used her flashlight to illuminate the interior of an immense cavern, easily three times the size of the one holding the bats.

With his own flashlight Thomas surveyed the hundreds of crystalline stalactites that hung from the cathedral-like ceiling. Many of these dagger-shaped formations extended for a good fifty feet, until they almost touched the pointed stalagmites that had formed on the spacious floor.

Altogether, it was an awe-inspiring sight, and had a certain reverence to it. For this was an alien, subterranean world, the likes of which Thomas had never experienced before.

"How much further is the river?" asked Captain Christian, the muffled roar of cascading water clearly audible in the distance.

"We only need to climb down to the floor of the cavern, and then we should see it," answered their guide, who added somewhat hesitantly, "please remember that this is as far as I've ever explored this system. My colleagues are the ones who kept on going at this point, and it's their reports of a decent trail along the river that I'm relying on."

Thomas looked at his watch again, then shared his thoughts with the senior MP. "Captain, I don't know about you, but I'm beginning to wonder if this route is in fact going to lead us to our goal."

Christian raised his compass and orientated it toward the river. "If the stream's course runs true, that's the general direction where we left Colonel Callahan and the Sappers."

"And hopefully, the facility will be somewhere in between," added Jody Glickman.

Thomas readjusted the fit of the nylon holster that was

clipped to his web belt. Then he somewhat reluctantly signaled the ranger to lead on.

Doc Martin instinctively knew that this was one engagement he would most likely never survive. He had already taken a pair of hits to his left shoulder and right calf. Having been shot several times before, he understood that his first challenge was to survive the initial shock. He did so with the help of a deep-breathing technique the Yards had taught him. A pair of cotton compresses temporarily stopped the bleeding, and he resolutely regripped the stock of his M60, ever ready to delay the oncoming enemy force the best he could.

Two members of his team had already gone down, leaving only a single trooper other than himself to return fire. From the characteristic report of the man's weapon, he realized that the survivor was Chief Roe. Against Doc's advice, the hefty Texan had selected one of the newfangled squad automatic weapons from the assortment of armaments they had recently stolen from Fort Leonard Wood. Though Doc stuck with a trusty M60, Roe was eager to try out one of the SAWs, which was the weapon of choice of today's high-tech Army. And so far, he had to admit, considering the constant fire that Roe was able to effect, the SAW was proving to be extremely reliable.

A grenade detonated nearby, and Doc waited for the shrapnel to expend itself before he dared to poke his head out of the rock crevice in which he was hidden. He quickly ducked upon spotting the muzzle flashes of at least six M16s. The soldiers firing these weapons were rounding the bend where the ambush had been initiated. They were moving quickly, in an assault-train formation, and were concentrating their fire on Chief Roe's position alongside the opposite wall.

After a deafening barrage was completed, Roe's SAW was silenced, and Doc knew he was all that stood between the assault train and their Op Center. Oblivious to the pulsating pain that coursed through his upper torso, he decided there was only one thing left to do. Ever true to the warrior spirit of the Montagnards, Doc wasn't about to go down without taking along as many of the enemy as possible.

From the back of the assault train, Ted Callahan acknowledged that it was an absolute miracle that they hadn't experienced more casualties. Of the eight Sappers who comprised the original formation, only two had been forced to drop out with various wounds. This was remarkable considering the heavy fire they had encountered, and had abruptly ceased, moments after their latest barrage was completed.

"Sappers, hold fire and reload!" ordered Sergeant Reed from the front of the train.

They did as instructed, and Callahan's hands shook so badly from the adrenaline rush that he had trouble inserting a fresh magazine. He needed to shake his right hand to relieve the pent-up tension, and as he regripped the magazine, all hell broke loose from the direction of the tunnel immediately ahead of them.

It started when two stun grenades detonated in quick succession. Callahan found himself momentarily blinded and deafened by this unexpected blast, which was followed by a resounding round of automatic weapons fire.

The Sappers reacted to this onslaught by dropping to the ground, and Ted followed them, motivated by a ricocheting round that passed only inches from his ringing right ear. Before he could raise his rifle, the blazing muzzle flash of a single M60 appeared out of the darkness directly ahead of them, fifteen yards away at most.

A lethal barrage of 7.62mm slugs tore into their ranks, and Callahan watched two of the Sappers get hit. He had yet to put his own carbine into play, and he looked on with ad-

miration when Sergeant Reed rose to one knee and answered
the fire with a tightly grouped series of three-round bursts on
his M16.

The M60 answered with a full thirty-second barrage that
sent over two hundred and fifty 7.62 rounds headed their
way. Callahan hugged the cold rock in a desperate attempt
to find cover, and he could hardly believe it when Sergeant
Reed actually stood up to answer this fire in kind.

Like two cowboys of old dueling it out on a Western
street, Reed and his opponent shot it out, face-to-face, man
to man. And when it was all over and silence finally returned
to the smoky, cordite-scented tunnel, the only one left standing—and, amazingly enough, untouched—was the wild-
eyed combat engineer who stood before them and forcefully
cried out:

"Sappers, lead the way! Onward!"

Vince found it hard to believe that for the second time that
day, fate had chosen him to run the very same underground
river that he and Miriam had traveled upon previously. Yet
this time he was a prisoner, at the complete mercy of the two
individuals seated at each end of the dark green fiberglass
canoe.

Like Vince, Andrew Chapman also found himself
sprawled out on the wet floor of the vessel. From this awk-
ward vantage point, it was hard for them to get orientated,
and they could only sit there soaked and chilled to the bone
while the canoe shot down the incredibly swift current.

The all-prevailing darkness did little to prepare them for
the frequent collisions with projecting boulders which
scraped their hull and dented the gunwales. They had to
hang on to each other for dear life when the canoe dropped
off the steep rock face of a small waterfall Vince remembered from his previous visit.

He also knew that most of the river was just wide enough

to carry the bobbing canoe. This made any escape attempt by diving out of the vessel both impractical and extremely risky, even though their captors hadn't bothered to bind their limbs.

Immediately after running a particularly fast-moving section of rapids, they encountered a relatively calm stretch of water. From his semiprone position, Vince gazed up at the huge stalactites that extended from the roof of the immense cavern they were soon passing through. During their mad dash to escape earlier, he hadn't had a chance to get a good glimpse of this huge, subterranean cavern, which stretched overhead for as far as the eye could see.

"Skipper, lights!" urgently whispered Richy from the canoe's bow.

Vince immediately sat up in an attempt to see what the green-faced commando was referring to. He didn't have any trouble spotting the sweeping beams of a collection of red-tinted flashlights. They were located approximately fifty yards downstream, and looked to be congregated beside the river itself.

From the rear of the vessel, Mariano dug his paddle into the current and guided them over to the nearest bank. Richy attempted to steady the canoe against a rock ledge, and while Mariano reached into his ruck and began assembling the pieces of a compact Ingram MAC 10 submachine gun, Andrew Chapman caught Vince's attention with a kick of his foot.

The VP discreetly beckoned toward the main river channel behind them, and Vince realized that he was thinking about a possible escape attempt. Vince thought any such effort ill-advised, and he was about to express his disapproval with a shake of his head when Chapman sprang up and dove headfirst into the channel. Without a second's hesitation, Vince did likewise, his body striking the icy water just as the first 9mm bullets arrived alongside him.

*   *   *

While the main Sapper party stormed into the cavern's centrally located Op Center, Ted Callahan and Sergeant Reed found themselves drawn to a dimly lit tunnel. It was there that they chanced upon four individuals, gathered behind the open cell doors of some sort of detention facility. Two of them were sprawled out on the floor and looked to be seriously injured, and it took only one look at them for Callahan to realize that they had discovered the Stoddards.

"Is the Vice President with you?" Callahan urgently questioned, not taking the time to join them inside.

"We need some medical attention, mister," pleaded the only female in their midst.

"It's on the way," said Sergeant Reed, who ripped the first-aid kit off his LBE and threw it inside, along with his canteen. "We're with the United States Army, and we're here looking for Vice President Chapman. Is he still alive?"

"As far as we know," answered the group's grizzled elder. "They grabbed him and that Secret Service fellow and headed further down the tunnel, to the river access down yonder."

The first evidence that they weren't alone in the cavern arrived in the unlikely form of a submachine gun firing. Thomas dove for cover, and as he anxiously scanned the cave in the direction that the shots appeared to be coming from, he readily spotted a muzzle flash. Strangely enough, it wasn't being aimed at them, but was focused on something in the river itself.

Since this position was immediately upstream, Thomas alertly crawled to the nearby bank. He arrived there in time to see a pair of individuals being swept downstream. Captain Christian also saw them, and it was his flashlight that illuminated their faces.

Thomas could hardly believe it when the first floating figure proved to be Vice President Andrew Chapman. While following close behind was none other than his own brother, Vince!

Both Thomas and Christian were forced to duck for cover when they came under fire from two figures seated in a canoe. As this vessel passed by, a pair of smoke grenades were tossed onto the bank, and the MPs were forced to hold their return fire.

"What the hell is going on out there, and who are those guys shooting at us?" asked Jody Glickman.

Thomas and Christian leaped into the river, leaving their Forest Service guide behind with her questions unanswered.

Vince never got a chance to see his brother dive off the river-bank, his attention completely concentrated on staying afloat and keeping Andrew Chapman in sight. It was as the current continued to pick up speed that this latter chore became increasingly difficult, Vince getting only an occasional glimpse of the VP's wildly bobbing head.

The water itself was numbingly cold, and Vince didn't know how much longer they'd be able to survive in this frigid torrent. Unlike the Eleven Point, there were no log snags to grab onto. It was also impossible to see more than a few feet ahead, the only illumination being a faint luminescent glow emanating from the crystalline stalactites that hung overhead.

The resounding roar of crashing water signaled their imminent arrival at the next series of rapids. The channel narrowed, and Vince was soon cascading on his back, down a chute of frothing white water. He tumbled over a low rock shelf and plopped down into a deep pool, where he began gagging from all the water he had just swallowed.

At the same moment, an excruciating pain shot up his left side as his muscles began cramping. He was unable to stay afloat, and he swallowed yet more of the river when his pain-racked body began helplessly sinking.

He desperately flayed at the water with his arms, but nothing could reverse the pull of the depths—except the firm grasp of Andrew Chapman.

"It's payback time, Kellogg," said the VP as he pulled Vince to safety on a shallow gravel bar at the edge of the pool.

Vince rolled over onto his stomach and retched. Once he had purged the last of the river from his system, he reached down to massage the cramped muscles of his upper thigh and lower back.

"I guess that does make us even," he grunted to Chapman, who sat shivering beside him in the shallow water. "Now how are we ever going to get out of this infernal place?"

"You're not, Sergeant Spit and Polish!" proclaimed Dick Mariano from the left side of the ledge, where a flat rock outcropping projected into the current.

Vince all but forgot about his cramp, his gaze locked on the leering eyes of the bearded ex-SEAL.

"Nice try, compadres," Mariano remarked with a smirk. "But no fucking cigar!"

Mariano's green-faced associate also appeared at the left side of the rock shelf, and together they dropped their canoe into the calm waters of the pool. Neither one of them bothered to board the vessel, preferring instead to jump off the five-foot-high ledge to the gravel bar below.

"Richy," said Mariano, "I believe we're just about to lose our hostages."

Before he could raise his submachine gun to carry out this threat, yet another voice sounded from a rock outcropping on the other side of the ledge.

"Drop it!" ordered Thomas Kellogg, who, along with Jay Christian, had his specially adapted tournament pistol trained on the two startled kidnappers.

Vince's eyes opened wide with utter amazement upon spotting the familiar figure of his brother. Yet before he could acknowledge him, Mariano yanked up the stubby barrel of his MAC 10 and swept the ledge with an intense volley of 9mm bullets.

Captain Christian had seen this coming, and he selflessly jumped in front of Thomas, taking slug after slug. By the time the MP's bloodstained, bullet-ridden body dropped lifelessly into the pool below, both Mariano and Richy had grabbed their hostages from behind, and had the hot barrels of their weapons jammed up against their necks.

Thomas still had his Caspian .38 Super pistol raised before him. He peered down the C-MORE electronic sight, alternating the passive red targeting dot from the furrowed forehead of the bearded kidnapper, who held the Vice President, to the green-painted forehead of the man holding Vince.

He knew he'd have time for only a single T-zone shot to end this standoff. But the dilemma he faced was whether to attempt saving the life of Andrew Chapman or that of his own brother.

"Come on, cowboy. Come on!" shouted Mariano.

"Save the *Man,* Thomas!" Vince urged.

Thomas had already made up his mind, and he sucked in a deep breath and pulled the trigger.

The .38-caliber slug hit its mark on the bridge of his target's nose. As the bullet penetrated the bone, it further expanded, creating a wound path one and a half inches in diameter. This destructive path led directly to the all-important cerebellum and medulla areas, instantaneously severing communication from the brain to the spinal cord, and effectively preventing any physically contractible response from the limbs below.

In other words, Dick Mariano never had a chance to execute the Vice President. And as the bearded ex-SEAL slumped to the ground dead, Thomas desperately swung the red dot to the right in a frantic effort to save his brother.

Long before he could center his aim, a shot rang out.

Thomas flinched in horror, and he looked down onto the gravel bar, expecting to see Vince's body lying there. But strangely enough, it was the green-faced kidnapper who was in the process of falling to the ground, a neat bullet hole smack on the bridge of his camouflaged nose.

"Hoo-ah!" exclaimed Ted Callahan from the other side of the ledge, the still-smoking barrel of his pistol held close at his side. "Not bad shooting for a desk-bound fast-food junkie, if I do say so myself!"

Saturday, July 3, 0740 Zulu

Nightwatch 676

"Nightwatch six-seven-six, this is Shuttle Landing Facility tower. We have you on visual. Emergency equipment standing by. Good luck. Over."

From his copilot's position inside the cockpit, Lucky acknowledged this transmission, while beside him, Coach addressed Jake over his chin mike.

"What's the status of number two hydraulic system?"

"It continues dropping toward critical, Coach, with pressure just barely in the green."

Coach looked to his right and briefly caught Lucky's concerned stare before redirecting his line of sight back out the cockpit window. The Shuttle runway's approach lights had just come into view. He could also make out the long line of halogen centerline lights, which were set into the entire length of the runway at two-hundred-foot intervals.

"Let's do it, gentlemen," said Coach, firmly grabbing the steering yoke. "Lucky, take us down to nineteen hundred feet at one hundred forty-five knots. Jake, it's time to tap the alternative electrical system and lower the flaps to twenty degrees."

"One hundred forty-five knots. Nineteen hundred feet," Lucky reported.

"Flaps coming down . . . and holding at twenty degrees!" added Jake, his relief obvious.

In the distance, the bright lights belonging to the Shuttle launch pad could be seen. Coach couldn't help but derive additional confidence knowing that the runway they were currently approaching was designed to service the most advanced flying machine on the planet.

"One hundred forty-three knots. Eighteen hundred ninety-two feet," informed Lucky.

"Let's go ahead and lower flaps to thirty degrees," said Coach, who knew that this was a critical adjustment. If the flaps didn't properly deploy, they'd touch down at too high a speed, causing the already damaged wing landing gears to most likely collapse.

Thus when Jake reported that the flaps were holding firm at thirty degrees, Coach realized that a major hurdle had just been cleared.

"Lucky," he said to his copilot with a bit more certainty, "take us down to two hundred feet at one hundred thirty-three knots. Jake, inform our passengers to prepare for landing."

"Take up emergency landing positions. Brace! Brace!" warned Jake over the plane's public-address system.

The moment of truth was almost upon them, and Coach reached out with his right hand and opened up the reserve brakes. The plane began to vibrate, and he pulled back the yoke slightly, to reduce their rate of descent, while nudging up the throttle, to compensate for the sluggish control response.

"Here we go," said Coach, who saw the runway suddenly loom right before them.

Nightwatch touched down heavily to the left of the first

halogen light, and immediately bounced back into the air. As gravity pulled the massive airplane back to earth once again, it struck the runway near the second halogen marker, and this time it remained on the ground.

Coach yanked back on the reverse thruster lever, realizing that the landing gear had, remarkably, held. There was a loud growling roar, and the flight deck began to vibrate violently.

"Only number four engine has gone into reverse!" warned Jake.

So that he wouldn't lose control because of asymmetric thrust, Coach pushed the reverse lever forward to negate the command. At the same time, he stomped down hard on the toe brake. Again the cockpit shook, and Jake informed them that the antiskid system had just failed.

Nightwatch began to veer sharply to the right of the halogen-lit centerline after seven of the remaining eight tires blew out. They were quickly running out of runway, and Coach fought to put them back in the center of the reinforced concrete strip by utilizing the plane's rudder.

They were still moving well over sixty knots when the last halogen light passed beneath them. This signaled the end of the main runway, and the plane bounded over the final section of concrete and headed smack into the thousand-foot-long overrun.

There was a violent lurch as what was left of their landing gear bit into the soft-soil/concrete paving material. Coach and Lucky were thrown forward, and it was as their restraint harnesses pulled them back into their seats that they realized the airplane had stopped. Against all the odds, Nightwatch was safely on the ground once again!

A round of spirited high fives were traded, with Major Lassiter leaving the navigation console to celebrate along with Brittany and Red. It was with great relief that Coach unbuckled his harness to join Lassiter in the upper-deck rest area. Yet as he stepped out of the cockpit, he found his backup approaching the sealed fire door.

"No, Major Lassiter!" screamed Red, who looked on with shocked horror as Lassiter hit the large red switch that triggered the door's unlock mechanism.

The door slipped open with a loud hiss, and in stormed Major Hewlett and the Chairman. Both of them carried pistols, and Lassiter quickly resealed the door the moment they were safely inside.

"Nice job with that landing, Major Foard," said the Chairman to Coach while waving the barrel of his .45 toward the pilot. "Too bad the medal will have to be delivered posthumously."

Coach ignored this veiled threat, and turned his anger on Owen Lassiter. "I can't believe you're one of them, Major. You're a disgrace to your uniform."

"Coach," replied Lassiter with a snicker, "you're just upset 'cause you picked the wrong side."

"That you did," agreed the Chairman before expanding his gaze to take in Brittany and Red as well. "All of you are part of a failed, morally bankrupt system. And though by its very nature revolution is painful, it's the only way to get our country back in the right direction."

For the first time ever, Brittany didn't fear directly meeting Warner's penetrating glance, and she addressed him forcefully. "The only trouble is, if we do it your way, Admiral, it will mean the end of everything!"

There was a loud rending sound when the overworked left landing gear suddenly broke down, and the deck below unexpectedly tilted in that direction. Everyone standing was thrown off balance, and Red was able to lunge forward in an attempt to knock the gun out of Hewlett's grasp.

In the resulting struggle, the Marine's gun went tumbling to the deck, and Coach alertly retrieved it, while the Chairman trained his pistol on Red and fired. The bullet hit her in the back between her shoulder blades, and she collapsed in a bloody heap.

Brittany saw Warner now turn his gun on Coach, but before he could fire, she grabbed the flare gun, aimed the blunt barrel at the Chairman, and pulled the trigger. The red-hot Magnesium/phosphorous round hit him squarely in the center of the chest. There was a sickening, sizzling hiss as the chemicals in the flare began eating into Warner's skin, and he let loose an anguished wail before falling to the deck himself, the bitter scent of burning flesh heavy in the air.

"We've got a Priority One transmission coming in on the FEMA emergency network!" informed Jake from the cockpit. "It's being simulcast on our video system."

Only after making certain that both Red and the Chairman were beyond their help did Coach lead the shocked occupants of the flight deck over to the auxiliary comm console. With Lucky guarding their two prisoners, Coach activated the video screen and patched in the same real-time, live video broadcast that was being transmitted to every television and radio station in America.

The crystal-clear video picture was captioned—LIVE FROM FORT LEONARD WOOD, MISSOURI: THE SWEARING-IN OF OUR NEW PRESIDENT.

The setting was an operations center, with a group of civilians and high-ranking military officers gathered around a flag-draped podium. Standing next to this lectern was Andrew Chapman, looking a bit out of character dressed in a pair of wrinkled khakis and a white Harvard polo shirt. Leonard Wood's immaculately attired Judge Advocate stood alongside him, and he held out a thick Bible, on which Chapman placed his right hand and then repeated an oath that came right out of Article II, Section I of the Constitution.

"I, Andrew Chapman, do solemnly swear that I will faithfully execute the office of President of the United States, and will, to the best of my ability, preserve, protect, and defend the Constitution of the United States, so help me God."

After holding on a close-up of the country's new President, the camera slowly panned the faces of the various onlookers, which included the very somber-looking figure of Speaker of the House, Andrew Pierce.

"The Speaker sure doesn't look very happy," noted Jake.

"What else do you expect from a man who came within a life of being our next President?" Coach replied. "A man for years denied his party's nomination, and who will probably never get it."

And as the camera momentarily remained on the determined faces of the two civilians standing beside the Speaker, Brittany let out an astonished gasp. On this tragic day that no American would soon forget, standing there at the new Chief Executive's side were none other than her dear friends Thomas and Vince Kellogg.

Sunday, July 4, 0003 Zulu

U.S.S. *James K. Polk*

It was with some trepidation that Brad Bodzin found himself knocking on his Captain's stateroom door. The hour was late, his presence here the byproduct of a formal request on his part to the XO earlier in the evening.

The senior sonar technician found Benjamin Kram seated at his desk, immersed in a pile of paperwork. Bodzin had a genuine liking for the old man, as he was better known to the junior ratings, and he tried his best to shake off his nervousness as he cleared his throat in greeting.

"Good evening, sir. Thanks for agreeing to see me."

"Not at all, Mr. Bodzin. And may I be the first to wish you a happy Independence Day."

Bodzin had totally forgotten that it was already the Fourth of July, and he listened attentively as Kram added, "I gather that you saw the videotape of President Chapman's swearing-in ceremony?"

"I caught a replay right before I began my last watch, sir. It was a very emotional moment."

"That it was, for all of us," said Kram, who pulled off his bifocals and set them down on his desk. "Now, I know you're tired and ready to hit the rack after your second watch of the day. So what can I help you with?"

"Sir, first off, I understand that scuttlebutt has it that this will be your last patrol with us. I wanted to personally say what a great honor it has been to have sailed with you."

Kram grinned and shook his head in amazement. "Why, thank you, Mr. Bodzin. And considering that I only just told the XO, COB, and Commander Gilbert that I'd be permanently leaving the Jimmy K when we get back to Norfolk, I'm impressed with your intelligence network. Is that all, son?"

"Actually, sir, it isn't." Bodzin took a deep breath before continuing. "Captain, I've been playing that tape we made of Sierra Seven's signature over and over. I know we didn't get much to work with, but I was able to enhance the signal, and pulled off a decent segment both immediately before they collided with the *Rhode Island* and right after they took that potshot at us. I then filtered out the highs and lows, and ran it through the computer for a positive identification."

"Don't tell me," interrupted Kram. "My money says that Sierra Seven is an enhanced Russian Akula."

"Sir," replied Bodzin while shaking his head that this wasn't the case, "the computer shows that there's a ninety-seven percent probability that Sierra Seven is a U.S. Navy 688I attack sub. Captain, that sub had to know we were fellow Americans. Why in the world would they do such a thing?"

Benjamin Kram was unable to reply. Until all the facts were in, and the entire cast of conspirators apprehended, knowledge of the coup attempt was to be restricted on a need-to-know basis. Even in the world's oldest practicing democracy, some questions were better left unanswered.

"The tree of liberty must be refreshed from time to time with the blood of patriots and tyrants."
—THOMAS JEFFERSON
1787

Acknowledgments

This novel would not have been possible without the invaluable assistance of the following:

Donald DeLine and Jordi Ross of Disney's Touchstone Pictures, who helped generate the creative spark that got this project off the ground;

Lou Aronica and Stephen S. Power of Avon Books;

Robert Gottlieb, Matt Bialer, Alan Gasmer, and Steven H. Kram of the William Morris Agency;

Philip M. Strub, U.S. Department of Defense;

Charles "Lucky" Davis of the U.S. Air Force;

General Eugene E. Habiger, Vice Admiral Dennis A. Jones, Captain Robert Pritchard, and Captain John Kennedy of U.S. Strategic Command;

Major General John G. Meyer Jr., Colonel Robert E. Gaylord, Colonel Mark Brzozowski, and Lieutenant Colonel Richard Breen of U.S. Army Public Affairs;

Major General Bob Flowers, Lieutenant Colonel Stephen Rego, and G. Michael Warren, my hosts at Fort Leonard Wood, MO;

Brigadier General David W. Foley, Colonel Wes Cox, and H.M. Chapman, my hosts at Fort McClellan, AL;

Captain Harold Christy and Robert Aylward of the U.S. Army Marksmanship Unit;

Terry Miller, Charlotte Wiggins, Ben Wyatt, Al Stevens, Jody Eberly, and Ron Asplin of the U.S. Forest Service;

Charles Jaco—my key to the Irish Wilderness;

Lieutenant Colonel Stu Pugh;

AFSOC's Captain Ty "Monzo" Alexander;

Keith O'Leary;

Director John McGaw and Assistant Director Patrick D. Hynes of the Bureau of Alcohol, Tobacco and Firearms;

Bruce Blair, senior fellow, the Brookings Institution;

Commander Strategic Communications Wing One;

Lieutenant A.A. "Flex" Plexico, USN;

The men and women of the 55th Air Wing and 1st Airborne Command and Control Squadron;

And last, but definitely not least, my dearest Carol Frances, for her patient love and constant support.

To all of you, my heartfelt thanks for sharing your fascinating worlds with me and my readers!